Jaded

Book Five

Mistress & Master
of
Restraint
Series

Jaded

Copyright ©2012 Erica Chilson

Wicked Reads
PO Box 29
Nelson, PA 16940

www.ericachilson.com/wicked-reads

Printed in the United States of America

First Printing, 2017

ISBN-13: 978-0692713808
ISBN-10: 0692713808

Rags to Riches…

The queen is not born– she is forged through survival.
You've read the Mistress and Master of Restraint series in present day. Join Regina Regal nineteen years in the past to where it all began with Jaded.

Even as a scholarship student, Regina Regal is the brightest at Hillbrook Prep, causing her to straddle two extremes between the destitute class she dwells in and the affluent she visits daily. Neither of which welcomes her with open arms, forcing her to choose between her people and her friends.

While dealing with insurmountable loss, Regina has more burdens placed upon her shoulders than the average adult could carry. With her mother dying, Regina has a difficult time crossing the line from caregiver to daughter in order to have both her mother's and her own emotional needs met. Regina is struggling to keep her head above water as she takes on more debt from her mother's mounting medical bills and living expenses, only to realize she is drowning.
At eighteen, with a college scholarship guaranteeing she will join the ranks of her one-percenter classmates, Regina should have the world at her fingertips.

Since she was young, Regina has been the provider, creating a young woman who has the need to survive and a hunger to be in control. But she finds herself falling apart, making horrible decisions that have lifelong consequences.

Regina Regal's life changes irrevocably when her best friend, Adelaide, invites her to study at the imposing Whittenhower Estates. Going against her instincts, Regina is compelled to visit Misery Castle.

The girl who entered Misery Castle's iron gate will not be the jaded woman who flees it almost five years later…

Dedication

Jaded is dedicated to all the females who have yet to find their true voice and the ones who have felt the power of exceeding their own self-perceived limits. Don't bother reaching for the sky when your fingertips already touch the stars.

Nineteen years earlier…

Chapter One

"Do you want to study tonight? We could go to my house and it would give you a break from your mom." Voice beyond hope-filled, my best friend– Fate Simpson –leans across the cafeteria table with a wide smile on her flawless face.

"I can't," I mutter, glad that I have an excuse. I love Fate and her little sister, Faith, but their mom makes it uncomfortable to visit. But my excuse is an even worse fate. "I have to go to Ade's house tonight for the first time. She's been pestering me, and I finally gave in."

Fate gives me the usual pinched look of disdain, and then rolls her blue eyes. She doesn't understand how I could be friends with someone who acts like Ade does. My best friends aren't friends at all– more like enemies of the highest order. As Dominion's original founders, the Whittenhower and Simpson families share bad blood, and their daughters perpetuate the cycle. It makes it rather uncomfortable to be me, because I have to split my time between the two girls, with both of them pissed at me for loving the other.

As the only scholarship student, having two friends at Hillbrook Preparatory School is necessary for survival, needing the queens of the elite to watch my back from deliberate attacks. Dirt poor, where I come from makes me the enemy amongst the budding world leaders. Rich mommies and daddies get their panties in a wad when a girl from the slums is smarter than their genetically engineered kiddies who were showered with expensive tutors from birth.

"Ade's a snooty bitch. I don't know how you can stand her." Fate slouches in her chair, bony arms resting on the tabletop. She pulls a grumpy look and pouts– too adorable for words.

Adelaide Whittenhower is an entitled monster who loves me because I accept her for who she is. Fate Simpson is a sweet, naïve, sheltered girl who *will* be consumed by the sharks in life, and I've made it my life's mission to protect her from the Ade Whittenhowers of the world. It's best if the dual sides of my life never collide.

"We're studying for the Latin final." What I say next isn't a dig, since Fate is a mathematical mastermind, but dumb as a rock with foreign languages, which Ade excels in. My best friends are complete and total opposites. "You didn't have to take it, so that's the only reason I'm studying with Ade instead of you. Ya know you could always study with us. I'm sure she wouldn't mind."

Flashing perfectly straight, predatory teeth, "Oh," Fate draws out, smile warping into an evil smirk. "But *I* would mind." She pulls her long, dirty blonde hair into a ponytail, and then wraps the hair tie around it three times. She gives it a tight yank and I wince. I'm surprised she has any hair left at all after the amount of times she adjusts her hair in a day.

"What kind of freak graduates at sixteen? Worse is that you hang out with someone two years younger than you. It's sad really." Eyelashes fluttering, Fate allows haughty pretentiousness to infuse her voice.

Wincing, I love my education and my two friends, but I can only take so much of the '*I am better than everyone else on the planet*' mentality. I deal with these people in short bursts, and then get back to my side of the city where the drug dealers and prostitutes dwell.

I live across the street from Dominion's crime boss. Stanton Green just usurped his own father, and he's only a few years older than I am. The elite think they hold the world by their wallets. But through ingenuity, we hold them by the balls. They may think we're trash, but we live in reality. While they live in their own universe and are ignorant to anything that doesn't outright affect them.

"Fate, lay off Ade," I warn. "We've been through this for the past four years. We're two weeks from graduating, so I think it's a bit late to change anything."

Eyes downcast, Fate turns sheepish. "It's always worth a try." Uncomfortable, Fate wringing her fingers together on the tabletop draws my attention. "I just want you to like me more than her, ya know? You loving someone so… nasty, it makes me wonder if I'm a good person or not."

"Fate," I sigh deeply, lowering almost into a snarl. I grip her fingers before she cuts off their circulation with her constant fretting. Softening my voice, "I need to study for finals tonight. You know I'll lose my scholarship if I slip with my grades. We all can't have our daddies buy off admissions and pay our way."

Fate's blue eyes tear up, and I'm instantly regretful for hurting her. It doesn't make the insult any less true, so I won't apologize. She's never had to worry about grades, or scholarships, or even financial aid she can't afford to pay back. Thomas Simpson bought his precious daughter her admission to the university of her choice and is paying her entire way.

Whereas, I'm not even sure I can use the scholarship I was awarded– the one I've earned by working my ass off for the past four years while suffering through these insufferable fuckfaces. I work and work, and study and study, but all I end up doing is treading water. Nothing will keep my dying mother alive– the only thing that would have saved my future was if her fight had ended before my eighteenth birthday.·

I turned eighteen last month.

I'm in an impossible situation, praying for every moment with my mother, but knowing the longer she lives, the more weight will be put on my shoulders. At the beginning of my future, I'll have creditors garnishing my wages and putting liens on everything I own to recoup my mother's mountain of medical bills.

One of the worst mistakes I've ever made was signing as the debtor on my eighteenth birthday– the administrators' way of using my ignorance against me to recoup their losses. I hadn't realized they couldn't turn my mother away. Using my love and fear against me, the hospital strong-armed me into becoming fiscally responsible for my mother's debts.

Without the backing of Dad's social security, with Mom having no job, I faced the impossible choice of either signing as the debtor, or having my mother's care cut off for defaulting on the payments.

What an awful daughter I would have been to have wanted a future versus a few more days with my dying mother.

I signed without hesitation, but the mountain of debt in my name will haunt me until every cent has been paid.

Brushing those fears away, I know I'll be stuck with Fate for life, so I best assuage her fears instead. "Fate, you know I love you. But I can love both of you, and it doesn't change either of our friendships." Arms spread wide, I display all six feet of my gargantuan body while wearing a smile on my face. "There's more than enough of me to go around."

"Of course there is," a syrupy voice flows above my head, breath fluttering my hair. "You have a large capacity for love, Regina."

Fate's eyes narrow and fill with bitter hatred. "I just lost my appetite. I'll see you in A.P. Calc. Later." She abruptly leaves her seat to walk to another table filled with taunting elitists.

A sheep, always following the herd, Fate begins to laugh with them and glances our way over her shoulder. No doubt I'm the brunt of some brutal joke, but it doesn't bother me anymore.

Individual.

Unique.

Strong.

A survivor.

A loner.

A leader.

Fingertips curling into my palms, my nails bite into my skin. My present may suck, but these assfucks are going to lick my boots in the future.

If it weren't for the fact that we have to wear uniforms, I'd be bullied more. My clothing comes from secondhand stores, not the pricy shops where you buy a pair of jeans worth no more than twenty bucks for a thousand dollars. The wealthy are the most wasteful people on the planet.

Without the aid of a salon or stylist, don't get me started on my frizzy strawberry blonde hair.

The irony is the fact that no matter what I do, I won't fit in anywhere, not when I'm bridging the gap between two cultures. Wearing my school uniform in the slums has slurs slung into my face on a daily basis, as would wearing my regular clothing around the Hillbrook elite.

Ade sighs above my head, no doubt glaring at Fate for her antics. After a reassuring clench to my shoulder, Ade takes a seat beside me.

With a wan smile, I look to the young girl everyone is utterly terrified of. Willowy, Ade looks like a runway model with her pale, flawless skin, natural blonde hair and big blue eyes– all Whittenhower genetic standards. With a mind rivaling mine, she may be controlling and demanding, but she does understand how I feel.

Ade speaks while looking down at her tray filled with a chopped salad and grapefruit segments, neither of which she'll eat. "The fresh-fish-freshman are doing their orientation today. They should be here any second. Father said there are nine new students."

With a minuscule student body, Hillbrook Preparatory School is preschool through graduation, but we're segregated by age group. The rectory across the back lawn was converted for the little kids, with the preteens housed in an outbuilding. With the main cathedral turned into classrooms, the seventh and eighth grades are all clustered into a segment away from the influence of the older kids.

There are few open slots for grades beneath ninth. Your parents can either afford for you to start at preschool, or apply for high school. The only concessions being made are for the students of an influential legacy family– there are no new kids at Hillbrook. You're either here from day one, or are admitted as a freshmen and beyond, where there is more space for the student body.

Freshman orientation is an event the proud mommies and daddies celebrate like a graduation, where legacies meet the kids who were rich enough to buy their way in, guaranteeing admission to any top university of their choosing.

Then there is me, the worst kind of interloper. Poor scholarship kid. The only scholarship student to ever grace Hillbrook's marble hallways. The parents raised a major stink, saying I was tainting their reputation. Proving myself, I outscored their children, which only made them angrier. Every semester they petitioned to remove me from their roster because I was knocking their precious babies down the ranks. Two weeks until graduation, I'm still here, never knowing who my benefactor was.

Nodding that I heard it trickling down the gossip vine, I snag Ade's multigrain roll slathered with a layer of honey butter. Only the best for the children of the one-percenters. Commuting to a school with a different zip code, wearing a uniform, having Catholicism shoved down my throat when I'm a Protestant, and dealing with shiny bastards wasn't as bizarre as the lack of sloppy joes, pizza, tater tots, canned corn, and instant potatoes on my lunch tray. In fact, we don't get a lunch tray with compartments. Plates. Real porcelain plates and stainless cutlery sit atop a silver tray. Hillbrook served high-quality, gourmet meals that are lost on my dirt poor palate.

I spear a fork into Ade's salad, knowing she won't eat it, and what I was offered wasn't enough to fuel my masculine-sized body. Another advantage of having two dieting, skinny white chicks for best friends– I eat their lunches, because my cupboards are bare at home.

Cheeks stained pink, Ade shocks me with what she says next. "I've had my eye on one of the incoming freshman for a while." Shock because I chat about boys with Fate, never Ade. Ade is my partner in academia and culture, whereas Fate is a gossip monger and pop culture expert.

Blush deepening, "It's too bad that I was so accelerated. I would've loved to stay here a year or two with him." Ade licks her thin lips salaciously, and I giggle out of discomfort. She's all talk and no bite. Worried about grades and our futures, neither of us have been kissed.

"Here they come," I say of the thirty or so new students that will grace the halls of Hillbrook next school year. Twenty of them have been here since they were three years old, but the rest have never entered our hallowed halls.

Arrogant, the legacies have eaten in this cafeteria for over a decade, but the newbies show no chinks in their armor. They don't enter as I did and still do on occasion– heads down and shoulders curled, shrinking into themselves.

Swallowing hard, a ball forms in my stomach, knowing a child in preschool, someone in my graduating class, or one of these freshmen could possibly be a future president of the United States, or go on to cure cancer, or create a revolutionary idea to change the way we live our everyday lives.

I'm witnessing history being made. A mark on a journey of a great man or woman. I'm an outside observer, never in a million years believing I'd be sitting here. I'll forever be Reggie from the block, earning my way but never believing I deserve to be here. I have the brains and guts to grab for it, but those positions of power are only handed to a legacy, never to the daughter of a second-generation Irish-American bus driver.

With great respect, I meet the eyes of every child who walks into the cafeteria. The students walk with their shoulders back and their heads held high. Sure of themselves, filled with pride and confidence, they are the future of our nation. They never get intimidated, even by the ninety kids in the cafeteria who are older and smarter. That isn't the currency they go by– it's green. Money is power. They aren't intimidated because most of the newbies' families have more money and power than the ones who are seated.

Stunned silent, I watch as a few students rise up and pull the new freshmen from their ranks to sit with them.

Fate runs up to her little sister, Faith, and hugs her proudly. Bony arms locked around one another, blonde hair flutters as the sisters rock each other back and forth while giggling and making happy sounds. Broad smile on her pixie-like face, the small girl waves at me, and I wave back.

Faith is a good girl. Born in Dominion but raised in West Virginia with her aunt. She hasn't developed the attitude of the Simpson family, yet to fall into the trap that the rest of these kids are already ensnared in. They're too blind to see that their fate has been sealed. It's too late for them to make their own way. Yes, they have money, but at what cost? Freedom. It's the cost of their true selves and their happiness.

Snapping me away from the scene playing out before me, "Hi," a cute boy with tan skin, huge gray eyes, and black hair greets me.

An odd smile tugs at my lips as I glance up at the newcomer. Covered in baby fat, the mixed race kid looks like he should be hanging outside of my building with Stanton Green's teenage enforcer, Julio Ramirez. Not to sound racist, but even I'm not white enough for Hillbrook, and I burn in the sun after five minutes.

Eyes twinkling with mischievousness, grin charming, I can't help but feel a pull toward the jailbait kid. He's another outsider in this pure, six-finger environment.

"Hi," muttering back firmly, I refuse to show any vulnerability. I've learned over the past four years that meekness is a weakness to these predators. No matter how much they think they're better than me, it doesn't mean they are.

Making himself known, "Stop leering at the lady," another boy chastises with a soft, punishing cuff to the back of the other boy's head. "That's rude." The charmer shrinks back, rejection flashing across his chubby face.

Baby fat already burnt off by puberty, the bossy kid looks similar enough to the charmer to be his brother, except their skin and hair color are at opposites. He's nearly albino white, meaning he's probably Dominion royalty, while the other kid is dark enough that one of his parents has to be of Mexican descent. The differences stop at skin-deep, because their smoky gray eyes and the shape of their bodies are identical.

Bastard brothers? Maybe Daddy stepped out on Mommy like Fate and Faith's dad did.

Tall and graceful, the pale one gestures to himself and then his pouting companion. "Hello, I'm Ezra Holden-Zeitler, and this rude bastard is Cortez Hunter."

Not brothers, then.

That hyphenated last name means both sides of his family are Dominion founders. Ezra's top of the food chain, which explains why over a hundred pairs of eyes are watching us with curiosity.

You could hear a pin drop in the cafeteria– all the better to hear the dulcet tones of Ezra's smooth voice.

Ezra extends his perfectly manicured hand for me to shake. I do so, and I'm shocked at how soft his skin is. Softer than mine was when I was a baby. He's never seen an honest day's work in his life. But then again, he's still a kid.

"She's Regina Regal," Ade says for me, pushing her way into the conversation, clearly already acquainted with these gentlemen. I don't mind. I'm not lusting after these cute boys. Not only because they're babies compared to me, but because I've never lusted after anyone.

"It's always a pleasure, Adelaide," the smooth voice rolls over us, eliciting a shiver. Not faked or acted, amazing genetics on display.

Cort rolls his eyes at me as Ezra speaks. Either he's making fun of the voice or Ade– I don't know which. I smother my smile by taking a sip of my water, eyeing the pair over the edge of my glass.

Slumping against her chair, completely unladylike, Ade melts into a puddle because Ezra acknowledged her. The guy must be the one she has her eye on. Good choice, girlfriend. When he grows up, he'll be devastating. I'm positive the sidekick charmer will be, too.

I have a few rules I abide by: I don't do the rich and no one is worth it in my neighborhood. I'm biding my time for college to find someone in the middle ground to date.

Ezra doesn't shake Ade's hand or touch her in any other way to avoid encouraging her. With a kind smile flirting along his lips, he humors her as she rambles on embarrassingly. She has a tendency to do that when she's nervous. However, Ezra does rest a possessive hand on Cort's back. The boy leans into the touch, face going from murderous intent to satisfied, and my eyes widen in shock.

No freaking way!

The brightness in my best friend's eyes informs me she has a massive crush on Ezra, and I don't have the heart to tell her how she isn't his type. Where I come from, you're either observant, or you get mugged, knifed, or raped. Here in the land of opportunity, you don't notice anything you don't want to see. I'm sure deep down, Adelaide must realize Ezra is gay, but she's in denial. Probably the rich are forced to marry anyway– maybe that's what she's hoping for. We're too young to worry about that kind of thing, but many of my classmates are already betrothed to keep the wealth in their families.

It's not a love match; it's a business merger.

"We should mingle some." With practiced ease of many dinner parties and public functions, Ezra orders Cortez as he squeezes the boy's shoulder affectionately. "We can't stand here with these graduates. Sadly, these lovely ladies won't be here with us next year and we must build reliable connections early on."

Both boys blaze brilliant smiles at me, flashing their pearly, bright teeth. The smile Ezra gives Ade is fond, whereas Cortez's is a feral baring of teeth. I bet he doesn't like her looking at his guy with marital intent.

Adelaide's thin lips stretch across her face in a huge grin. She tosses her shoulder-length blonde hair, trying to bring attention to it, and it doesn't have an impact.

I watch as the boys approach the table where Fate and Faith are sitting. Both girls give them a cursory half-second look to see who it is, and then go back to chatting with their friends. They aren't impressed, but most of these kids have grown up together since birth. It's too much like siblings to get excited over one another.

"I'm going to be Mrs. Ezra Zeitler someday," Adelaide declares with a great wealth of pride. "My father has been negotiating with Diane Holden for the past few months." Her eyes glaze over with an insane level of want. I don't know if Ade wants Ezra as a person, or just wants to know she can acquire him.

"Doesn't the kid get a choice?" I scoff, appalled. "He's a child." I have more freedom as poor white trash than these rich children have.

I'd rather be poor than owned.

"No, Ezra doesn't," Adelaide states firmly. "We marry who our parents tell us to marry. Katherine was lucky because she fell in love with her best friend's big brother, so that made the betrothal easy-peasy."

"Easy-peasy?" I bite back a few choice words, but I am happy for Ade's older sister.

Katie Whittenhower– now Katherine Preston –was a pleasant girl to be around, genuine and compassionate. I wouldn't wish an arranged marriage on my worst enemy. Ade loves retelling the story of how when Katie was only fourteen, she was visiting her friend while the brother was home from college. Katie fell head over heels, but Kent didn't show any interest until after Katie turned eighteen. It was a whirlwind romance with a lot of publicity.

Lucky in love, Katie did have the bad luck of her husband becoming a Junior Senator.

Politicians are smarmy maggots.

"It's human trafficking of one's children, is what it is. The gang occupying my neighborhood has more ethics than that."

"Oh, Reg." Ade washes the air away with an outstretched palm. "I was smarter than my brother– Grant waited too long, dragging his feet, and didn't get to pick. So Father did instead, and Grant is downright miserable with Cora. I picked who I wanted, and Father was pleased it was his closest friend's son."

Ade responds like this is normal and perfectly acceptable behavior. The world doesn't operate like this, and she is ignorant to that fact. You don't just order up a spouse like you're catalog shopping.

Hello? Yes, I'd like to order a pale as paper one-percenter. I'd prefer if he had light eyes and hair to complement my own, and a bank account with so many zeros I lose count. Do you have one with political ties from a Dominion founder line? Please and thank you. Easy-peasy!

My eyebrow hitches high. "What if you pick someone and your parents say no?"

The fact that I'm making fun of her goes straight over Adelaide's head. "You have to trust that your parents know better than you do. If Father says no, then it wasn't a good match. Father said it was a perfect match for Ezra and me, and Ezra's mother, Diane, is excited as well. But she hasn't told him yet. We have to wait for him to grow up some." She preens like a bird under the parental praise.

My eyes cut to the table where Ezra and Cortez are squeezed in next to Divina Hastings. She's a pretty brunette who was this year's freshman. Divina must be a relative of Ezra's or Cortez's, judging by the ease of how she touches them. Not possessively so, like you'd razz a bratty little brother. Everyone is chatting animatedly around them, while the boys seem to be lost in their own world, holding a preternatural, silent conversation.

Any woman who steps between Ezra and Cortez is staring down disaster.

"What about Cortez, though?" The looks the kid keeps tossing Ade's way scream that he's planning her demise and enjoying the thought.

"Cort's a nobody– his mom just died," Ade offers flippantly, and my heart beats double-time.

Gazing at Cortez, I recognize the same pain I'm holding deep inside, and it bothers me that Adelaide can talk so freely about the death of the most important person in your life, especially when my mother is dying. I curl my fists, barely restraining myself from punching the smug off my friend's face.

"Celeste Hunter was Diane's companion– Ezra's mom. They fed from her hand and now she has taken in the orphan. It's disgusting that Cort's family was looking for a handout, but it was very sweet that Diane would be so charitable. She's an incredible woman. I would be proud to call her my mother-in-law." The haughty tone in Ade's voice deepens as she speaks. I do love her, but she is the most pretentious person on the planet.

"No, not marry Cortez. What about Cortez if you try to marry Ezra? They look like a package deal." I say about the obvious couple. Neither is hiding their mutual affections for the other. Right now they're holding hands. On top of the table.

"It's just a phase," Ade says with surety, and I do a double-take. Hands still holding, pretty much screaming they're a couple to every person in this cafeteria. "The rich are never gay. They marry and have a family. I don't care what my husband does in private as long as it stays private. Those are the rules."

Ade looks at me like I'm being slow, and I look right back at her incredulously. Private? The boys keep caressing each other. In public. In a Catholic church. There's no re-stabling that horse.

What a fucking way to live. I cringe.

"I gotta get to my next class– I'll see ya around." I stand and toss Fate's discarded lunch on top of my tray. It's gross that they never pick up after themselves. I glare at the back of Fate's head, drilling my disappointment into her brain.

Knowing I'm pissed at her, "Do you still want to study tonight?" Ade's big blue eyes look hopeful. She can't stand to be alone for a second, while I revel in it.

"Yeah. Sure– come over after dinner tonight." I say quickly, hoping she falls for it and misses the fact that I asked her to my apartment, not wanting to set foot onto her estate. I grab her garbage, knowing she would just leave it for the staff to pick up.

"You're coming to my house." Ade's command is laced with the sickly sweet tone she uses to cover her true voice. I don't like the calculating gleam in her eye.

"Why?" I ask in suspicion. "Why do you keep forcing the issue? Every time you ask it's more demanding than the last. You sound desperate."

"I… I…" Ade hesitates, and I can see she is struggling to find something that will assuage me. A small V forms between her eyes.

"Just tell me the truth, Ade." I huff. "I need to get to class."

Pain flashes over her perfect features, then she blurts a truth that hurts, but one I also feel to the core of my soul. "I don't like seeing your mother. Okay? It freaks me out." She says of my cancer-riddled mother, causing my heart to break. Her words make her look like an unsympathetic asshole, but I can see Adelaide's point.

I'm my mother's caregiver, and it pains me every time I look her way, hear her labored breath or the faltering of her heart.

Adelaide isn't used to seeing anything that isn't perfect. Also, I don't doubt that she hates visiting my beaten-down apartment in my shitty neighborhood, too. Some people don't like having harsh realities shoved into their faces, showing them how much they have to lose should they fall from on high.

"Fine, I'll come to you." I stare down at the tray, biting back how I truly feel. "Your father doesn't like me, remember? He was carrying the proverbial torch at the last school board meeting, trying to get my scholarship revoked."

"That was *not* what was going down," Ade stresses, and the terror in her eyes clues me in that she's telling the truth. "My mother is your biggest supporter, and Father will never go to battle with her."

Shuddering, I mutter to the trays in my hand, "Maybe we should go to the library instead." I've never been to Whittenhower Estates, and I don't think I want to, either.

"I'll send my driver to pick you up at five. You can eat dinner with us." She looks excited and I don't want to let her down.

"No on dinner. I have to cook for my mom, you know that."

"So make Ella something to eat, but don't eat with her. I'm not trying to be insensitive, but you need some space, Regina. Every moment with her is precious, I get that. But I can see the shadows beneath your eyes." Ade's face goes as soft as her voice. "You're my best friend, and I want my family to meet you. It's been four years– I think it's time, don't you?" The command is back in her voice, and I want to disobey it instantly.

"I'll meet Albert out front of my building at five sharp," I say over my shoulder as I scowl at my best friend. I dump the trash in the garbage, stack the plates and bowls, stow the flatware, and then rinse off the trays with the sprayer. The kitchen staff looks at me with kindness while simultaneously glaring at the rest of the student body in the cafeteria.

"Hillbrook– educating the next generation of pompous assholes."

Chapter Two

I'll be ecstatic when I'm finally finished with Hillbrook. The Cathedral is at the very edge of Dominion's business district, placing it closer to Crestview's gated community. Like Mount Olympus, Crestview overlooks Dominion, where the legacies are tucked safely behind wrought iron and stone in their founders' mansions. I've never been farther than Fate's mansion, only seeing pictures of the hidden, sprawling estates in our history books and museums.

Whittenhower Estates, Adelaide's home, is the largest residential property in the tristate area, if not the country, dwarfing most of our institutions, and I'll be visiting it tonight.

With a foot in two different cultures, it takes a lot of effort to bridge the gap. A twenty-minute subway ride and walking ten blocks to my apartment in a Catholic schoolgirl uniform is pure torture. Daily I deal with constant leers and propositions because I look like a grown woman on her way to work at the strip joint, or the plaything to a deviant with a school girl fetish. A few construction workers mistook me for a guy in drag– I flashed them my nut-free panties to get them to shut up. One guy told me I was an expert '*tucker*' and my huge tits looked natural.

The farther from Hillbrook and the closer I get to home, the worse the abuse I suffer. My people don't like anyone who tries to rise above their station, and I've been verbally and physically attacked for trying to better myself. The only weapons at my disposal are my bitch glare and my strong body screaming **Back Off**.

In times like these, I'm no longer envious that my body isn't petite like Fate's since I need to be able to protect myself. I'm towering over six-feet and curvy. Big boned. Wide hips. Birthing stock. Huge tits perfect for a wet nurse.

I'm not tiny and pretty, which is what a man needs from a woman. They love helpless, fragile, stupid and giggly creatures who feed their male egos. I can never be any of those things, but the thought of coupling with a weak man who needs me to take care of him leaves a bitter taste in my mouth.

I loosen my strawberry blonde hair from its bun, releasing the mass that refuses to curl or lie flat. I'm a sight with my wild hair, green eyes, and girly, virginal uniform. Mid-freshman year, just before my last growth spurt, I was repeatedly groped on the subway. Just after I moved into this neighborhood, I was nearly raped on my walk home. A group of homeboys dragged me into an alley and assaulted me.

Experience has changed me.

Hardened me.

No one bothers me anymore.

Reaching my block, my eyes cast over the dealers hanging out on the corners, the crackheads' zigzag strides, and the whores' dead eyes. I wave to the big, handsome sweetheart guarding the building across the street, and Julio waves back while flashing me a grin.

"Keeping the hood safe, buddy boy?" I call across, projecting my voice over the sound of traffic. I like teasing the burly guy, because I know he has a hand in the fact that I've been untouchable for the past few years.

"Reggie!" Julio brightens because I acknowledged him. No way is he much older than I am. Hell, he might be younger than me for all I know. The streets have a way of aging you before your time. "I visited Ella earlier, brought little Bianca with me."

"Ah…" I press a hand to my chest, eyes watering. I've never spoken to our crime boss, but as his enforcer, when I speak to Julio, I speak to Stanton Green himself. Stanton's a single father, and since I have a way with kids, I've watched Stanton's toddler daughter a few times when Julio was busy.

Employers trust the scholarship kid, and my on-and-off babysitting gig has kept me safe thanks to Stanton putting the word out to all of his employees. If only the elite knew I moonlight for a crime boss…

"So sweet– I bet it brightened my mom's day. Tell Binks I said hi." With a wave, I cut into my building, ignoring the piss-stank smell, used syringes, and broken bottles. Security is real tight here in the hood– there's no front door anymore. I wished Mr. Green owned this side of the street, because he takes care of his property and people.

A baby begins to wail– alarmed, dogs bark from several apartments. Once one kid starts to sob, it's like a siren call to the others. Infants and toddlers join en masse.

Televised, rapid gunfire is paused. "Shut that goddamned kid the fuck up!" shouts an enraged dad who should be working instead of playing on his brand-new Nintendo 64.

"Feed, change, or hold your own fucking kid, asshole!" With the side of my fist, I pound on the lazy idiot's door since it was his baby who alerted the entire building. The kid continues to cry, but the game is restarted. "Jesus, you assholes need to be castrated."

Trudging up the three flights of stairs to my apartment, a litany of bitching plays out in my head. With me going to school, Mom unable to work due to cancer but not eligible for any assistance because I'm eighteen and able-bodied without kids, and Dad's pittance from social security ran out last month when I reached the age of majority, we can't afford the rent in a building with an elevator. It's been really difficult for my mother to make the trek. After Mom's last doctor's appointment, I had to carry her up the stairs like a small child. She can't weigh more than seventy pounds at this point, but it was still a struggle.

I refuse to think about how that was most likely my mother's last time to go outside of our apartment for the rest of her too short life.

But that able-bodied asshole in 1B can live off the system while playing the latest video games.

Taunting, waving at me in the light breeze from the broken window, the red eviction notice is a mirage in my sight. Growing larger and larger, becoming reality, it's all I can see as I walk closer. I yank the offending piece of paper off my door, crumple it up in my fingertips, and then pitch it down the hallway, aiming for the manager's door. I'm not angry with him or the building owner.

I'm furious at my circumstance.

My mother is too ill to work and the medical bills keep piling up. Every time we've filed for assistance, the response was that Dad's SSI should cover us. No medical card, no food stamps– not a dime from the very system my father paid taxes into from the time he was fifteen years old. I barely make enough money to afford food for us to eat by working on the weekends, helping the manager do odds and ends around the building, and picking up some babysitting money from Stanton or one of the mothers on the block. Those baby mommas are broke, trying to make ends meet while their baby daddies are sitting on their asses, sucking everyone dry like a bloodsucking leech, so sometimes I'm paid in a handful of food stamps.

Girlfriends need to get some self-respect and kick the bums to the curb, put the food in their children's mouths instead of a grown-ass man, and never fall victim to the same bullshit, or else they'll end up with another kid on their hands and a second deadbeat daddy.

But I have larger worries than the economic devolution of my neighborhood.

Mom's debt is daunting– a quarter of a million dollars in medical expenses that will fall onto me when she passes away. They've cut us off at the pharmacy, obligatorily sent Hospice our way, will no longer schedule my mother for any doctor's appointments, and have written my mother off as already being dead and not caring about her comfort and pain-level.

Our life used to be very different. We lived in a slightly safer neighborhood, a few blocks over, with the rest of the paycheck-to-paycheck, working class. I grew up in a row house with our neighbors being families with both mommies and daddies. There was a gaggle of kids I used to roam with, all of us going to school together and playing in the park afterward. No gunfire. No drug dealers. No women selling their bodies to pay for their habit. No filthy, health-hazard cesspool of an apartment that is speeding up my mother's demise. While we may have not lived in it, we could see it from our front doors, going everywhere in groups to be safe.

We were poorer than poor, struggling to get by, but Mom and Dad worked hard so there was money from the Tooth Fairy, the Easter Bunny dropped off a candy-filled basket as he hopped by, and we had a fireplace Santa would slide down on Christmas Eve to fill the stockings and place presents under the tree.

My parents would go without to make sure there was family game night, movie night, Taco Tuesdays and Pizza Fridays. Dad's green eyes would light up and his freckled face would pink when he looked Mom's way, then he'd ask her to dance while I played the piano in the front room.

We took vacations to Upstate New York and camped in the Finger Lakes every summer. Dad was waiting on his fifteen-year salary increase from the Transit Authority, promising a better future filled with a home to call our own in a lower middle class neighborhood, a puppy for me, and a used car for Mom to drive to her job at the supermarket.

Dad earned his raise, and we celebrated by going to the A.S.P.C.A and looking at throwaway puppies, pointing out sporty cars we'd pass on the street, and by sitting around in the evenings looking at the real-estate section of *Dominion's Insider.*

Dad was no dreamer, a hard-working man with a family as his incentive, and he was determined to make it a reality. Then tragedy struck, destroying a future that would never become reality.

A drunk asshole ran a red light, plowing into the side of Dad's bus, right where he was sitting. Since no one else was critically injured, there was no fuss made– no restitutions paid.

Curtis Regal was just a bus driver, and his wife and daughter were worthless when it came to the City's list of priorities.

Dad's pension would've kicked in at the twenty-year mark, our insurance was cut off the day Dad died, and we were left to fend on our own with a monthly pittance from SSI.

Life can change in the blink of an eye, and I'm only eighteen. How many more times will I have to deal with the shift in my lifetime?

At least once more, I remind myself when my mind wanders back to my loving mother. I think she tried to hold out long enough for me to become legal, ensuring I wouldn't be placed with Child Protective Services.

A mother's will to survive is only strengthened by her children, and I appreciate how much she loves me. Long ago, I came to terms that her death was looming– nothing will stop it. But it would have been better for my future if she had let go last month when I was still seventeen. I feel awful for thinking it, like the evilest of human beings. Every day she is with me is a blessing, but my future is now shit before it has even begun.

Sure, I could get a lawyer and fight the hospital for the debts owed, but I have neither money for the debts that will go to collections, nor a lawyer to make them go away. I'm stuck.

I try to be quiet as I enter our apartment, knowing Mom sleeps more than she's awake and I don't wish to disturb her. The door squeaks on its rusted hinges and I startle, as if freezing will erase the sound.

If we had any furniture, at least it would act as sound absorbers.

"Is that you, Regina?" Straining, my mother's raspy voice echoes from the only bedroom in the apartment.

"Yeah, it's me, Ma!" I yell back. "I'll be with you in a minute. I have a few chores to do on my way."

Leaning with my back against the door, eyes slipping shut as my heart breaks wide open, I try to fortify my nerves. Seeing our dilapidated apartment, with all of the precious treasures my father worked so hard to provide long gone, isn't as difficult as facing my mother. With a deep breath, I shove away from the door.

If there is a chore to complete, I do it because it makes me feel like I'm accomplishing something– anything. I hate feeling helpless, and there is nothing worse than the powerless feeling of impending death.

I clean up the stray clothes, water bottles, and plates that my mother and her visitors left around the living-space. Rich or poor, cleanliness is an issue for both. I see someone spilled tea on my blanket, and unadulterated fury slams into me out of nowhere, and I immediately regret my resentment. It's not Mom's fault that her mobility is shit– but it's not my blanket's fault, either.

I can't blame her, but that doesn't take away that it did happen. Frustration and guilt are the root to most of my mood swings. I pull my blanket and pillows off my bed– the couch– and tuck them safely behind it.

Our apartment has three rooms: a small bedroom that barely holds the single bed. There are no nightstands, or dressers, or even a closet. We pawned all of our old furniture when we moved into this apartment, with my childhood bed taking up residence in the only bedroom. The bathroom is big enough for me to sit on the toilet taking a shit while simultaneously washing my hands in the sink while soaking my feet in the shallow tub. The living-room-kitchen-combo has a couch, no T.V., a two-seater table, and a dinky kitchenette with rundown appliances.

The rent on this hellhole is ridiculous, as is everything else in Dominion. The cost-of-living is exponentially higher in the slums because we're unable to afford moving to a nicer neighborhood because there are no jobs that would support it.

We're born here, and unless you claw your way out, we're stuck here. I've been clawing my ass out since birth, while my neighbors have been grabbing at my ankles, trying to pull me back down to their level.

I have barely enough to cover the rent and utilities. I missed this month's rent a few days ago because it was either that or no pain medication for Mom. I have no way to pay the rent, or next month's rent. We have sixty days before they gather up our stuff, where they'll place it on the curb like garbage, and then lock us out. I have no clue what to do.

Mom's dying. I'm still in high school, and about to be homeless until I start college in the fall. I shouldn't have to worry about this shit at my age.

With a deep fortifying breath, I peek around the doorframe. "Ma, how are you feeling today?"

Ella Regal is a shallow shell of her previous self. Her blonde hair is no longer silky and long. Now wispy puffs of pure white hair no thicker than a spider's web freckle her scalp. The rounded cheeks and button nose of youth are now gaunt and sunken in. Her once voluptuous body is now a skeleton of skin-covered bones with a network of protruding blue veins.

I try not to look at Mom and have it affect me. I've had to distance myself emotionally, or I would've gone insane. There is no way I could ever be my mother's caregiver and allow myself the chance to breakdown. I don't have the luxury of feeling grief and pain when the most important person in my life is wasting away, her body cannibalizing itself, with every nerve in her body signaling pain to her brain.

If things had been different, if we could have afforded hospitalization and caregivers, the bond between mother and daughter could have been preserved. I try to give her warmth, but it's difficult when I have to remain cold in order to be clinical when it comes to washing her body, helping her to the bathroom, and feeding and clothing her. I need someone to hold me and take the pain away, and the only person who can do that needs it from me instead. My needs do not matter, so I have to distance myself in order to survive. I've been in a constant state of grief for years on end.

Dad passed away two years ago in the accident. At the same time, my mother was at the hospital being diagnosed with late-stage breast cancer. I had to take care of funeral arrangements while helping my mother cope with the loss of my father and her inevitable demise, all the while grieving in private without a shoulder to cry on.

I've never spoken the words aloud that I can't wait until this battle is finally over, with both of my parents at peace and hopefully together. But I can't help thinking it on a daily basis. Does that make me a horrible person? Probably, but don't judge until you've watched a person decay before your eyes, both mentally and physically. It's a form of hell reserved only for the living.

I paste a blurry image of my once healthy and full of vitality mother over her present decaying version.

"I'm doing better today than yesterday," Mom lies, voice weak and thready, like she needs a drink but no amount of water will ever change it. Noting every change in her body, I can see a pronounced difference from last week. Especially in her eyes, her green gaze is glazed over in intense pain.

"Ma, did you take your pills?" Voice soft, I approach the bed. I know she didn't when I see her white knuckling the flannel blanket, a shiver working a way through her body. It's eighty degrees outside and a good ninety in the stifling environment of our apartment, and my mother has three blankets covering her and she's still shivering.

"Yes, Regina," she lies poorly– forever the mother provider, even if it lessens her comfort. "I took my medicine just a few minutes ago. Let it run its course." Struggling to shift on the small bed, she sits up partially to distract me from the obvious. "How was school today?"

Mom's pain pills cost more than a month's worth of groceries, or the price of one designer, silk sock worn by a Hillbrook legacy. She's been skipping doses because we can't afford the refills. This is her last time on earth, and it should be pain-free– luxury or not.

Ignoring Mom's attempts at connecting with me, I go into caregiver-mode. "Did you run out again?" I ask over my shoulder as I walk into the bathroom to check the medicine cabinet. Fingers clutching the amber bottle, I give a shake and hear no rattle– empty.

Jesus Christ.

"I'll be back in time to fix your dinner." I say as I hurry from the apartment before I change my mind. There aren't many way to gain some quick cash, but I'd do anything for my mother.

My feet slide along three flights of steps on autopilot, taking me to my destination even if my mind and heart are warring. Exactly where I knew he'd be, I find Roman Alexander holding up the side of my building in the alleyway.

As a member in Stanton Green's criminal army, Roman isn't much older than I am. But around here, by the time you're my age, you're on your own. Thank God, he isn't bad to look at if you're into the sexy bad boy– I'm not... or so I lie to myself. Jawline sharp enough to cut glass, his Native American ancestry created an exotic creature with a fall of black hair brushing his broad shoulders. His intelligent blue-green eyes take in everything within 180 degrees of him.

"Miss Regal regales me with her presence." Widened eyes shine, traveling over my body from head to toe, then his lips curl into a naughty smirk.

Groaning with mortification– I forgot to change out of my school uniform.

Roman has been after me since before I grew boobs, but not in the predatory way others have been. Kindred spirits. It's a miracle if you keep your virginity until you're twelve around here. I'm an anomaly at the ripe old age of eighteen.

"Roman, I need a favor." I ignore my voice when it breaks. However, Roman misses nothing. "Mom's out of pain pills, and if I were to take a guess, this will be her last refill." Eyes held wide to stop the flow of tears, I look at Roman, silently admitting that Mom won't last until the bottle is empty.

I don't want to admit it out loud. I feel relief thinking that it would be easier when she's gone, but I dread it too. I wouldn't change a thing, as long as she stayed with me, but she's in immense pain and her suffering needs to end.

I'm not *that* selfish.

Face softening, stance sagging against the building, Roman projects sympathy but no pity. "I don't traffic that kind of thing, sweetheart. You know that. I'm sure your mom has a prescription for them." His voice is a soothing wash over my throbbing emotions, and I know he's merely placating me. "It would take Stan a couple days to track down a supplier, and I assume you need them immediately."

"I know," I admit while scrubbing a hand over my face. "It's not that– we have a few refills left, but I don't have any money and she's in horrific pain right now."

Frustrated, on the edge of either murdering something or holding up a convenience store, I stomp my Mary-Jane on the pavement. Roman's sharp bark of laughter turns into a grin. He thinks I'm being cute and it pisses me off. This is life or death– I'm not asking him for a date.

"Are you saying you want to work for it?" He arches a perfect, black eyebrow at me in surprise.

Shaking my head left and right, I plead with him. "I'm willing to do *anything* I need to do to take her pain away."

"You know I can't put you on the streets to sell even if you changed your clothes." Roman tugs at my skirt. "We all know the smartass Regina Regal goes to Hillbrook and has a fancy scholarship. No fucking way would they buy anything from you, sweetheart." He leans against the building and folds his arms over his chest, bulging the muscles. It's impressive, but I'm not impressed.

Losing the pleading tone, I get down to business. "I need two hundred and thirty bucks for a refill, and I'll do anything you want to get it."

Roman's eyebrow hitches sinisterly high with interest. "Anything?" He drawls, curling the word around his tongue, and I nod my head yes in reply. "Then follow me…" He pushes from the wall and swaggers away.

Shoulders back, head held high, eyes looking straight forward, refusing to show defeat, I follow Roman behind our building to a metal door. He leads me down the cement steps and into the small basement apartment he rents. It's the same size as mine, but the windows are at ceiling-level and he has more furniture. Dealing pays better– he even has a television.

"This will be the most expensive blowjob I've ever had and probably the worst." Roman's blunt about our transaction, and his businesslike attitude comforts me some. "But deflowering your mouth will be worth it– everyone already thinks we've been fucking for years. It's time I had those ripe lips wrapped around my cock." Salacious, words taking on a filthy cadence, Roman is trying to scare me away.

I flinch as Roman mentions his cock. I've never even kissed a guy, let alone handled a dick. I'm thankful, though, because I thought he'd demand sex. I know how much the girls ask for on the street, and it's nothing in comparison to what I'm getting for a simple blowjob, which will probably suck in a bad way for Roman.

I don't want to do it. *At all.* But I will. I waited to do this with my first real boyfriend, but it could be worse. Roman, although a lecherous dealer, has been my friend for a long time.

I will do anything to make my mother's last moments on earth peaceful and pain-free.

Anything.

In the middle of Roman's kitchen, I drop to my knees in front of him as he stands impassively by. I try to ignore how cold the linoleum is against my bare knees. A slash in the flooring is digging into my skin, leaving an impression that will fade quickly but the moment will forever be branded into my soul.

Childhood lost– no longer a daddy's girl. I transform into a survivor.

Staring at the bulging crotch in a pair of secondhand jeans, I experience another shift in reality as my world tilts on its axis. Two hours ago, I was sitting in Advanced Placement Calculus, going over the questions on our upcoming final. I earned half a college credit from the course before ever stepping foot out of high school. All eight of my senior classes were A.P., so I'm starting college with a head start. Now I'm kneeling before a drug dealer, prepared to give him head.

Chest rapidly rising and falling, nearly gasping for air, my teeth begin to chatter. With shaking fingertips, I fumble with the zipper at Roman's fly. All of a sudden, my fingers feel swollen with fear as they try for the tiny bit of metal holding back the demanding bulge in his pants.

My eyes roll up to his just as I find purchase with the zipper. I slowly drag it down as my emotions turn from dread to anticipation. Incredible, a rush surges in my veins. Right now, I want to do this for some reason, and I want to do it to Roman. I don't want this to be the most expensive, worst blowjob he's ever had. I want to do a good job like I do on everything else. I want to suck Roman better than anyone else has ever sucked him before.

Moving in my periphery, his hand draws my attention away from the glimpse of navy boxers peeking at me through his fly. He whips out a roll of cash from his pocket and peels off three bills. Around here, that's rent money. But where I spend my days, it's a daily allowance.

"Keep the change," Roman murmurs as he hands me three hundred bucks. I take the money with shaky fingertips, and then shove it deep into the cup of my bra.

My fingers resume their fumbling at the button on his jeans, oddly eager and curious. Stopping me, Roman's grip surrounds my wrist, so softly I barely feel any pressure. With a smooth jerk, he pulls me to my feet, my knees sticking to the dirty linoleum– a popping noise sounds as they break free from the sticky floor.

More so than confused, I feel disappointed for some reason as I stand before Roman.

"Regina," Roman breathes my name, hand rising to brush a strand of my hair off my cheek. "That's because you're my friend."

"I-I-I… I don't understand," I stammer, cheeks blooming with a crimson kiss of embarrassment, humiliation, and rejection.

"Don't ever whore yourself out to anyone, do you understand me?" Roman's voice breaks on the demand. "After your mom passes, I want you to reach for your dreams. You're too good for this Godforsaken life." His turquoise eyes are filled with tears, and I can't stop mine from leaking out the corner of my eyes to fall down my cheeks.

What have I become?

I wanted to suck Roman off, and it hadn't even crossed my mind that I was whoring myself out for money.

What is wrong with me?

Roman reaches up and wipes my tears of shame away with his rough fingertips. "Remember me someday when you're a big-time computer whiz." He kisses my forehead, leads me out of his apartment and up the stairs, and then pushes me outside. "Better run along– the pharmacy on 68th and Carmichael closes at five." His kind smile is the last thing I see as he disappears back into the depths of his apartment.

In a haze of confusion, I rush to the pharmacy and back as quickly as possible. I have to meet Ade's driver at five outside of my building. I bought some groceries with the leftover cash Roman gave me after I paid for the pills. Using chores to blank my mind, to erase the consequences of my almost-actions, I quickly prepare Mom's supper. She can barely hold anything down anymore. I warm up some beef broth and fix her a grilled cheese sandwich. I place it on a tray along with a cup of tea laced with honey and lemon, and bakery shortbread cookies.

"Here ya go, Mom." I place the tray on her lap, and then hand her two pain pills with a full glass of water. One pill will no longer numb her pain away, and I worry two may not be enough anymore, either.

"What did you do to get this money?" A strong accusation heavily laces her thready voice. I don't answer her– it's none of her damn business what I have to do to make her comfortable. In the past two years as she was slowly declining, I know Mom did many things she's ashamed to admit.

It's called survival, and there is no shame in that.

Gingerly resting my hip on the edge of the bed so I won't upset her tray, I turn from caregiver to the daughter Mom is starving for more so than food. "School was eventful today– freshman orientation. Hillbrook was bloated by nine non-legacy students, readying to take the Ivy League by storm."

"You fail miserably at keeping the bitter edge out of your tone," Mom admonishes me as she dips her spoon into the broth, but her tone is wicked sarcastic.

Sharing a rare smile with my mom, a laugh flutters from my chest. "I'll never deny that I've had the best education in the country. If I knew who my benefactor was, I'd give them a big hug. But that doesn't take away from the fact that the kids at Hillbrook are more lost than the crackheads zigzagging down our streets."

"No one asks to be born." The dull crunch of Mom's teeth cracking through the toasted sandwich is a pleasure to my ears. Anything that gives Mom strength is a godsend. "No one should be judged or envied on their station in life. It's their behavior that dictates whether they are a good human being."

Smirking, "Is that your way of saying I'm being nasty to my fellow students because they're asshats?"

"Their parents are asshats," Mom mimics me, smirking back. "Your peers are asshats-in-training, just as your peers in the neighborhood are users-in-training: drug using, using their bodies with disregard of self-respect, and using the system to the point there is no money for those who truly need it. We're all victims of our stations in life– it's up to the individual to drag their own asses out of it."

"Ah! You definitely saw Julio today. That boy has some odd notions about community revitalization."

"Stanton," Mom floors me.

"What?" I gasp, voice tight like I'm speaking through a straw.

Making me earn the information, Mom continues to dunk her sandwich into the broth, then chews thoughtfully. "Stanton came with Julian and Bianca. He's always liked to visit with me because my personality mirrors that of his mother."

"You mean from not around here, don't you?" Cocking my head to the side, I really look at my mother, trying to see beneath the disease. Two years ago, my mother was a stunning woman to the point that if she was in the room, Dad couldn't take his eyes off her. At thirty-five, she now looks like a body long buried in the ground.

"Stanton Green is oddly moral for a criminal," my mother muses. "His family lives in Upstate New York on a farm. His stepfather was described as looking like your father. Burly, red-haired and green-eyed, with a strong work ethic. A Marine. Since we've moved into the neighborhood, Stanton's enjoyed my company when he needs a burst of reality, because I don't thrive on… destructive behavior."

"Whoa…" I whisper, mind blown. Roman exhibits some of the very traits of his employer. It's a good thing he does, because I was wandering down the inescapable path of destructive behavior. The soup my mother is eating was nearly bought and paid for by the rhythmic suction of my lips wrapped around an eager cock.

Shuddering, I change the subject. "Did you have any other visitors today?"

"A few neighborhood ladies." With a clank, the spoon falls into the soup bowl. "Their constant hovering and gossiping exhausts me so. I'm unable to rest when I need it."

"I'm sorry, Mom." I reach over to fish her spoon out of the broth bowl. After wiping it dry with a napkin, I press it back into her hand. "After graduation, I'll be able to monitor your visitors so they don't overtax you."

"All mothers should have a daughter like you, Regina." Mom sounds wistful as she dips her spoon back into her broth, coming away with barely a sip. "Your father and I were truly blessed when we had you."

"Dad didn't think that when he was swatting my ass for being a brat." I try to use humor to shift the conversation.

"You'll make an incredible wife and mother someday– your children will lack for nothing that's important. I wish things would have been different, where I could've gotten you ready for prom, been at your graduation from Hillbrook and University… your wedding day. The excitement of finding out you're pregnant for the first time. Holding my grandchildren in my arms and seeing your father reflected in their eyes."

"Mom," I gasp out on a gut-wrenching sob, spine bowing from the force to keep it silent. "Please don't. Please."

Caregiver is lightyears easier than daughter.

Ignoring my protests, "Even if I'm not here in body, I'll be here in spirit. If you ever miss me or your dad, just look to your children."

Unable to take this for a moment longer, I turn to the side to mask the horror etched across my face. In theory, I can't wait for this to be over. In practice, I haven't even grasped the concept of Mom's death. When it finally hits me, I'll feel like I'm the one who died.

I finally understand what Ade meant earlier, about how I needed to get away and be *me*. Every second is an added blessing with my mother, but constantly staring down the Grim Reaper is killing me as surely as he is killing my mother.

"I'm going to Ade's house for dinner tonight, and we're studying for our finals after. Albert– her driver is picking me up and taking me home, so you don't have to worry if I'm late."

I rub Mom's bony thigh as I speak. It feels like massaging a dried up twig through a cheap, threadbare blanket, but I can tell the contact makes her feel better– loved. I try to ignore the tactile sensation that leaves me queasy.

I sit with Mom while she slowly eats her meal, and we chat about everything that's going on at school and random bits of gossip around the neighborhood. This is our routine. We used to do it at our kitchen table, now we do it while she rests in bed.

I clean up after supper and tell my mother goodnight. Then I charge down the three flights of stairs, knowing I'm late. With an *eek!* of surprise, I burst out the front door, one that didn't exist an hour ago. Slamming it against the outside wall, I avoid the rebound, but just barely.

What greets me is a black Town Car idling at the curb with Roman interrogating the driver. Julio polices one side of the street, with Roman on this side. If you're not from these parts, don't expect a warm reception.

"Miss Regal," Albert greets me, looking relieved. The Whittenhower's driver is a kind, patient man in his late thirties. I've ridden around with him for the past four years. I've never met the Whittenhower family besides Ade and Katie, but I know their driver well.

"Hello, Albert. Sorry to make you drive all the way over here just to pick me up. Adelaide always gets what she wants– you know that better than anyone." We share a conspiratorial smile. "Here," I say to Roman as I hand him four sandwiches and a few shortbreads. He stares at me in amazement.

I can tell Roman thought I would be angry with him for what he did to me in his apartment. I know he was trying to teach me a valuable lesson on how easily we can stoop to get what we need. How asking a friend for a hand-up is not a handout. I understand why he sells drugs to survive. I don't judge, and I never will. I always thought myself above it all, though. I was wrong, because even I'm willing to whore myself out to survive.

Using humiliation as a learning tool, Roman knocked me off my self-created pedestal and showed me the error of my ways with kindness. How the hell could I be angry at him for *that*?

"I seem to have extra this evening after my good fortune. Thanks, Roman. Mom is sleeping peacefully because of you. I will never forget your act of kindness."

Leaning forward, I kiss Roman on the cheek in thanks, and he jolts as if I've electrocuted him. He flashes me a goofy grin that I haven't seen grace his face since I first arrived in the neighborhood. I kiss him on the other cheek for the simple pleasure of seeing the real Roman filter through his tough guy image. I allow myself a brief touch of his shiny hair, after always wanting to know what it would feel like to sink my fingers deep into the silky strands. His hair has always fascinated me because it's so unlike my wiry mass. It's even softer than I imagined.

Stepping away from me while wearing a sad, little grin, "This is your future, sweetheart." Roman gestures with the sweep of his hand toward the expensive car idling at the curb. "Don't let anyone take it from you– *anyone*. Ever."

I flash Roman a shy smile in reply as Albert helps me into the car. The door cuts off my view of his face, and by the time the driver moves, Roman is already walking away. But I can tell by his jerky movements that he's eating my sandwiches. I smile to myself and enjoy the smooth ride.

Chapter Three

After a few minutes of idle chitchat about my school performance, Albert sinks into his duty with practiced ease, leaving me to my private thoughts. Leaning on the armrest, cheek pressed against the cool glass of the window, I mull over Roman's words.

Is *this* my future? Riding in an expensive car with a driver behind the wheel? While the luxury of it is beyond decadent, it feels more like a trap. The absence of freedom. Merely being the passenger in your life while someone else drives.

If I stay on the academic track I'm on, I'm positive I could afford this at some point, but I'd never buy it. Everything happens for a reason, and as I watch street after street of the slums roll by, I know I was meant to be where I am today to keep myself humble in the future.

Instead of buying an expensive car, I could buy four reliable cars to pass out to those who need a way to get to work. It's the difference between rewarding the bum sitting on his couch and actually helping the mother trying to feed her family. The indulgence and waste is disgusting. While I don't advocate the redistribution of wealth because it teaches no one anything, the hoarding of money when it could better lives is sickening.

While my classmates passed notes and mooned over each other, I truly paid attention in economics class. But I paid greater attention to the world surrounding me. Money has greater value to the starving than it does to those who hoard it.

Idling at a stoplight, at the intersection where the lower income section meets the business district, I watch the suit-clad business people eye the service workers as if they're going to be mugged– the very people who scrub their toilets and serve them their seven dollar coffees. Not tipping their server could mean the difference between making rent and living on the street for the server. When desperate, crime happens.

As the Town Car rolls down the street, the buildings get taller, grander– steel and glass. Chrome emblems on the hoods of expensive cars shine bright in sunlight– the elites' form of a cock-measuring-contest. On the sidewalks stride women wearing stilettos and pencil skirts, receiving wolf-like hungry gazes from men wearing three-piece business suits.

These people are just playacting at being rich. There is *having* money, and then there is *being* money. Owning the suit, having the degree, and working at a corporation means nothing in Dominion unless your name is *on* the building.

The Green Building is up ahead– Stanton Green prefers to live in the slums across the street from me because it's safer to live with honest criminals instead of sociopathic philanthropists. Humble. Not fucking audacious ridiculousness.

Like a gorgeous eyesore, ominous black-tinted glass surges from the ground with a sense of contained violence, The Edge Building rises three stories higher than any other building in Dominion.

In the heart of Dominion's business district, the founders play global domination– my classmates' parents and families. Closing my eyes to the excess, I agree with Stanton Green. I'd rather be back in the hood.

Reality.

Albert accelerates, causing my eyes to pop wide open. He meets my gaze in the rearview mirror with a tiny smile of reassurance. This isn't the first time I've ridden down this particular highway, and not because my father used to take us on family day-trips and vacations. This road is not the road out of Dominion– it's the only way to Mount Olympus.

Crestview gated community is a few miles out in the middle of nowhere, resting higher than the low-lying business district and residential neighborhoods. The land Dominion's founding fathers first settled looks down upon the city like a disapproving parent.

We slow to a stop for the first of a series of wrought iron gates, surrounded by miles and miles of impenetrable fencing. Just like how having a driver forces you to be a passenger in life, the fence and gate keep more people in than out.

Albert rolls down his window to speak to the guard. "Pleasant day, isn't it, Robert?" He gestures to the backseat. "I have Miss Regal joining me."

"Very well, then." The bearded face of the security guard comes closer as he leans into Albert's window. At first I fear he's making sure I'm who I say I am, but then I see his lips move. "I'm sure I'll see you again when one of the darlings force you to run an errand for their entitled skinny asses."

Albert's abrupt laugh is immediately smothered, warping into a repressed snort-like sound. "Oh, no doubt I'll see you at least four more times on your shift. Off at midnight, are you?"

"And your shift never ends." The guard leans back until he's upright, then walks away with a wave, disappearing into his shack.

Albert continues to chuckle underneath his breath as we traverse the wide, straight as an arrow street. Identical mansions dot the street at even intervals, offset, so their gates don't faceoff with one another.

From what I've gathered from Fate on my few visits, the closer you are to the gate, the less power you have in Dominion. Even inside their cage, the founders fight for power.

The Simpson home is the first mansion to greet you upon entering Crestview, meaning Fate and Faith's family has the least power. The street bisecting the community feels like it runs for miles, but that doesn't mean there are a lot of residents. The spacing between mansions is thousands of feet wide. Their neighbors share the street, but they are most certainly not their next-door neighbors.

I've never been past the first house, so it's a bizarre experience to pass opulent lawns behind the security of wrought iron fences and intimidating gates. Rolling slowly, I have a sneaking suspicion Albert is setting a pace for me to absorb it all. With my face twisted in disgust, Albert seems to be warming to me by the second, no doubt thinking it all sickening as well.

Abruptly the street just ends, forking three ways. On the left and right, there is another set of gates with guard shacks like at the entrance to Crestview. But in the center is a gothic gate draped in a black, death shroud.

"What happened?" I gasp, heart beating uncontrollably, mind venturing a city away, in a neighborhood the complete and total opposite of this. My mother's gaunt face flashes before my eyes. "Did someone die?"

Albert draws the car to a stop, shifting into park. "Behind these three gates, and miles and miles of woods, are the original founding fathers, with those they brought here filling the houses behind us."

Mind reacting to Albert's verbal cue, my head whips around to stare at the mansions towering behind us.

"The center is Zeitler– the shroud is almost two years old, replaced monthly in homage to Rebekah Zeitler. Way before

Dominion was anything but woodland, the Zeitlers were the ones who took charge, getting their hands dirty with the others to build the first home erected in the area. Sanctuary housed everyone while the village was built."

Nodding, because that's exactly the history I learned, I watch as pain crosses Albert's features.

"Sanctuary was razed to the ground almost two years ago. It was a sad time, as not only did we lose an important part of our history, we lost the woman who kept them all… human."

Throat tightening, eyes tearing up, all I can do is stare in horror at the black shroud's wind-whipped tattered edges.

Shifting back into gear, Albert pulls to the right. "The left is Holden's Shadow Haven. Marcus Zeitler married into the family, but he's still a man without a home."

"Ezra Holden-Zeitler," rolls off my tongue as I gaze out the window, trying to see the new freshman's home, but there is nothing but the gate and the woods lining the hills behind it.

On the right, the gate opens before us, allowing Albert to drive past the guard shack with only a tilt of his chin in greeting. We're immediately swallowed by trees. Gazing out the back window, I watch as the gate shuts. The resounding clank locks us in more so than intruders out.

"The founding fathers are a vicious lot," Albert warns as the car navigates the switchbacks, cutting the wooded mountainside at a fast clip. Dizziness overcomes me, trees whip by, and the road disappears behind us as we drive higher and higher above Dominion. Fighting off vertigo, my ears pop.

An ominous feeling descends, forcing me to swallow my fear. On some level, I instinctively realize I won't leave Whittenhower Estates as the same person I was when I entered.

Albert continues to speak as I struggle to keep my equilibrium. "Miss Simpson and young Miss Simpson are good girls, but their father is a worse criminal than our Mr. Green. In the two hundred years of Dominion history, Thomas Simpson is the first to be allowed into our community by anything other than marriage, blood, or bloodshed."

"Bloodshed?" My heart patters out of control, and I finally realize it's not the change in altitude. I'm on the cusp of a panic attack.

"Our founding fathers had roles to play in the creation of Dominion. The Green role was organized crime, no different than any other business erected. It was for our protection to police all levels of society, to ensure our reign was never overthrown. All business is criminal in nature, and our Mr. Green is revered with the same level of respect as the Whittenhowers are for their contribution to civilized society."

"I'm a good student, but I don't want to admit I understand what you're saying. Nor do I want to contemplate why you're warning me in the first place."

"Good girl, Miss Regal," Albert murmurs as we crest the mountain.

"Jesus Christ!" I nearly shout, aghast. "I think I'm going to be sick." Slumping forward, I rest my head between my knees with my hands over my eyes, but nothing will erase the split-second view from my memory.

Owning an entire high-rise in Dominion is the very definition of power. Whittenhower Estates? I thought it was a goddamn joke when they'd toss out the word castle.

It's no wonder I felt like the trees were swallowing me. It's like I'm being transported more than two hundred years into the past as the tortured heroine in a gothic novel.

Dumbfounded, unbidden, my head jerks up to take it all in. The nausea abates if I ignore the castle and gaze out at the miles and miles of Dominion sprawled beneath.

"The front of the estate welcomes you, the rear overlooks her people. It's a sight on a clear evening from the back lawns," Albert whispers in a soothing tone. "Lights as far as the eye can see. The Holden's Edge Building winks off and on, as if it's calling out to its master, knowing he can't see her."

"What?" I gasp, still ignoring the castle in favor of squinting my eyes to see if the slums darken Whittenhower Estates' back lawn.

"Each of the three large estates have an advantage. Holden looks directly onto Crestview. Zeitler has its own lake, a natural fortification the originators used for a natural resource and protection. But Whittenhower Estates has the uninterrupted view of Dominion on the whole."

"This isn't feudal England," I snarl, thoroughly disgusted.

"And where do you think the founders came from?" Albert smirks at me in the rearview mirror, enjoying my discomfort. "Well, the Whittenhowers are descendants of highborn."

"Clearly the Greens weren't," I mutter sarcastically.

"Clearly. It's quite possible they were indentured servants to the Whittenhowers and Holdens, but were smart enough to break their chains. As punishment, they were reduced to lifetimes of crime." Albert has a wicked streak. "Are you going to look at the castle now?"

"No," I mutter begrudgingly like a child. "I don't want to– it makes me sick."

"It's impressive in the way a car accident or a compound fracture is," Albert teases me. "But I've learned to look at it as the architectural wonder that is Whittenhower Estates. On the flip side, realize generations of more than two hundred souls would not have employment without this monstrosity existing. Realize, that without the founding families, life would be far worse for all those who live in Dominion."

"Fine!" With defiance, my stomach flips over as I take in the house where Ade lives. Ade is *inside* a gigantic fucking castle.

We're parked at the arc of a circular driveway leading up to a building so large I'd have to exit the vehicle and walk backward, and then farther backward to take it all in. I'd have to walk into the woods to have an unimpeded viewpoint.

Gray stone as far as the eye can see, with buttresses supporting the structure. The innumerable leaded glass windows have high arches. Menacing gargoyles gaze down at me from the roofline.

"What could the Whittenhowers have possibly done to deserve this?"

"Luck? Being born into a legacy. The three *I*s. Intelligence. Ingenuity. Industry. They shaped our great nation, isn't that deserving enough?"

"No." With clinical eyes, I see the history, not the excessive display of wealth.

The Castle is definitely a '*her*', because she is watching over her people's safety beneath. The outbuildings are fortifications meant not only to protect but to defend its master. It's the law of nature that someone has to be in charge, has the responsibility for the safety and welfare of those they protect, feed, and educate. It's a continuing cycle, every part having an equally important function. Where it goes off the wheels is the fact that no one should live *inside* a fucking castle, unless it's packed to the seams with the very people it's protecting.

Gothic, dark and depressive, a malevolent force settles over me as I look at the façade of Whittenhower Estates, as if it hides pain deep within its mortar and devastating secrets behind its walls.

"Misery Castle," I whisper beneath my breath as Albert opens my car door and releases me into a world I could never envision.

Chapter Four

One of the wooden double-doors to the imposing stone mansion flies open and makes me jump backward with a startled *meep!* Leaning against the car, clutching my backpack to my chest, I stare into the brightest blue eyes I've ever seen in my lifetime.

Clack. Clack. Clack. Tiny leather shoes run down the front limestone steps, where they come to a stop on the cobblestone drive. Cocking his head to the side like a hawk sighting down its prey, the small towheaded boy smiles until a dimple dents his cherub cheek.

"Aren't you the cutest thing I've ever seen?" Chest aching with how pure the little boy is, I can barely stand it. "You're like human sunshine."

"My name is Daniel Whittenhower II," the little boy announces formally, bowing his head. "Daniel is one of the old men of the house, so everyone calls me Whitt."

The child's hand is held out for a shake. He's a polite little boy with the mind of a grown man– how peculiar. Wrapping my fingers around his, I shake Whitt's hand. Flexing, he tightens his grip on me. He's strong too, but not as strong as a gargantuan woman. I smile as he pouts for not getting the desired reaction out of me, his lips twisting with resignation.

"Physical strength isn't the only quantifier of power, so don't pout." Releasing his hand after a gentle squeeze, I introduce myself as formally as the little man had done with me. "It's a pleasure to meet you, Whitt. My name is Regina Regal."

Eyes glowing even brighter, "Do you have a nickname?" His voice pitches high with excitement.

I shrug, thinking of the lame 'sweetheart' Roman calls me. "No one has ever given me a nickname tailored just for me."

"Can I call you Queen from now on?" Voice hopeful and innocent, he tugs on my hand to pull me up the stairs toward the front doors.

Queen? I give Whitt a confused look in return. So engrossed with the tiny man-child, I don't realize we're in a three-story foyer until my sneakers begin tapping on the marble flooring.

Walking backward while tugging me forward, Whitt looks me deep in the eyes. "Both your names mean Queen. I just learned about how Regina means queen in some language– I can't remember which." He scrunches his eyes together just as Ade does when she's concentrating or confused. He looks at me so seriously that I know he isn't joking.

"How do you know this stuff already? I thought you were only five." Ade talks about her little brother all the time. She thinks he's annoying. This is one more thing I will disagree with her on.

Whitt's a lovely boy.

"Doesn't everyone learn this stuff?" He looks at me as if I'm from another planet. I guess I am– planet reality. I forgot for a moment that they have their own community and don't venture out to learn about anything else. "I've been going to Hillbrook since I was two and a half."

"Okay, from now on my nickname is officially Queen." Whitt smiles widely, showing off his set of dimples and a missing front tooth. His eyes shine conspiratorially. But as cute as it is, it kind of creeps me out. What does he know that I need to know?

Whitt grabs my hand tighter and pulls. He doesn't speak, but by the way he's yanking on my hand, I guess he's going to show me instead.

Whitt tugs me along a museum-quality furnished hallway. I missed the detailing in the foyer, and now the hallway, because the tiny man is pulling me briskly toward somewhere. He stops next to a slightly open door, and I nearly collide with him.

Whitt puts a finger to his lips and smiles, showcasing his dimples. His eyes glow with a devious light as we eavesdrop on his family.

A chill runs down my spine and my skin breaks out with goosebumps as I'm swept over by a startling premonition. I don't like the ominous feeling pouring from this house.

Whitt gazes up at me, pleading with me to listen. Suddenly woozy, my hand finds the mahogany-paneled wall and my fingers tighten over the molding. I have to hold myself in place or I'd run as fast as possible from Whittenhower Estates and never look back. But I fear I'd never make it out of the two gates separating me from the outside world.

Trapped.

The small but strong hand grips tighter. Whitt's either lending me support, or he's making sure I don't make a run for it. Eyes downcast, the little boy taps his ear, and then leans forward to press it against the crack in the door.

Following his lead, I hear more than I bargained for. "Grant, after young Daniel's outburst during Adelaide's betrothal negotiations, we need another heir." An older gentleman is speaking, concern thick in his voice.

I look down at Whitt, our eyes connecting. He mouths *'Father'*, trying to hide the tears glistening in his sunshine eyes. I realize *young Daniel* gained a nickname of his own today.

"Generations of Whittenhowers cannot hinge on the possibility that young Daniel won't provide an heir because of his proclivities."

With a question in my eyes, I gaze down at Whitt. But he hides his face from me by turning completely around with his tiny back bowing in shame. Hand gripping his shoulder, I give a few reassuring squeezes, having no clue what I'm overhearing.

"You have to do something about your wife. You can't divorce Cora, because that would be too much of a scandal. We combined our family with the Spencers for a purpose, and they would take half of our net worth. Our family *must* remain in safe hands."

"We got the results back this morning." Melancholy, I've never heard a voice as smooth or sad in my entire life.

The sound flashes through my body and reverberates down my arm to Whitt's tiny hand. He smiles up at me like I pulled a neat trick– creepy. I don't look to Whitt to figure out who's speaking. I know who Grant is from Ade talking of him constantly with an affection that is borderline hero-worship. Grant is Ade's older brother who just turned twenty-three. He's also the brother who failed to place an order with 'Father' on his marital choices– fucking weirdoes.

I realize I'm witnessing history being made. This is how the elite create another generation, not in a bedroom between a married couple who loves one another. I get the gist of the conversation. They find their young Daniel lacking– after a few minutes, I know *my* Whitt is perfect just the way he is.

Hand curling around mine, Whitt's palm heats my skin and torches my heart.

"Daniel, it's bad news– Cora's barren. Dr. Livingston called it Polycystic Ovarian Syndrome."

"Christ!" Daniel calls out, voice breaking. A soft thump issues from the confines of the room. "Cora was the last hope. The Spencer line has been snuffed out. Two hundred years of hard work gone. *Poof* because the cunt can't pop out a damn kid."

"What? I-I-I... I thought," Grant stammers, voice going softer and softer. "I know Henry's an old bastard, but what about Cora's little brother? Boyd's sixteen now. I'm sure he'll make many sons."

Boyd Spencer? That geeky kid is Grant's brother-in-law? The sophomore is in A.P. calculus with me. Hillbrook ran out of math to teach him, but just like Fate, Boyd is nearly failing out of classes that aren't math, science, or history in nature.

Boyd and Fate sneak off together, always pressing their heads together like co-conspirators. Once I asked Fate if she fancied Boyd and she laughed for days.

"Grant, get real," Daniel growls. "Henry's almost ninety years old. It was a miracle Cora was born thirty years ago. Do you honestly believe the *Whore* didn't get knocked up by the *Crook* for the third time? I hope to God none of them procreate– those money grubbers are a pestilence. We either have to imprison Thomas, or commit Gwen to stop the blight."

"Don't *ever* speak of Gwen like that again, Daniel," low and seething, Grant forces a shiver to work its way down my spine. Whitt, the oddest child on the planet, channels Grant's obvious violence by baring his teeth– comical with him missing his front tooth.

I try to gain Whitt's attention, but he's glaring through the crack in the door.

"You and that annoying heart of yours. Wilhelm would have never chosen your mother had he known she was a walking charity case. Fine," Daniel grumbles begrudgingly. "We'll imprison Thomas, because we can't suffer any more of his spawn. *Your* Gwen is safe."

"I swear to God, Daniel... I'll pull a Jackson on your ass at Mass."

"Threats. Threats. Threats." Daniel taunts. "Always with the threats. I'm happy your balls have finally dropped, after that punch you threw when I slapped young Daniel, but let's put them to a better use... like getting your sperm into a fertile female."

"You. Are. Disgusting." Grant voices words directly from my mind.

"I'll think of a resolution, Grant. You're godawful at choosing for yourself. The Whore, really? I thought Jackson's heart would cease when he shared that news. First Whitt tries to fight Adelaide over Diane's queer mental patient of a son, and now your wife is barren. We need to find you a woman built like an ox at this rate. I will not allow the Whittenhowers to die out like the Spencers."

"Good riddance," Grant's soft voice is crystal clear.

With his face tight to the crack in the door, Whitt's muscles are taut with fury. The child understands more than he should– a hell of a lot more than I do.

"You're the one who forced me to marry Cora. I'm surprised you didn't give her a gynecological exam yourself before the wedding."

A loud pounding sounds through the door, causing me to jump out of my skin. Whitt doesn't even flinch.

"Fisted the desk," Whitt mouths. Must be it's a usual occurrence around here.

"Don't be a self-righteous prick, Grant. I've planned something that doesn't involve you divorcing Cora. My daughter is taking care of it. Be prepared to do whatever I say," the deep voice of the eldest Daniel Whittenhower commands, expecting to be obeyed.

Confusion rings loudly in Grant's voice. "What does Katie have to do with this?"

"Who said it was Katherine?" I can feel the air of smugness wafting from the room beneath the closed door.

I pull Whitt away from the door before we're caught. It sounded like the discussion was over, and I can't listen for another second.

Poor Cora. I understood enough to know that she is in the same position I am. The last of her family. Whereas I want children so I can see my mother and father reflected in them, Cora has the weight of generations of wealth to protect.

Poor Grant. Daniel sounds like a self-righteous, arrogant prick. I understand his fears, but I have a feeling he's more underhanded than the whole of Stanton Green's criminal empire.

What the hell is Ade going to do to help this situation? It has to be Ade– Grant only has two sisters.

"My father doesn't think I'm normal," a small voice says near my hip. I had forgotten the child as my mind processed everything I overheard. "I messed up and said I wanted Father to find me a husband instead of a wife. I didn't know there was anything wrong with it."

Mind wandering, reliving what Daniel must have said to him in that moment, the light in Whitt's blue eyes fades. He's worrying his bottom lip with one front tooth, so I kneel down and draw the child into a hug. Too trusting, he burrows against me, tiny fingertips clutching at my back.

Who could be mean to this darling little boy?

"You're only five years old. You haven't had time to be a disappointment to anyone. I think you're too young to know if you like boys or not, but there's nothing abnormal in that. Your buddy, Ezra, he seems like a pretty normal kid. It's your father who doesn't sound normal at all."

I try to reassure the child by drawing my fingertips through his baby-fine hair in a soothing rhythm like my mother used to do to me, and I now do to her when she's sleeping. Whitt's hair texture reminds me of the downy feathers of a duckling– the same color too.

"There you are." Ade's voice is sharp and piercing, like she's scolding a misbehaving pet. "Whitt, quit pestering my guest– scat!"

The boy doesn't say a word, but he does pull out of my arms. Without a backward glance, he runs down the hallway, zigzagging around expensive obstacles in his path. I feel bad for Whitt because he has to live in an adult environment without anyone making adjustments for him.

I'm furious with Ade for being such a bitch.

"That wasn't very nice," I scold my best friend. "I'd love to have a baby brother, and it's never going to happen. You need to appreciate him." I have to bite my lip to force myself from adding anything else I really want to say to her.

"I've got two brothers. Do you want one of them?" Ade says jokingly, but it rings with truth.

Ade starts to head in the same direction as Whitt, and I follow after her because I have nowhere else to go. My eyes go fuzzy with tunnel vision, refusing to look at my opulent, disgustingly wasteful surroundings. Whittenhower Estates could house the homeless, or remove some of the burden off hard-working American's shoulders. But instead, the money paid for a tall vase sitting on a pedestal, which probably cost more than I could ever fathom.

We enter a huge, narrow dining room, large enough to host at least thirty or forty pretentious bastards. In fact, it's twice as large as Hillbrook's cafeteria. There's more molding on the vaulted ceiling than I have in my entire apartment building. Gold-leaf is rubbed into the pattern on the navy and cream wallpaper. Five chandeliers hang from the center of the room, highlighting the table and its occupants. I imagine two dining in this lavish room, each sitting on an end of the table with twenty-plus feet separating them–

yelling as loud as their lungs will allow just to be heard during their conversation. But I'm relieved to see only one end has table settings.

A woman in her late forties is seated in one of the two chairs that occupy the end of the table. I assume that she's Ade's mom, Priscilla Whittenhower. A young woman is seated on her right. They both look to us expectantly.

I'm too nervous and freaked out to do anything but gawk.

"Mom, Cora," Adelaide says to her mother and sister-in-law. "This is my friend, Regina." She slumps into the seat across from Cora, giving me no direction to go in without guessing.

Sometimes I have bigger balls than brains, because I know I'm smart, and these rich fucks are just as human as I am. Deciding to be polite since Adelaide is apparently unable, I walk over and offer my hand to her mother. "Mrs. Whittenhower, it's a pleasure to finally officially meet you."

"Priscilla– please," she says as she shakes my hand lightly. I repeat her name and she smiles at me. She's nothing as I expected. Whitt's sunshine comes from this woman. "I know much about you, Regina. It's been a pleasure to follow your academic career these past few years. It pleased me to no end how you and Adelaide befriended one another."

"Ade's been a good friend," I murmur almost silently, rethinking my position on that topic.

I repeat the Mrs. Whittenhower and present my hand to Cora– she's immaculate with her bleached-blond hair, narrowed light blue eyes, and thin, pale skin. No doubt the dress she's wearing is her high-priced armor.

Cora bleeds insecurity and bitterness.

I contain a shudder as Cora takes my offered hand and shakes it gingerly, barely moving her dainty, ladylike hand. She also doesn't offer for me to call her Cora. Her face holds a pinched expression as she releases my hand, then she wipes her fingers on her linen napkin as if to remove the low-income disease I brought with me into Whittenhower Estates.

I can see why Ade's father chose the woman– Cora is perfect for the reserved nature of this family. Everything is about appearances, no matter how false they may be. I'm not sure how Priscilla and Whitt's wild natures survive this environment.

Unsure where to sit after such a cold reception from Cora, I slide into the seat next to Ade, hoping to find comfort with my friend. Taking in a deep breath, I turn to look at Ade, but the men joining us draw my undivided attention.

A handsome, imposing man in his late forties comes in first. Ageless, he's in his prime. If I was in a restaurant and he came in, I'd know he was someone important just by how he carries himself. The air of power emanating from him is as suffocating as it is intoxicating.

Daniel's intelligent, predatory gaze assesses everyone in the room. The scrutiny burns my flesh, and I cringe, not because it intimidates me, but because it pisses me off. Ade has that same look when she bosses people around and I hate it. She and her father look just alike and no doubt act alike too. One look, and I already know this man and I will *never* get along.

Without greeting anyone, Mr. Whittenhower moves to take his seat. After Daniel is finished sucking up all of the attention in the room, I notice Ade's brother, Grant, is sitting across the table from me.

Breath catching in my throat, to my horror, all I can do is stare. Grant is what Whitt will look like when he grows up. A tousle of sandy blond hair crowns a devastatingly handsome face. Piercing blue eyes stare at me with unveiled interest. Even the slope of his jaw and the curve of his neck are perfect. I can't take my eyes from him and he seems compelled to just tilt his head to the side and gaze back at me unflinchingly.

I feel a gaze burning into the side of my face, and turn to see Daniel's assessing eyes flicking between Grant and me. A small smile plays around the edge of his lips. It's a disturbing expression on such a serious man.

The tension breaker, Whitt shadows into the room to sit next to me. He wiggles into the high-backed chair with some difficulty. I notice no concessions are made for the child. He sits at the table as a grownup. He pulls his napkin from the table and snaps it. I recoil in my seat at the sound. He politely lays the fabric on his lap and mouths "*sorry,*" out the side of his cupid bow mouth.

"Who are you?" Mr. Whittenhower orders rather rudely to me. I wait for Ade to introduce me or jump to my defense… it would be a long wait before either happens.

"Daniel?" Priscilla sighs in exasperation. "Don't play coy."

Balls. I have balls. "As you know, my name is Regina Regal." With respect and formality, I refuse to play his game. "I go to school with Adelaide. It's nice to finally meet you, Mr. Whittenhower–outside of a school board meeting, that is."

I know he already knows who I am. Daniel's testing me, just as Ade does with anyone she comes into contact with. I see where she gets that annoying habit from.

"You're that scholarship student, aren't you?" Disdain envelops every word that flows from his sneering lips.

"Yes, sir," I say proudly, refusing to be 'put in my place'. I've earned my position. I didn't have it handed to me or bought. Daniel glares at me for a second, and then turns to speak to his wife as if I'm of little consequence to his dinner.

I feel eyes on me again, but from a different source. I look directly across the table at Ade's brother. Amused by my presence, but shadows are lurking beneath the surface, Grant receives an elbow to the ribs from Cora– excuse me, Mrs. Whittenhower. She doesn't like me much. He smiles wider at Cora's jealous reaction, showcasing a devastating set of addictive dimples. Whitt must have inherited his dimples from Grant.

"Hello, Regina–" Grant's voice is quiet and soothing, rolling over my skin like a caress. "Ade talks of you all the time."

"It's nice to meet you too, Mr. Whittenhower." I don't mean for it to come out meekly, or to sound so much like a question, but it does. "Ade speaks of you nonstop," I mutter wryly.

Grant's full, pink lips stretch into a satisfied grin. I shake my head to break myself out of the spell he's cast over me. I see Ade's fascination with hero-worshipping her brother. I want to worship him in another sense… or maybe I want him to worship me.

"You can–" Grunting sharply, Grant's elbowed again– hard to the ribs, to the point I fear Cora had to have bruised herself. I think he was trying to offer for me to call him Grant.

Now, I'm only on a first-name basis with Ade, her baby brother, and her mother. That's not uncomfortable– not uncomfortable at all.

"Family!" a deep voice echoes through the long and narrow dining room, causing my head to snap up. I look around, noticing no one at the table had spoken. Daniel looks pissed, Grant is silently laughing, and Priscilla is glowing.

What. The. Fuck? Are there ghosts in Misery Castle?

A small nudge to the side of my breast gains Whitt my undivided attention. "Jack," the boy whispers, voice trailing a giggle. "He's toying with Daniel from the passageways."

"What?" I glance around, trying to figure out what's happening. Sure enough, I spot a huge man squeezing out of an open panel at the head of the dining room. Wild blond hair sticking out in every direction, he's wearing a pair of jeans and an old, ratty t-shirt.

"He's not as crazy as he looks," Whitt whispers against the side of my arm. "He's smarter than all of us collectively."

Squinting, I try to figure out what the boy is trying to tell me without actually asking. "Collectively? Whitt, act like a little boy. You're freaking me out."

"Don't all families have a crazy relative?" Grant murmurs from his side of the table, thoroughly enjoying my discomfort. "I promise he's not escaping from where we locked him in the attic."

"Huh?"

Enjoying his dramatic entrance, Jack, whoever the hell he may be, taps the panel shut with his heel, and then strides across the endless dining room. "Family! How are we doing this fine evening? I see Miss Regal has finally crossed our threshold, terrified we'll never allow her to leave."

"He's joking," Ade promises, but I notice Whitt and Grant sharing a conspiratorial look.

No longer silently laughing but now releasing a string of sadistic giggles, Grant readily accepts the welcoming kiss from the lunatic man. He tilts his head back and receives a kiss directly on the lips.

Eyes narrowed, Jack bypasses Cora, strolls around the end of the table, walks behind Ade and then me, to where I shiver in fright, and then gives little Whitt the same level of affection. Jack tickles Whitt until he's giggling breathlessly.

Jack is like a whirlwind of energy in the dining room, leaving me feeling dizzy and confused. Quite the greeter, Jack kisses Priscilla on the lips, then leans over Daniel while glowering.

"You're sitting in my seat," Jack murmurs like a spiteful child. "Move."

"Jackson," Daniel growls, refusing to move.

A huge man in his late forties is pouting. *Pouting.* "My house. My family. I feed and house and take care of you and your girls, and you take my seat."

"Brothers," I mutter, earning a chuckle from Grant. "Men never grow up, do they?"

"Never," Jack replies without breaking the staring contest with Daniel. "Fine! I'll sit next to our guest," he threatens, and I shudder in fear. "You never know what secrets may spill while I'm all the way down in the center of the table."

"Jack?" Priscilla admonishes. "Behave."

"Fine. But I'll use salt!" Jack strides across the room, and then dramatically sits next to Grant, across from Whitt. "I like it better down here anyway– better company. Pass the salt, girly."

"No, Uncle Jackson," Adelaide mutters, quickly grabbing the shaker, and then passes it to her mother.

"Lost the damn genetic lottery, I did." Jackson speaks directly to me, like he's not terrified he'll be infected with my low-income disease. "Heart defect. My ticker could just give out whenever the dang thing feels like it."

Movement catches my eye, and I see true fear reflected in Grant's gaze. Jackson gazes at him, face softening with affection. "No fear, the boys have tested clean of my taint."

"That's not–" Grant tries to explain why he's upset.

But Jackson cuts him off. "I know." Cupping his hands to his face, he bellows. "Martha! We're ready for some grub."

Unsurprised this time, another panel opens in the wall, and a tiny woman steps out and to the side, followed by several maids carrying trays. I may not be a racist, but clearly the Whittenhowers are. The older woman and the girls all have tan skin and dark, silky hair.

Jackson Whittenhower, the master of the house, fries my brain. "I have an old-school valet. A white asshole who has my number, if that's what you're thinking– he's trashing my closet as we speak because I had the audacity to put on these jeans," he mutters while wearing a roguish grin. "Our father was a bastard of the worst sort. All of our staff are descendants of his. But Martha and her daughter–" he points at Priscilla. "Martha came with the lady of the manor." Leaning across the table, he whispers conspiratorially. "Don't let the old bag fool ya– she barely works."

"Sir," Martha, neither an old bag or amused, places a plate in front of Jackson. I note the faint smirk on the forty-something woman's face as she steps away.

Gazing down in disappointment, I have no idea what the hell is on my plate, but Jackson is a welcome distraction. "Goddamn you, woman!" he bellows. "If a man could die at any time, he ought to have some red meat, some spirits, and a willing bed warmer!" Jack makes a gagging sound. "Salad. Uh! Wanna trade, new girly?"

"Um…" I look down, contemplating it.

"Jackson," Priscilla murmurs, clearly this is an everyday occurrence and not just because I'm their guest. "Behave and you can have two of the three," she teases.

Eyes flicking around the table, I beg for someone to tell me which of the three his sister-in-law is offering. Clearly it's not red meat, judging by the amount of green on Jackson's plate.

"How's your mother?" Grant leans forward, trying to block out Jackson while ignoring the jab in the ribs by his disgruntled wife.

"Death is a fact of life," Jackson mutters around a mouthful of greens, but the tone of his voice is not unkind. "When dying, you no longer care about life. Your child's future eclipses all else."

"You'll never die," Daniel teases. "All you have to do is avoid Mass." Everyone laughs, sounding uncomfortable over a family joke. But Jackson and Grant laugh like it's the funniest thing they've ever heard.

"No fear, brother– my son would never slaughter his father during Mass because his father isn't a bastard like ours was." Jackson puffs out his very broad chest, confusing me further. "My son loves me and knows where his bread is buttered."

Reaching forward for his wine glass, "So arrogant," Daniel breathes, sounding very much like a jealous baby brother. Then he chugs the entire glass of crimson liquid.

"You have a son?" slips past my lips before I can stop it.

"Biologically," Jackson doesn't even hesitate, while Daniel chokes on his wine, sputtering for air.

"Your mother?" Grant tries and fails to change the subject.

"She's–"

I'm interrupted by Martha. "Master Whittenhower, Pierre Fontaine and Jonathon Wilson have arrived unexpectedly."

Slamming his napkin on top of his plate, "Christ!" Jackson and Grant share a look. "My brother's namesake isn't to be alone until they leave the house. Do I make myself clear?"

"Yes, sir," Grant and Whitt mutter in unison as Jackson leaves as abruptly as he arrived.

"What is this business about?" Daniel demands of Grant.

"Little Daniel is their favorite flavor of candy," is all Grant will say on the subject. Terrified, I wrap my arm around the boy.

"After my brother's death," Daniel's voice breaks with grief, "Those men are never allowed on the property."

"Agreed," everyone but me mutters, with Grant adding, "And not because you said so. Because *I* said so."

While Grant and Daniel engage in silent battle, I look a question to Ade. But she avoids eye-contact by staring at her fascinating plate. I turn the other direction to the little boy who is usually a fount of information, yet this time he is wolfing down his food like a starving puppy.

Without Jackson, all the life in the dining room flees, and I fear what will happen to the Whittenhower family when Jackson passes. My mother is my life, but Jackson seems to be the heartbeat and humor to an entire dynasty.

I sit politely throughout a dinner that tastes like paste while Daniel dominates all conversation. Just because it's expensive, doesn't mean it tastes good– I'd kill for a New York slice or a Philly cheesesteak right about now. An Italian sub.

The truffles shaved all over my plate cost more than I was willing to whore myself out for and they taste like a dank basement– moldy. My mouth waters at the thought of a grilled-cheese sandwich, or maybe it's watering because I can barely keep the food down. I guzzle from my water glass until it's empty.

I look up to see Grant silently laughing at me, dimples on full display. My eyes flit around the table, and I'm thankful that everyone else is engaged in the boring story Ade's father is regaling us with. I smirk into my linen napkin.

"Will you read me a story, Queen?" Whitt asks from the seat next to me, and it surprises me that he requested something so… normal. I start to say sure but Ade interrupts.

"No, Daniel." Ade practically hisses at the boy. "Regina is my friend, not yours. Never call her Queen again."

"Adelaide," Grant tries to stop Ade's tirade.

"And you can read– read your own story. We have to study."

I take Whitt's hand in mine underneath the table and vow to get away long enough to read him a short-story. He squeezes my hand and my eyes prickle with tears. Fucking bitch.

Grant smiles at me like he has x-ray vision and can read my mind. "Ade, it's not the end of the world if you miss a few questions on your Latin exam."

"My GPA versus Daniel getting a story at bedtime shouldn't even be equated." Adelaide tosses her napkin on top of her dinner plate.

Priscilla leans forward, hand on her daughter's arm. "Breathe– breathe deeply and calm yourself. Your summer abroad and your place in California are not at risk, even if you fail all of your classes."

"It's all I can control." Adelaide snatches her hand away, voice breaking with panic. "It took four years to get Regina to visit, and you all embarrassed the hell out of me– you promised to show her we're just normal people... and now Reg only likes Uncle Jackson."

Knowing how Adelaide can turn into a terror, I hope I'm not breaching any protocols I don't know exist. "May Ade and I be excused?" I stand, placing my hands on the back of my chair. "She'll feel better after we get a few hours in– she's struggling and needs me to tutor her."

"Of course," Priscilla flashes me a relieved smile, making me wonder who Adelaide is more like: Daniel or Jackson.

"You're excused." Daniel dismisses us, refusing to even look me in the eyes. I get three steps from the table. "Miss Regal, my daughter better score high, or I'll blame you."

"Of course," I mimic his wife, but my tone takes on another note, giving off the opposite meaning.

Without another word, I follow Ade up to her bedroom. I'm momentarily hit with shame because we left the dining room a mess for those young women to clean up. I now understand where the kids at Hillbrook get their sense of entitlement from– their parents. It's bred into them.

Chapter Five

After a long walk down a paneled hallway, we reenter the foyer I missed when Whitt pulled me through the house. Vestibule is a better term. The large, three-story space is the size of my apartment times five, and no one inhabits this space.

An impressive set of double staircases curve around the outside of the vestibule with a hallway leading to the rest of the house situated between them. There are two more hallways at the landing of each staircase, leading left and right to separate wings. Adelaide chooses the left-hand side, and I follow her up. Pausing, I look up, amazed to see the staircase continues to weave up two more flights.

Misery Castle is so large I can't even fathom its true size. There is no description adequate enough to describe a castle three stories tall with a labyrinth of interconnecting hallways, not to mention that bizarre secret passageway Jackson popped out of in the dining room.

Ade knows I'm not pleased with her, so she's quiet while surreptitiously flicking her eyes in my direction to gauge how angry I am. After what has to be at least ten minutes of walking, when it literally takes me thirty seconds to walk around my entire apartment, we pause outside of Adelaide's bedroom.

"Don't secretly hate me, okay?" Voice breaking, Ade is truly afraid I'll think less of her. Like a Band-Aid being torn off, she carelessly flings open the double set of doors to her bedroom.

I gasp in horror as I follow Ade into her room. It's three times the size of my apartment, with ten-foot ceilings with walls dripping with molding and expensive wallpaper. When my father was still alive, I had posters of famous paintings– Ade has the originals.

Ade has every piece of furniture imaginable: king-sized bed, dressers, nightstands, sofas and arm chairs, a coffee table and an honest to God coffee maker and mini-refrigerator. Shelves lined with books and a desk overflowing with gadgets, a desktop and a laptop. Speakers as tall as I am bracket a stereo that should never be outside of a club.

"Is that a plasma television?" Voice filled with wonder, I'm drawn forward to find myself caressing the smooth lines of Ade's gigantic television. "This isn't even on the market yet. Mr. Gibbs couldn't even get one so we could dismantle it and put it back together in class."

Spinning around, my hands seek out Adelaide's gadgets. Heart beating like I'm caressing a lover, my mind is cataloging how I could improve every digital and computerized device in Ade's room. "A DVD player? Those are like... a thousand fucking bucks. Did you get it imported from Japan?"

Ade smirks at me, and then tosses me an object. I catch it without hesitation. "A Nokia 5110? In red? These aren't even supposed to go on the market until next year. I thought they were still doing research on these?"

"God, Regina..." Ade laughs throatily, sounding like a grown woman and it freaks me out. "I imagine this is what it's like when a boy discovers porn– you should see your orgasm face right now. You look like you're about to pop your cork."

"Ade." Flabbergasted, I'm tempted to toss her mobile phone back at her, but my hand won't unclench from around it. Shaking, it takes everything in me not to sit down in one of Ade's many chairs and never move until I discover all the secrets inside the device. Mr. Gibbs makes sure I have an unending supply of mobile phones to tear apart, knowing it's where my passions lie.

"You can have it," Ade offers, and she's wearing a queer grin I can't understand. Her face is flushed, like she's hot and sweaty.

"I can't," I deny myself, voice breathy. My fingers twitch, hard-pressed to let the device go.

"I don't use it." Ade chuckles, producing my backpack. Obviously Albert had it delivered from the car to Ade's bedroom. "I don't see the need to have a phone strapped to my ass. I mean, who would want their mother to be able to track their asses down. Seriously?"

"That's blasphemy." I flinch like she hit me, and begin petting the Nokia because Ade insulted it. "I wish... but I can't..." I wistfully purr at the beauty. "But I can't keep it."

"Fine." Ade snatches it out of my hand, and I'm bereft at its loss. "I'll give it to Mr. Gibbs, and he'll sic you on it."

"I only tear apart nonfunctioning phones," I grumble, heart fluttering with the possibilities.

"That can be easily arranged," Ade threatens, and my heart stalls. "Just kidding. I'll donate it to Gibbs for you to trash. Maybe someday you'll make a mobile that makes sense to me. Until then, I don't want one."

Without the phone in my hand, I'm finally able to think clearly. Ade's room is a disaster of epic proportions, and that sickens me more so than its size or the contents. The room is in complete chaotic disarray. Clothes upon clothes are thrown on the floor, items that probably cost more than I need to pay off all of Mom's medical debts. I'm disgusted by the disrespect and total lack of appreciation. Ade doesn't deserve anything if this is how she treats her belongings.

Suddenly furious, and not an ounce of that is from jealousy, I sit in the leather office chair at her desk– a desk that should be in an office, not a sixteen-year-old girl's bedroom. With hasty movements, I pull my books from my bag and push all my anger down to my gullet.

"I know you're mad at me," Ade approaches me with her hands held out. "But you have to give me a clue why?"

"You have so much money you no longer respect what it buys." Refusing to look at her, I point over my shoulder to the ten thousand dollar mountain of discarded clothing on her floor. One shirt would have paid for Mom's pain meds, and here I was, trying to hand out blowjobs to lessen a dying woman's pain while Ade throws away money like it's trash.

"Um… I-I-I–" While stammering, with hurried movements, Ade begins hanging up her clothing. "You're right, as always, Regina."

"Forget it," I mutter, hating how Ade's voice keeps breaking. "Here's my notes." I toss the notebook behind me in Ade's general direction. "You can use them for the final."

"Okay," she turns meek, collecting the notebook from the top of the clothing pile. "Thanks."

I start to study in spite of how furious I am. I don't pay attention to Ade when she tries to talk to me. I don't engage her in any way. Eventually she shuts up and starts to study too. No way was I answering her question: *Why are you mad at me?* There aren't enough hours in a day to answer that question.

Am I jealous?

Am I judging Ade for being born into a situation she didn't ask to be born into?

No.

I'm judging Ade for wasting her money instead of using it for good. Maybe she's a bit young to begin donating to charity, but she could refuse gifts and stop asking for things she doesn't want or need. At the very least, take good care of it– that's all on Adelaide.

A few hours later, with an aching neck and a muddled brain, I slide from my seat and shove my books into my bag. Ade is fast asleep, curled into a ball in the center of her king-sized princess bed, softly snoring. I decide now is the perfect time to read to Whitt if he's still awake.

Never have I seen anything like it– the corridor is long and menacing with patches of darkness broken from tiny lights set along the baseboard of the floor with sconces bracketing each door. The burgundy walls are embossed in gold, and the gold carpet is highly padded to dampen the sound of footsteps. My shoes don't even whisper as I ghost down the hallway at this late hour.

I creep down the hallway, trying to figure out which room belongs to the boy, deciding it's probably a hopeless task. To ensure I don't get lost, I count the amount of doors lining the hallway from Ade's bedroom, but I lose count. The spacing between each door isn't the same. Some rooms are large and others are small. Maybe the small rooms are storage or guest quarters.

Smile curving my lips, I spot a door that has a brown teddy bear plaque on it. I turn the knob slowly, not wanting to disturb the child if he's sleeping. I'd worry that I was walking into someone else's room, but who else would have a bear on the entrance to their bedroom? I'm shocked the hinges don't squeak like mine do as I slowly crack the door.

Alerted, Whitt looks up at me and smiles, showcasing his dimples while flashing his missing front tooth. He's sitting cross-legged on a queen-sized bed in a room that looks like it belongs to an adult, not a five-year-old child. No clothing is scattered on the floor. No toys on display, and without a toy box in sight. But he does have a desk and chair, with a bookshelf filled with reference materials and a few children's books.

Small, Whitt looks out of place as his huge bed swallows him up in the center. He has a pad resting on his lap and a pencil poised and at the ready in his hand. Curious to see what he's working on, I walk over and check it out, assuming it's his homework.

"It's you," Whitt says brightly as he shows me the sketch he's working on. Turning the pad around so I can view it, there's a girl who's rendered to look like me, but she's wearing a crown on her head. Even the hair is a wild mess of light strawberry blonde.

"I'm impressed, Whitt." I can't believe he's only five, and I can't believe they treat him as they do. He's a very special boy. "*Really* impressed."

"It's nothing," he mutters with a shrug, blushing. "Just something I dabble in."

"Dabble?" Whitt and I share a grin. "Are you sure you're not older than me?"

"I'm a very old soul, Jackson says all the time." Whitt shoves over, making room for me to join him on the bed.

"Why do you call everyone by their first names? Grant, does too," I observe. "Except for Priscilla."

Tiny blond eyebrows knit together in the center of his forehead, in an expression I've seen Ade pull thousands of times over the past four years. "Because we can't mess up and call someone the wrong name in public," is Whitt's bizarre answer, but I can tell he'll refuse to elaborate.

I locate a book resting at the foot of his bed– I'd bet it's his favorite. "Somebody knew I'd visit them tonight," I tease. "Shall I start on page one?"

"Yes, please." Eager, downright giddy, Whitt's voice is the sweetest thing I've ever heard. "And if I fall asleep, you can stop reading. We'll just pick up when you come back next time," he ensures I'll see him again, the little sneak.

"Where the Wild Things are," I murmur as I settle my back against the headboard. I wait for Whitt to crawl up to me and cuddle. With my arm wrapped around the little guy, his body fitting snugly to my side, I begin to read to him, and I fall in love for the very first time.

Chapter Six

After falling asleep with Whitt cuddled in my lap, I have no idea what time it is. This, of course, has my mind spinning with the possibilities of how resourceful a mobile phone truly is. You could check the time if you're stuck in a labyrinth deep within castle walls, with no way of looking outside to know if it was night or day. If you're lost, you could call for help, or phone a friend for directions to their bedroom. I truly have no idea why Ade said it was useless.

I wander aimlessly down the hallway, startling when I see it branches off in three directions. I remember it being a straight stretch from the staircase to Adelaide's room, and straight again from Ade's door to Whitt's bedroom. I thought I was heading in the right directions, but lost is what thinking got me.

The doors appear ominous now, and I swear the hall lengthens as I walk. There must be people behind them, right? How freaky is that? Where are all these people coming from when I met so few at dinner?

It's like I'm trapped in a horror film as my earlier feelings of premonition flood my system. My mind goes into fight-or-flight mode, where I'll end up running these hallways for all eternity.

Eyes sighting far in the distance, I blink away the visage of the Redrum Twins holding hands at the end of the hallway. Shuddering, I envision a flood of crimson to flow in a torrent to wash me away.

Getting twitchy, time is a big deal for me. I have no idea what time it is or how I'm getting home. Powerlessness is not my friend, which is why I hate Ade right now. I know that Albert must be asleep, and I don't know how to contact him. No busses run to Crestview, as that would mean the low-income disease would spread to the upper echelons.

I'm not above tapping the walls for hidden panels, should worst come to worst. But I'd piss my pants if crazy Uncle Jackson popped out and said *boo!*

Since there are no strategic house phones in the hallway, if I had a mobile phone, I could call a taxi, but I have no money. I guess I should solve one problem at a time. Problem one is finding my way outside before I worry about how I'm getting home.

I'm a rat in a maze.

Then there's bypassing all those gatekeepers. I know we're trapped inside, not the other way around. Even if I called a cab, he'd be stuck about five miles down the mountain from here at the gate leading into Crestview.

If only I could get to Fate's house, but I'd still have to walk three miles down a mountain, then wrestle my way out of the gate leading from the driveway to Crestview's only street.

Shitcicle– I'm screwed.

In the far off distance, I see a shadowy figure coming down the hallway toward me, and I get excited. Heart beating a rapid tattoo, the closer they come, the sooner I will go home and never revisit this expensive house of torture again. Within seconds, the shape of a man coalesces before my very eyes.

"What do we have here?" Grant slurs at me. "My lucky night– I've found a wandering, lost sheep." Ade's big brother seems different than before, and it raises warning alarms in my mind.

"Misery Castle is a terrifying place, even for me, and I was born here." Grant's fingertips wrap around a section of my hair, and it scares the living piss out of me.

Face flushed red in a blotchy pattern, with his eyes glassy and bright, I can smell the smoky scent of whiskey or scotch rolling off Grant's tongue as he speaks and breathes heavily.

"I'm lost, and I need a ride home." My voice wavers as I speak. I hate this helpless, powerless situation I've placed myself in. Twisting my hands in the hem of my blazer, I play the blame game.

What Regina Regal should have done if she'd only known it would turn out this way...

There's no such thing as a time machine. There's only dealing with your mistakes and learning from them. I just hope and pray Grant is a good guy, but there's no guarantees. Back home, the criminals keep me safe from the 'good guys' who want to take what isn't theirs.

With Ade's big brother looking sleepy yet sad, I instinctively know Grant would never harm me– I'm being a stupid girl, I'm sure.

"I'll get Albert for you, Regina. But first, spend some time with me," he begs, slurring his words, sounding like his tongue is too large for his pouty mouth.

As if sensing my attention, the tip of Grant's tongue sneaks out to slide along his supple bottom lip. Eyes bright and shiny, glossed over with drink, he smiles as he tastes the alcohol staining his mouth. Dimples dent his cheeks, but they no longer remind me of Whitt. The innocent divots seem sinister and dangerous– promising something I'm not ready to experience.

Twisting while humming to himself, the feel of Grant's fingertips playing with my hair has goosebumps beading my flesh. Unable to stop the movement, I shiver as my scalp tightens, sucking up the pleasant attention. I do the first stupid-girl moment of my life. I shamelessly crush on a guy, a completely unobtainable and unavailable older guy, and let it turn my thoughts to mush.

"Okay, if you promise to call Albert first." I try to negotiate with Grant, and he gives me a naughty smirk for agreeing– a twist of perfect lips that leaves my knees weak.

Although he's an inch or two shorter than me, Grant backs me up with his physical presence, until his front touches mine– chest to breasts. Lips parting, he breathes the smoky, whiskey scent onto my chin.

Stunned at the sensation of my lower stomach clenching with want, my back hits the door behind me with an audible thump. My eyes hold wide open in wonder, as if in slow motion, Grant reaches around me. I don't wince. Blood boiling, I anticipate him touching me until I begin to crave it.

Tilting his head to the side, Grant watches my obvious reactions. Instead of touching me as I expected, his hand twists the doorknob by my hip. Before I register what's happening, I'm falling backward into a dark room.

Feeling fuzzy-headed, my legs connect with the edge of a bed. I can't see anything and the only sound I hear is our combined breathing. Buzzing alive with caution, I'm hyperaware of every nerve ending and hair on my flesh. My senses are so in tune that I can feel my system pumping the blood through my veins to nourish my whole body.

Light blazes, nearly blinding me, when Grant flips the light switch. Curious to know where I've wandered, I look around a room that's larger than Ade's, minus the over-the-top double-doors. But I'm surprised to find it sparsely decorated and extremely neat. Antique yet sleek, the roll top desk covered in notebooks doesn't look as out of place as the corporate desk looked in Ade's room. The oak bed, nightstands, and dressers are separated from a leather-clad seating area. The room's missing a television, but has a stack of books on the coffee table instead. I wonder if this is a guestroom, probably dubbed the '*Blue Room*' because of its many hues of blue.

Answering my unspoken question, "This is my space," Grant says as he smiles at me. "My wife and I don't share a room. We don't touch. We don't talk. We don't fuck or make love. We would have had clinical sex to procreate, but that's never going to happen now."

"I'm sorry?" flows out like a question as my knees give way. Like a stupid girl, I sit on the foot of Grant's bed.

"I'm not," he mutters flippantly. "The Spencers are maggots, and I'd never want their taint to mix with Whittenhower blood."

"Boyd seems like a good guy... I mean," I stammer, at a loss. "I don't know your wife at all, but I've taken classes with Boyd."

"Boyd's not a Spencer. Demonic kid, but in a good way." Grant clears the thread of conversation away by gesturing his hand through the air. Drunk and animated, he reminds me of crazy Jackson right now. "You'll never believe what Daniel suggested to me– no, not suggested. *Commanded* of me. Then, of course, Jackson got on board with the plan, so now I have to do it. No one can refuse a dying man anything, you know?"

Before I can reply, Grant's answering for me. "Of course, you understand– your mother." His features twist up in misery, with his glassy eyes filling with tears. "The *bitch* thought it was a splendid idea. Being bossed around by your father is one thing– by your fucking wife is another."

"I'm sorry," I mutter again, having no idea what else to say.

The seemingly tidy Grant is not how I assumed he'd be. His blond hair is wild, sticking up in every direction, like he's been tearing through it with his fingertips out of frustration. His jacket is long gone somewhere, with his shirt unbuttoned to nearly his belly button, giving off flashes of pale, firm skin. His shirt sleeves are rolled up past his slim forearms, with only the smattering of hair lending a masculine edge.

Palm cupping the crotch of his dress trousers, Grant squeezes his manly bits. "If it wasn't for the fact that I can grab them, I'd swear Cora's shorn off my balls."

"Cora doesn't like me, either," I try to soothe Grant so he'll stop manhandling the family jewels. He's really wrenching on the poor things– it has to hurt.

"Don't ever get married," Grant issues as a warning, giving one final punishing squeeze to his bits before letting go. "I never wanted to get married. None of the families give two shits if the kids are born in wedlock, or even if they're your actual kids, just as long as they have founding families' blood running through their veins. Look at Boyd– Henry just took him and claimed him as his own. So why did I have to get married?"

"Uh…" at this point, I don't even think Grant realizes he's speaking to me, so no response is necessary. Grant's expression is clouded, so I wonder if he even knows he's talking to me, or if he thinks he's talking to himself, or maybe he doesn't even hear himself and he thinks he's thinking it.

Mad drunk, Grant turns in a circle, wobbling to the side. I want to be annoyed, but it's amusing after the night I've had. If Whitt brings sunshine to this house, Grant brings unexpected humor. Both brighten up Misery Castle.

Grant is a very peculiar man.

"What was I doing? I was supposed to do something. What was it?" He turns in a circle again, talking to himself this time for sure. "Oh! I know!" He proudly shouts. He hobbles over to the phone on his desk, and then presses the number three with more force than necessary.

"Albert, I found Miss Regal wandering the halls looking for a way home." Grant speaks slowly, trying to hide the fact that he's drunk. "Could you please meet us in my room so you may take her home?"

Grant hangs up before he even gets a reply. Clapping excitedly, evidently he's happy about how he was able to speak a complete sentence without slurring any words. He sits on the foot of the bed next to me, like we're the best of friends and this isn't the most bizarre night of my life.

"What was I saying?" Grant pats my knee a few times, then his own. "Oh, right. They didn't give me an option of with whom, but Daniel and Jackson have my number. On this, Cora went ballistic. Seeing her that way made me say I wouldn't do it unless it was *you*. My father picked up on my reasoning, and he looked proud that I was being defiant of the bitch. I won't be cowed by a woman ever again. My elder, sure. But not some low-level daughter to the Spencer's dying bloodline."

Grant continues to ramble on about things I can't decipher, just like Ade does when she's nervous. But in his case, he's drunk as a skunk. He reminds me of the deadbeat dads who weave their way down my street at two a.m., coming home from the bar after spending their paychecks. I have no clue what he's actually saying, or what he means. It's all slurred together into gibberish. But I can guess drinking and Grant aren't usual companions.

"There is something about you," Grant's voice rolls over my skin like a silken caress. I've never heard such a tone in my entire life. His voice holds melancholy, to the point I long to make him happy. But at the same time, it's the smoothest thing I've ever heard.

Even drunk and slurring, Grant's a charming bastard, and not the kind of charm that Cortez kid tried to pull off during lunch this afternoon. Very male but not, like he'll protect me but he needs my protection too. Grant's charisma has an effect on me, and I'm trying my damnedest to ignore it.

Grant's an adult– a grown man. The combination of his piercing blue eyes and wicked mouth, flashing the innocent yet sinister dimple when he smiles, are my ultimate undoing. I reach epic levels of stupidity.

"We've met before, Regina," Grant draws me up short. "You were interviewed for your scholarship by my mother and her mentor. Do you remember?"

"Shit," I hiss, realizing Grant's right. "I can't believe I'd forgotten that. Neither lady gave me their name. But now that you mention it."

"Rebekah Zeitler and Priscilla Whittenhower interviewed you."

My mind spins, and then my stomach twists in pain. "The older lady is the one the black shroud is for, isn't she? The one whose house burnt down. God, I hope not. She was so nice to me."

Grant looks the other way, a pained sound rumbles up from his chest. "You walked by us that day, more than four years ago. I was waiting for my mother, and my best friends were waiting for their grandmother. But sadly, you don't remember us."

"I... I-I-I–" I stammer, not knowing how to respond to him.

"There's definitely something about you, and I can't put my finger on it," Grant murmurs as he slides a fingertip along my bottom lip. My breath hitches in my throat and my lips part in shock.

I've never had anyone touch my mouth before– *ever*. My lip quivers beneath Grant's expert touch, begging for more contact. Capturing my gaze, I can't blink away. Hurried little pants expel from between my parted lips as my lower stomach cramps, screaming for something I don't understand. A part of my body that has laid dormant my entire life blooms for this man. It's so wrong, and yet I want something just for myself.

Intent on every reaction he evokes in me, Grant's fingertip traces an outline of my lips. Pulling away, the absence of his touch leaves me feeling empty inside. Still holding my gaze, Grant licks his fingertip, then closes his eyes as he sucks on his finger.

A whimper is torn from my throat as I watch the tip disappear between Grant's full lips. He slowly draws it out, and then slides the damp digit over my lips again. The intense contact has me jumping as if electrocuted. His fingertip slides silky smooth and tastes like whiskey when it comes in contact with my tongue.

Grant.

With a deep moan, my legs clamp together on the feeling building between my thighs. I hiss when a sensation I've never felt grows from the pressure. I clench my thighs a second time to see if it happens again. I moan loudly in surprise when it does.

"Are you a virgin?" Grant abruptly asks me in a rolling, seductive tone— coaxing me to answer. I nod my head yes, too embarrassed to admit the truth out loud.

"Oh, God!" Grant hisses, and then trails his moist fingertip over my chin, sliding it down the column of my neck, where he settles it between my breasts. The damp pathway lingers on my skin, burning me from the inside out.

Slowly, with deliberate movement, Grant leans forward to kiss me. His eyes and lips get closer and closer, and it's maddening. Heart racing, I'm finally going to have my first kiss, and it's going to be with Ade's married brother.

I *should* protest, but I don't want to. There's something about Grant. Something broken that has created an undeniable need inside me.

Smoky breath fluttering against my lips, hair brushing my cheek, I lean toward Grant to take that kiss.

"Grant? Miss Regal?" Albert announces as he knocks loudly on the open door, but he doesn't enter.

Spell broken, Grant snaps back from me with a look of utter shock etched across his features. Flustered, he runs his fingertips through his wild hair, putting it back to rights.

"Um— we'll be right there, Al," Grant calls back. "What's wrong with me, dammit?" I can tell it's rhetorical when he runs his hands across his face, trying to scrub his drunkenness away. "I can't do this. I shouldn't be doing this. But I want to do this. What kind of man are they making me?"

I get up from the bed in a daze, and I don't dare look back at Grant. I feel ashamed of myself for what I almost did– what I almost allowed Grant to do to me. Stupid girl that I am, I would have allowed him to have anything he asked of me, and now I understand the girls in my neighborhood better.

Trying not to blush, I open the door the rest of the way, and then walk over to Albert. As hired help, he's several feet down the hallway, as to not be seen or see anything untoward.

Albert flashes me a confused look and asks if I'm ready to go. But I barely hear him, sounding as if he's speaking through water. I watch in a daze as Grant hands Albert my forgotten backpack, while keeping a large distance between the two of us.

After what feels like miles and miles of confusing hallways, and a flight down the right-hand staircase, I follow Albert out to the car. The entire ride home, my mind is in a complete fog.

Chapter Seven

"Ma, here are your pills for the rest of the day until I get home from school." Trying not to jostle anything, on her lap I place a tray with several bottles of water, her toast for breakfast, crackers and shortbreads for a snack, and the pill bottle. "I may be a few hours late tonight because I'm looking for a job for the summer."

In caregiver-mode, I make sure everything that needs to be fixed before I head out is perfect. Without a telephone, Mom has no way of contacting anyone if she goes without or needs assistance. So I try to get everything set up for her, while depending on the neighborhood ladies to pop in and out at intervals throughout the day.

"Take two at a time from now on– three if that doesn't help." I adjust the pillow behind Mom's back, helping her sit up. "I know the prescription won't last as long, but that doesn't matter. I'll work part-time after school until I graduate. We'll be okay– I promise."

Leaning over the bed with my hands on her shoulders, I gaze into Mom's pain-clouded green eyes, and I'm not sure if she truly understands me anymore. The cancer is progressing at a faster rate than just a few weeks ago.

Pulling away as daughter tries to overtake caregiver, I hide the tear that leaks from the corner of my eye. After I kiss the top of her bare head, I walk to the closet in the main room to grab a satin scarf. With more than two years' worth of practice, I wrap the fabric around Mom's skull so she won't get cold, even if it's eighty degrees in the shade. I tuck her blankets around her tightly, and then wait to make sure she takes her pills and swallows a few mouthfuls of water.

"I'll be fine until you get home, Regina." A bony hand with paper-thin skin cups my cheek. "Take your time and find a good job, and good luck at school today with your finals." Mom's voice is rough from her illness, no longer holding the melodious edge I heard as a child. Now there's a hollowness, almost an echo. In the future, I hope to God I can forget the agonizing sound and overwrite it with the loving voice of the mother I had for the first fifteen years of my life.

I don't know where I find the courage to look at her, to listen to her voice, and to smile as if she's the most beautiful creature I've ever laid eyes upon. My mother is, but the disease draining her is not. It hurts so much to look at the once vital beauty reduced to a living skeleton.

Ella Regal is only in her mid-thirties, and she *had* a long life ahead of her. She should be working, dating, going out with her friends now that I've reached the age of majority. She should be living a life, not lying in bed.

Dying.

Ninety years old and several years in the grave is how my mother looks right now. Playing imagination land has never been my strong suit, so it's nearly impossible for me not to see my mother for who she is now, not who she used to be.

On a daily basis, people tell me how lucky I am that I've had two years to say goodbye. As a child who's had one parent die unexpectedly and one die a slow death, lucky isn't the word I'd use. People assume that cancer allows you to say goodbye to your loved ones, but an accidental death has one advantage. You get to remember your loved one as they were, not who they turned into.

Quality versus quantity.

Mom and I have had many days together, days I didn't get to spend with Dad. But Dad wasn't in pain, unable to be my father, while slowly losing himself more and more each and every day. Dad had it easy, saying goodbye and I love you– leaving on a high note after we'd spent the night before excited about our futures. Mom had the agony of not only losing Dad but of her own loss, and the inability to mother me while her daughter had to be the caregiver instead.

Then there's me, the one who gets to live the rest of my life in the aftermath.

Alone.

My mother is a breathing corpse, and every second I spend with her, I'm checking to make sure she's still breathing.

That is *not* lucky.

That is pure fucking torture.

I don't want Mom to feel any of my discomfort, so I still look her in the eye and touch her as I've always done, but it's not without a steep cost to my soul.

Every day I spend my ride to school shoving the pain deep down into a hidden, private place within myself, and I lock it away the best

I can. But sometimes it tries to escape its confines to suffocate me, and today is going to be one of those days. There is no ignoring the harsh reality of my life and my mother's death. After last night, my nerves are wearing thin from being creeped out.

"I have an interview at the electronics store. Mr. Gibbs wrote me a recommendation and I'm taking my grades from my computer programming class as credentials. It should be enough to get me the job." I prattle on as a way of ignoring my mother white-knuckling the blanket in pain. "If not, I have an interview lined up at the coffee shop down the block. I may apply for both and hope they can work together to create a schedule that doesn't conflict with each other. I gotta go, Ma. I don't wanna be late."

After another quick kiss, I rush down the stairs, escaping the harsh reality of my life by running to the fantasy I see for my future. I will make it, and I will do it with my brains. Nothing will stop me from leaving this shithole in the past, even if that means my mother will only be a fading memory.

"Whoa... sweetheart, where's the fire?" Roman drawls as he catches me before I take a header off the bottom step.

"Sorry," I mutter, cheeks blushing bright red. I grip the front of Roman's t-shirt to find my footing, and my blush migrates all the way to the roots of my hair when I realize I'm touching him. Mortified, I pat his shirt down, and then step away. But his hand remains on my left shoulder.

"I'm already late, and I have to hit the subway." Panic setting in as a silent timer ticks in my mind, I gasp breathlessly. "It's a long trip to get to Hillbrook from the hood."

Tilting his chin thoughtfully, Roman tucks a lock of hair behind his ear. Refusing to behave, it swings right back to curve against his jawline. I find his hair fascinating since it's the complete opposite of mine. He tries again and finally the silky strands stay put– too bad, I liked watching them caress the side of his face.

What the hell is wrong with me? I blink to release my insane obsession with Roman's black hair. I've got a billion things more important than this awestruck girly bullshit.

Lips curving into a smile, like he can hear my private thoughts, Roman gestures behind him. "Shall I be your chauffeur this morning? I'm not as seasoned as old Albert, but I can get you to school early." He releases me from his grasp after holding me longer than necessary, leaving me feeling cold where his hand had heated my shoulder.

"You have a car?" I mutter in shock. If you can afford a car, you don't live in this neighborhood. The bank repossessed our car right outside of the supermarket while Mom was working inside. All because the loan was in Dad's name. Back then, we could afford the payments, but Dad was dead and we legally couldn't have the car. But that was another lifetime ago.

"Of course I do," Roman utters with a naughty smirk. "I have pickups to make, or else I'd have nothing to sell. Stanton doesn't make the buys himself. The men on top have to be protected at all costs, with the soldiers doing the heavy lifting. Come on, sweetheart."

"What happened to Stanton's brother? Caleb used to go to Hillbrook with me." I miss the kid. It was nice not being the only lowlife entering Hillbrook's hallowed halls. "I haven't seen him around."

"Stan sent Caleb Upstate to his mom and stepdad's farm," Roman replies hesitantly.

"Why?" shock is heavily lacing my voice. "The kid was a sports nut."

"In a rage, Caleb beat the shit out of four of our dealers last month– put them in the hospital," Roman says stiffly. "It took both Julio and me to take the kid down. Stan stuffed him in a car not ten minutes later, leaving his ass to be straightened out by the Marine stepdad."

"Oh." I try to wrap my head around Caleb being violent, and fail. "I hope he's okay."

"Caleb will be fine now that he's no longer in Dominion." Roman leads me to the rear of the building near the door to his apartment.

I've seen the car sitting there, but never associated it with Roman. It's a primer-colored, old beater that has more Bondo than metal. No one would bother a shitty car around here. Anything with any value would have been stolen instantly. Plus, it would stick out like a sore thumb, especially for a dealer.

I hop inside and get settled, finding the car surprisingly clean for a twenty-year-old guy from this area. But over the past four years, I've learned that money doesn't buy manners. The elite are gluttonous, filthy pigs too.

"How come you were out so late last night? I began to worry the Whittenhowers were going to keep you." Roman smiles at me while facing forward as he maneuvers through traffic. His eyes cut to the side to see how I reacted. "If that happens, at least make some time to tell me goodbye."

I try not to show my alarm at the petrifying thought. Grant creeped me out last night, or rather, my reaction to Grant did. I never want to go back to Misery Castle ever again.

"Ha!" I laugh off the thought because Roman's comment was too close for comfort. "I fell asleep studying because my Latin final is this morning." I pause, for the first time allowing the nervous jitters and graduation excitement to creep in. "I can't believe I'm about to get off a thirteen year education train."

"And ready to hop aboard the higher education plane," Roman teases, voice light and carefree.

"I've loved my education, but I'm looking forward to the day I never have to set foot back into Hillbrook." I shiver from the thought, and button my cardigan for warmth.

"Now, c'mon. It can't be that bad." Roman's eyes cut in my direction again. The corner of his lips lift in a slight smile, and the stirring in my stomach that was awakened last night returns with a vengeance.

The curve of Roman's upper lip and the slope of his jaw hold my undivided attention. I hope this sick fascination with anything male evaporates before I get to school. Maybe it's only targeting those who fascinated me before my body woke up. No matter how much I try to deny it, Roman was always on my radar. And who could resist Grant?

My worst nightmare is Grant and Roman sitting in class next to me as I take my final exam.

What's the word people call this feeling? Horny, that's the word– gross.

With that revelation, my mouth decides to run a mile a minute. "The education is excellent. No way would I have gotten it at public school. It's not even the kids that attend. It's the attitude that affects them. You and I have more freedom than they will ever see in a lifetime. I know it sounds crazy, but it's true. Really, it is."

"If you say it's true, then I believe you," Roman says sincerely. "I'll drop you off a block from the school. I don't want to embarrass you." He glances over his shoulder and starts to pull over to the curb.

"No, don't." I order softly as I place my hand on his strong forearm. Roman peers at me with surprise written across his face. "I won't deny who I am. It's important that I never fake anything for these assholes. I earned this. It wasn't a birthright."

"Okay, sweetheart. Doorstop service, as requested." Roman swings into a spot directly in front of the ancient stone cathedral that houses the Hillbrook Preparatory School. The kids milling around outside of the school stare at us and gawk in superiority.

"Thanks for the ride," I say as I gather up my bag. Before exiting, I lean over to kiss Roman on the cheek, and he jolts just as he did last night. Lips lingering longer than they should, I imprint to memory how his skin is soft while baby-fine whiskers poke me in the lips. I wonder if he can even grow a beard. My mouth curves into a smile against his cheek, and he laughs in response.

"Good luck on your test, sweetheart." Roman flashes me a self-deprecating smile. "Show 'em how you're a force to be reckoned with."

"I plan to do just that," I mutter deviously as I step out of the car.

With my head held high and my shoulders back, I walk up the sidewalk to the front steps. The insistent burning from students staring at me propels me forward. I chuckle underneath my breath when I hear the awful noise from the broken exhaust on Roman's car. He drives away with a loud *pop*.

Roman doesn't need the car to attract notice, as is apparent by the first thing out of Ade's mouth when she strides right up to me.

"Who was that?" Ade demands of me, getting right into my face, and I can see the interest lingering in her eyes. We're almost the same height, but I'm twice the size of Ade. Her demands immediately piss me off, to the point I have to swallow down the need to break her in half like a brittle twig.

It's going to be one of those days. My life is a never-ending tour of the inner circles of Hell. We're all waiting for the day I snap.

Roman is off limits. He isn't something to be acquired like Adelaide's Ezra. He's a human being, and for some reason I feel protective of him– territorialism, maybe jealousy.

"He's no one you need to worry about, Ade." I try not to hiss at her, but it comes out as snotty as she usually sounds. "He isn't in your circle– your father would have a stroke."

"Reg," Ade sighs my name like I exhaust her. "One day, you're going to actually see me for who I am, and you'll realize how moronic it is that you think I *want* your friend. I was asking because I care about you. I don't want to see you get hurt by some homeboy looking to get into your panties."

"Pouring guilt on my open wounds now, are ya?" Fury pushing me, I don't even flinch when every student I pass snickers at me, and then turns to whisper loudly about all of my faults.

"Oh, so you're talking to me now? I wasn't sure." She looks concerned with why anyone would ever find her less than exceptional. "You know how much I hate it when you freeze me out, and now you know why. I live in an ice castle in the sky."

It's my turn to sigh her name. "Ade." But I do it because I can hear the hurt ringing in her voice, but not as loudly as the loneliness and longing.

"I love you, Regina," Ade says with unflinching honesty. "I couldn't survive if you hated me– I need you."

"Shit!" It takes no effort whatsoever to pull Ade into a hug.

Clutching me tightly, fingers digging into my back, Ade whispers into my ear. "Maybe someday you might forgive me."

"Ade?" I question her, but all she does in reply is to hug me tighter. "Forgive you for what?"

"Goddamn dykes!" is bellowed from an asshole, freezing everyone in the atrium. "Get a room– can't you see we're standing in a church."

"Nice." I huff a laugh at the idiocy of pointing out our location while taking the Lord's name in vain. "Blasphemy is frowned upon." I *tsk-tsk* the dumbass while containing a struggling Ade.

Feral, a snarl echoes down the hallway. "Fuck off!" Ade turns in a heartbeat, enraged and no longer looking like the friend I've known for the past four years. "Did you inform your friends how you're actually a scholarship student? Did you? Did you tell them Whittenhower money is financing your daddy's dealings because he's as stupid as his dickless wonder of a son?"

"You cunt!" The boy charges like a bull, nostrils flaring. "Take it back!"

"It's true." Fate comes out of nowhere, mitigating a disaster. "My daddy is your family's financial advisor, so shut the fuck up!"

Pushing their differences aside, Fate clutches Ade's hand and tugs her away from me, like she knows my best friend's deepest and darkest secrets and I'm the one yet again standing on the outside looking in.

"Thomas Simpson is a crook who stole all of our money!" is bellowed after us. "Thief!"

Both of my best friends transform before my eyes. Fate turns, evil glowing from her eyes. "Tell your daddy thanks– I love the new car, my sister loves her Hillbrook tuition, and Mom is wearing your legacy. She's positively dripping in carat after carat."

Muttering, I back away slowly. "You're speaking a foreign language to me. I've got my own shit to deal with. You guys can settle this on your own." I practically run away as the upperclassmen turn on each other in a boiling wave of unsettled power.

Chapter Eight

Seven hours of misery, where all of my classmates turned on each other, with Fate bloated with satisfaction over their hatred. I never thought I'd see Fate and Ade presenting a united front. Our teachers assumed the animalistic nature erupted because of the end of the school year stress. On the plus side, the disruption lowered everyone's concentration during finals, ensuring I'll stay at the top spot.

From what I've gathered, Fate's dad, Thomas Simpson, has been running a Ponzi scheme and draining Dominion's elite dry. Snippets of conversation from last night filter into my mind. Daniel called a guy a crook, and said he was going to have him imprisoned.

Ade and Fate's newfound friendship will fracture in a heartbeat as soon as Daniel has Thomas arrested.

I've had nothing but time to worry over Fate since I stayed after school to find out what my grades were on my final exams. More than a perfectionist and obsessed with time, my teachers are happy I'm graduating. In a cycle, I stood over my teachers' desks as they graded our exams. If one wasn't ready, I stalked the next, in an endless cycle until they gave up and graded my tests in front of me.

I nearly screamed when I received perfect scores across the board. Mr. Gibbs laughed, saying I didn't intimidate him into the grade. One more final to go, and I can bid this educational institution goodbye forever.

My diploma will probably have extra script added to it: *don't let the door hit you where the good Lord split you.*

Giddy with excitement, I practically skip down the front limestone steps, only to collide with a firm body. "Whoa…" Hands steady me before I land face-first onto the sidewalk.

Immediately an apology forms on my lips because everything I do at Hillbrook is my fault according to the student body. Fingertips press into my skin, strong hands grip my shoulders and move me a step back.

A gasp is torn from my chest when I gaze into Grant's eyes. "What the hell are you doing here?" My voice is tight with accusation.

My earlier enthusiasm evaporates as I stare into crystalline blue eyes. No sign of inebriation lingers in Adelaide's big brother. I expect to see remorse at our almost-kiss, but Grant gives me guileless eyes filled with hunger instead. A hunger I try to squelch inside my lower body.

"I don't need to explain myself to you, Regina." Grant's voice holds uncertainty, but he doesn't look angry by my accusation. In fact, he looks eager to talk to me, and that frightens me more than anything. "I'm a Hillbrook legacy. But in case your brain is suddenly addled, Adelaide is one of your classmates, and I needed to speak with the dean after today's events."

"Yeah, that was a nightmare," I mutter while staring at the sidewalk. "I have no idea what happened, but Ade was livid and Fate turned psychotic all damn day."

"Don't worry about Fate, Regina." Grant reaches out to rest a hand on my shoulder, fingertips flexing to reassure me. "Whatever happens with Thomas, Fate and Faith will be taken care of."

"Why?" slips past my lips. My father was killed while on duty, and no one gave two shits about his wife and daughter. Here is a man bilking his colleagues out of their money, and the injured party is promising to take care of his children.

The hypocrisy is mind blowing.

"Their mother is a personal friend of mine." Grant's eyes dart away when I try to catch them.

"Lara?" I grunt, mystified. "She's the biggest bitch I've ever met, and I attend Hillbrook."

Chuckling, Grant shakes his head no.

"Oh, Faith's *biological* mom," I draw out, suddenly curious. Faith was the unexpected product of an affair. The day Faith was born, she was handed to Thomas to raise. Lara wasn't too pleased, and shipped Faith off to live with an aunt in West Virginia. But Hillbrook freshman orientation trumps jilted wife, and Faith is back for longer than holidays.

I've spent a lot of time at the Simpson household over the past four years, and I actually like Thomas. He's a hands-on dad, really attentive. Not many dads would sit on the floor and be Ken to their daughter's Barbie. In my wildest imaginings, I never would have guessed him to be a crook.

"We take care of our own, Regina," Grant promises, and my heart clenches in pain.

I'm not one of their own, not that I want to be. But I don't belong anywhere, not with me as the only living member of my family.

I take care of me.

"Goodbye, Grant," I barely whisper, but the permanence of my words rings clearly.

Walking away, I make it a dozen feet down the sidewalk before Grant stops me by snaring my wrist. His hold is loose enough I could break free, but I'm not sure if I want to. When I'm around Grant, I feel like I've known him forever, like we could talk or just be silent around each other.

Grant bleeds give and take, like he'd meet me halfway. But then again, that's just the stupid girl in me hanging onto infatuation because she's so fucking lonely she's choking on it.

Reading my mind, Grant smiles at me, and those damn dimples reappear. He reminds me of a puppy that followed me home. Do I keep him? He's a gorgeous purebred, not a mixed-breed mutt. If Grant were a mutt, I wouldn't need to worry about a pissed off owner knocking on my door, demanding I return their pet. But Grant is a purebred with an owner. An owner who would not only knock but break down my door.

"What do you want, Mr. Whittenhower?" I use Grant's last name, trying to snap him out of whatever the hell he's up to. I know he wasn't at Hillbrook for Ade. He shouldn't be lurking outside of a school, trolling for girls. I'm legal, but just barely.

"I need to speak with you, Regina." Still holding my wrist, he gives a tug to pull me closer. "Please call me Grant– I think we're acquainted enough, don't you?" His voice is soothing and trusting– good politicians have that type of voice. And you know what they say about politicians…

"Regina?" Grant tilts his head to the side, trying to zero in on my private thoughts. "May we converse for a moment? After all, it's such a small request after what we shared last night."

Cheeks blooming in remembrance of our almost-kiss, my gaze flicks to Grant's lips. At the same time, he's doing the same dang thing. I squirm, heart and mind filled with confusion.

"I believe Mrs. Whittenhower wouldn't be too happy with me calling you by your first name, Mr. Whittenhower." I bring Grant's wife into the conversation to halt my weird fascination with him, and apparently his with me.

"What does my mother have to do with it?" Grant genuinely looks confused for a split-second. "Oh, you mean Cora." He waves his hand, clearing the air, obviously annoyed that I brought his wife up. "I don't think of Cora that way."

"That's really gross, Grant." I stride down the sidewalk toward the subway entrance, and he keeps pace with me. "Knowing your family, you took vows before God and man in a giant cathedral, and that's how you talk of your wife."

"Cora's just like my sisters and Daniel. Who wants to sleep with their family?" Grant's face twists up into a repulsed expression, and I barely hold back a laugh. "I told you I never wanted to marry."

"Cora's your problem, not mine." Face turned to the side, I stare Grant down while continuing to head in the direction of the subway. "You're not my problem either, Grant." He's an inch shorter than me, so my stride is larger than his, but he keeps pace easily.

Grant makes a peculiar sound in the back of his throat. "Hurry up, buddy. I've got a ride to catch, then ten blocks to walk. We all don't have personal drivers named Albert. You're wasting my precious time– I have two job interviews before I can get home to see my dying mother."

"If anyone can imagine how you feel about the loss of your mother, it's me, Regina." Grant's insistent hand is back on my shoulder again, this time patting me in sympathy. "Watching your lifeline slowly die. Not wanting to release them, but knowing they will be better if you do. Imagining scenarios of their loss, but knowing nothing will prepare you for when it ultimately happens. Anytime you want to talk about it, I'll listen."

"Grant," I snarl in exasperation, but not because he doesn't mean it– because he does. "What the fuck do you actually want from me?"

"I do want to talk to you about Ella." Grant's voice turns sullen– every emotion he experiences flows off his tongue like a verbal lie detector test. He'd be better off keeping his mouth shut.

"I know you do, but that's not all you want from me. I can read you like an open book."

"Okay, so you're partially correct." Grant stumbles because I refuse to slow my pace, but I do grab a hold of his hand to keep him upright. "I have a proposition for you, Regina. Well, you really can't deny me. So you may as well hear me out."

The arrogance is astounding. I shake my head at him incredulously. "WOW, just wow! You arrogant fuck. I will deny you for the sake of denying you. It must be fabulous to always get what you want when you want it." I quicken my pace, nearly jogging. I can see the entrance to the subway a few blocks up– my destination.

"Don't do this, Regina. You need to hear me out. The consequences are bad. Don't underestimate a determined Jackson and Daniel," he pleads with me. "I don't want to do this. But as you know, you'll give a dying person anything they request."

"Jesus, Grant. Like I don't have enough shit on my plate." I just stare at the gorgeous idiot while wearing a gobsmacked expression. "After last night, I want nothing to do with your whole family. I'm contemplating never seeing Ade again after graduation even. You're all fucked in the head. That child should be taken from you."

"They won't take no for an answer, Regina," Grant pleads. "Usually Jackson and Daniel are at odds, which makes my life infinitely easier, but in this they are in perfect agreement. Which means they will be as relentless as they are ruthless."

"Well, bully for them," I mutter begrudgingly.

"Regina." Grant grabs for me but I sidestep him. "I don't want to do it this way– I don't want to do it at all. I'm trying my damnedest to take the brunt of the fallout, but you have to meet me halfway by just doing as you're told."

The suffocating sensation of last night's premonition radiates up my spine. I can see it as if it were happening right now. The gate to Misery Castle closing behind me– the clank of finality. The illusion of being protected from the outside world, but in reality I'm trapped on the inside. A giant cage. The trees closing in around me as we ride the switchbacks at a rapid speed. Young Daniel greeting me as if he were waiting for me– expecting me. He nicknamed me Queen, while taking the moniker Whitt for the very first time. The dizzying sensation as Whitt tugged me to the cracked open door, because the discussion was about...

ME!

I have your sister on this.

What does Katie have to do with this?

Who said it was Katherine?

Someday I hope you might forgive me, Adelaide whispers.

Cora's barren– they call it Polycystic Ovarian Syndrome.

We have to pick you out a woman built like an ox...

"You sonofabitch!" Palms balling into fists, I pummel the center of Grant's chest. Leaving him momentarily stunned, I grab the railing at the top of the stairway leading down to the subway, and then jog down the steps away from him.

If Grant wants to speak with me, he has to earn it– catch me if you can.

"Regina, stop! Please!" Grant screams out in desperation, voice holding every emotion he's feeling. Panic etches across his features, tightening around his eyes and drawing his lips into a thin line.

I do stop, but not because he said so, because the subway hasn't arrive yet– or so I tell myself.

I shout, defeated. "What the fuck, Grant?" Voice utterly hopeless, knowing I've already lost the battle before it has even begun. "Why?" warps into a cry. "Why?"

Seeming to feel my pain more so than hear it, Grant looks lost. "My father is disappointed in his son and grandson." I try to reason out what he's saying, but he continues before I can solve it. "We're too much like my mother, not enough like him. He hopelessly loves us, even knowing we're not strong enough to shoulder the burden of generations upon generations of evil deeds."

"That's the point of guilt, Grant. Every good Catholic boy knows that." I roll my eyes, because the alternative is shoving Grant on the third rail to electrocute his perfect ass.

"The Whittenhower bloodlines must be preserved, Regina. Jackson knows I'm incapable of following in his footsteps, and young Daniel may like boys."

"So what? Are you a bigot, too?" I snarl, spittle flying from my lips. "*My* Whitt is perfect."

Grant smiles beatifically at the vehemence in my tone. "He is– I'm doing this to protect *your* Whitt. If he's gay, do you really want women shoved at him because it's his duty to propagate the bloodline?"

"Grant," I gasp breathlessly. "Don't ask this of me– don't. I can't. I won't."

"This is killing me, Regina. The spare always has it easy, but I wasn't so lucky with two sisters born after me. It's like the only thing I was born to do was to breed another generation. Then I was told it wasn't good enough, and forced to repeat it. I won't do that to Whitt, because I've barely survived it and I know he won't–"

"Grant?" The screech of the train stopping drowns out whatever he's professing. I can see his lips move, but I don't know what he's saying.

I back up as the door slides open. The last thing I hear is, "Surrogate." I run into the train and move until I'm several cars away from Grant, because I refuse to contemplate what his family has planned for me.

Chapter Nine

"Thanks for coming home with me today, Fate. I know my mom really wants to see you– to say goodbye." My voice breaks, and I try to cover it with a cough.

The past week has gone by in a blur. I managed to land both jobs, and I've already started them. I work alternating days on school nights and half days at both on the weekends. Between work and graduation preparation, I haven't seen much of my mother and the guilt is killing me.

Now is when I should be spending every waking second at Mom's side. But I need to pay for her medicine to make her last moments as comfortable as possible. I paid for a week's worth of rent to get the landlord off our manager's back, but I worry Mom will run out of medicine before my next paycheck now.

Someone else I haven't seen much of is Ade. She looks at me with guilty eyes, and I know that she knows her brother is hounding me at the behest of her father and uncle, and why.

Every night at work, Grant comes in and pesters me to listen to him. Begs and pleads. So far, all I've allowed him to say is the word surrogate. I know enough of what that means, combined with the conversation I overheard between Grant and Daniel.

My ox-sized body will not be used to birth another generation of Whittenhowers– I don't even like them.

Okay, so that's not entirely true. I love Adelaide. Priscilla seems like a generous woman. Whitt is a darling boy. Uncle Jackson is crazy yet amusing. Daniel is evil incarnate. Grant... is Grant.

Last night I had Grant thrown out of the coffee shop. I'm curious to see if he tries to visit *Digital Nation* tonight. We close early on Friday nights so the owners can have their date night. I wish I could see the look on Grant's face when he shows up and I'm not there.

"Your mind is spinning a mile a minute, Reg," Fate remarks as she keeps pace with me on the walk from the subway.

Another major difference between Ade and Fate– Ade has a driver drop her off while Fate rides home with me, trusting me infallibly to protect her.

"I have too much on my mind and no way to put it in order," I admit, sounding defeated.

"You do know…" Fate twirls until she's facing me, getting a few appreciative looks from the boys hanging on the street. "The best friend gig is not one-sided. I can hold my own if you want to vent."

Smirking slyly, I murmur, "I know."

"Good." Fate twists until she's no longer walking backward, much to the disappointment of my homeboys. Petite blonde in a Catholic schoolgirl uniform is a hot commodity. "School's pretty much over– your mom is a given. So it must be boy trouble. Right?"

So perky, I hate to burst her bubble. "Grown man trouble, and it goes deeper than that."

"Good God, woman!" Fate's eyes bulge from her skull and her mouth is gaping wide open. "Look at that blush. You like a boy! That's a first."

"NO!" I protest too forcefully as we reach my building.

"Sweetheart!" Roman whistles from the alleyway, no doubt hearing my protests. Fate pulls on her ponytail, straightening it, making sure she's picture-perfect.

I smile at Fate and mouth, "Roman's not the grown man trouble," to head her incessant questioning off at the pass.

"Oh," she pouts, disappointed. "Hottie would be worth the trouble."

"Hottie, you say," Roman purrs as he steps from the side of the building to join us.

The energy that infuses me every time I see Roman is starting to grate on my nerves. I don't know how to turn it off now that the switch has been thrown. It happens a thousand times stronger around Grant, but no one else. I'm thankful my body isn't going batshit crazy around every male.

Smoking hot and built, and not doing a dang thing for me, I tested my theory out on Julio yesterday, but he caught on. I learned the young mob enforcer is gay.

Epic fail.

Now Julio Ramirez thinks I have a dang crush on him, and he has taken to avoiding me.

I experience a full-body flush that leaves me feverish as I check out Roman. Today he's wearing a tight black t-shirt stretched across his chest, shoulders, and arms, and worn-in jeans encasing his thighs and cupping his bulge. On anyone else, it would look on purpose. On Roman, it's like a second-skin.

"Hi-ya, Roman." Not ashamed of my roots or my friendship with a criminal, I introduce them, and Roman's resulting smile curls my toes. "Roman Alexander, this is my best friend, Fate Simpson."

"Hi!" squeaks out. Fate is practically drooling on herself as she looks at the guy– bright-eyed and bushy-tailed. But she'll behave like the young lady she was bred to be. I smirk, wondering what she'd think of Roman if she learned he was a drug dealer.

"How'd your last final go today?" Roman leans down and gives me a kiss on the cheek. I gasp and Fate's eyes bug out of her skull. My cheek tingles where his lips made contact with my skin– dampness kissing the air. The pleasant sensation lingers. I still my hand before I touch my cheek with my fingertips.

Roman grins at me– his aqua eyes shining with mischievousness.

"Perfect score. One week from tonight, I will be an official graduate of Hillbrook Prep." I announce with pride, adding a bounce on my feet as I speak.

"Next week is going to be awesome," Fate says to join the conversation. "No classes at all because we have to practice for graduation."

"No work sounds like fun until you get bored, girly." Fate lights up like Christmas when Roman gives her a pet name. Too bad it's the one he calls every female when he can't remember their names. I'm sweetheart. Half the time I want to ask Roman if he actually knows who I am, but I know he does.

"How's your mom?" In the wake of Roman's solemn voice, my enthusiasm deflates.

"Not good– everyone in the neighborhood has stopped by this week to say their goodbyes. Truthfully, I think Mom's waiting for me to graduate. She needs to know that I reached that goal at least."

I discreetly swipe a tear away, but Roman is highly observant. He pulls me to his chest, and I suck in a huge breath of his clean, masculine scent. Feeling safe and comforted, I allow a single sob to release from my throat.

"It's fucking horrible– pure torture," is muffled against Roman's shoulder. His hands rub my back for a minute, and then I pull away and wipe my eyes with the back of my hand.

"We better get up there. I don't want to miss a minute with her, ya know? My time is too valuable to waste right now. Not that you're a waste–"

Roman cuts me off, and I grip his shirt when I realize how that sounded. "Go– I know what you mean, sweetheart. Spend all the time you have with Ella. I'll visit her tomorrow while you're at work. Go on now," Roman coaxes as he pushes me into the building.

I grab Fate's hand and look over my shoulder. I give Roman a look of thanks, and he flashes a sad smile my way. As I turn away, I swear I see him drag a thumb underneath his left eye.

This is why I love Fate so much. Even though she has the propensity to turn on her entitled attitude in a split-second, she's still one of the sweetest, kindest people I've ever met.

I always assumed Ade wouldn't visit because she's repulsed by my mother, but maybe it has more to do with the prospect of losing Jackson. But Ade can't suck it up for a half hour and lend me some support as I go through the worst time of my life. I'd do it for her, but she can't do it for me.

But Fate, she manages to see my mother as the beautiful woman she met when we were freshman, back when both of my parents were alive and well. Fate helped me make dinner while I picked up the mess in the apartment. I was shocked to notice how much pride she took in cooking, and she laughed and said Faith gets on her ass for being a spoiled brat so she learned some things.

Now, an hour later, Fate takes to the role of daughter so I may continue on as the caregiver. She sits on the edge of my mother's bed, holding Mom's hand as if it wasn't skin over bones, while wearing a genuine smile on her face and hiding the tears in her eyes.

"Ella, you should feel so proud. Regina is the top of our class, and even the alumni are jealous."

Pale, blue lips tug into the facsimile of a smile. "Curtis and I could never figure out how she got so smart. I'll never forget the day I put Regina in her highchair. I went to grab the milk after placing the Cheerios on her tray. I turned back with the milk, only to find my toddler reading the cereal box to me. She was smarter than me from that moment on."

"Mom," I sigh, smiling fondly at a snapshot in time I didn't remember, but will now file away in my memory bank.

"Your intelligence scared your father because your teachers didn't know what to do with you. Curt would drag home broken television sets he nabbed off the curb for Regina to dismantle and put back together. The day she managed to get one to work, was the first time Curt was brought to his knees."

"Dad and I were just playing a little game, is all." I look away, blushing. "I plugged the TV in and got a fuzzy screen, but Dad's ass landed on the floor when the news started playing."

Chuckling, Fate looks between my mom and me. "What was wrong with the TV in the first place?"

"When Curt brought it home, it was missing a screen," my mom whispers with pride. "Regina used four of her other projects to make one work."

"Jesus," Fate hisses, awed.

"It was nothing," I mutter with a shrug. "I was eight by then."

"Eight?" Fate slaps my knee because she thinks I'm joking– I'm not. "Ella, how did Regina get her scholarship? My dad doesn't even know. Scholarships are actually forbidden at Hillbrook– a way to keep our legacies pure, so to speak. Even the few non-legacies who buy their way in freshman year have to have ties to the founding families."

An uncomfortable laugh rumbles out my throat. "Well, we sure as hell share no ties with you guys."

"Well, let's see…" Mom gets a faraway look in her eyes, and I fear we're not managing her pain well enough. "Seventh and eighth grade were the worst for Regina. She was in middle school and they wouldn't allow her to take high school courses. Regina's math teacher– Mrs. Brody volunteers at Transcend, and she found Regina a scholarship."

"I was already spending most of my time at Transcend anyway, since they had a computer lab. I was in the middle of writing code for a word-processing program, so I could do my homework faster, when Mrs. Brody dragged me out and pushed me into a room with an older woman, who I just learned was Rebekah Zeitler, and Priscilla Whittenhower."

"Holy crap!" Fate leans forward, fully engrossed. "So what happened? Who is Regina's benefactor?"

Shrugging one shoulder, I mutter, "I talked to the ladies for about an hour, and that's all I know."

"Mrs. Zeitler was your benefactor, Regina." Mom's eyes turn glassy with tears, so I assume she knows the woman passed away.

"Her estate was placed in the hands of her grandsons. Dexter Hayes was written on the last few tuition checks. But your college scholarship fund had another name written on it… what was it? Dang it, my mind is always blanking on me."

"Marcus Zeitler," Fate supplies. Stated, not said as a question.

"Yes! That's it," Mom sounds relieved that she's not losing her mind.

Fate catches my eye, brows knitted in the center of her forehead from worry. "Your other BFF gave me the lowdown on your boy troubles," she warns, shocking me. "Your tuition may as well have been coming straight from Whittenhower coffers, with as tight as they are with the Zeitlers. If you catch my drift."

"Jesus, not now," I issue a warning of my own. "We're on Mom time."

"I'm fine. You girls go be girls while you still can." My mom's eyes fade out for a second, and I know the pain is hitting her again. "Too many visitors today and not enough sleep." I jump up and grab her pill bottle off the dresser. I pop the cap and stare into the amber tube in morbid disbelief–

Empty.

Heart beating out of control, I'm at a total loss of what to do now. "Mom, I gotta run to the pharmacy to fetch you another refill. I'll be back as soon as I can."

I dart from the room before she can answer. I don't have a fucking clue how I'm going to pay for it, and I won't beg off of Roman again, even though I know he'll give it to me. Realistically, I know Stanton Green would be the one paying for the prescription. He's the type of man who will help you if you truly need it, but you have to have balls big enough to ask for it first.

I'm an eighteen-year-old girl with the Whittenhowers on my ass. I can't be beholden to Dominion's twenty-something lord of the underworld too.

Jesus! I can't ask Fate, and not only because I refuse to hurt our friendship over borrowing money. The FBI has been hounding Fate's dad, so any money borrowed was stolen from someone else.

I look around the apartment and realize that nothing in here matters. Materialistic possessions with no sentimental value. Bedridden, Mom won't be with me long enough to ever see this stuff again. As soon as I start college in the fall, I won't be living here anyway.

Everything my father ever bought us is long gone in our quest to survive. What's left is just cheap replacements bought at secondhand stores. Depressed, on the verge of a panic attack, I drill into my psyche that it doesn't matter. They're just inanimate objects– they hold no emotions and have no soul.

Everything but love and life is replaceable.

I'm capable of earning back anything I need in the future. But, today, we need money.

Sliding to my knees in the only closet in our apartment, I locate the loose floorboard covering my hidey-hole, knowing there was always a high probability of being robbed in this building. I pry the board up with my house-key and lift the cigar box from its cubby. Inside is the only jewelry to the Regal name. With shaking fingertips, I hold my father's watch– the one he was awarded when he reached fifteen years of proud service working for the Transit Authority. There are only three other items in the box: Mom's diamond engagement ring and their wedding bands.

I could pawn the bands, or the diamond, or the watch. The choice is like choosing which of your children to keep, kill, or give away.

I sit on my ass, half in and half out of the closet, with tears streaming down my face, contemplating which to pawn when Fate finds me.

"Reg?" Her tiny palm cups the back of my neck, trying to soothe me. "What are you doing?"

"The watch is Dad's– the engagement ring is Mom's, but Dad gave it to her." I show Fate the jewelry as I speak, knowing she'll never understand when everything in her affluent world is disposable.

"It's a no-brainer. I'll keep the bands." I come to a decision, even though they are worth the least. "Mom and Dad bought them for each other as symbol of their undying union. So, in turn, it's both Mom's and Dad's rings, and also given by them to each other."

Fate looks at me in bewilderment, not understanding why I'm contemplating my only assets. I hop up from my crouch and grab her hand, while shoving the flimsy door closed with my heel.

"Regina? What's going on?" I leave the apartment, dragging Fate behind me in a cloud of confusion. She's about to learn what it means to live in reality. "Talk to me, Reg."

I don't answer Fate because I'm incapable. If I were able to make a sound, it would be an agony-filled death knell.

We don't have to walk far. Every few blocks or so is a pawnshop in this part of the city. The worse the living situation, the more pawnshops you'll find.

We're ogled and catcalled the entire walk to the shop. Most of the grown men are simply teasing us for shits and giggles, no threat to be had, but the boys haven't learned the value of personal space yet. The younger ones have the nerve to follow us up the block, tugging at our skirts.

"Hey, baby?" A small hand reaches out to tug Fate's ponytail. "Do those lily white preppy bastards have big enough balls to reach up under your skirt?" Poor Fate slaps the boy's hand away from her skirt.

Chuckling underneath my breath, "Go away," I mutter to the boy, shoving a palm at his forehead. Stringing together an inventive list of slurs, the boy slips back to his friends, only to get razzed by them for being a dumbass.

Fate cowers, trying to sink into the pavement. "Leave me alone," her voice breaks.

What's an everyday occurrence for me, is a terrifying nightmare for Fate. Her hand finds mine, and clutches me in fright.

"Just ignore them like you would a child– to engage them is to give them attention. The more attention they get, the worse they behave."

"They're awful." Fate clutches me tighter.

"They're picking on you." I swallow back my laughter. "You should see your face, and how you're clutching at my hand like a scared child. They see it as an insult, because where you're from, you call everyone down here lowlife criminals. So they're showing you lowlife criminals to frighten you away."

"That doesn't make sense," Fate whispers, practically hugging me she's so close.

"Makes perfect sense from my position. Treat them like human beings, and they will treat you like one. Sure, there are muggers and rapists. But not every man on every street is looking to steal your virtue and leave you dead in an alley."

"Don't joke about shit like that." Fate crowds me more.

"Most of the guys are pretty cool dudes, even if they are thieves and dealers– they're still normal dudes."

Just now, I realize how jaded I've become. This is my daily life, but this is a once in a lifetime moment for Fate.

"You should realize–" I almost stop myself from saying it. *Almost*, because I'm more than insulted too. This is *my* home turf. "You should realize, thieves and rapists wear suits and drive fancy cars, too. My people are more likely to commit crimes in order to survive. Yours are more likely to commit crimes for the sport of it– which act is born of evil?"

"Regina?" Fate gasps, but I interrupt her tirade by dragging her into the shop.

The bell over the door rings with finality as we enter *PAWN*. Yeah, just Pawn. No need to be creative around here. Shop signs announce what you are looking for: Pawn. Loans. Clinic. Diner. Grocery. Laundry. Tattoo. Cigarettes. Beer. Wine. Liquor.

We're a literal community.

You can spot one of Stanton Green's businesses simply because he used artistic license and actually gave them a name, usually inventive ones at that.

Mind spilling 'round and 'round, I rush through the transaction, not wanting to think of the ramifications of what I'm doing.

This is the end.

The Regal family is *game over*.

I sell the most important items we own and save mere trinkets. It's sentimental value, not monetary value that I place on my parents' wedding bands. If it comes down to it, they're next to go. I try not to get too attached to anything anymore, including people.

Everything is disposable. The only person I can rely on is myself, because everyone leaves when they die.

Fate's teeth chatter so loudly that I can barely negotiate. She's scared shitless. What does she think the shopkeeper is going to do, knife her? We're just normal people living our lives. Violence doesn't only happen in underprivileged areas. There's just more of us crammed in here together to bring up the statistics.

"I could have given you the money." Fate reminds me as we walk to my apartment after leaving the pharmacy with the prescription in hand. "Why didn't you tell me where we were going, what we were doing, and why we were doing it? I'd do anything for Ella– *anything* for you!"

Walking past the same boys who pestered us before, we've lost their interest. Fate has calmed down some now that her *ordeal* is over. I would love to explain why I had to do this the way I did it, but Fate would never understand.

One thing that makes me the angriest is knowing that my father was gypped on his watch. Those pieces of shit gave him a piece of shit for his fifteen years of service. It comes as no surprise, seeing as how after his death, they took no interest in the wife and daughter he left behind.

"I don't want to be indebted to anyone else, least of all to a friend. You have your own problems at home right now, and I'm not going to compound them with mine. So just be here for me like you were today with my mom, because that's what I need from you right now."

Chapter Ten

Sitting in the middle of the floor, bent over the computer stack Mr. Gibbs wants me to fix, a knock on my door startles me into jabbing myself with a flathead screwdriver bit. "Fate, didn't your driver show up?" She only left five minutes ago.

After scrambling to my feet, I swing the door open, only to find Grant standing on the other side. He looks decidedly uncomfortable.

"What are you wearing?" is the first thing to blurt past my lips.

Eyebrows knitted together, Grant glances down at himself. Clad in a white wife-beater and navy track shorts, his naturally pale skin is glowing tan with a little help from the sun. I concentrate on a pink spot near his right shoulder, ignoring the rest of his delectable flesh.

"Contrary to what they say about us in your neighborhood, businessmen don't wear suits while playing tennis." Grant fists his palms on his hips while trying to catch my gaze.

"What do you want?" I spit out, sounding surly and annoyed because my eyes refuse to ignore how strong Grant's thighs look in his shorts. He's small and lean for a man, but there isn't an ounce of fat on him and every muscle is taut and defined. The sparse hairs on his chest and his nipples beaded against his tank are far too intriguing for me to handle.

I need to shut these hormones down.

"Aren't you going to invite me in?" Grant smiles, employing his dimples, but it doesn't work this time.

"What do you want?" I repeat, voice dripping with rage– at myself.

I have to hate Grant. I *need* to hate him. But, for some reason, I can't seem to do it. Damn it!

Shoulders slumping, Grant gazes at the floor like a sad puppy begging to be let in from the cold. "How are you, Regina?" His soothing voice caresses my name.

Shivering, I pretend I'm unaffected. "What. Do. You. Want?" I fist my palms on my hips, mirroring Grant. But it doesn't have the same effect since I never changed out of my uniform.

Stubborn, we both turn into children. "How. Are. You?" Grant repeats, mirroring me as I mirror him– the bastard.

Engaging in a standoff, we just stare at one another. Grant breaks first by curling his lips, eyes drinking in the apartment at my back.

"Yeah, welcome to how the other half lives." I have nothing to be ashamed of, but I don't want Grant knowing how I live. I do have some pride left. Okay, a ton of stubborn pride left. "What are you doing here, Grant?"

Giving in, I move to the side and allow him entrance. No sense denying him, he'd just barge in anyway. I hold a small amount of control if I invite him in versus him just doing as he pleases.

Grant looks around my squalor as I shut and bolt the three locks on the flimsy, paper-thin door. "You weren't at work, so I came to visit. I need you to hear me out, Regina," he demands, voice soft yet compelling.

Grant looks desperate and maybe a bit crazed. His blond hair is standing on end as if he has repeatedly run his fingers through it in frustration. His crystalline blue eyes are as dark as storm clouds.

"Why should I, Grant?" I walk away from him, not far obviously, since the apartment is tiny.

Grabbing a dishcloth and the spray bottle filled with a mixture of vinegar and water, I begin wiping off the counter. There isn't much to clean in the apartment. The past few months, I've pawned just about everything of value. If we had something nice, I pawned it and bought a replacement at the thrift shops. It's pitiful, but I think I was letting go of everything that held a memory of Dad or Mom. I've been grieving the loss of my parents for two years straight.

"Take a look around at my reality, Grant." I gesture behind me with the spray bottle. "I sleep on a couch I dragged in from the curb, in a cockroach infested hovel. Go peek into the bedroom and introduce yourself to my decaying mother. And then ask yourself why you're bothering me."

"Regina–" Grant's voice breaks.

Glaring, I turn on Grant, hating how he has tears glistening in his eyes. "Ask yourself why you're suddenly infatuated with someone like me. You have a huge mansion and a rich family. Go home to your wife, and thank God that you had the fortune to be born to your parents and not to mine."

Grant steps forward, frustration ringing in his voice. "It doesn't work that way, and you know it."

"Luck is the only difference between us, Grant. *Luck*. It's like the lottery. We're born into a family– rich or poor, white or black, gay or straight. In this country or any other. It's all luck, and we shouldn't be punished for where, how, and who we are when we're born. The only difference is that I will rise above this, whereas all you can do is fall. I think you should be more appreciative of your station in life."

"If *you* didn't pick where and how and who you were when you were born, then neither did *I*!" Grant glares at me, begging me to disagree with him. "You're more judgmental than you believe me to be."

Throwing the gauntlet down, I rush over to the bedroom door and crack it open in invitation. Surprising me, Grant strides across the apartment and slips inside my mother's bedroom without a backward glance.

I thought for sure Grant would leave like his sister would have, but he disappears inside after closing the door in my face. With a deep breath, I turn the doorknob, and then follow after him.

"Mrs. Regal, it's a pleasure to meet you." I hear no pity in Grant's smooth voice, and his eyes don't flinch as he looks at my mom. I feel proud of him, and as much as I don't want to like him, I can't help it in this moment.

"Call me Ella– you must be Ade's brother. Very handsome– you look so much alike." Mom clears her throat several times, so I hurry over to give her a sip of water. I dab her chin with a cloth where she dribbled some that didn't make it past her lips.

Ignoring my caregiving, "Yes, ma'am. I'm Adelaide's brother, Grant." He sits at the edge of the bed and takes her hand like they're the best of friends.

Bewildered, heart thudding for some unknown reason, I walk backward to the door, not wanting to intrude on their conversation– or maybe I'm just too much of a coward.

"How is your sister? I haven't seen the girl in months. I was worried that Regina and Adelaide weren't getting along anymore." Grant's eyes tighten around the edges when he hears how Ade won't visit.

That's the last straw– my nerves can't take it.

Unable to work on my project, I sit on the couch and begin to worry as I watch the time tick on our cheap, plastic wall clock. The minute-hand is broken and now shorter than the hour-hand. The ink on most of the numbers has faded to a pale gray. I stare at the secondhand as it makes its twenty-seventh revolution around the numbers. The ominous *tick… tick… tick…* of my life changing by the second drowns out any noise from within the building or on the street.

Blocking out Grant and Mom's whispered conversation, the silence becomes deafening.

Eyes flicking from the clock at the fifty-four minute mark, "What took so long?" I ask Grant when he sits next to me.

The ratty couch is clean, but I'm embarrassed to see Grant sitting on something that should be on the curb for garbage collection. I blush when I realize he's sitting on my bed with me as I had last week with him on his.

"Since you wouldn't listen to my proposition, I asked for permission from your mother." Face pinched, Grant is decidedly perturbed at my avoidance tactics. "To say Ella wasn't pleased is an understatement."

"Yeah, stealing a dying mother's only daughter's womb will do that to a woman."

Grant ignores my sarcasm. "I didn't want to upset your mother, but she and I understand one another. After a lifetime of dealing with Jackson, I know the only thing she wants is for you to be taken care of, happy and healthy, and loved. To not be alone."

"Stop!" I snarl, fingers curling into a fist against my palms.

"Ella wants to know that you have security before she parts our earthly plane. She gave permission when I told her what my father has in store for you if you don't come willingly. As I've said, Jackson and Daniel joining forces will lead to ruthlessness. Jackson wants for me what Ella wants for you– and he'll do anything to get it."

I have no idea how the man can make my plight sound like it's his punishment because he's hurting for me, but he's a master at it. Weakened by the cadence of his voice, I give in when he tries to hold my hand.

The innocent gesture of his fingers wrapping around mine lights up every nerve ending in my body, and I hate it. I hate that I react to someone I should despise. I despise everything Grant Whittenhower stands for. Most importantly, I shouldn't respond like this with my dying mother in the next room.

Why should I experience pleasure when all Mom feels is pain?

Why should I enjoy anything when she will cease to exist?

I pull my hand away and tuck it under my thigh, where Grant can't get to it. It doesn't matter though, because he places his hand on my knee instead. The touch isn't sexual. I can tell he means it as a comforting gesture– one that will connect us as he tries to talk to me. But my body is making more out of it than it should.

I disgust myself.

"I don't want anything from you, Grant. I wouldn't even accept my scholarship if it wasn't for the fact that I earned it. I don't want a handout, but I sure as hell don't want one from a Whittenhower."

"I will never argue over the fact that you have earned your scholarship, but I'll point out how my best friends are paying for it."

Flipping around to face Grant with a sneer on my face, "You bastard," I growl. I hate how I can envision how this will play out if I don't obey. But I can't stop fighting, even if I'm destined to lose.

"Be angry, Regina." Grant bares his perfect teeth. "I'm angry too!" He pounds the center of his chest. "You're not the only one in this situation. If you'd give me an inch and meet me half way, we could be allies instead of adversaries."

"Fuck you!" My fist flies out to punch him where he was taking out his own frustrations just moments ago.

Moving so fast, I can't track the movement, Grant's gripping my chin and wrenching my head sideways, forcing me to look at him. "Hit me again," he demands.

Startled, I flinch backward. "No."

"Do it," Grant snarls. "Hit me– I'm destroying your life. Do. It."

"What the fuck?" The calm, soothing man is replaced by a younger version of Jackson Whittenhower. "What?"

"Do. It."

All I can do is stare into his wild eyes, seeing my own confusion reflected back at me. "You don't know the half of what my elders have planned for you," Grant warns. "If you think what's happening now is bad, refuse me."

"I won't do it!" Wrenching my head to the side, I break from Grant's hold. Chin burning, I know a bruise will be left behind. "I won't give my child to you assholes."

"We'll see," he mutters in defeat– mine, not his. "We'll see."

"I can take whatever they dish out," I hiss right into his face.

The biting fingertips are back, but this time they're gouging into the back of my neck, restraining me. "No, Regina." Grant's soothing voice is at odds with the violence sparking from his eyes and the command radiating from his fingertips. "You can't," is breathed across my lips.

Enraged, my fist flies out to cut across Grant's jaw, whipping his head to the side. Knuckles stinging, stunned, I sit frozen still as he twists his head left, then right, adjusting his neck.

"Do it again!" Grant orders, and my fist obeys. With a snap, the hollow thud of flesh meeting the center of his chest snaps me out of it. "Again!"

Broken, I ball my fists up, pummeling his chest and arms, not realizing tears are streaming from my eyes and sobs are pouring out of my throat. Body shuddering as I release two years' worth of pent-up anger, frustration, and grief, I find myself pulled into Grant's lap with my face tucked against the side of his neck.

"Let it out, Regina," Grant coaxes, hands moving in a soothing rhythm along my back in time with his words. "Don't try to quiet your pain– your mother needs to hear it. She needs to know you'll be okay."

Hiccupping, "How could hearing me cry make Mom feel better?" With renewed sobs, I clutch Grant like he's my lifeline.

"Because Ella needs to know her daughter is human," Grant whispers against the top of my head. "Your robotic routine is without emotion– I love yous said in a dead voice ring false. Hearing the devastation at her loss will hurt Ella, but she knows it's the only way you'll heal."

"Bullshit," I snarl. With force, I try to tug out of Grant's arms, but he's a lot stronger than he appears. Arms constricting around me like steel bands, I'm not going anywhere until he allows it.

"I'm sure you've figured out that my sisters and I don't have the same father– so we weren't raised the same way. At another time, I'll tell you most of my secrets. But not tonight, because right now I need you to know I not only feel for you, but I *hear* you. I understand you."

"No," flows out on the end of a sob.

"Yes. I love my father more than I love myself. I've done all he asks of me because when faced with death, I'd do anything to keep him with me. Jackson's heart could give out at any moment, and I don't want guilt layered on top of the mountain of grief. I won't be the tipping point– the stressor that ends his life."

Greedy for support, I fall into what Grant is offering in the moment. Strong arms to hold me, shoulders to support my burdens, and ears that hear my pleas. Melting into his embrace, I soak up the sensation of his hands running over and over my back in a soothing rhythm.

"You and I are one in the same in this– don't fool yourself, Ella wants exactly what Jackson does. The ability to live after death. As human beings, there is only one way to accomplish this feat of immortality. By becoming allies, we both win."

"I haven't even graduated from high school yet. I have two jobs and a scholarship. I have goals in life, and nothing will stop me from reaching them," I say with conviction. "I just turned eighteen. I'm too young to have a baby, especially someone else's."

"Jackson loves me exactly as I am, but Daniel is terrified for the aftermath. Once Jackson dies, everything Whittenhower is mine, and we all know I don't want it. Your lottery comment was the perfect analogy. While I was born into the position, I'm incapable of surviving what it entails."

"Then it will pass to the next in line," I offer the logical resolution.

"Jackson and Daniel don't believe Whitt will be able to survive the title. In this, I agree. I want more for my children than how I've had to live, but I understand how this is bigger than I am. Generations of Whittenhower history and our future legacy is in my hands."

"Then don't do this," I beg, hating Grant because he and I are stuck in the passenger seat while two vicious assholes drive us into Hell.

"Don't you think I would if I could?" Shaking me, his fingertips bite into my back. "I don't want this life." Enraged, he no longer sounds like the Grant I've begun to know. "I told you I never wanted to marry, and yet I find myself married. I never wanted to be a father, yet look at where this is leading…" he squeezes me in example. "I never wanted to run an empire. But no one ever asked me what I wanted– no matter how loudly and often I speak, I'm silenced."

"You're angry," I make a statement, pressing closer to him. Stupid girl that I am, it suddenly feels like Grant '*gets*' me.

"Yes," he whispers against my hair, arms pulling me closer. "And hurt."

"You're frustrated."

Grant's hand grips my thigh, pulling my leg over his hip until I'm sitting astride his lap. "Yes. Very."

"You're grieving for the living." I settle on his lap, never having sat with anyone like this before. The intimacy is mind blowing.

"You feel like you have to be strong because there's no one left to support you." Grant's voice is deeper than ever. I pull back to look at him, only to discover he's been crying right along with me this entire time.

Terrified, our eyes connect as, "Powerless," passes my lips.

"I hear you, Regina, because you're my echo."

Have you ever wanted to hear something so badly, it didn't matter if it was true or not?

Have you ever experienced the sensation of trying to stifle a cry, to the point your skin tightens, your eyes prickle, and you feel like you're going to suffocate?

"What do you want, Regina?" is said at the same time I say, "What do you want, Grant?"

I have.

Suddenly supported, we break.

Clutching at one another, neither trying to quiet our sobs, we grieve our future losses and mourn what will never be. We seize one another, fingertips holding the violence of suppressed anger and a lifetime of frustration and injustice.

Faces pressed tightly to one another's neck, tears dampen our skin. Hands roaming, seeking comfort. Hips rolling against one another, finding pleasure.

An hour or more later, we part. Feeling lighter, Grant's promises aren't able to intoxicate me into buying what he's selling. "I can't."

Crawling from his lap, I try to stand on wobbly legs, and have to clutch the arm of the sofa to stop myself from falling to the floor. With all the dignity I can muster, I wipe my eyes on my shirt sleeve, and then smooth my skirt back down, ignoring the fact that Grant and I found peace *and* pleasure on the sofa.

"No one has ever asked me what I wanted. No one ever listens when I speak. So I showed you what I wanted, and I know you heard me," he warns. "An ally."

"I can't," I repeat, rationality banging around inside my skull.

Grant straightens to his full height, not bothering to hide the wet spot on his shorts by pulling his t-shirt down. Striding across my apartment, he flicks the locks and opens the door. "You will," he says in parting.

"I'm too young to be a mother!" I scream at the top of my lungs, reverberating off the walls.

The door reopens, and the only thing I see is the knowledge lurking in Grant's eyes. "As you've no doubt figured out– *your* Whitt is *my* son."

My shocked gasp ricochets around the apartment.

"I didn't have a say in it then, just as you don't have a say in it now." Grant glares at me, and then shuts the door. His words resonate from the stairwell like an alarm. "I'm too fucking young to be a father *right now*," his voice breaks from the force. "But I became one when I was fifteen when my father shoved Gwen in my bed, even if it didn't come to fruition until I was almost seventeen. So suck it the fuck up, Regina!"

Slumping to the floor, my fists pound as I shout, "FUCK!" at the top of my lungs. Moments later, my neighbors are screaming for me to shut the hell up.

"Goddamn, you're a manipulative bastard, Grant Whittenhower." Unable to face my mother, because no doubt Grant spelled every single thing out to her during their hour, and because she heard more than she should have a few minutes ago, I clutch my screwdriver and get back to work.

Chapter Eleven

Not ready to face the music, I stand outside of my mother's bedroom with my head resting on the door. Graduation was a nightmare from all sides, but worsened by the presence of the Whittenhowers. All of the legacies stared at me as if I was the brunt of some cosmic joke, and they were all in on the punch line but me. They *knew*.

Look! It's the scholarship kid, when there shouldn't even be a scholarship kid! The Whittenhowers are going to destroy her already shitastic life if she doesn't give them the use of her womb, and then pass her baby off to the wolves.

Shame, which I'm sure will never go away, has had me lashing out against Grant every time I've seen his face for the past week. He's been everywhere, making sure I don't forget him. Calling me his ally, asking me how I am, and not once pushing for what I'm not willing to give. So when I saw him at graduation today, I rejected him outright by ignoring him.

The one thing I know Grant will never do to me– reject me– I did to him, and I feel disgusted with myself for feeling bad that I did. Other than trying to help me through this disaster, he allowed me to take the lead. I was the dumbass who got caught up in the moment and was grinding on him.

Grant's hands had stilled. His body had vibrated with the need to move. Patient and needy, as if he could wait forever for permission… and like a fucking stupid girl, I gave him permission to move, to grind back against me.

No, not permission– I ordered him.

Grant will never say yes to me without being asked first, but I instinctively know he'll never, *ever* say no to me either, even if he should.

I almost feel like I took advantage of Grant. How fucking disturbing is *that*?

Mind twisted, even if I don't see Grant, I still can't stop thinking about him. But I couldn't avoid Whitt. After graduating, I immediately crouched down and took the tight hug the little boy offered, with Grant standing at my back, silently begging me to talk or touch him, to stop ignoring him. I'm stubborn, so I didn't accept that there is someone out there who is willing to put me first, because I can't trust it. It feels too much like I'm giving up in defeat.

I have to fight, even if I can't win.

I'm already ashamed of myself; I refuse to add disrespecting myself on top of it.

With that final thought, I push through the door into my mother's room, and share this pivotal moment with her.

"I did it, Mom!" I sit on the edge of her bed while proudly waving the leather case holding my diploma in the air. "I'm officially a Hillbrook graduate. This diploma will give me access to the top universities." I smile at my mother brightly– falsely. "Have to give the elite props for educating me so well."

Mom's pain-free tonight. We've upped her dosage to four pills. I'm not sure she can feel anything at all, when I know she can't feel her legs or feet anymore. Weeks ago, I had to help her to and from the bathroom, but now that isn't even an option. I had to ask a few of the ladies from the building to take care of her when I wasn't around. They never leave now. Several are camped out in the living room. We all know it's time.

"How did the ceremony go?" Emotional pain is reflected in my mother's gaze, all because she missed my graduation ceremony. She isn't well enough to move from room-to-room, let alone leave the apartment. I don't blame her and she knows it, except she blames herself.

Step one in showing Regina Regal how her life will be systematically torn to bits unless she complies: The ceremony was a joke. Obviously I was top of my class, yet the next in line had the honor of recognition and the pleasure of addressing the crowd with his speech.

I play pretend, by believing Hillbrook couldn't have their scholarship student show up their rich children. Those parents paid a huge fee to hear one of their own give some lame speech about how graduation wasn't an ending but a beginning. It was the same speech that was given at countless schools over the years. They wouldn't have tolerated the speech I would have given.

Yet, I know that that wasn't the reason. Jackson and Daniel had me blackballed because I've refused to allow Grant to tell me their demands.

To pour salt into my already infected wound, I was surprised as I walked across the stage to hear several people clapping. Not the whole auditorium as the students before and after me received, but a few from Fate's and Ade's families. I nearly burst out laughing when Whitt squealed *Queen* at the top of his tiny lungs. I received one standing ovation from Roman. He was camped out at the exit, and as soon as I walked across the stage, he vanished.

"It was fabulous, Ma. I gave my speech and everyone loved it." I lie to Mom, and I don't feel bad for a second. She'll never find out the truth, and I'd rather have her believe that I was given the respect that I was due.

"Bullshitter," Mom mutters, calling me out on my lie. "Grant has been visiting me every morning while you're at school."

"Why–" Fists clenching, I smash my lips closed to the nasty things that want to expel.

"Regina, you need to hear Grant out." Mom tries to hold my hand, and even with her dying, I yank away.

Betrayal.

"Mom–" I count to ten before I continue speaking, trying to organize my words into something other than profanity. "Let me get this straight. You want me to go with Grant, get inseminated, and then pass my child off to some vile bitch to raise? The Whittenhowers are making my life a living nightmare, and I refuse to bend to their extortion attempts."

"Attempts?" Mom tries to raise her eyebrow, but she has no hair on her body. Wrinkles form in the paper-thin skin on her forehead. "Regina, I need you to hear me out then."

"Mom." I turn from her, unable to stare at the hope written across her face, especially while betrayal simmers in my veins. "I'm eighteen. I want to fall in love one day and honor my future husband with our children. Not have a father forcing his son to coerce me into something I don't want to do."

"I have few words left," Mom says, and agony clutches at my guts. "So what I say has to count. I can't coddle you by telling you what you need to hear."

"I don't blame you for anything, Mom." With a deep breath, I turn back to face her. "Hit me with it– go on. You know I can take whatever you have to say."

"Regina, I love you." Mom reaches over, and this time my fingers are curling around hers and squeezing. "I'm proud of you. But you're my daughter, so I know exactly how you think."

Mom's struggling to speak, so I lean forward to give her a sip of water.

Once her throat is lubricated, she continues. "You're stubborn. Your life is a series of goals. Once one goal is accomplished, three more take its place. You'll never fall in love and give that imaginary man children, because you'll be too busy reaching out for another goal, and another, and creating another and another and another."

Annoyed, I want to stop Mom, because she's hit the nail on the head. Shit.

"Extortion. Coercion. You're the most stubborn person I've ever met. You need to be around people who stop and listen, who take in everything around themselves and live in the moment– someone who can derail you from your goals long enough to live life."

"Mom, that man is *not* Grant," I bite out. "I don't love him because I don't know him. He's a stranger."

Green eyes clouded with death pierce my soul. "Life is too short. You don't want to be on your deathbed and realize all you've accomplished in life is a series of goals that are meaningless. Goals do not keep you warm at night– they don't hug you, or kiss you, or hold you when you need to cry."

"Kisses won't put food in my belly," I mutter underneath my breath. "Hugs won't put a roof over my head."

"Regina," Mom says my name sharply, so I know she overheard me. "Even the strongest people need to be mothered– they have partners and friends and confidants. You can't live life–"

"Don't!" I protest, not wanting to hear it. "Don't."

Mom ignores me. "Alone. Regina, I can't leave you alone. No matter how capable you are, you'll need a support system. Roman is a wonderful man, and he'll try to help you once I'm gone. But what you'll need from him will drain him dry. I'm not asking you to love Grant. I'm not even asking you to give him a child. I'm asking you to hear him out, because he has what you need, even if you don't realize it."

"Mother," I say sharply. "I can't hear this– not now."

"There is no later for me, daughter. So I don't give a shit if you don't want to hear it." Anger sparks in my mother's thready voice– the first sign I've heard in years. I get my strength from my mother. While she battled cancer, she mourned the loss of my father privately. She's never complained while suffering in silence.

"I've spent hours a day with Grant for the past week, getting to know the man who will have an impact on your future. You're so damn stubborn, we both know you'll watch your life burn to the ground before you give in."

"Damn straight," I whisper quietly enough so she won't hear.

"Remember how much you hated everyone at Hillbrook, and you promised to suffer through it because the payoff was larger than the cost? Now you're facing a similar situation. Stay with the Whittenhowers while you further your education. Deal with it while they make you stronger. When you're educated, when you have your feet beneath you, walk away knowing you can survive anything."

"What about my children?" I gasp, very real pain constricting my heart. "Just leave them like Whitt's mother left him?"

"Grant said her name was Gwen, and that she is very much a part of Whitt. Regina, no matter how horrific the Whittenhowers may be, they are offering you something you'll never achieve without them. Power. The ability to change more than just your future."

"It's not selfish to want to keep my own children."

"No, it's not. But what's selfish is that if you don't agree, they will decimate your life. The past twelve years of your education will mean nothing. You'll attach yourself to Roman, and then you'll never do anything with your life. Use your education, use your roots to make a real difference in this life. It's the only one you're given. I know that more than anyone."

"We're talking about *my* children." My voice breaks with outrage. "Your grandchildren."

"Whether you raise them or not, they will always be a part of you and you a part of them. Your father and I didn't make you stubborn— you were born that way. Your children might be more than what the Whittenhowers bargained for." Mom laughs evilly— the first laugh I've heard from her in months. "Your children will have the money and power to do good in a bad world."

"I'll want them— they're mine," I whine about children that haven't been conceived, let alone born. I ache for something that is imaginary.

"I'm a good judge of character. Grant doesn't seem like the type of person to deny you anything. He might not be strong enough to fight his family, but you sure as hell are. You need him. He needs you. I think it will do you some good to use your dusty empathy."

"I'm not deaf— I hear the words you're not saying," I grumble. "You're calling me stubborn. Selfish. Harsh and cold— a bitch."

"I'm dying," Mom says, but there is humor infusing her voice. "You don't get the luxury of me comforting you with lies. Go have Grant coddle you some more."

"Grant doesn't coddle me," I sputter, completely offended. "Mom, this is the end of your life, do you really want to spend it arguing with me? Especially when the topic is as ridiculous as this one is."

"Regina." Mom uses all of her strength to pull me down to her side. As big as I am, I barely fit on the twin-sized bed. But Mom is a skeleton, so we both fit on the bed together. She tries to hold me like a mother would her daughter.

No more Regina the caregiver. I'm transported back to when I was fifteen, and the world was brighter– happier. But I'd rather be jaded, because Regina the daughter hurts too much.

"I heard you and Grant," Mom murmurs while petting my hair. "If you didn't trust him, you never would have cried with him. You're my daughter, and I know you. Let me be your mother one last time, and do as you're told."

"I can't," is forced between my gritted teeth, as I try to contain a sob. "I can't– not even for you."

"I know." Mom's bony knuckles rasp beneath my eyes, clearing tears away. "No matter how much you fight, you'll end up in the same place. You may as well give in, unless you enjoy the misery of watching all you've worked so hard to achieve be destroyed. That's your only choice."

"There's always another choice." Voice grave, I feel horrible for arguing with my dying mother, but I can't give in.

"There's always another choice for those who can feed themselves." Mom squeezes me tightly, so I know I'm going to hate what comes next. "You can work hard to earn your meal, but Grant told me his family will tear the food out of your hands before it makes it to your mouth, until you'll either starve or take from their hands. There is no harm in yielding until you're strong enough to not only fight back, but to conquer."

"You sound like Dad," I mutter fondly, ignoring everything else Mom said.

"They say you see your dead loved ones when your time is near." Mom's words strike fear in my veins.

"Today's a good day, so I assume you've yet to see Dad and Granddad and Grandma." I try for teasing as I snuggle closer, ignoring the fact that hugging Mom is like cuddling with a pile of twigs.

"Today's the last good day, Regina." My eyes flick up to meet empty pools of cloudy green. "I spent the last two weeks hoarding my energy for this conversation."

Pulling away slightly, "I… I-I-I–" stammers from my numb lips. "I don't understand."

"It's true," Mom whispers as her energy fades. "Your dead loved ones comfort you at the end. I don't know if it's a hallucination, or if it's truly their spirits welcoming me home. But Curtis has been visiting me for weeks, and I saw my mom while you were being handed your diploma."

I mouth, "Mom?" in horror, heart breaking.

Slipping into delirium, "Your father's with us now, standing in the corner. He's watching over you, waiting to tell me when it's okay to let you go."

Ear pressed against Mom's chest, I can hear the fluid in her lungs rasp with every labored breath she takes. I will never forget the sound for the rest of my life, or the way I can see her eyeballs twitch beneath her translucent eyelids. My nightmares will feature Mom's paper-thin skin with its spider web network of blue veins, and how I've worried for months that if I touch her too hard, I'll bruise or wound.

Voice barely audible, "Let me hold you one last time, Regina. Be my daughter for a little while longer."

"You'll always be my mother," I breathe. "I'll never forget you. Ever."

Chapter Twelve

Sliding down the bedroom wall, I prop my elbows on my knees and settle in for the long wait. Lately, I don't really sleep– I can't remember the last time I slept through the night, and it's been years since I had a bed to call my own.

Alive and healthy, I've been living on my mother's borrowed time. Just as I have for the past few weeks, I sit vigil in Mom's room, watching her sleep– eyes targeted in on the movement of her chest rising and falling.

Apparently Dad doesn't think I'm ready, because it's been a few hours and Mom hasn't let me go yet.

When our neighbor, Maggie, checked in on us two hours ago, she clasped a hand to her chest, already thinking Mom was gone. After some convincing, Maggie believed Mom was still with us.

I wasn't surprised when Hospice arrived after Maggie disappeared. They didn't tell me anything I didn't already know– Mom's candle could be snuffed out from one heartbeat to the next. I simultaneously dread and pray for it to come to pass. Mom's suffering needs to end, and nothing hurts more than watching it.

Powerless.

Hopeless.

Alone.

Light filters in every time the neighbors open and close the door to check on us. I get slightly annoyed by the interruption in my meditation. I'm resting in a calm that isn't sleep nor wake.

I should be worried that our front door is wide open, but what's the worst that can happen? There is nothing to steal. They can't kill us, and if they did, it would be faster than the pace we're going right now. It would be a godsend. They could harm me, but really, it would pale in comparison to the hell I'm experiencing right now.

"Are you asleep?" Roman whispers from the cracked bedroom door, worrying he'll wake my mother. But can you truly wake the near-dead?

"No, I haven't slept in a very, very long time," I whisper back. "The time was too precious to waste."

I gaze up at Roman as he quietly shuts the door. I get a quick glimpse of the side of his face before the closing door cuts off any available light from the living room, leaving us in near darkness. I grimace at the grim expression marring his face.

The streetlight casts across the room, lighting Roman's blue-green eyes as he walks toward me, and I hold his gaze like it's my lifeline.

I could do this alone, but it's better having someone with me who wants nothing, expects nothing.

Roman slides down the wall to sit next to me. Without thought, I find his hand and hold it tightly. I relish the warmth of human connection– the strength, health, and vitality as Roman's fingers clasp mine, giving a squeeze. A harsh sob is torn from my chest all because the hand in mine isn't a living skeleton.

I don't want to go through this alone, yet my so-called best friends aren't the ones to go through this with me. I know Fate would sit here with me until the end. Adelaide probably would if I asked. Grant would be here, no questions asked. But I don't want to ruin their day. I want them to have what I never will– knowledge only in the aftermath.

Roman– he's been here with me from the very start. We moved here after Dad's death, and Roman has only known Ella Regal on the Grim Reaper's time.

"The government should use this torture as a form of interrogation. I would spill anything, confess to things I've never done, just to end this misery. I will never condemn the Dr. Deaths of the world. How a doctor could see this day in and day out and not want to end the suffering is unfathomable to me."

Roman doesn't reply, because he understands how I'm just talking and there's nothing he could ever say to change anything that I'm going through. It's a comfort that he doesn't feed me pretty lies.

I curl up to Roman's side, and sit wrapped in his warm arms while silently praying that the end is near.

"I have an ethics problem, Roman– a crisis of conscience. The Whittenhowers want something from me that I'm not willing to give, and they have threatened to destroy me if I don't give in. If I don't do it, I don't know where my life will end up. I have worked so hard to get where I am after losing so much, and they could make it vanish in the blink of an eye. I don't know what to do."

"What is it?" I can hear the intense emotion in Roman's voice, and it reminds me of what I heard from my mom's mouth.

My parents, and Roman especially, they've never known anything but hardship. They would be willing to sign their lives away for just a chance to live in a different class. They've never seen the elite from the inside. They have a fantasy built in their minds. I've walked both paths, and neither is worth your soul.

"They want me to be a surrogate. I'm not sure why me, other than they want my intelligence and stubbornness flowing in their heir's veins."

"I could see it, sweetheart," Roman whispers. For the first time, I understand what Mom was trying to tell me. Everyone handles me with kid gloves, worried they'll offend me and I'll go ballistic. The only one who has ever challenged me is Adelaide, and most of the time I hate her for it... then there's Grant.

"You're so fucking smart and strong– sometimes you scare the living piss outta me. I feel like I ought to be bowing down to you in awe. Your brain terrifies me."

"I'm just a girl, Roman– nothing more," I mutter, feeling bizarre at the reverence lacing his voice. "I don't know if my mind works differently than yours does, because it's my normal."

"Trust me." Roman snorts. "You do *not* think the same way I do. I've met that Grant fella a few times this week, and he doesn't think like you or me. So I could see why his family is sniffing after you. But your hair is a total disaster." Ruffling my hair with the tip of his nose, Roman laughs, and the light sound is music to my ears. "I hope to God your kids inherit their father's hair."

"Thank you for that, for allowing me to hear you laugh." I snuggle closer to his side. "It's been too long."

"Regina, you're the most beautiful creature I've ever seen." Roman holds me tighter, and then kisses the top of my head. "The Whittenhowers would be lucky to have your blood running through their family."

"I don't think I can do it, Roman." I pull back far enough to look deep into his eyes, thankful for the stream of light coming in from the window. "It's my child we're talking about here. *Mine.* A piece of me."

"I can't–" Roman's voice cracks. "I can't imagine. I'm so sorry, sweetheart."

Shaking my head in agreement, "I've never backed down before, so I think I'll wait and see what they throw at me. I wouldn't be able to respect myself if I don't at least try, and they'd never respect me if I just gave in."

Deft fingertips brush my hair from my forehead. "All I know, I don't want you to stay here. I'd love to keep you for myself, but that's selfish. I've spent the last few years avoiding the attraction I feel toward you, because I've seen how stupid women can be when it comes to a man. I'm not saying that a few endearments and some money would blind you, but I know how I feel for you, and it can be intoxicating."

"You think very highly of me." I laugh without humor, remembering how Grant held me while I cried, and I turned into a stupid girl and stole sexual gratification instead.

I've seen it too. When I was younger, the girls in my neighborhood said they wanted to get out of here, how they wanted more out of life. Then between the ages of fourteen and sixteen, they lost their minds to raging hormones and false I love yous. All of them have a kid or two, and they aren't with the guys they originally fell for. They're just perpetuating the cycle, and their children will as well.

The Regal's cycle ends with me.

I could see how easy it would be to love Roman. I try not to look at him and see who he truly is, but it's a struggle. I don't mean lusting over his exotic good looks, or judging him because he's a dealer. I can see the inherent goodness in him. It's intoxicating because he makes me feel innocent and carefree, and I can't afford either.

With Grant, I'm jaded.

Just as my mother feared, if I allowed myself, I would continue the cycle with Roman. But I'll never allow it, and neither will he.

Even as we sit here, we both know the odds of Roman leaving this neighborhood are slim to none, and neither one of us will let him hold me back.

Instead of expressing any of the chaotic thoughts raging through my mind, I kiss Roman's cheek so close to his lips that I can feel the heat radiate from his mouth. I try my hardest not to move that last centimeter and kiss him. He freezes beneath my touch, trying not to give into the temptation.

I move slowly, intending to steal my first kiss, but a hollow gasp has my blood running cold.

I bolt upright and run to my mother's side, arms braced against the bed on either side of her failing body. Raspy and shallow, I suffer through the sound of Mom's labored wheezing as she tries to breathe through the fluid drowning her.

Numbed to my soul, I grab my mother's hand just as Roman grabs my other. Connected, we both stare down at my dying mother as she struggles to use the last of her words.

Without thought, I'm speaking what she truly needs to hear, what Dad was waiting for me to say before he told her to let me go. "Mom, I'll be okay– I promise." I know those words are more important to her than anything else I could possibly ever say.

"I'm so proud of you," Mom tries to wheeze out– the words are broken, but I fill in the gaps, instinctively knowing what she's trying to say.

I've always tried to make my parents proud, and I always will.

Mom's translucent eyelids flutter several times, until her eyes roll up into her head, leaving behind whites turned red from burst blood vessels. A loud expulsion of air is released from her chest, and then her fingers go lax in my hand.

Stunned– numb. Pulling away, I allow my mother's fingers to slip from between mine, and then I gently fold her arms over her chest above her heart.

Empty.

Alone.

Staring down at Ella Regal, in body only, my mother is no longer with me. I'm no longer caregiver nor daughter, and I don't know what to do now. Gasping, on the edge of panic, I can't feel Mom with me. There's an empty void inside of me where she used to be.

Mom has moved on from the agony and misery. It happened in the blink of an eye. One moment she was with me, and gone the next. I never told her I loved her– I never said goodbye. It went without saying. Our last words were filled with all the things left unsaid.

I want to cry, yet no tears come.

I feel sickened that a smile breaks across my face. The expression isn't from pleasure or happiness. It's because Mom is finally free– free of the pain. Free to move on and join my father in the afterlife.

In my grief, I'm unable to do anything but believe in an eternal existence. The alternative of fading into dust and floating on the wind is too devastating to contemplate. This can't be it. Please, don't let this be it. Our trials and tribulations must lead us to where we deserve.

I will believe– I *do* believe.

My mother's last gift to me was allowing me to move on too.

"No mother has been loved by their daughter as much as Ella Regal was."

Roman's voice is rough with grief. Unshed tears glisten in his sympathetic eyes– tears that refuse to leak from mine. His words release me by saying exactly what I was thinking, exactly what I needed to hear.

Chapter Thirteen

In the movies, this is where they jump forward to the wake, the funeral, to the friends and family who refuse to leave shoving an endless supply of casseroles and cakes into your hands. But this is reality.

The earth revolves around the sun at supersonic speed as I stand in the center of my living room. Vision a hazy gray, showing all movement in muted lines. Hearing muffled, until all I hear is nonsense rumbling and the thud of my own heartbeat.

Wading through life on slow-speed while everyone else is moving on fast-forward, I watch with morbid fascination as the coroner wheels out a gurney laden with a black body bag– inside is my mother's *body*.

Inside that impenetrable bag is my mother.

My. Mother.

Trapped inside a bag, unable to breathe or see– terrified and alone.

No, my mother's gone. All that's left is a lifeless vessel being wheeled out into the hallway and down three flights of steps, and transported to be stored in the city's morgue.

It's times like these that I wish I was ignorant about what comes next. But this is my second time around, and I'm now an expert on every step that occurs once the coroner takes *the body* of your parent away.

At least this time, I don't have to identify the mangled and broken body of my larger-than-life, formidable father.

Lost. Alone. I stand, watching but not absorbing. My neighbors run in and out of my apartment, most crying– all wearing similar expressions of horror etched across their faces.

Hands push tissues into my curled palms– tissues meant to dry tears that refuse to fall.

Hugs are given. Words are spoken. But I feel nor hear either.

What's next, I ask myself.

Arrangements must be made– arrangements that cost money I don't have.

…And with that, I unfreeze and move into action.

With a pop, I can hear again. "Regina!" Adelaide is screaming into my face. "Regina!"

Voice groggy, slurred, "What? I'm thinking."

"Reg?" Fate's tiny hands wrap around my biceps, and then feeling returns in a rush so potent my skin burns with flame. "Goddamnit, breathe!"

"I am," I mutter, annoyed that they're interrupting my thinking. "I've got shit to do, but I've got to figure out what comes first. Does the coroner need to speak to me, or do I call the funeral home where they'll embalm *the body*?"

"Ouch!" I shriek when fingers brutally twist into my hair and yank my face to the side.

Red-rimmed, crystalline blue eyes come into sharp focus. "Stop being a taskmaster for two minutes and allow yourself time to grieve." Grant's soothing voice is at odds with him angrily fisting my hair. After a strong shake, Grant's way of making sure I'm no longer zoning out, he releases my hair, then pats the wiry mess back into place.

"How did you–" I spot Roman leaning against the wall with a washcloth clutched in his hand. Beside him, Julio lounges with his arms folded over his impressive chest. "Oh," I huff. "They called you… wait a minute, they don't know you!"

"I know Grant," Julio mutters with a shrug, then he turns to Roman. "Washcloth– you're leaking again."

"Julian," Grant issues as a warning in an authoritative tone I'd never imagine possible from his voice.

Ignoring Grant, Julio smiles at me. "We go waaaayyy back, me and Grant do. Businessmen are bigger criminals than my boss."

"Julian, a little respect. Please," Grant murmurs, sounding more like the man I've come to know. "Stanton is my age, whereas Jackson is not. Remember that."

Julio's warm, brown eyes roll so far back into his head I fear he'll never see again. "I'm *sooo* scared of the crazy Whittenhower." He allows his voice to warble mockingly, and I'm unsure if he's calling Jackson or Grant the crazy one. "As Stan's shadow, I went to Hillbrook with your *friend*– that's how I know Grant."

"Small world." Eyes flicking around, hysterical laughter flows from my throat. A Mexican mob enforcer, a Native American drug dealer, and three blond-haired, blue-eyed prince and princesses are standing in my mutt-ass, white trash living room.

Has Hell frozen over?

"What's wrong with Regina?" Fate's voice warbles with fear, which makes me laugh harder for some reason. Bent over at the waist, I press my palm against the stitch in my side.

"She's in shock," comes muffled from behind Roman's washcloth as he blows his nose. "Lord knows the last time she's eaten or slept."

Strong hands curl around my waist, pulling me upright. Ade tries to manhandle me to the couch, but I won't budge. "Knowing Regina–" Ade speaks like I'm not even in the room. "She hasn't eaten since lunch at school– days ago."

Voice coaxing, hands soft as they cup my cheeks, Grant tries to comfort me. "Regina, come home with us and let us take care of you– it's what Ella wanted."

Breaking free, I snarl like a rabid animal, "Leave me alone." I stomp away, as far as my tiny living room will allow. "I've got shit to do."

"Regina, no!" Grant paces me as I try to get away from his influence. "You need to stop long enough to grieve." His arm hooking around my waist fractures my false calm.

"Goddamn it!" I shriek so loud my eardrums warble. I fall to my knees and scream like I've never screamed before. Empty and hollow, I release a death knell. "This is the only life I've known for two years. A heartbeat later, it's over. Now what? WHAT THE FUCK DO I DO NOW?!"

Arms try and fail to contain me as I scramble and fight against Grant. Stronger, I easily overpower him to get away. "I don't want to *feel*! I have to do something– I need to work." I try to crawl to my feet so I can run, but I'm not the biggest person in the room.

With a sharp bark of, "Goddamnit, Reggie!" Julio's hauling my ass off the floor by a hand wrapped around the back of my neck. The instant my feet connect with the floor, his fingertips curl around my hips. With a plunk, I'm shoved onto the couch, releasing a plume of dust motes into the air.

"Stay!" Julio issues like I'm a dog, then he turns to face everyone else. "What do *we* do with her now?"

Grant crouches down to my level, tragic-struck face coming into view. "Come home with us, Regina. Please. We've even arranged a room for Fate so she's close by."

"Stop coddling her!" Ade barks, and then a notepad and pen are thrust into my hands. "Reg hates that shit."

Laughter bubbles up from my throat– this time it's the real deal. "Mom… only a few hours ago, Mom told me that if I wanted to be coddled, I should go find Grant." Eyes held wide in disbelief– "Wow… that's in past tense. I can't believe she's gone. Forever. Not just in theory."

Adelaide smiles down at me with tears streaming down her face. "If you want the brutal truth, you'll find your best friend." Eyes flicking to Fate, "*Me*, in case there was any confusion."

"I just want to make Regina feel better." Fate swallows a sob.

"No," Ade says firmly. "You can't be Regina's shoulder to cry on because she's too busy coddling *you*." She reaches down to pluck the pen out of my hand, then she taps the notebook. "Get to work, girlfriend. You've got a list to write. Delegate– it's what you were born to do."

"Thank you," I whisper, feeling more confident now that I have a purpose.

Lost in thought, I scribble line after line, creating a detailed list. Feeling someone gazing over my shoulder, I look up to find Julio memorizing my list. "What?"

"Ella spoke to Stanton about her burial expenses– the neighbors took up a collection to make sure your mother could be buried next to your father, with Stanton pitching in the rest."

Throat tight, eyes stinging from tears that won't manifest, I nearly suffocate on the bubble of emotions erupting with no outlet to release them.

Julio's heavy palm rests on my shoulder, then gives a quick squeeze. "We'll take care of two through six on your list." Stepping away, he hitches his finger in Roman's direction. "Say goodnight, Romeo. We've got work to do, and Stan already warned you about stepping in another man's territory."

"I got the memo." After drying his eyes, Roman stumbles to my side. "I won't be far, sweetheart." With a fleeting kiss to my forehead, he follows Julio to parts unknown.

"Food," Grant and Fate mutter in unison. Each trying to rush to the kitchen to do their part, only to discover bare cupboards. "Grocery store?" Grant says immediately, while Fate mutters, "Take-out?"

"They'd be lost without me. None of us but you has ever set foot into a grocery store in the first place." Adelaide sits next to me, then takes charge. "Grant? Go fetch Regina an Italian sub from the deli on Seneca Street." In reply, her brother makes a mad dash for the hallway. "Fate?" Voice quieting, becoming softer, "Please dispose of the bedding, and then lean the mattress against the wall– the underside facing out."

Voice quivering, I mutter, "Thank you," and then get back to work, refusing to acknowledge the mess death leaves behind.

"You have two options: come home, or fight to the end," Ade begins, but I stop her.

"You already know what I'll do, so don't bother." Slumping from exhaustion, I barely have the energy to fight with her.

"Oh, I know. Grant knows. My father and Uncle Jackson expect no less. Watching you suffer will kill a part of me, Regina." Never one to be affectionate, Ade actually rubs my back. "The outcome will be the same, but Grant and I will be left to watch you suffer, while my father gets off on watching you try to win a losing battle."

"Daniel and Jackson wouldn't respect me otherwise."

"Who cares?"

"I do, because I wouldn't respect myself otherwise."

Voice grave and tight with frustration, "You've been warned. Don't make me say I told you so."

The night of my graduation from Hillbrook– the night of my mother's death – I won my first battle of too few when I refused to go home with Grant and Ade and stayed in my own apartment.

Alone.

Chapter Fourteen

A wish granted is one you realize you'd never made. I honestly believed I'd feel better once my mom died. The selfless part of me understands how this is better for her, but the selfish part that I call daughter is lost.

The concept of alone is nothing like you'd imagine. Alone is not a state of being. Alone is when I'm at work, and one of my coworkers tells a funny story I can't wait to share with my mom, only to realize I can't.

I can't.

Mom's not here to hear me, to share the laugh with me. Mom's not here to hold me, to listen to my problems, or to call me on my shit.

Mom's not here anymore to be my mother– without Ella Regal, I'm no longer a daughter.

Identity in tatters, with no direction to take, I'm completely lost.

I've fought many battles this week. Alone. I won them all, proving I'm a strong bitch when necessary.

Grant's been inches from me at all times– silently begging to help. I ignore him at every turn. Furious that he's my problem, but then I feel horrible for treating him inhumanly.

It's not hard to hate Grant Whittenhower when faced with Jackson and Daniel. Both, separately and together, have haunted me this week, beginning with my mother's funeral. They were passive during the small service, where my mother was laid to rest next to my father– only a metal plate with their names and dates signifying who was interred in the ground. But afterward, I was cornered.

Technically, I didn't win that battle, as it took Stanton Green to call them off me. I'd only seen quick glimpses of the mafia boss in passing, but he showed up to my mother's funeral, and showed true emotion at her loss.

Stanton pulled Jackson away for a powwow while Daniel continued to berate me in front of my neighbors, my friends from school, and the Whittenhowers in attendance. After a minute,

Jackson called Daniel off because of whatever Stanton had threatened.

This past week, Grant showed up to my jobs, then when I came home, I found one of his relatives on my doorstep, warning I couldn't do this alone. Daniel had the nerve to say everything I have he'd given to me– my education is all I have, and it was bought and paid for by a faceless entity whose hand signed the checks at the Whittenhower's behest.

Whittenhowers giveth, and they can taketh away.

My education, my entrance into Dominion's elite was not without cost. I may possess the intelligence, but they gave me an education to flex and hone it. Jackson said I am to Grant as Julio is to Stanton– services bought and paid for, no matter what the service entails. In this case, my womb.

These quiet hours drive me insane. The hours when most people sleep or relax. The quiet hammers home how alone I truly am. I have no one– NO ONE –to rely on. Not my best friends, because they are one of *them*. Not Roman, because Stanton issued the edict to leave me alone, no doubt handed down from the Whittenhowers. Plus, I can't drag Roman into my problems. Then there is Grant…

This entire situation has set it up to where I'd have to seek Grant out for comfort, for safety. That is *not* going to happen, no matter how much their manipulation has made me want just that.

Truthfully, Grant's a victim just as I am, which makes me feel like shit.

It's been over a week since Mom passed. I went to work the very next day, trying to move forward the best I could. My world has surrounded Mom's life since her diagnosis and Dad's death. Now my days and nights feel empty without all the extra work and companionship she brought into my life.

Every resting moment is filled with *what now?*

I come home, expecting Mom to call to me from the bedroom. I miss sitting on the edge of the bed, discussing the events of my day. I will always miss sharing my hopes, dreams, and fears. I don't think I will ever find someone to share those with. I don't think I could ever truly trust someone to accept me as she did. She was my mother, and no one can ever take her place.

I'm walking this earth alone. I have no family. From now on, I have to be my own *everything*.

It's a fight to believe that, no matter how much I think it or voice it aloud. Deep down, I know Mom wanted me to have a support system, and I don't trust anyone anymore because they will ultimately leave me– die on me.

I rest my head on the back of my couch, waiting for the clock to signal it's time to go to work. All I feel is numb, using work to deaden any emotions that try to erupt. As soon as sadness tries to sneak into my consciousness, I get up and do something productive. When there is nothing productive to do, I pretend that the comfort Grant has offered me isn't the very thing that helps me through the pain.

I haven't said one word to Grant since my mother passed away, but he haunts me by leaving notes beneath my door. It's hard to ignore when I secretly look forward to his written words.

Pages worn soft from repeated reading over the course of every night this week, like an addict, I try to ration them.

Eyes flicking up to gaze at the clock, I groan in a mix of pain and indecision. Why now has my life decided to crawl at a snail's pace?

With shaking fingertips, I unfold the notes I'd be better off burning on the stovetop.

Regina,
You never stray far from my thoughts.

Quickly, I refold that note, shoving it into my pocket, hating the emotions that single sentence elicits.

Regina,
I know you blame me– Lord knows, I do. Would you believe me if I said your life could always be worse? No? Probably not, huh? I know it sounds ridiculous, but believe it or not, your upbringing was safer than mine. So believe me when I say that it can most definitely get worse. Bury your pride, get your behind to Misery Castle, and then wait to enact revenge.
That's what I do.
–J

Grant always signs his notes *J*, and I have no idea why. But I've concluded that Grant is most definitely the *crazy* Whittenhower Julio was joking about.

Regina,

In my quest to get to know you, I could ask your favorite foods, what you like to watch on TV or read about. But after you've seen someone cry over the death of their mother– after you've watched them rally against their enemies... after you've shared extortion and coercion with another human being, the benign question of what is your favorite color becomes a moot point, doesn't it?

It doesn't truly matter anyway, as I have your best friend as a tapped source of information. By the way, my sister will not be swayed, even if she thinks I set the moon and rise the sun. Fate, however, with a few well-placed, pretty words, she spills like a sieve.

Purple is such a royal color. No wonder it's your favorite.

Blue is a very complementary color to purple, even if my best mate said red is more suited. But we'll ignore the fact that his favorite color is red. Who wants their home to look like a tacky Valentine's card? Overhearing our conversation, my other mate decided to torture us both by saying he's going to renovate his home in those very colors– in velvet! Can you imagine sitting in your study when it looks like a low-class whorehouse?

Sometimes Grant jumps the tracks on the crazy train and enters insanity territory. If I didn't find him harmless, I'd be utterly terrified. Most of the time, I find him humorous, and I pray that's why he writes me these insane letters.

Regina,

Your silence hurts me. I'm a very quiet person myself, so I understand the need to be private. But your silence is screaming animosity. I get it– I do. But it doesn't hurt any less. Do you like my notes? Do you want me to stop? You never say stop, so I continue. Jackson said you called me a stalker. You're probably right about that.

I don't like many people. Just my family members (even Daniel), my two friends I've had since birth... Gwen won't talk to me. I seem to have that effect on those who give me children.

Jackson said you threatened to have me arrested for stalking. That's not wise, Regina. Jackson was very upset about that, and I feared for his heart. Besides, it's not as if you're in a position like Gwen, where she has her enforcer shoo me away. Oh, that sounded bad, didn't it? Gwen is not a member of organized crime. We'll say he's her bodyguard, but not because of me.

I'm not actually a stalker… I just get depressed because no one wants to hear me.

"Jesus Christ, Grant." I tuck that note away, never able to finish it in its entirety because it shows just how lonely Grant truly is, and it resonates with me in a way I refuse to acknowledge.

I have this bizarre tradition, where I have to read all of the notes in order before I can read the newest one. I worked the morning shift at Digital Nation, where I had a two hour break before heading to the coffee shop. When I got home, a new note was waiting for me since Grant didn't show up to the electronics' store– Daniel had though.

Another battle fought and won in an unwinnable war.

Paper trailing between my fingertips, I actually debate not reading Grant's words because each note gets more desperate than the last, and it terrifies me. But then I hear Grant saying no one listens to him, and I can't not read it.

With a deep breath, my eyes peer down to take in what Grant has to say today.

Regina– my ally,

Letter-writing is a dying art. As you've discovered, I have a problem voicing my thoughts into words. Add another discovery on the ever-growing pile, I'm able to voice everything on paper.

I trust you value your future and will do as you're told, ensuring you will embark on the final leg of your educational journey. This is a warning, not a threat leveled against you from me, since emotion can be misconstrued in writing. Panic and fear are causing my handwriting to tilt as my fingers shake.

Since I've learned about you via your best friends, your actions, and by stalking you, I decided perhaps I should show you who I am. I hope you actually care to learn more about me– most don't.

Who is Grant James Whittenhower?

He's just a man with wishes, dreams, and wants that go long ignored. When I sit and think, when I write, that name doesn't even register with who I truly am, to the point when someone calls me Grant, I don't answer.

I was born to fulfill a role, whether that role fit who I was or not. For the first twelve years of my life, I thought my father (Daniel) hated my guts. Requiring his validation, I'd work so hard to please him, but he'd always look at me like I wasn't good enough. I didn't understand why Uncle Jackson was always coming to my rescue, making me feel loved and understood– accepted.

Regina, has your destiny ever shifted? It's the sensation of the floor dropping out from beneath your feet, where you hover suspended in the air for a heartbeat, and then you drop. The freefall is as exhilarating as it is terrifying. When you land, you're no longer who you thought you once were.

The first shift was when I was five years old. If you need a visual, imagine your Whitt, but make him ultra-sensitive, quick to cry, and acting like a five-year-old should. My grandfather was murdered before my eyes during an act of patricide, and my childhood ended. That was the night I learned what my Whittenhower legacy truly meant.

The second shift was when I was twelve years old. I had come of age, and I had duties to uphold. Small, fragile, Daniel was disgusted every time he looked at me, saying ten-year-old Katie and five-year-old Ade were stronger than I was. What he meant, my sisters– his daughters – deserved the legacy I was born into but incapable of handling.

After Uncle Jackson healed from his first heart transplant, he took me to my first founders meeting, where he told me how and why he was my father, and then forced me to choose a girl with Dominion's founders' blood flowing through her veins to carry my heir. If you could possibly empathize how jarring this was for me, you could understand me better.

The third shift was at fifteen, after Jackson's second heart transplant when the first was rejected. At this point, with the fear of my father's death looming over my head, I'd do anything for Jackson. If I hadn't complied, Daniel would have probably murdered me as a consequence. Daniel and I don't get along, but we understand each other perfectly as we love Jackson with the same level of devotion.

Even when I was fifteen, it was common knowledge that I wasn't the right person to lead generations of Whittenhowers. Jackson and Daniel were rushing to make a worthy heir. My chosen was delivered to Misery Castle, where I was ordered to perform.

This would be another time for you to pause and imagine this scenario from my point of view, and how writing this is beyond difficult for me.

I fell in love for the first and only time, only to have my lover torn from my bed after she became pregnant. I've spent every year thereafter trying to get her to acknowledge my existence. Hence the 'shooed away' comment in my last letter. Gwen wants nothing to do with me, even though my intentions are honorable and innocent.

The fourth shift was at sixteen, nearing on seventeen, when my son was delivered to Misery Castle after his birth, where I was told he was to be my brother. Appearances are everything– Mr. & Mrs. Daniel Whittenhower I are the legal parents of Daniel Whittenhower II.

The fifth shift was less than a year ago when I was told to marry Cora Spencer, with the weight of two legacies on my unworthy shoulders, with both patriarchs dying.

The final shift, and the last straw, was the triple-whammy from nearly a month ago. Money can buy everything but love and life– Jackson's heart is failing yet again, and he's ready to leave us behind. He wants my mother and Daniel to find peace without the constant level of fear over his death clouding every breath we take.

In this, I know you of all people understand how I feel. Jackson is larger than life, and I can't imagine living my life without him. I can't. I don't want to, even though he says I must. How do you do it, Regina? How do you survive the loss?

Then Whitt innocently had us questioning his sexuality. Just as Jackson loves me, I love my son unconditionally. Just as Jackson knows this life is not for me, I know it's not for my son. So the rush to create another heir commenced, only to discover Cora was barren.

You had the misfortune of being the girl my mother watched over for her mentor- Rebekah. Your academic record and your will to survive piqued Daniel's interests, Whitt's interest in you piqued mine, and my interest in you piqued Jackson's

Blame me– Lord knows, I do.

I know what lies in your and my immediate future. As for the long-term, my son has an uncanny ability at eavesdropping. The brothers are at war over the Whittenhower Legacy. Yes, they fight often but always present a united front. After his death, Jackson trusts my abilities to lead while waiting to pass off the torch to our son– the one he knows will be made because I'll do anything he asks of me. Angry at being the spare and thinking he knows better than I do, Daniel wishes to push me from the nest, steal my rights to my own sons, and lead as he waits for our son to reach the age of majority.

I'm in a house divided, one in which you'll be delivered just as Gwen was, only you won't be removed because of your value and worth to the Whittenhower name.

Who is Grant James Whittenhower?

His own family deems him unworthy to carry the Whittenhower name, as they do his only heir.

But do you know who they do find worthy?

You.

I may not understand myself, but I understand you, Regina.

Your life echoes mine– I hear you.

But the difference between you and Grant Whittenhower is that you're strong enough to be Queen to Misery Castle's King.

The silenced one– J.

Page fluttering to the floor, I'm struck with a realization. "Jesus– fuck," rolls off my numb tongue. "This is real." Unable to allow the note to get sullied, I quickly retrieve it, fold it, and then tuck it into my pocket. "This is real."

In a way, I've been living in a fantasy world for far too long. I was so worried about my mother's life ending, I'd forgotten I had to live my own afterward. In my game of avoidance, I'd missed the trees while only seeing the forest.

Eventually I will lose– then what?

I'm at a turning point in my life, and I have to wait. Treading water and getting nowhere is frustrating. My only escape– I don't start college for seven more weeks. I've survived one week without my mother as the Whittenhowers hit me from every direction. I don't know if I can survive seven more with my sanity intact.

If only I could room in my dorm before school started, then I'd be okay. But I can't. I have to endure the torture of residing in the very place I watched my mother die while deflecting direct attacks.

With a quick glance up at the clock, it signals that I can finally make my escape to the coffee shop. Escaping to work is not how most people would see it. I make sure my thrift shop black pants are wrinkle-free, walk across the living room, and then open the door.

Grant is on the other side with his hand raised at the ready to knock. Momentarily thrown off guard, I shut the door in his face after catching sight of his sad, blue eyes.

With a not-so silent curse, I'll be late to work if I don't leave right now.

I'm not a coward, and I will not be treed by a Whittenhower. With a deep breath, I put my hand back on the doorknob.

"Regina, let me in." Grant tries and fails to sound commanding– he doesn't have it in him, which is exactly why we're in the position we're in. "You have to hear me out."

Wrenching the door open, "What do you want, Grant?" I mutter as I rush by him. "Oh, I know– my child. I don't fucking think so." I lock the deadbolts from the outside, and then run down the steps, trying to get away before he can catch up to me.

Avoidance is my middle name.

Tenacious and Patient are Grant's– he gets two because the rich seem to have too many names at their disposal.

Grant's in good shape, but he hasn't run up and down these stairs for more than two years. I almost get away from him, but he catches up with me down the block.

"Stalker, much?" I flip around to glare at Grant, hating how the lost look on his face makes me feel guilty. Then I feel ashamed of myself for not having enough self-esteem to ignore Grant's many needy facial expressions.

Damn that handsome fuckface.

Mouth twisting up with seldom-seen impatience, "I'm not stalking you, Regina. I'm trying to warn you, but you won't listen." He reaches for my hand, but I deflect his touch. "This ends. Today."

"Leave me alone, Grant. I fucking mean it. I have nothing to lose of any importance. Don't tempt me."

"You have a lot more to lose then you realize. I'm trying to help you," Grant hisses out in frustration, with sincerity and fear for me warring in his voice. "Just come home and get this over with. You're only stringing out the inevitable, and I don't want you to have to go through this– it's making me sick watching it."

"I'll take my chances." Running down the sidewalk, I rush into the coffee shop, flinging the door so Grant has to either catch it, or get hit in the face with it.

"Is Mr. Whittenhower bothering you again?" My boss asks in concern. He's used to Grant, but not the expression of fear on my face– fear over Grant's "*This ends. Today.*"

"Yeah, he is," I gasp breathlessly, holding onto my side. I want Grant gone from my sight, because looking at him will make me face the reality I can't overcome.

I know in my heart I will eventually relent, but not until I've fought as hard as I can, and then harder still.

Curtis and Ella Regal did not raise a weakling of a daughter.

Rob– my boss turns on a man who could quite possibly ruin his business. "Sir, you need to leave now. You're not welcome in here again."

 I haven't worked here long, but Rob's fond of me already. A good, reliable employee is an asset. We've all seen Grant every day for weeks, and we're all sick of his handsome, sincere face.

Grant, proving the Whittenhowers didn't raise him to be a weakling either, even if it's in his nature– "Regina, when the car comes, you best get in the fucking thing." His voice is firm, and I wince. "Make no mistakes, that's a threat and a warning. I can't save you if you don't allow it."

I've never heard Grant speak with such authority. I ignore him and go behind the counter to tie my apron on. Pretending I couldn't care less, I watch as Rob pushes Grant out the door. I see their lips moving rapidly as they argue on the sidewalk. I feel bad– no one should have to deal with a Whittenhower because of me. I should deal with my own problems without having someone do it for me, especially my boss. It's cowardly. I push forward to intervene just as Grant points at me through the shop window. He looks crazed as he mouths "*BE READY.*" Then he abruptly turns and walks away.

Chapter Fifteen

This didn't end today, as that was six days ago...

No Daniel or Jackson sightings. No Grant always being in my face. No notes pushed under my door– which was disappointing, especially when I needed the distraction from grieving.

Six days of total silence. Just long enough to make me think I'd won every battle and the war.

I'm a stupid girl.

An eighteen-year-old, stubborn girl is no match for rich businessmen who make a living out of destroying lives and finding sport in it.

Retreating is not cowardly if you do so to rally the troops, so to speak. It doesn't matter if you win every battle; you only have to win the final one.

I just rode the wave of a six-day silence before the epic shit-storm.

Today is one of the worst days of my life, and considering how my recent past has been, that is strongly saying something.

I'm late for work because of the tantrum I threw when I received a letter from the Zeitlers who donated my scholarship. *We regretfully inform you that we're no longer offering the scholarship you were awarded. Please accept our deepest apologies.*

It said something along those lines. As soon as I saw that my scholarship was revoked, I didn't give a shit what else it said. I tore the paper into a thousand pieces, and then ransacked anything within arm's reach in my apartment.

I no longer have any dishes to eat off of, not that I have any food to place on said dishes.

I immediately called Ade and told her that I never wanted to see her again. Needless to say, she wasn't surprised by my outburst. Recognizing the Zeitler name, I told her I hoped she married that gay Ezra kid and they lived miserably ever after, and that Cortez Hunter murdered her in her sleep for stealing his man. Then I added how one day, Ade would come home to find Whitt in bed with her husband, but it would be okay because it's hidden behind closed doors.

There was nothing that would have stopped the verbal vomit. Too bad Ade was laughing as she said, "I'll see ya at home," and then she hung up on me.

Losing my parents was horrible, but there isn't a guarantee in life that you'll have those you love walk this earth with you. I know I have to rely on myself, but I have no idea how I'm supposed to get to school with no money. I can't get financial aid since I owe a fortune in medical bills. I don't fucking know– maybe a roommate and try to pay for community college? That idea is ludicrous since I'm one of the top ten in the country with a place secured at our local university that caters to my love of the digital age. I know better than to try to get another scholarship, even though I could get one quick as shit with my shiny Hillbrook diploma. Those fucking Whittenhowers would just take it away again.

Mom warned how there are only options for those who can feed themselves. Even if I earned the meal, they'd take it right out of my hand before it reached my mouth. Mom's telling me *I told you so* from the grave.

Entering the coffee shop, I try to appear upbeat so I can keep my job. "Hey, Rob. Sorry I'm late." I walk behind the counter to get ready for work as my boss gives me a peculiar look I can't decipher in reply.

Leaning over the counter, "Paycheck," Rob slaps the envelope into my hand.

My stomach stirs in anticipation over the prospect of money I *need*– there are no wants in my life, only needs. Wants are frivolous things that I have no concept of ever receiving. I have worked both jobs fulltime, so I should have enough money to pay the monthly bills and still have some left over for a bagful of groceries.

Acting strangely, Rob gives me a look full of sympathy as I rip open the envelope.

I stare in utter shock at my paycheck. Just to be sure, I bring the check closer to my eyes, squinting while tilting my head sideways so I can see it better. But my reality doesn't change.

Has your destiny ever shifted, Regina?

Yes, Grant– it has. Again. Right now.

Zero. Zip. Zilch. A few bucks shy of four hundred dollars. All. Gone.

Withheld for collections.

Lowering my head in defeat, I breathe deeply through my nose, trying not to scream in frustration. I have a bad feeling about this. I know that my paycheck from Digital Nation will be zero as well.

I will not work for nothing.

Why should I pay those bills when I don't even have a mother? I would have paid millions of dollars if I still had Mom, but I don't.

It's sickening how I'm to pay for a service I never received. No mother, but I get punished for the rest of my life by having my wages garnished until I pay back every last, rotten cent.

"Regina, I'm so sorry. I know how hard you work." Rob reaches for me, but his hand falls to the counter when he sees the tragic look etched across my face. "Frantic, Ken called, and said your check at DN is the same. I'm going to save you the agony of indecision. I won't allow you to work for nothing, and neither will Ken. I'm sorry, Regina– you're fired from here and the electronics store. It's for your own good."

Rob flashes me that look again.

I don't cry, scream, or throw a fit. I slowly untie my apron, and then hand it to my ex-boss. I know deep-down that Rob's doing me a favor. I'm not being fired because of my performance. Tears prickle at my eyes as they have for the past two weeks, but they don't manifest.

I walk away from my jobs with my head held high and my shoulders back.

Dignity.

Dazed, I wander down the block. You never walk down my streets without being on alert. I could be targeted for a mugging, and I wouldn't realize until it's too late. Actually, go ahead– I have nothing left to lose.

The Whittenhowers have backed me into a corner. Grant tried to warn me, and I might as well have waved red in front of a bull. Jackson and Daniel aren't people you can deny.

I knew this all along, and yet I had to try. I don't know why they picked me, other than assuming it's the very traits I've exhibited during the game they've played with me. The stubbornness I displayed and the inability to give in are probably virtues they want added to their bloodline, so my recent behavior only added to their desire to possess me.

If I were older, more experienced, and had money on my side– if I hadn't been born into the life I was given, I could have taken Jackson and Daniel on head-to-head. If it were a battle of wills, I would win hands down. I know this, and it allows my head to rise, my shoulders to go back, and my iron-will to infuse my being.

I put one foot in front of the other, and walk into what I have left in my life. I will persevere, because I will accept nothing less. It's the journey that may be very uncomfortable.

I have nothing left now. I had told Grant I had nothing to lose. I guess he was right– I did. Now I have no source of income, no prospect of going to college, and I'm at a precipice where I could make a horrible decision out of spite.

What a Whittenhower doesn't understand, because they have never been where I am as they have too much to lose, when you have nothing left to lose, you have nothing left to fear.

Rock bottom either brings out the worst, or the best in you.

I scuff my feet the entire way home as I scroll my resources through my mind, trying to find a way out of this shit. Resources? What resources? I could get another job, or fifty, but my pay would still be garnished. I could apply for financial aid, and then be turned down for defaulting on my debt. I could apply for more scholarships, and then watch them poof into thin air.

The scene before me stops me dead in my tracks. I stare in utter disbelief. I shake my head, not understanding what I'm seeing.

No way am I seeing what I'm seeing. It just cannot be.

It's just one more thing to add to the list–

Homeless.

My rent was paid up, but I guess that doesn't matter when someone bribes your landlord. All of my meager belongings are in a pile on the curb. Roman is standing sentry, making sure no one steals anything while keeping the garbage collectors at bay.

It looks like trash. It *is* trash– worthless possessions that people rely on for happiness and comfort.

It's all just pretty lies.

I walk up, purposefully avoiding Roman. He stares at me in wonder as I pull the only photo album I have from the heap. The images mark the passage of time with visual memories when my mind no longer supplies the finer details.

When you're a kid, and your parents are trying to describe the concept of death, no one explains how you'll forget how your loved ones look and sound. Some days, I can only remember expressions that would scroll across my father's face, and I can't remember what he sounded like with the exception of the tone in his voice when he said my mother's name.

Clothing, jewelry, television sets– meaningless. Photos are the most important possession when memories fade– it's too bad there isn't audio saved when capturing the moment.

I'll invent that when I get the chance– mark my words. I'll invent that. Not a video, just two seconds of audio in the time it takes for the camera to capture the image. Imagine the sound of a laugh imprinted over the file to be shared on a device.

Would Ade find a mobile phone worthy if it could do *that*?

As a coping mechanism, my mind checked out, venturing to a place where I could problem-solve. Emotions can't be solved, and I have no idea how I feel in this moment when I don't want to feel at all.

"You can have what you want, Roman. Make sure everything else is distributed to my mom's friends." I gaze down at the stuff my mom and I had accumulated over the past few years, none of it my father had touched. "I won't need it where I'm going. They fucking win!" I scream at the top of my lungs until they burn as hot as fire with my fury and desperation.

Reaching to calm me, "What happened?" Roman asks, concern warping his voice. Blue-green eyes are intent on my face, and it breaks my heart.

Refusing to allow Roman to comfort me, I snap. "Let's see– I lost my scholarship." I tick off my fingers as I hiss out how my life just went to hell. "I was fired from both jobs because my wages were garnished to nothing– N O T H I N G!" I scream as I wave the check stub like a flag of defeat.

Moving my hand in a circle, gesturing around the mound of shit I call mine, "And now I'm homeless. Oh, and my mom's dead." My voice cracks. "Pick one– just one would be horrible. Combined together, it's life-shattering. I hate those fucking Whittenhowers."

Conquered, I kick a box of my clothing until they dump and scatter into the street. A car drives over them, tearing hysterical laughter from my chest. A pretty blouse I wore to the movies with Ade and Fate sticks to the tire– spinning 'round and 'round –only to be left behind a block away. Meaningless. But at the time, I worked my ass off to afford the two-dollar blouse at the Salvation Army so I could feel feminine and comfortable while hanging out with my elite friends. It meant everything.

"I will show them one day– they will kneel down to me and give me the fucking respect I deserve," I declare maniacally.

"Shh… it's okay, sweetheart." Roman pulls me into a hug and squeezes me so hard I hear my joints crack. He murmurs words of comfort– all lies. I try not to soak up the comfort and attention, not to seep into his embrace and his clean scent. I wish I could cry. I think it would be appropriate in this situation, but I have no way to release my pain and frustration.

A glint catches my eye from my mound of belongings, and for a moment in time, I imagine myself taking the paring knife from the knife block and slicing my forearm– watching the crimson bead on my flesh to flow down my skin and puddle on the pavement. A visual manifestation of the pain and frustration eating my soul. I think about it until my senses scream '*NO! Pain is weakness leaving the body.*' If I were to cut the pain away before I've earned the relief, I would be a coward.

Weak, I am not.

"I'd offer for you to stay with me, but it wouldn't be a good idea." Roman squeezes me tightly, trying to take the sting of rejection away. "We'd end up together in a forever sort of way, and you'd never get out of here. I'd happily do this, but you deserve better than me– better than here." Roman has no problem shedding the tears that won't break free from my eyes, and I envy his release as much as I ache for his pain.

"It's not that I deserve better than you, Roman. It's that we both deserve better than this." I point down the block, and he knows what I mean. "Right now, we would enable each other and go nowhere fast."

"I agree, sweetheart," is murmured against the side of my face, sending shivers down my spine. "You deserve better than a drug dealer. If you stay here, you'll end up a whore."

"I'm trading one kind of whore for another, Roman." A humorless laugh is pulled from my chest. "Trust me. I'll still be whoring myself out." My voice grows heavy with my fear. I dig my fingernails into Roman's back, and I pull him to me as tightly as I can manage.

"I couldn't stand to see the light fade in your eyes. Your soul would die a little each day if you stayed here." Roman's shaking fingers caress my cheeks, and then slide through my wiry hair, pulling it away from my face. His penetrating gaze pierces me, pouring his soul out through his eyes. Hugging each other tighter, I clench my fingertips against his shoulders, trying to anchor myself to my friend because I don't know what will happen when I finally let go.

"It's a question of the devil you know. My soul would slowly die here, or I will sign it away to the Whittenhowers. I guess I need to figure out which is easier to escape." Reason tries to break through the panic, but my voice still wavers in fear.

"I think it's already been decided," Roman murmurs as a black Town Car pulls up to the curb, and then Albert climbs out of the driver's side.

"Regina, when the car comes, you best get in the fucker." I mimic Grant in a nasty tone.

"Miss Regal, would you like me to load anything for you?" Albert asks, and I can see the sympathy etched across his face.

Great– I don't want pity. I hold no responsibility for my circumstances. One day, I will be in control of my own life and no one will ever take that from me.

"No– nothing!" I screech, voice sharp and lashing.

Albert flinches and Roman's arms tighten around me in restraint. It isn't Albert's fault. I nearly apologize, but then I think *'Fuck it!'* I deserve to be able to lash out at whomever I please, especially if they work for the very people who are destroying my life.

"I guess this is goodbye, sweetheart." Roman's voice breaks, and the tears are no longer a threat glistening in his eyes– they're rapidly falling down his cheeks to wet his hair.

Even that agonizing sight won't bring on mine. Am I dead inside? The pressure building behind my breasts is an ache for his pain. It's agony to see Roman breakdown before me, taking my breath away with its intensity.

My fingertips seek out Roman's chin, and I hold him firmly in my grasp. Moving without thought, I steal something that should only belong to me. I kiss Roman, and we gasp as the electrically charged current that has been flowing between us for weeks is finally connected.

I saved this first kiss for someone important. I don't know what's going to happen where I'm going, but one thing is for sure– Roman deserves to have my first kiss. He deserves to hold that small part of me. This way I know I will never forget him, and hopefully he will never forget me, even if I'm his hundredth kiss.

"Regina," Roman whispers against my lips. Feeling oddly light, freed, I smile. See, Roman knew my name all along.

Leaning in, I kiss Roman deeper and hold him as tightly as I can. He's an inch or so taller than me, and it makes me feel like a woman. This is a man who deserves to be in charge, and I would let him. I know without a shadow of a doubt, that if I had stayed here, I would have fallen hard for Roman Alexander.

I kiss Roman with an intensity that frightens me– an intensity that I didn't think I was capable of giving. I always felt numb until Grant unleashed something deep inside of me that is frightening. I use that newly risen, powerful force to show Roman just how much he means to me.

Lips parting, I turn from Roman and rush to the open car door. I can't look back, because I wouldn't get into the car if I did. Sliding doors– the fork in the road where one lane leads you on a journey at complete odds with the other, but you never know which is the correct path until you walk it.

Rich or poor, both have a cost I'm not sure I'm willing to pay.

The building prickling behind my eyes becomes a misery that won't let loose. Albert holds the passenger door open, and I crawl into the unknown.

"Regina!" Roman yells, and my head whips to seek him out. Arms stretched, as if deciding whether or not he should try to pull me free from the car.

Albert shuts the door before I can bolt. I hear the click of the lock engaging and it confuses me, but Roman holds all of my attention. I stare at him through the tinted glass of the window, while somewhere in the recesses of my mind I hear Albert get into the car.

"Regina, I believe in you." Roman professes as he jogs forward as the car rolls from the curb. His hand is firmly rooted on the roof. "I love you, sweetheart! You'll blow their minds!"

The car swiftly pulls away before I can reply. The last thing I see is wide blue-green eyes and the swing of silky black hair.

Chapter Sixteen

A guttural sob spills from between my kiss-damp lips– the imprint of Roman staying with me. I wipe the back of my hand over my eyes, surprised to see that my fingertips come away with no moisture.

"Do you love him?" Grant's voice flows softly from the front passenger seat. I instinctively know that Grant was the one who imprisoned me by locking the door when Roman yelled my name.

"I don't know," I answer honestly, voice sounding dead even to my ears. "I didn't get a chance to find out."

"And you never will," Grant replies as he turns and straightens in his seat. It sounds mean, but his voice is bleeding remorse. "Roman Alexander is not the man for you."

"And you are?" Snarling, fingertips curling into claws on the seat, I lean forward with my breath skating across the back of Grant's neck.

"I didn't say that, Regina." As patient as ever, Grant waits me out. "Never once have I said that– if anything, I've said the opposite. But what I do know, Roman Alexander is *not* the man for you."

"Fuck you, Grant!" Furious, a hairsbreadth from raging inside the confines of the car, I glare out the window.

My emotions are pinging all over the place, not unlike the last time I took this same ride through Dominion and into Crestview. Now it's no longer a terrifying premonition– it's my reality.

It's hard to imagine how much has changed in the past month. I'm not the same girl I was. I'd thought myself jaded then… I was dead wrong.

In complete silence, none of us engage in conversation. Even as we pass through the first gate, the security guy doesn't say anything, as if he can sense my fury wafting through the car. As we pass Fate's house, my fingers curl around the handle as I contemplate jumping from the car.

Grant unintentionally hurt my feelings when he asked about Roman, so I do the same in return. Intentionally. "Where does your

Gwen live?" No note of jealousy in my tone, just as none was present in Grant's when he mentioned Roman. Curiosity and pain.

Grant's pained sigh ricochets through the car, and even Albert shows signs of discomfort. "Right there," Grant points to the left-hand side of the street, directly in the middle of Crestview, which means Gwen isn't the richest or most powerful but centrally located to drive Grant insane.

"Interesting," I murmur, getting off on Grant's pain. But since Ella Regal didn't raise a cunt, I immediately feel horrible for it. "Why do you do that to yourself?"

Turning to face me as we roll at a snail's pace down the street, Grant raises an eyebrow. "Who says I have a choice?" He turns away from me, as if it physically hurts to gaze at me. "If you read my notes, you'd remember me saying you're my echo. In this, neither of us have a choice."

"There's always a choice," I mutter petulantly. "Always."

"Not always, Miss Regal." Albert's eyes bore into me from the rearview mirror. "Not always."

Catching on too slowly for me, but swifter than most. "Gwen has a bodyguard you called an enforcer. I assumed Julio was Stanton's because of the mafia, but then he said he went to Hillbrook as Stanton's shadow. So, who's yours, Grant?"

Albert's lips curl into a devious smirk as he gazes at me in the rearview. "I belong to Jackson."

"I belong to no one," I grit out between bared teeth.

"No one said you did," Grant reminds me. "Your tenure isn't forever, unless you wish it to be."

"What about Fate? Does she have a *bodyguard*?" I lose my train of thought when I catch sight of a huge Victorian house that sprung up out of nowhere in the past month. Situated at the fork at the end of Crestview's only street, exactly where the death-shroud-covered iron gate used to be. "What the fuck is that monstrosity?"

Albert, being a sadistic bastard, actually stops the car so I'm forced to stare at three stories with a massive turret. Grant is bellowing laughter from the front seat, amused beyond measure.

"Is that where my fucking tuition went? Goddamn you, Grant!" I kick the back of his seat, eyes unable to look away.

Chuckling uncontrollably, Grant tries to speak while choking on his own laughter. "That's Dexter's house– he's rebuilding his own version of Sanctuary in clear view to annoy the families. You may remember the name Dexter Hayes, as he's the guy who signed your tuition checks to Hillbrook for the past two years."

Forehead pressed to the window, I watch as the construction crew acts like deranged worker bees. Dozens of men complete the finishing touches on the home, including those who are carrying purple and red velvet furniture inside.

"Dexter Hayes is your bestie, I bet. The one who said he'd spite you by turning his home into a low-class whorehouse."

"Oh, Regina!" Grant's laughter reaches an all-time high, causing Albert to actually vocalize his amusement. "You did read my notes." Slim, elegant fingers motion for Albert to continue on.

Turning sharply to the right, away from Dexter's Victorian nightmare, the gate opens automatically. I wince, waiting for a panic attack to hit me once the gate closes behind the car and the trees swallow us whole.

"No fear, Regina," Grant's soothing voice doesn't tell me what I want to hear, but what I *need* to hear. "The moment you got into the car, your scholarship was reinstated. Marc already sent in the payment, minus room and board, as you'll be staying at Whittenhower Estates."

"Poor Albert is going to be spread pretty thin carting my big ass around," I mutter sarcastically.

Ignoring my tone, Grant continues as if I never spoke. "You are not being held hostage, Regina. This summer, I'll teach you to drive, just as I did Ade. You'll be given a car with unlimited access to Crestview's main gate and Whittenhower Estates' gate. You can drive yourself to class and to visit friends. It won't be long before Fate will be moving into the house with us to keep you company."

"Don't you mean away from the FBI Daniel sicced on Thomas?"

Albert makes a choking laugh, eyes bulging with surprise.

"Please be mindful of what my son eavesdrops and relays to you– all information comes at a steep price." I shudder at the intense terror infusing Grant's voice.

"Understood," I grumble as a shiver of trepidation works its way up my spine.

"You must remind young Daniel to keep his tiny mouth shut," Albert whispers so low, he assumes I can't hear. "Or else you will be forced to take him as your heir after Jackson's death."

"Don't!" Grant barks, causing me to jump in my seat. "My son will not suffer through the life I've lived."

"Then stop speaking with Daniel, and if you do, stop doing it when your son is hiding behind the draperies," Albert warns, like he's in charge, not the hired help. "How often do I have to repeat myself?"

"Duly noted– I'll take that under advisement." Realizing I've heard way too much, Grant turns in his seat to face me. "The founding families have a great deal of power, so that is why we have people like Albert who protect us in all areas, especially from ourselves. Just as Julian does for Stanton."

"Um… okay." I decide to leave that alone, since Grant was clearly placating me. The area of Dominion I just left behind taught me to mind my own fucking business. "Whitt would look adorable with a bell around his neck, then you could hear when he's lurking in the shadows."

Albert laughs outright this time, seeming pleased with my bizarre sense of humor, but this time Grant doesn't look amused. Visibly uncomfortable, shoulder muscles taut with stress, Grant looks about ready to jump from the car to escape either Albert or me.

"Welcome home, Regina. I hope you find it more pleasant than I do." Grant says as the car rolls up the circular driveway to stop in front of the massive stone mansion known as Whittenhower Estates. I can feel the malevolence flowing from the mortar.

"Welcome to Misery Castle," I mutter underneath my breath.

Grant swiftly exits the car and opens my door. A gentlemanly hand appears in my line of sight, wishing to help me from my seat. Stubborn, I avoid the sweet gesture and crawl out on my own.

No matter what, I will always do it on my own. I stand in the driveway and look at the imposing building that I will call home for at least nine months. My fingers seek out my parents' wedding bands that are tied around my neck with a ribbon.

I promise you, Mom and Dad, that this is only my present– it will never be my future. I send my oath to the heavens.

I grab my album from the backseat and make my way up the front stone steps, ignoring both Albert and Grant. Albert gets the hint and leaves to park the car. The front door bursts open and I flinch, showing just how thin my false calm truly is.

Sunshine brightens my day in the form of a five-year-old little boy. He bounds to me and hugs me around the waist. "Welcome home, Queen," Whitt says in a small voice that never fails to make me smile.

I know that this is the best welcome I will get anywhere on earth. I hope I can remember it as the rest of the Whittenhowers welcome me. I'm sure it will be anything but pleasant, judging by the pained expression marring Grant's handsome face. I hold the boy's hand as I open the massive door and step into my unwelcome future.

Chapter Seventeen

"Follow me," Grant says gruffly. I want to disobey, but I might as well get this over with as soon as possible. He tries to take my elbow, but I sidestep him.

"No touching unless I initiate it," I hiss. Grant nods his head in agreement, and moves his hand in a gesture for me to walk before him. I shake my head no.

Every time I set foot into the gigantic foyer, I'm blown away how it's the size of four apartments in my building. Ancient tapestries and precious works of art hang from hardwood paneled walls. The marble floors have a gold vein running through the tiles.

Dual, curved, marble staircases meet at a center balcony that takes you to two separate wings of the mansion. A shudder waves its way up and down my spine as I remember being lost in the labyrinth of hallways.

A crystal chandelier the size of a car hangs in the center of the room from three stories up. Beneath the twinkling light fixture is Whitt. He peeks at me from behind a ridiculously large floral arrangement resting on a useless table in the center of the foyer. He winks at me, and I can't help but smile. What has me doing a double-take is Grant smiling affectionately at the boy, like Grant thrives on watching Whitt act his age.

Every time I try to hate Grant, he does something that makes me like him more.

Looming ahead, situated at the end of the hallway, resting beneath the massive staircases, is a pair of arched double-doors. My intuition tells me this is my destination– the Whittenhower study. The place, where weeks ago, Whitt had me eavesdropping at the cracked door.

Leaving Whitt to his own devices, no doubt where he'll go eavesdrop on someone, I follow Grant into the infamous Whittenhower study. The walls are mahogany, not veneered paneling– real wood. The ceiling is high enough to be two stories tall. Hand-carved bookcase after bookcase rises to the ceiling. In different circumstances, I would love to explore every title in their library. A narrow balcony and a sliding staircase give access to an upper floor of shelving, which is full of ornate books that are probably priceless. The scholar in me wants to climb those treads and pry the books open, devouring their hidden knowledge.

A ginormous crackling fireplace warms the frigid room, even though it's summer outside. The beautifully gothic library is dark and cavernous, leaving the room cool compared to the outside heat. The fire is inviting and makes me want to live in this room with all the knowledge lining its walls.

I come to an abrupt stop when I see Daniel Whittenhower sitting at a baroque desk in the middle of the room. I change my mind; I hate this room because he is in it. It's *his* room. Lips twisted with arrogance, he smirks at me from his leather chair. Holding a binder of papers in his hand, Daniel waves it about.

"Sign this paper, and then Grant will explain what will happen next." Daniel's voice is commanding but not as booming as his older brother's, but it's laced with something I can't name– uncertainty, maybe? I narrow my eyes at Daniel in suspicion.

"I'd like to read the contract first, if you don't mind?" I say firmly to the older man as I try to take the papers from him, but he snatches the binder away.

Daniel's eyes widen in surprise. Until this moment, he saw me as an impressionable young woman. He hasn't lived as much life as I have– even my innocence is jaded. Daniel looks at me with an expression of disbelief and a small amount of grudging respect.

"Sign it, Miss Regal," Daniel bites out from between gritted teeth. "Don't make me remind you how I will throw you back on the streets. Every time you get back up, I'll knock you down farther than you were previously. No matter how long it takes, I will make you hit bottom. My power is far-reaching, and you'll have nowhere to hide and no help to be given, in this country or others. So save us all a lot of grief by stowing your pride. Sign the contract."

Adversaries, Daniel and I lock eyes. Instinct taking over, my green eyes glare into his blue, establishing a hierarchy. Dark globes reflect the pits of Hell with all the horrid things he has planned for my future. I don't need a psychic to know that I will never win against Daniel. At least not today in the present. But the future…

Without blinking, I do as Daniel says. I stow my pride by harshly grabbing the expensive pen from his fingertips. Then I do the stupidest thing I've ever done. I sign the paper without reading it first. I know that whatever it says, there will be no negotiating between us. I have nowhere to go but the streets thanks to them. I roughly sign the paper– the pen tip skates across the document, snagging as I gash the paper.

Relieved, all the muscles relax in Daniel's body at once. "Thank you, Miss Regal. I will leave you to discuss your duties with my son. Kristal is preparing your room for you, and I had my wife and Adelaide pick out things for your stay." Filled with pride, Daniel rises from his seat while presenting his hand. Having no other choice, fingers wrapping around his, I shake his hand firmly. "Welcome to Whittenhower Estates, Regina."

I'll find something to wipe the smug from Daniel's face. I have at least nine months to accomplish it– I'll bide my time while plotting hellish situations.

I stand frozen in shock in the middle of a room, one that at any other occasion I would find fascinating. The only sound I hear is my labored breath and the rapid tattoo my heart is impressing inside my chest.

"I'm so very sorry, Regina. I can't say that enough, just know I truly mean it." Grant's voice holds emotion, as does his expression and his eyes. This man couldn't ever get away with lying, not even if his life depended on it. "Please sit with me and we'll talk." He gestures to the leather chairs facing the roaring fireplace. "Again, I profusely apologize, as you aren't going to like what I have to say."

Instinctively, I know Grant is telling the truth. Growing up as I have, I've learned to read people. The naïve don't live long in my neighborhood. I can tell that Grant isn't smug and gloating as I'm sure Daniel and Jackson are right now.

Grant's soothing presence helps me relax and release the tension that has been riding me since my father's death. I have no other option than the one I'm living right this very moment. I accept my circumstances, and that is freeing in a way. It's all I can do.

I follow Grant to a seating area and pick out a Cordovan leather chair. I rub my hands down the buttery smooth arms as I sit, mulling over how it's the color of dried blood. I choose the chair over the sofa because I want to face Grant while we talk, and I didn't want him to be within touching distance. When he's too near, my mind goes hazy and I don't react as I should.

Grant clears his throat several times, yet he still doesn't speak. We sit for what feels like hours in total silence. My mind reels as I come up with scenarios about what my *duties* are. Obviously I looked up what surrogacy meant. I know it'll mean doctor's appointments, having his *stuff* pushed up inside of me, growing our child in my womb, and ultimately giving our child up at birth for Grant and Cora to raise while Jackson and Daniel direct their every action.

The agony behind my eyes returns with a vengeance, yet the tears refuse to fall. I take deep breaths– one right after another, trying to calm the pressure building. I have no outlet now that crying is impossible, and it's slowly killing me.

"This will not be a traditional surrogacy." Grant shifts in his chair, refusing to look at me. The glow of the fire highlights the planes of his face. "That's why Jackson and Daniel went about this as they did. It isn't legal in that way– however, it isn't *illegal* either." He stresses the word illegal, and sweat begins to bead along my spine.

Hands clammy, the shakes radiate up my arms. "No pretense, Grant. Just say it, and get it over with. It's too late now, isn't it?" I glare at him, trying to loathe him and finding it hopeless.

Leaning forward, Grant rests his elbows on his thighs, and then wraps a palm around the back of his own neck, clearly tortured. "The child you'll carry will be yours and mine– *ours*. But no one will know it, same as with my paternity and my son's. As soon as you're pregnant, Cora will announce her pregnancy. The child will be born at home, and everyone will think Cora birthed it."

"I-I-I–" stuttering, I'm at a complete and total loss.

"Surrogacy will not work, and neither will adoption. Jackson wanted his legacy to remain in control, even if everyone believes it to be through Daniel."

"I don't understand this Daniel bullshit, Grant." Eyes scrunched together in the center of my forehead, I can't wrap my mind around it. "Why didn't Jackson just claim you, and you Whitt?"

"We'll discuss the torrid secrets of my paternity at a later date." Grant sounds beyond perturbed. "Right now, I think what's going on between you and I–" he gestures between us. "Is more important."

"We *will* speak of it," I command, and Grant nods his head in agreement.

"Jackson's been on borrowed time since birth, but a legacy has always been passed down from the first born son to his first born son, and so on. But legacies are meant to be broken for the sake of the bloodline. Wilhelm– my grandfather feared Jackson would pass his defect on. Two sons were always the ideal– the heir and the spare. Wilhelm had two: one who was dying and willing to do the dirty work, and one as the public face of the family. I was an accident, which I'll explain later, so I'm legally Daniel's heir. After giving Daniel two daughters, my mother had a hysterectomy."

"I don't know whether to feel pity for Daniel or relief for Priscilla because her use as a broodmare ended," I mutter sarcastically, vitriol thick in my voice. "I have the insane need to find your mother and hug her because she was in the same position as me."

Tilting his head back, peals of addictive laughter flow from Grant's flawless neck. "Regina," he chuckles my name. "My mother loves my fathers– never doubt that. She's hopelessly in love with them, as they are her."

"Shit!"

"Regardless, there was only me with an entire dynasty hanging over my head. Jackson's always been dying, and Daniel's always been terrified our legacy will fall into another family's hands. That's how my son came about." Grant leans farther forward, then taps my knee with a single fingertip. "I hadn't reached the age of majority yet, Regina. I couldn't legally raise little Daniel as my son. As the public face, Daniel and my mother took on the legal responsibilities of both of us. The need for two male heirs was satisfied."

"But Daniel and Jackson felt neither of you were enough?"

"Jackson's always felt I was enough, but Daniel resents the softness in me, thinking me incapable to lead. He was perfectly happy with my son until the announcement that Whitt wanted to marry another boy. You may not see it this way, but we're all trying to save Whitt from the life I've had to lead, where the only thing important about me is my sperm. If Whitt is gay, he shouldn't be forced to bed women."

"But you'd subject *our* child to it?" Curling my fingers into my palms, my fingernails draw crescents of blood.

"Regina," Grant utters my name in a soothing tone. "I'm the son who can do the dirty work, but not the one who can lead– my soul is so tainted that it doesn't matter if I can handle it or not. Whitt is the purest soul I've ever met, and he deserves the right to grow into his own man. Any child of ours would be able to lead an invading army while leaving peace and tranquility in his wake. I have no doubts that our creation will not only be equipped to run the Whittenhower legacy, he'll thrive on it."

Ignoring Grant's faith in me, I go in for the kill. "What was the document Daniel had me sign? Why?"

Every muscle in Grant's body turns bowstring taut. "In essence, you just signed a contract to give up all legal rights to any children born between you and me. It's also a confidentiality contract. You will never be able to speak of this with anyone who isn't already privy to the agreement."

Sadness and shame wafts from Grant's every pore, and it annoys the piss out of me. I lean forward in my chair and pin him with my stare. He flinches as if struck by the force of my gaze. "So, let me get this straight. I'll bear you a child, you'll take it from me, and that's it." I say with incredulity. "What if I'm like your mother and only give you a girl. I'm assuming you need a child with a dick. Will you go out and extort another woman if I fail to deliver a male heir?"

"No," Grant murmurs so quietly I can hardly make out the word. "Only you– my obligation, as is yours, will be met after this. You signed a five-year agreement."

A heartbeat away from jumping up from my seat and tearing Grant's family jewels from their sack, his pained reaction stuns me stupid. Back curving, Grant rests his head in his hands and issues a sound that only the dying are capable of making.

"What if I can't have kids? Maybe you should have tested me like you failed to do with Cora."

"It's a five-year-agreement," Grant repeats. "You have to try for those five years, unless you have a medical ailment." He rests his head on his knee, cradling it with both arms, and I can tell that it only gets worse from here. The lost expression on his face makes me scared to hear any more.

"It's not just one kid, is it? It's however many I can pop out in five years?" Shocked, I realize that if I'm a very fertile person, I'm handing these freaks several of my children. I'm going to be sick– the back of my hand covers my mouth, trying to hold the nausea at bay.

"Yes…" Grant groans, sounding like he's on the cusp of being sick too. "I ask that you see this from my perspective as well– how we're both being forced to do this."

"Oh, I feel so *sorry* for you," I snarl snottily, and then instantly regret treating Grant like shit. I'm incapable of being angry with him, no matter how justified I may be.

"Please don't kill me." Arms wrapped around the back of his neck, protecting his skull, Grant looks terrified. "I don't want to say this because I know it will incite you. Every child will net you a million dollars. I know that you won't take money for selling your children. I wouldn't want you to, and I respect that you won't. But my fathers don't think like we do, nor does Cora."

"Kill you?" I seethe. "How about you become the head of this goddamn family? Tonight! I'll help you– anything you need."

Grant ignores my murderous proposition, and the fact that I offered to pull his strings. "I did set up a bank account for you that they don't know about. Not a dime is Whittenhower money. It's money I've earned working, and it isn't tainted by my fathers. Look at it as a thank you and a safety net should something happen to me and you want to take our children from here."

Eyes narrowed, voice holding barely restrained violence, I begin to respect Grant. "I see you do know me."

"Yes, Regina." Frustrated, Grant tugs at his hair. "I may be soft, but I'm not a moron. We're stuck in this situation, and I do have contingency plans that no one else is privy to. But I also believe we need to make the best out of this situation. I know you'll be helpful to my mother, my sisters, and my son. You'll be good for us– a grounding force. Reality."

"I don't think your family will appreciate my version of reality," I mutter with fiendish delight.

Grant has an exceptional ability to ignore my bloodthirsty attitude. "Your bank account, I'll only be able to access it to deposit money. It's your account, for you and the children should you need to run. I also paid off Ella's medical expenses with my own money. Again, not Whittenhower money. I understand you better than you think, Regina."

Emotionally, mentally, and physically exhausted, I fall back against the chair in utter disbelief. I don't know if I can do this. Panic washes over me in a tidal wave, forcing me to rapidly suck in air between my clenched teeth.

"You can do this, Regina." Grant tries to reassure me, as if reading my mind. "I love my family, and I have responsibilities, which is why I have never run. I understand loyalty and duty, and I accept this. But I don't want to cut you off from your future. You can go to college until your pregnancy is noticeable, and then we'll work something out with the dean so that you may continue here at home until after the baby is born. You're a genius, and have a lot to offer, and I refuse to allow anyone to harm your future. Had I known this was to happen, I wouldn't have allowed Adelaide to bring you to dinner. I'm so sorry."

"And your apology and gifts of money are supposed to make it right?" I seethe– I don't scream the words, even though I want to. Instead I get deadly quiet, forcing Grant to struggle to hear me from three feet away.

"No, nothing will ever make this right for either of us." Exhausted, defeated, and angry, Grant sounds exactly as I do.

"You could have stood up to them and told them no!" I yell directly into Grant's face. "You could have told them you didn't want me. That you didn't want your children to have my ugly, huge DNA running through their blue-blood veins."

"And you don't think I did that?" Grant shouts right back at me, pale skin turning a brilliant shade of pissed off. "I fought Daniel, knowing I couldn't fight Jackson. But nothing I said would sway them. I think you've learned that lesson by now, Regina. They do whatever they wish, your needs and wants be damned. You either comply, or they drive right through you. You have to accept defeat, try to make the best of the situation, and wait patiently until you can change your own fate."

"I'll never accept defeat." Shaking my head, disgust is etched across my face. "It's not in my nature to lie down and die. They'll regret this, Grant. I promise you."

"I know." Grant grins at me, white teeth flashing menacingly. "I'm counting on it, my ally. I'm counting on Daniel underestimating your drive, Regina."

Grant's beautiful face charms me, the hope in his eyes traps me, and his soothing voice coaxes me... and I'd hate him for it if I could.

Voice blank, emotions lost, I'm alone even if Grant and I are on this ride together. "So, life as I know it, the life that I've worked so hard to build for myself, is over."

"It doesn't have to be that way, Regina. Go to school– get your degree. Try to see me as a friend and ally. Don't be angry with me, but I knew you'd want Fate by your side, so she signed a confidentiality agreement of her own this morning. Now she'll be able to keep in contact with you. I want you to maintain your friendships and your schooling. However, I don't want you to interact with Roman Alexander. He is an absolute no. I hope that after our five years are over, you'll remain with me and our children and not seek Roman out."

Oh, those are fighting words. Eyes narrowed, I give it to Grant with both barrels. "What? Like I am some kind of IVF mistress, or something? Grant, you're married and I'm not your mistress." Grant cringes at the venom in my tone. "So you can't tell me who I can and can't see."

"I can." Anger flashes over Grant's features. Leaning forward, he grips my knee, squeezing to the point of bruising. "My children come out of your body, and I will not allow another man to stick his dick inside of you and contaminate your womb while my child is in there." Jerking backward, Grant looks surprised at the words rolling off his tongue.

"My mother didn't know which brother was my father. Was I full-term or premature? At eight pounds, Jackson was the lucky bastard who had the honors of being my biological father. I will not do that to my child, which is why Gwen was not out of anyone's sight until she was pregnant. But I respect you, knowing you'll honor loyalty and not betray me by having sex with anyone during our five-year contract."

"Jesus Christ. Fucking bloody hell." My mind swirls with madness, and it's filled with profanity. "When's my first doctor's appointment?" I want to get to the heart of the matter. If I'm to be an incubator for the Whittenhower offspring, I may as well get it started. I'll try to remain detached. It isn't my child even though it's my egg– it's Cora and Grant's child. I'll have to repeat this mantra constantly for the next five years.

My egg. Only my egg. Only my uterus growing my egg combined with Grant's sperm. Only my egg. It's Grant and Cora Whittenhower's child.

"Regina." My name is filled with agonizing pain, laced with deep regret and shame. "There will be a doctor who makes house calls and a midwife. But you will not step foot into a hospital since it will be incriminating. Everyone has to think the baby is Cora's child."

"How then?" My eyes bug out in confusion. All the information I could find said that it was a complicated procedure. I can't fathom how they could do it here unless they've installed their own clinic. It wouldn't surprise me, since in my experience, the rich do as they please.

"In a bed, Regina." Grant's face goes from pale to crimson in a heartbeat. "Our children will be made the old fashioned way."

Chapter Eighteen

I have the dignity not to run from the room, but I do leave rather swiftly with a palm holding vomit in my mouth.

I can never face Adelaide with her knowing that I'm to be her brother's mistress.

WHORE!

How do I look Priscilla, Katie, Ade, and Whitt in the eye, and then go off to Grant's bed while he's married to another, especially when there's no love between us? How can I survive the look of victory in Jackson and Daniel's eyes? It's no wonder Gwen sics her bodyguard on Grant when he bothers her.

My God, I'd cut his balls off the first chance I got. Grant would need Albert to stop me.

It's one thing to sell your body on the street to survive. Not only am I selling my body, I'm selling my unborn children as well. I'm worse than a whore, so much worse. Prostitutes do it to survive another day on this earth. Some of my friends from when we were in elementary school now turn tricks to feed their children. Yet here I am, selling my children.

Grant was right. I will never take payment for my children. I'm doing this for my future at the expense of my children. I think I'm going to be sick.

I rush to the nearest powder room, directly off the dining room. I barely make it to the toilet before the dry heaves start. Now moisture floods my eyes. It stings like acid after concentrating in my tear ducts for weeks. But it isn't a real cry, so it doesn't count. I gain no cathartic release from it. Psychology or not, no one can stop tears from rolling uncontrollably down their cheeks as they retch into a toilet. It's an impossibility.

Midway through a heave, I idly wonder if Grant is gagging over what his fathers and wife are making us do. Grant is a whore, too.

I imagined myself tolerating being a surrogate, telling myself I was giving a married couple a gift of life. But to hand Grant my virginity, to lie in bed and make the child with him, and then to turn around and give it to a woman who had no hand in the making of the child…

Hugging the toilet, tremors wrack my body. I'm not going to lie to myself. Being intimate with Grant wouldn't be a hardship. But what if he doesn't want me at all? He wanted Gwen– he *loved* her. He's in love with her still, yet married to another.

My brain is my biggest asset and it's not exactly sexy. My body is huge and mannish. I'm not blonde and blue-eyed, or petite and beautiful. I'm built exactly for what I was purchased to do. Birth children. Work like a bitch. To survive whatever is thrown my way. None of which is arousing.

Why do I give a fuck if Grant wants me or not? But, hell, I can only imagine the blow to my self-esteem if Grant can't get it up enough to perform. Then again, he didn't complain during our grinding session on my sofa.

After making sure my belly is empty, I crawl to my feet. While I wash my face, I promise myself that I'll do this on *my* terms. I'll find something that Grant will stand up for. Naïvely, I wonder if the birth of his children will garner him a backbone to stand up to his wife and father– doubtful. Been there and done that with Whitt and Gwen, and I know he loves both of them. I just have to find something that he values more than love or money.

I'm going to make Grant mine, and then take him away from Daniel and Jackson. If not in body, then in will. I'll become their heir's puppet master and use him against them.

I have the ability to be ruthless and brutal. I've always contained it, fearing who I'd turn into. I'm a good person and I will do good deeds, but that doesn't mean my mind doesn't know how to perform those evil acts. It's a choice. I will be ruthless to survive my stay at Misery Castle.

"Regina," is called out behind me as I leave the powder room.

I instantly recognize the nasal voice laced with pretention. Flipping around, "Cora," I appear welcoming and happy to see her, even if I'm anything but. Another reason to thank my Hillbrook education.

"*Mrs. Whittenhower,*" Cora reminds me with obvious annoyance and haughty arrogance. "You're an employee– nothing more. Don't get visions of you and Mr. Whittenhower falling in love and running off. It'll never happen." Cora's thin lips twist up into a disgusted smirk as she looks me over from head to toe. The expression on her pinched face says she finds me lacking.

"I believe since your husband will be fucking me in his bed, it's a bit too formal to call Grant Mr. Whittenhower, *Cora*." I stress her name on purpose.

I hate myself, I truly do. But nothing will stop the words from erupting from my mouth. No one. No one looks down their nose at me. Money means jack. I'm doing this bitch a favor at the expense of my own future happiness, only because I'm being coerced, which is a crime. Which makes Cora Spencer a criminal. Fuck her.

"Cora, don't look at me with that expression. If you find me ugly, then why would you want to raise my child as your own, when he will undoubtedly look just like me?" Leaning down, I get directly into her face. My four years at Hillbrook taught me some lessons other than academia. I can't let her see the smallest fissure in my resolve, or she will pounce on me.

"Your vulgarity isn't surprising, Regina, and highly distasteful," Cora says snidely, nose turned up like something stinks. "You're an employee, and you will call me Mrs. Whittenhower, Regina." My name rolls off her tongue like garbage bags thrown into a dumpster.

"Cunt," I hiss underneath my breath. "This poor, white trash mutt will be contributing half of your child's DNA." I taunt Cora, and impressively she ignores me. She continues to talk as if I hadn't just called her the c-word.

"I don't care what you call Grant while you're availing yourself to him, but in my presence only Mr. Whittenhower will fall from your lips. Do you understand me? I'm the one who will pay you," she threatens.

I shake my head at Cora. Leave it to her to think my currency is green. Maybe her conscience is lying by calling me a gold-digger instead of telling the truth. She's refusing to acknowledge I'm being coerced and forced to give up my children, and money doesn't even factor into the equation.

"First of all, any monies I'm paid will come from Whittenhower coffers, *Ms. Spencer*," I stress to make a point. "I'm the commodity you need. I'm not only providing you a service. I'm providing the entire Whittenhower name a service. Don't talk down to me when I'm doing something you're *incapable* of doing. The only name to fall from your lips better be Miss Regal. Do I make myself clear?" I back her up to the hallway wall with just the commanding intensity in my voice.

"Miss Regal," spits from between Cora's firm lips. With an about-face, her heels clack down the tile.

Pride swells my soul and runs through my veins. A smile forms on my lips. Even though none of this is fair, I'll do my damnedest to turn the tables on all of them.

My celebration is cut short when I sense the attention of someone. I whip around to see who is staring intently at me. Daniel is looking at me strangely from the doorway to the study. It's an equal mix of awe and fear.

I refuse to speak to Daniel, especially after everything that has gone down today. Instead, I home in on the one safe place I can think to go– Whitt's room. I can't face Ade or Grant yet, and I have no idea where my room is located.

I need a healthy dose of sunshine.

I stalk the second floor, both the left and right wings, looking for the lone door with the teddy bear plaque on it. I needn't have worried. Whitt's room is open and I can hear him humming to himself.

Glancing up with a dimple-inducing grin of welcome on his face, I take that as an invitation. I settle on the bed next to Whitt and look over his shoulder at his work.

"What do you have there?" I don't bother to paste a phony voice over my sad tone. I won't ever treat him like that.

"I like to draw, but Father doesn't approve." Whitt's so serious and formal, he sounds like a grown adult in a child's body.

I'll have to remember to ask Grant if Whitt knows who his biological father is, so I can make sure I don't fuck it all up. The use of '*Father*' has to be Daniel, because I instinctively know Grant would foster any passion of Whitt's.

I guess, and hope I'm right. "It's not about Daniel, now is it?" I breathe a sigh of relief when the little fellow doesn't correct me.

I look at the rendering of Whitt's family, and I note that I'm standing with Grant while holding Whitt's tiny hand. Adelaide is leaning into me, smiling happily. Priscilla's hands rest on Grant and Katie's shoulders. I deduce the handsome man next to Kate is Kent. Jackson and Daniel are bracketing Priscilla, with Cora's shadow standing off to the side. The symmetry is not lost on me. Whitt is a very astute child.

"Have you met Katherine? She's my oldest sister." Whitt's fingertip taps on Katie, and then on Kent. "She just got married." He gazes up at me with impossibly bright blue eyes as he speaks.

"Katie was a senior when I was a freshman," I mutter in reply, just now realizing Grant must have seen my walk of shame during orientation. He would have been a senior when I was fourteen. Just ending my eighth grade year, not knowing a single one of them, I had to walk into Hillbrook with my head held high knowing they didn't want the dirt poor scholarship kid staining their reputation the following school year. Grant had to have been present during my orientation– how did I miss him?

I can see the disconnect between Whitt and his family. The nearly twenty-year age gap must put a large strain on him, like he has multiple sets of parents and no true siblings. No grandparents. The little guy needs someone his own age inside Misery Castle.

Stop it, Regina! I shout inside my mind. *Don't let this child manipulate you into thinking it's okay to have a kid just to please him.*

Whitt flips the pages on his drawing pad until he comes to a blank one, and then he starts to draw again. I watch him in utter fascination as the pencil whispers across the paper, creating an intricate design.

"I guess I'm staying here with you for a while. Are you okay with that?" I know that Whitt's answer won't make a difference with my staying, but I'd feel better if he wanted me here.

Unlike his father, Whitt's face shows no emotion, but I can feel his annoyance tainting the air. "Father told me weeks ago that we were waiting for you to graduate, and that you would live with us after. After graduation, I waited for you during Adelaide's party, thinking you would show up, but you didn't. I finally gave up waiting." Whitt's voice is stormy, clouded with sadness, but then the sun comes out and he brightens. "Then you finally came this afternoon."

"My mom was sick, and I had to be with her." Without realizing it, my hand is rubbing soothing circles into Whitt's tiny back, and it's a comfort to me as much as it is to him. "That's why I didn't come, because she needed me. But I can guarantee I'll be here for the next five years. You'll be ten by then."

Wow, that really puts it in to perspective. If I manage to get pregnant immediately, I will spend over four years with my child. Will I watch over my children as they are mothered by another, as I act as their father's mistress, or will I be an active participant in their lives? What happens when the five years are up? Do I just leave my children behind?

I feel sick again, but I'm empty to the point I don't fear vomiting.

Breaking me out of my panic attack, "Eleven," Whitt murmurs quietly while he draws.

"What?"

"I'll be eleven in five years," he says matter-of-factly. "My sixth birthday was a few days after I met you back in May."

"Did you have a party?" I say in a bright voice, and surprisingly it isn't forced. I would love to hear the details, knowing there were happy times inside Misery Castle.

"No, only adults have parties." He shrugs and goes about his designing, not realizing his answer deflated me.

Seeing Whitt reinforces my resolve. I will do what I must to survive here, but I will escape eventually. I can't allow my children to live here, either. I'd take Whitt with me if I could.

"Miss Regal?" A smoky voice calls from the doorway. I peer up, expecting to see a grown woman and startle. A teenage Latino girl looks expectantly at me.

"Yes?" I ask in question.

"I'm to show you to your room," she says politely.

"Okay," I stand from the bed, and Whitt captures my hand, latching onto me before I can leave.

"Do you want me to go with you? I know how scary this house can be." Chivalrous, he looks at me like a little gentleman full of concern. Someday he'll be a very protective male.

I smile at Whitt, knowing I have to do this alone.

"No, thank you though." Unable to stop myself, I peck a kiss to each of his dimples. "Will you draw me something I can put in my room?" I squeeze his hand and smile at how the request brightens Whitt's eyes.

"I'll try really hard to make it special." Whitt crawls off his bed, and goes directly to his desk to fish around in his drawers, looking for something.

Even though Whitt decided his moniker should be Whitt, he named me Queen. It's only fair I bestow Whitt with an endearment of my own. "I'll see you in the morning, Sunshine. I'd read you a story tonight, but I'll be busy. Tomorrow– I promise."

I know Whitt hears me, but he's so absorbed with his task that he simply nods his blond head at me in reply.

Chapter Nineteen

"Young Master Daniel is a different little boy when he's around you," the girl whispers shyly as we walk the labyrinth of hallways. She makes the observation but doesn't elaborate, and I don't dare question her. After a minute, I recognize this area from when I was lost the last time I visited.

This isn't a visit, I have to remind myself.

Noticing my eyes darting around, imprinting the path from Whitt's bedroom to my destination, the girl gestures to a door, but ushers me into one next to it. "Master Grant requested that your room be adjoining," she mutters bashfully, blushing like she took a swift trip to Hades.

"How convenient," flows in the form of pure sarcasm from my lips.

Snorting, but trying to hide it, the girl opens the door. I walk into a large, pale gray room that's sparsely furnished with white-washed wood furnishings and lavender bedding. It's cold and utilitarian, and I instantly feel at home. Grant was smart not to regale me with too much stuff. I would have felt more bought and paid for than I already am.

"This door leads to Master Grant's rooms." She points out the door near the dresser.

My heart starts to beat out of control, a bead of sweat trickles down the nape of my neck, and my palms curl with a mixture of anger and fright. Jesus Christ, Grant wants easy access like I'm his goddamned mistress.

Aren't I?

Noticing my impending panic attack/destructive tantrum, the young girl soothes me with facts. "Master Grant had a deadbolt installed on your side of the door and the main door to the corridor."

She pulls a key from her pocket, and then hands it to me. I don't doubt for a second that there are several copies held by people in this household. I appreciate the gesture, but I will secure my doors further.

"What's your name?" I ask more than out of sheer curiosity, sick of calling her '*the girl*' inside my head.

I'd rather place my undivided attention on the girl than think about what I'll have to do inside this room– nightly. As much as I don't want to be pregnant, it will mean I won't have nightly duties for almost a year. I estimate that I'll have to lay with Grant only a handful of times if we're very fertile. I can handle that. I think.

The irony isn't lost on me. I tried with all my might not to end up like the girls in my neighborhood who make a living out of being pregnant, and yet…

"I'm Kristal Harris," she says meekly, but I can tell she's anything but.

Kristal is short and curvy, with coppery skin glowing with youth and health. She has the thickest hair I've ever seen– chocolate brown and luscious. I wonder where the ideal comes from that tall, blonde, blue-eyed, pale, and sickly-thin is attractive. It's an ideal that both Ade and Fate have aspired to reach. I couldn't care less. I'd rather look like the girl standing before me. Kristal Harris will be stunning when she's a grown woman. Too bad Ade and Fate will be showcased in society while this lovely girl will be hidden in the shadows of their castle.

Why can't we just accept who we are and stop trying to fit into someone else's perception of perfection? It would be a travesty if Kristal bleached her hair, and on the same token, Fate would look ridiculous with brown locks.

"Hi, Kristal. Please, call me Regina." I shake her hand, and she acts as if she's never had anyone use the gesture on her. I gaze at her quizzically as she stares open-mouthed at our joined hands.

Flustered, "I really shouldn't call you that," she mutters in a rush as I release her hand.

"Who will know?" I whisper conspiratorially, nudging her with my shoulder. "May I ask what you're doing here?"

"I'm your personal maid," she smiles sweetly, but her discomfort is showing in the strain around her pouty lips. "May I turn down your bedding and draw you a bath this evening?"

Kristal moves toward the king-sized bed that takes up the majority of the room. Lavender bedding lies like a cloud on the white-washed wooden frame. The headboard has ironwork inlaid into the wood, creating a sunburst pattern. It's the most beautiful thing I've ever seen, and I know right away that Grant picked it out.

It's as creepy as it is sweet.

"No, Kristal. I'll do those things myself. How old are you, sweetie? Why are you here?" I ask her again. I stay her hand as she pulls the coverlet down, and then I sit on the edge of the mattress and wait for her response.

Kristal looks surprised that I care. Her brow furrows as she decides on whether or not she should answer. "I'm fifteen," comes after a long pause, as if she never talks of herself. "This is what I do, Miss Regal. I'm a maid. My mom is the head housekeeper. Martha Harris. Whittenhower Estates is where I live." Her forehead scrunches up in confusion, and it only makes her all the more devastating.

"Don't you go to school?" I wouldn't put it past the Whittenhowers to use slave labor.

"I'm tutored, but most of my training is with the keeping of the house." Kristal tries to fold the sheet down, but my large ass is in her way. I don't move.

"Listen, I won't use you as my maid."

Kristal backs up as if I've struck her. "Did I do something wrong, Miss Regal? Do you want someone else?" She tries to hide that she's offended, but it's etched across her pretty face. Her hazel eyes flood with watery tears.

"No– no, it's not that." I hold my palm out to Kristal, wanting to take that tragic look off her face, yet not knowing how. "I want to do for myself. We'll just say you did it, but I'll do it myself. I'd rather we just spend time together than you cleaning up after me."

"Oh," Kristal looks confused by the suggestion, but I know she'll comply. Subservience is imprinted in her DNA. Yet her skittish demeanor screams she doesn't truly trust my motives– smart girl.

"I'll show you that I mean it, and I'm glad that you don't immediately trust me," I praise her.

I stand up, and then fold the sheet down myself. I locate two doors on the inside wall, and guess which one is the closet. I guess wrong. Inside is the bath. The room is the size of the living room at my old, rundown apartment.

Was it really just a few hours ago when I left that world behind?

In order to deal with the shift, I compartmentalize my old life and dive head-first into my new one. Dwelling on it won't change a goddamn thing, even if I do feel like I'm out of my element.

My new bathroom is like paradise– soft blue and frothy white. I've never seen a Jacuzzi tub before. This one isn't really mine, but

I'm renting it for the next five years with the product of my womb as currency. I might as well put the bathtub to good use.

I know my face shows the unadulterated lust I feel for the biggest bathtub I've ever seen, and I feel no shame for it either. "I think I'll take a bath," I drawl in a throaty voice that doesn't sound like my own.

I caress the goose-neck faucet as if it's my first lover. I blush bright red when I realize what salacious act I'm mimicking. I mustn't fall in love and jerk off inanimate objects. I vow to buy a tub like this with my own money in the future. A girl should have a few frivolous things to enjoy.

"I'll need something to sleep in…" I trail it off as a question. I have no clue how to operate the tub, or if I have any clothing for that matter. I try and fail to forget the memory of my blouse spinning 'round and 'round on the tire as the car drove away, losing it like a piece of trash nearly a block later.

"Would you like me to do it, or just show you how?" Hesitant, Kristal asks me of the various knobs on the side of the Jacuzzi. Her hazel eyes glow with amusement. Miss Smarty Pants Regal is a moron when it comes to the rich and famous.

I can rebuild a television set with my eyes closed and one hand tied behind my back, but I can't figure out a bathtub. I laugh good naturedly at my plight, and Kristal smirks with me, but she's still unsure if she's welcome to laugh too.

Kristal shows me how to work everything and lectures me on how I'm not to add too much soap or bubbles will cover the bathroom floor. After imprinting her instructions to memory, I do as she said.

While the deep tub is filling with warm water, I follow Kristal to a pocket-door that is nearly hidden by an orgy-sized shower stall that's larger than my old bathroom. She slides the door open, revealing a walk-in closet filled with clothing, and I hope to God they didn't belong to Grant's last mistress.

Ignoring that horrific thought, I concentrate on the facts. I would have guessed wrong on door number two inside my bedroom being the closet.

"Where does the other door out there in my bedroom lead?" I ask of the door in question.

"It's the nursery," Kristal says matter-of-factly, trying her damnedest not to pass judgment. I can tell it makes her feel awkward because I feel awkward.

Questions I should never ask, as the answers would probably have me committing multiple homicides, sit on my tongue: was this Gwen's room? Was that Whitt's nursery? Did these clothes belong to Gwen? Was that bed and all the furnishings picked out for the woman Grant is pining after?

Am I just a replacement for the original?

I sigh heavily. Well, on that note...

"Could you give Grant a message from me? Tell him to be here in an hour." Kristal's pouty mouth drops open in astonishment.

"Master Grant is a very nice man. Patient and kind." My request seems to have Kristal spouting Grant's virtues. "He won't force you. If you're not ready, he'll understand. He'll give you all the time you need." Her voice trembles with concern.

It's bizarre. I'm three years older than Kristal, and she's talking to me as if she's the one with more experience, and I can tell she's being genuine.

I believe that Grant would give me time. Not five years' worth, but at least a few weeks. I can't afford to wait, because I don't want to do this after I've formed an attachment to Grant. I have no doubt that his plan is slow seduction, until I'm so enamored his manipulations would look like love and caring. While it may be more palatable versus the truth, it's total bullshit. I won't follow the path of my fellow teenage stupid girls from my old neighborhood.

"I'm not a procrastinator. If I wait, it will fester in my mind and drive me crazy. I'm ready," I utter courageously, and I feel strong in my decision. Even if it's the worst decision I've ever made, it's the only choice I can make. I might as well get it over with. Tonight.

"It's not so bad after the first time." Kristal leaves the closet and walks back into the bathroom, and I follow behind her.

"You're not? I mean, you've done it before?" I gasp in astonishment. "You're just a kid."

If I was a young guy, I'd go nuts around Kristal– any man would. Nausea overtakes me in a rush as an unwelcome thought pops into my head. What if it was Daniel, or Jackson, or Grant who banged Kristal? My resolve shatters, and the fight-or-flight reflex pours through my body with a vengeance.

Panicked, heart beating uncontrollably, I need to get out of here. Now!

"Whoa! Regina! It's not what you think." Kristal's hands are surprisingly strong on my upper arms. Her fingernails bite into my skin, and the pain drives my panic away. "Grant's a nice guy and all, but I'd never touch him that way. He's like my big brother–gross."

"Grant's a smoking hot big brother," I remind Kristal, and my rabid response has her grinning like a Cheshire cat.

"I work and live here, but I do have a life outside of Whittenhower Estates." Kristal's grin turns naughty with a sexual edge. "Mistress Priscilla is big on charity, so my mother drags me around. I met a guy down at the community outreach center–Transcend. Do you know the place?"

"Yeah, it's just a few blocks from where I live– well, where I lived as of late this afternoon. I used to go to Transcend almost every day before I had to work all the time."

I take a cleansing breath, and then another, and then another, until I'm finally calm again. I clamp down on the thoughts trying to flit around in my brain. Memories of my dad and mom having us volunteer to feed the homeless on Thanksgiving when I was ten. All the memories after that involve my mom, right down to how excited she was when I was given a scholarship to Hillbrook because my presence at Transcend was noticed.

Okay, so I can't seem to turn the memories off, but Kristal's one-track mind when it comes to sex helps distract me.

"It was uncomfortable the first time, but it didn't really hurt. It gets *a lot* better after that." Hazel eyes glowing, Kristal turns animated as she describes sex– fucking bizarre. "There's nothing to fear. Grant is too much of a gentleman to hurt you," she tries to reassure me. "You take the lead, and he'll follow."

I hear Kristal's reassurances, but it falls on deaf ears. All I can see is this beautiful, bright girl before me, falling into the same trap as the rest of the girls I grew up with. Tragic.

"You're not in love with him or something, are you? Are you safe?" I ask in real concern. I've only known Kristal for a few minutes, but I feel a real connection to her. She's someone who also walks the fine line between two classes– dirt poor and filthy rich.

"Nah," she laughs, warming to me as my mother-hen attitude reaches an all-time high. "He was just my first. There have been two others since. Once you start having sex, it can be addictive. If it's good sex anyway," she teases. "I'm always safe. I won't let a few minutes of pleasure fuck up my future. Just my luck, it'd be the time it's dull that I get knocked up or pick up an STD. It wouldn't be worth it."

Talk of knocked up and STDs has me shuddering in terror. Shit! We can't use condoms if the result has to go inside me. Is Grant clean?

Kristal reaches over to turn off the spigot, then she taps a few buttons and the jets come to life, creating a whirlpool. Mesmerized, I stare longingly at the churning water.

"You don't have to do it tonight, ya know?" She tries to dissuade me again.

"Tell Grant one hour," I command, unable to stop myself from turning bossy. "I'll be ready. I *am* ready," I say to convince myself more so than Kristal.

I toe my sneakers off and strip out of my thrift shop trousers and blouse. I pull off my ratty underthings with a shrug. I'm sure Kristal will see me naked many times as my pseudo-maid.

Kristal doesn't look away. Her eyes take in every imperfection on my six-foot-tall body: my thick thighs, the paunch that developed as I sat vigil by my mother's bedside, the excess hair all over my body because razors are a luxury I couldn't afford, and finally she comes to rest on my wild, out-of-control hair. I put the straw in strawberry blond.

Without comment or judgment, Kristal hands me a fresh razor—no plastic, disposable razors for a Whittenhower Estates resident. No, it's stainless steel and super sharp. I idly wonder if Kristal has one like it, or if the servants have different living conditions?

I was so dang poor, I couldn't afford cheap Bic. Using disposables from the Dollar Store, I only shaved during the semesters we had P.E. My mandatory knee socks hid my hairy legs the rest of the time.

I slowly sink into the whirling water and sigh out in pleasure. My God! It's the best sensation I've ever felt, warm and intoxicating. The jets of water beat against muscles I didn't even know were sore.

"Ah… Kristal, this is incredible." I moan softly as I close my eyes in delight.

"My mom and I always see who can beat the other to the tub every night after our duties. I usually win since she's called out for all kinds of things at odd hours." I can hear the smile hidden in Kristal's voice.

I guess that answers my question: only the best at Whittenhower Estates.

"Soak for at least a half hour before you shave. It will soften the coarse hair. Here is something Miss Whittenhower picked up for you." Kristal hands me two bottles. Real glass. Shampoo and conditioner that promise to tame my frizzy hair.

"Sleek," I mutter with much skepticism. "We'll see. I'd even take curly or kinky. It does nothing but fuzz." Self-deprecating, I make fun of myself.

"A flat iron would help. I'll show you tomorrow." I study Kristal's silky locks, and wonder if she uses an iron on it. Doubtful.

"I'll get you a nightgown, and then go tell Master Grant you wish to see him in forty-five minutes."

I say thank you to Kristal's back as she disappears into the pocket-door to the closet. I close my eyes and try to push away thoughts of the duty I'll be performing in forty-five minutes.

If I do it right, Grant won't last long. I just don't have any experience to know what right is.

Chapter Twenty

After a bath, a session with the sharpest razor I've ever held, and sliding into a nightgown that was most definitely purchased for me, I feel like a different woman than the one who arrived a few hours earlier.

Nice things are nice, but that doesn't mean deep down inside I'm not a smoldering fire of pissed off. But I'm a practical person, and I know when I've been cornered. My mind spun my situation around and around until I was able to find a resolution that I could live with.

There are members of the Whittenhower family I truly care about, so spending time with them will not be a hardship, including Grant. My future children will definitely have all the things I've never had, and I don't mean in the materialistic sense. It will be my sole focus to make sure they learn the lessons my parents taught me. As long as I'm in this house, I will be their mother, Cora be damned.

Grant is easily bent, and with the Whittenhower heir in my belly, I'll be able to bulldoze right over the rest of the Whittenhowers. I best be pregnant the majority of my stay, or I'll be quite literally fucked.

I clear away the thoughts of replacing Gwen. After the jealousy faded, I realized I've never met another woman my size, so there is no way in hell these clothes were purchased for anyone but me.

I smooth my hands down the front of my virgin white, silk nightgown. Who knew a woman could feel secure behind such flimsy armor? I'm embarrassed by the lack of fabric holding my breasts, because they're far too big for the lacy bodice. I've seen all eyes seeking my tits when I walk by, so I best use the only sexual weapon in my arsenal to my advantage.

Gazing into the floor-length mirror, I look at myself and try not to see all my many imperfections. With a heavy sigh, I leave the bathroom, ignoring how nerves are causing all of my muscles to shake as if I'm freezing.

Gazing around the bedroom, noting things I missed during the first tour, I think Grant stood me up because he isn't on the bed lying naked with cock in hand while growling like a rabid animal. After never having a boyfriend, or even a guy interested in me, I don't know what to expect, but I surely didn't expect what I see.

Like a gentleman, with his hands folded in his lap, Grant's sitting in a chair while wearing a black bathrobe with black and gray striped pajama bottoms on underneath. The robe is belted tightly into place with a peek of white t-shirt at the neck.

The corner of my lips lift infinitesimally because Grant looks more terrified than I feel. "Hi," I whisper when he finally looks up at me.

Grant returns my meek *hi* with one of his own. Cheeks flooding with pink, he ducks his head, watching me through the fall of his white-blond hair. Blue eyes darken as he studies me from beneath his lashes.

I'm the virgin, and Grant's the one acting coy.

With great effort, I stifle a laugh.

"We don't have to do this tonight." Grant shifts in the chair, his movements betraying his words. The boy looks ready to burst from his own skin. "We could just get to know each other better. I don't want to rush you." His usually smooth voice is rough and raspy. He clears his throat a few times, but I stop him before he can say more.

"I'm ready." Walking across the bedroom to the bed, I truly mean it.

"Regina—"

"Grant," I retort, all fear dissolving in an instant. I'm dealing with Grant Whittenhower. The guy is harmless, easily manipulated, and all mine to play with.

"The nightgown is gorgeous— you're gorgeous." Grant shifts in his chair again. Is he ready to bolt from the room?

Words are pulled from my throat in a voice I don't dare call my own, and I have no idea what's come over me. "Did you pick it out?" I smooth my hands down the silky fabric as I ask.

For some bizarre reason, I want it to be Grant who picked it out. It would mean less if someone else had. I want to know the silk slid between his fingers as he thought of me wearing this gown.

Eyes casting downward to gaze at his hands, "Yes, I picked it out," he murmurs bashfully.

Grant's response hits me directly between the thighs, and I clench my muscles from the sensation. I nearly moan. Has this idiot not had sex since he was fifteen? Sixteen? He's acting like the virgin, and I suddenly feel like a predator, which is oddly turning me on.

"We can wait, Regina." He tries to make this right between us. It's a wrong situation; there is no right.

"Grant," I groan out in mystification. Can't this man see that I'm ready? "When was the last time you had sex?"

Startled, he bolts upright in the chair. "What?"

"You're acting like a virgin, when I know you're not."

"Well, at least you didn't call me a pussy." A smirk tugs at my lips when the fire in Grant's words reaches me. "Six years and nine months ago, give or take a few days– Gwen, obviously. When we got married six months ago, Cora and I never consummated it because she has female issues– that's why she was having tests run beforehand."

Taken aback, "Jesus. Why not have sex with her?"

Pinning me with his stare, "Have you met my wife?" Grant mutters sarcastically.

"Yeah, okay. I get that." My words are trailed by a chuckle. "I mean, you just turned twenty-three. I thought all guys your age were horny bastards."

"We are." Grant turns, refusing to look at me. In profile, his cheek is crimson. "My sperm is worth a billion dollars, Regina."

Head jerking back, peals of laughter spill from between my lips. "I-I-I... damn–" I'm laughing so hard I can't get the words out. "Should I be thanking you? Putting your sperm into my womb is like drinking champagne out of a store-brand Solo cup."

With narrowed eyes, Grant glares at me, but his lips are trying their damnedest not to curve into a smile. "Did you ever wonder why your Hillbrook classmates weren't screwing each other?"

"Fear of having six-fingered children?" I tease, leaning my hip against the dresser. I don't want to enjoy razzing Grant, but I do. I always thought the non-legacy freshman fish were to clean the gene pool.

"Probably." Grant rumbles a chuckle. "You're more right than you realize. My son has too many siblings, and only the oldest two know it. Thank God, the boy is probably gay so he won't impregnate his sisters."

"I'm not stupid, Grant. Whitt taught me how to eavesdrop, so I've met all of Whitt's siblings I bet, and the odds of him ever lying with his sisters is zilch, even if he's straight. Major age gap, there.

Which means Gwen is a lot older than you– why would a grown woman be with a young boy?"

Swallowing thickly, "Correct you are," Grant allows, shock written across his features. "There are rules all of us must abide by. We have to keep the money in the founding families. We're not allowed to just marry someone because they could be after our money, or they could have been sent to spy on the family. We're smart enough not to fuck around because condoms break and girls lie about being on birth control, then we have some greedy woman controlling our children. Our legacy. Dominion relies on us, and we can't let it fall into unworthy hands."

"Guess I passed the greedy, unworthy hands test," I tease, finding this entire conversation ludicrous. But the logical part of me understands. "That's not very fun, now is it? Cheap trash like me has more freedom than you do."

"Truth," Grant mumbles, then a horrified expression etches across his face when he realizes how that sounded. "Not that– not that you're trash, Regina. You're not. But you do have more freedom than I do, even when you're trapped in Misery Castle."

"Relax." I smile to show I'm not offended. "You can grovel better than most, I'll give you that. So the horny rich teenagers are told to abstain– that works real well where I come from. The more abstinence is pushed, the more sex is had. My stairwell was called the devirginator. Stepping over fornicating teenagers is what had me abstaining."

"Accidents happen," Grant admits, but then he turns green around the gills. "Catholic or not, our legacies matter. All of our parents act like Jackson and Daniel. Pragmatic and brutal. Let's just say, if you fall in love and knock your girlfriend up, your girlfriend will be shipped halfway across the country after your father cuts her a check for having an abortion. It's best to toe the line, or you'll end up hating your parents and having a broken heart."

"Seriously?" Voice tight with barely suppressed fury, I spit the words in Grant's direction. "You guys are fucking animals."

"I told you I wasn't cut out for this life," Grant nearly whines. "I made the mistake of falling in love with the woman sent to give me an heir. I do believe Gwen genuinely enjoyed our time together, but it's been no contact since, even when I'm face-to-face with her." Wearing a tortured expression, Grant rubs a palm over his face. "Regina, that was an amicable arrangement– imagine one that wasn't."

"You mean like ours?" I say just to be a cunt. Wincing, Grant looks ready to cry. "I'm sorry. If the guy I was supposed to have kids with was anyone but you, this would go down differently. I'd be in prison for shearing off your billion dollar nutsack. But you're Grant, and I can't imagine anyone who wouldn't find you charming and enjoy spending time with you. No matter how hard I've tried, I can't seem to be mad at you."

"Sorry," he mutters. "I understand how difficult this is. Trust me on that. This is round two for me, and there will *never* be a round three." Sometimes the turbulent emotions flashing over Grant's face terrify me, like he'd harm himself.

Voice stiff with fear, "What do you mean?"

"After Jackson's gone, my obligation to the family is finished. I'll be able to go, knowing my children will be better for the legacy than I ever was. I've– my only purpose was this, Regina." Face a mask of indifference, but nothing could overshadow the agony written beneath, Grant gestures to us and then the bed. "Not that being with you will be a hardship. I want you to know that. I really do want you."

"Because you're a twenty-year-old guy who's gone far too long without sex?" I tease to lighten the mood, understanding Grant more.

My parents are gone. My father was my rock, but becoming my mother's lifeline saved me from sinking. Grant is dependent on his dying father, whereas no one is dependent on him because of his nature. Without Jackson, Grant's entire identity dissolves.

We're going to change that, starting tonight.

Speechless, Grant really doesn't have a clue how to respond when I twist his words and toss them back at him. It's no wonder Jackson and Daniel walk right over him. I must be sick in the head, because I enjoy the fact that I fluster Grant, and a teensy tiny part of me wants Grant to be dependent on me.

"I'm ready," I repeat again, even more sure about it than the first time I said it.

"I don't know," Grant hesitates. "Isn't it too soon? You're a virgin, and I wanted to seduce you into enjoying this with me. This should be good for the both of us, not just me."

I want to say that seduction won't be necessary, but what comes out instead surprises us both. "Get on the bed, Grant." I order, husky and forceful. His pupils dilate as he finally reads the naked hunger etched on my face. No, it's not hunger– starvation.

I enjoyed our couch grind session way too much. Like a drug, I forgot everything for a few minutes, and for someone like me whose brain never shuts down, that's a gift.

"Don't forget the robe," I remind Grant as he drags a knee onto the mattress.

I watch in utter fascination, as if everything is moving in slow motion. Grant tosses the robe to the chair he just vacated. A rough gasp is torn from my throat when I see the front of his pajama pants. I've never seen an aroused guy, and Grant is *very* aroused. Thighs clenching against the need spawned at the sight, I whimper.

Grant's eyes dart downward to check out what I'm looking at. Taking in the tent outlining his cock, he swallows roughly in reply.

"Take off your shirt and lie down on the bed," I command.

Empowered. High on the control I wield over a very pliant Grant. I don't know where my courage is coming from, but something deep inside of me is awake and roaring for obedience. I'll do this tonight, but on my own terms. I've been starving for weeks on end, and I'm about to feast.

Puffs of air fleeing parted lips, Grant is breathing so hard his chest is rapidly rising and falling. He looks at me for direction, making sure this is what I want. Reassured, he quickly tugs on the back of his t-shirt, and then lifts it over his head.

Fascinated, my eyes follow the wake of the white fabric as it reveals Grant's flawless skin. Fingertips shaking, I long to trace the pathways of his flesh.

In the blink of an eye, I'm breathing just as fast as Grant. He's an inch or two shorter than me, but he makes up for that in lean, corded muscle. Now I'm the one who's swallowing roughly.

Made confident by my reaction, Grant looks at me again, and then does as I asked. As he lies down on the bed, I can't take my eyes from the front of his pants.

I'm in big trouble.

Grant lies flat on his back, hands clasped over his chest, patiently watching me. His eyes track my every movement, but he's otherwise still. I crawl up the foot of the bed and sit on my heels near his calves.

"How do you want to do this?" His voice quivers with need.

"Put your hands on the headboard. I can't have you touch me yet." My eyes bulge out as the commanding words spill– words that flow from my mouth that I didn't even think. I don't know where they're coming from, but they demand escape.

Intimidated, Grant looks confused and worried, but he doesn't say anything as he wraps his fingers around a wrought-iron finial inlaid in the headboard. He bites his lip, then looks wide-eyed at me.

Lost in arousal, "Come up here and let me taste you," voice dripping with need. "My face belongs to you– ride it!"

"No," I utter sharply, shocked because I always thought guys did that as a means to an end, but Grant's genuinely going insane for it.

Head cocking to the side, "Never?" He arches his perfectly groomed eyebrow, voice laced heavily with surprise and a healthy dose of disappointment.

"No," I say softer this time. "I don't want to do that while I'm still a virgin. That isn't something virgins should do."

"Who says?" Grant challenges me.

"You can munch to your heart's content after we get my virginity out of the way." What the fuck, why do I keep saying shit like that? Whose voice is flowing from my mouth?

"How will I make you ready if I can't touch you at all?" Grant lifts his head up so he can see me better, but doesn't let go of his handhold. "I don't want to hurt you."

"That won't be a problem," I assure Grant. I clench my thighs together on the bead of moisture that's trickling down my skin. The more he complies, the wetter I get.

"I brought some lubricant if you'd like to use it." He turns his head to the side and glances pointedly at the nightstand.

How presumptuous yet thoughtful.

Watching Grant hang onto the metal ornamentation, obeying me without question while looking so uncertain, it has me blooming. I want him. Good God, where are these thoughts coming from?

I rasp, "It won't hurt. I made sure of it, because I didn't want my first time to hurt. Taken care of– no fear."

"What do you mean?" Grant stares at me with curiosity and no judgment, while holding onto the headboard as if it's his favorite pastime.

How do I explain my habitual masturbation? *How?*

I rattle off before I can stop myself, "I've fingered myself since I was like… four or five."

Mouth parting, Grant releases a whimper while shifting on the mattress. Voice gruff, losing all its smoothness, "No shame in that. I have a constant need to get off, and I can't deny the urge. If I'm not working, my hand is wrapped around my cock, but sometimes I multitask."

"It's the only way I can shut my brain off," I reluctantly admit.

"Same here," Grant commiserates. "But that doesn't explain how losing your virginity won't hurt, Regina." Tilting his head to the side, he decides if it's worth the risk to go on. I nod so he will. "Rubbing your clit isn't the same as having a cock pounding into you. Over and over. God–"

Front tooth digging into his pouty bottom lip, my mind takes a vacation as I watch the sexy as fuck expressions scroll across Grant's face. Body flowing in a wave, he never once relinquishes his hold on the headboard.

Grant's reaction has me spilling more than I should. "When I was fourteen, I penetrated myself with a curling iron," flows rapidly without any command from my brain. My hand flies up to cover my mouth as my deepest, darkest secret spills unbidden. I blush bright red against the pale white of my nightgown.

"I don't understand." Grant's brows draw together in confusion.

"Two reasons: one, I was curious to know what it felt like, and ended up getting addicted to fucking myself on the curling iron. I've done it for years– it was my *me* time, where I'd shut myself in the bathroom. No guys did it for me, but I was horny all the time. The curling iron probably saved me from turning out like the rest of the girls in my building."

"Regina–" Grant's voice cracks, and then one hand flies off the headboard to cup the tent in his pants. "No more of that story until after we've both had a dozen orgasms."

"Hand," I remind him, simply because I like watching his dick jerk in his pants and his hand is blocking the view.

With a pinched expression, Grant slowly removes his hand, and then wraps his fingers around the finial like a good boy. I can't tear my eyes away from the growing damp spot on the front of his pajama pants, remembering how much more came out after our grinding session.

It was so goddamn warm against the seat of my panties…

"Regina?" Grant reminds me there's more to him than the imprint of his dick against his pants. "You said two reasons."

"Oh, yeah." I blink, catching Grant's satisfied grin in my periphery. "How much does that set me back?" I mutter saucily, pointing at his ever-growing wet spot. "On the streets, I'm guessing an ounce of Whittenhower juice is priceless."

Head hitching backward, Grant loses his shit. God, he's gorgeous when he lets go like that. Pale skin, sad blue eyes, he always looks on the verge of slitting his wrists if you're mean to him. I feel good making Grant feel good.

"That's why there's a strict no blowjob and handjob policy. A few years ago, one of the founders caught a woman spitting his jizz into a cup for *later*. Another time a woman tried to steal the used condom, and no good came of that. Our fathers teach us to keep our dicks in our pants, and to make sure what's in our nuts stays in our nuts."

"No grinding?" I tease, smirking. "Because you left some Whittenhower Gold behind on my underwear."

"I know– I wanted you to have it." Movement catches my eye, fingers white-knuckling the headboard. Sobering, Grant pins me with his melancholy stare. "It's lonely, and I've had to make concessions. I've had two mates since birth, but they're related. One has no issue cuddling while we jerk ourselves off."

"What?" I squawk, finding that strangely hot. My mind takes a vacation as I envision it, trying to remember what Julio looked like when he was sucking face with one of his dealers.

'Related mates' has a ping going off in my head– Rebekah Zeitler's grandsons. "The fuckface who took away my scholarship, or the assmunch who's building the gothic nightmare for all to see? I'm guessing Mr. Velvet Whorehouse. He seems to have a good sense of humor, since he has no problem making fun of himself."

Grant's smile is back, just as I was trying to achieve. "Fuckface," he says with a straight face. "I love pussy, and he's something, but I don't know what. It's strictly platonic, enjoying the connection and intimacy. He's tried to exchange grips during, but no fucking way."

Popping an eyebrow in question, "Homophobic, are ya?"

"No, straight." Grant doesn't even blink. "I wanted to keep my hard-on, not give him his jollies. I have a mind like a steel trap, Regina. Quit trying to distract me and answer the second part of why you used the curling iron in the first place."

"Fine!" My eyes seek the ceiling, simultaneously hating and loving the fact that Grant caught me on my crap. "Reason two: my friends were losing their virginity in droves. I heard lots of stories about how a guy will know if you're virgin or not by how you feel inside, and whether or not you bleed. So I took care of it." I clamp my lips shut and growl. I didn't want to tell Grant this, so why is it coming out of my lips?

"In my limited experience, I don't know if that's true or not." Grant mulls that over for a bit. "But I really don't see why it should matter, unless you're a guy who wants a rough fuck and doesn't want to harm your partner."

"Oh, it matters in the hood," I drawl. "Being pure is a blessing and a curse where I come from. The honest, good guys won't sleep with a virgin, fearing you'll want them to take care of you for life it they have sex with you. Then there are the guys who prey on virgins because popping cherries gets them off."

"Human sexuality is a fascination of mine since a few people close to me are not what you'd consider the norm. In my research, I've seen just about everything, and sadly, there are men who prey on virgins."

"I know," slips past my lips, voice cutting with violence. "I penetrated myself with a curling iron to save myself from a few assholes who lived on my block. It hurt like hell, and I bled. I did it night after night until it started to feel good."

I bite my tongue. SHUT UP, REGINA!

Studying me, Grant doesn't look at me with judgment, and it loosens my tongue, no matter how hard I may be biting it.

"When I first moved to the shithole part of Dominion, I was harassed constantly for wearing my uniform home from school. One day, while I was walking home, two guys from my building cornered me in the alley. Everyone had their panties in a wad, saying I was a goody-two-shoes who thought I was better than everyone else. They assumed I was a virgin, and got off on tainting my lily white ass– wanted to knock me off my pedestal."

The creaking of the bedframe draws my attention. Grant's white-knuckling a finial, and I notice it's loosened from the wooden headboard. I hope he doesn't destroy the artistry with what I have to say next.

"I was terrified." Lost in the past, my voice warbles. "One of them held me down on the pavement behind a dumpster, while the other shoved his hand up my skirt. He sank three fingers inside of me, and when he didn't meet resistance, he stopped." Gulping, I pretend it didn't happen to me, while learning how to make sure it never happens again. "Pissed off, they started kicking and punching me while I fought back. The whole time they demanded to know who I was having sex with. I told them it was Roman, and he was going to kill them for assaulting me. On the fly, it was the best threat I could think of."

"Was the threat effective?" Grant grits out from between clenched teeth.

"Yeah." I nod my head as I speak, still reeling from the surprise of it working out. "Afterward, everyone assumed I was Roman's girl, and they left me alone. Without ever discussing it, Roman went along with it. That's why Julio calls him Romeo."

"I will have to thank your Roman someday, somehow," Grant muses, talking to himself, not me.

"So– yeah, that's why I know it won't hurt when we–" I swallow audibly, feeling awkward. "When we have sex, it won't hurt. I'm still a virgin, just a hymen-free one."

Innocent versus jaded, the dual sides of my personality clash. I blush so brightly my skin tightens and prickles as if I just caught fire. While at the same time, part of me is feeling brazen and in control. It's discombobulating.

"What happened to those men?" Grant asks so coldly a shiver works its way along my spine.

"They apologized to Roman immediately, but he didn't know what they were talking about because I hadn't caught up to him yet. The next day, I came home from school, and Roman called me into the alley. He held the bastards down on the dirty pavement while I kicked them with my penny loafers." My face splits into a huge, sadistic grin as I relive all the emotions that struck me on that day.

Vengeance is exhilarating.

"My shoes had metal tips on the toes, and they were most excellent at bruising ribs and smashing balls. I was bothered a few more times after that, but eventually I grew up. A pissed off, six-foot-tall girl in a Catholic schoolgirl uniform with wild hair is a scary sight."

"I'm rather fond of Hillbrook's uniform," he murmurs softly, affection coloring his voice.

Grant displays his dimples, and I can't help but smile back because I'm struck dumb by the sight. Pretty boy Whittenhower has a bloodthirsty side that's calling to me, making me hot when it should terrify me.

"I'm proud of you. I don't know how anyone couldn't be. Your strength amazes me as much as it intimidates me. Your will to survive and your instincts are incredible to behold." Grant looks *at* me instead of through me, and it makes me want to cower. I don't.

Instead, I hold his gaze back. I don't bask in his praise, because I take it as it was meant. Grant's being real with me, showing me how he really feels, and I won't make it less or more than it was given.

Reaching down with sure fingertips, I tug Grant's pajama pants at the waistband. He lifts his hips, never taking his hands from the headboard, and my respect for him grows. After a bit of an awkward struggle, I pull the pants off him, and then toss them with the shirt and robe.

The entire time, I never take my eyes off Grant's crotch.

Grant lies before me completely naked, and my eyes devour the sight. He trusts me enough to make himself vulnerable. He's gorgeous: smooth, flawless skin covering taut muscles. I can't believe that Grant wants to have sex with me– this smart, witty, handsome, affluent man wants me.

The situation is absolutely wrong, but there's no denying the power I feel knowing that he desires me. I could get all girly and think that it's my looks or that he wants me more than his wife, and this somehow means I'm better than every woman on the planet. But I know that Grant just needs me. It's illogical and has nothing to do with looks or station in life. Something unexplainable attracts me to him and him to me. Knowing that we may or may not make a child tonight adds to the thrill.

"You're big." I moisten my lips with my tongue. "I mean, are you big? You look it to me, but I've never seen an aroused guy before." I blush harder than I ever have.

"Does it matter?" Grant murmurs, light and teasing.

"I'm just curious." Suddenly bashful, I turn my face away.

"Am I bigger than your curling iron?" Grant taunts, his blue eyes twinkle in the light.

"Yes." I trail a laugh. "Are you the average?"

"Ah– yes. Scholarship Girl rears her head, I see. I don't know." He tries to shrug, but leaves his hands on the finials.

"Come on! You're a guy. You have to know if you are or aren't. I'm guessing you aren't, since you're being so closed-lipped." I tease him back. I scrunch up my lips and pout. I really want to know for some bizarre reason.

"How about you, Regina. Are you average?" Eyes zeroing in on my hard nipples, Grant leers at my breasts.

"Nope– not average. I'm a double D– cup size is a no brainer. We walk around with our boobs on display no matter how hard we try to cover them up. Guys are luckier."

Leaning forward, until suddenly his warm breath caresses my chest, "I'd love to see you in your Hillbrook uniform with your blouse unbuttoned to your waist. I would devour those healthy tits of yours. I nearly spill thinking of our son heartily nursing at your nipples," rapidly pours out from between his lips in a deep, husky voice.

I suck in a gasp as I envision Grant's fantasy, clenching my thighs against the ache his voice creates.

We stare at each other, frozen in need.

Grant's eyes darken, pupils blown from arousal and need. The tip of his penis beads with moisture and turns ruddy. The veins bulge and beat with his heartrate. I don't know if it's the thought of me nursing or of me having his child that arouses him, but if he's turned on, so am I.

"The average is around six inches, and you can't fathom how big one can get. Cunt-rippers. After hanging around my friends, I should be self-conscious. But Dexter complains how he hurts women on accident, and Marc... he has issues. Anyway, I'm a modest eight and a quarter inches long." He announces proudly, chest puffing out.

"I knew it– ya liar. All men measure their dicks. I bet that quarter inch makes a *huge* difference," I tease with a roll of my eyes.

"You'll find out as soon as you scream my name in ecstasy," Grant rasps out roughly. "That quarter inch will drive you to heights your curling iron couldn't possibly reach."

"Challenge accepted," I whisper while meeting his gaze.

Heart beating out of control, adrenaline coursing through my veins, Regina Regal has huge motherfucking metaphorical balls.

Shifting on the mattress, I straddle Grant's hips. No nerves. No shaking. No fear. This is Grant, and I'm the one in charge. Grinding, it feels the same as before because fabric is acting as a barrier. Finding my nightgown in the way, I roughly tear at it until it no longer separates our pelvises. A spark shoots up my spine and ignites in my mind at the feel of his bare flesh meeting mine.

"Jesus Christ," we hiss in unison as I swivel my hips, with his billion dollar precum paving the way to slickly slide us together.

Running on instinct, I rock back on Grant, and all I manage to do is to slide him up and over me. I groan in a combination of frustration, want, and pleasure. Grant's cock feels incredible sliding against me, but it isn't what I want. I need him *inside* me. Changing the angle, I do it again, and his dick doesn't magically slide up inside of me.

"Regina," Grant utters gently, a slight chastisement in his voice. "This is why I suggested foreplay, which I love doing by the way. Selfish men may not, but I'm not one of them. This isn't just about getting my rocks off. I want to please you more than anything."

With a deep breath, I explain something to Grant I don't even understand myself. "This first time, I have to be in control, or else I might break. Okay?"

Insanity is doing the same thing and expecting different results. With my palms gaining leverage in the center of Grant's chest, I roll my hips again. We moan together, finding the sensation exquisite… but his cock isn't inside me.

A few more tries, and I'll end up coming before losing my virginity. Reluctant, fearing Grant will think me inept, I look down at him, worried his facial expression will show buyer's remorse because he got stuck with an incompetent imbecile. But I'm amazed to see his face is slack with need as he gazes back at me tenderly.

"I could help, but I know you want my hands to stay put. May I offer a suggestion?" Grant's tone is level, like he's worried he'll upset me. Instinctively he knows that I *need* to do this myself, but it can't be too pleasant watching me fail.

"I've never done this before," I squeak out in frustration. "I usually pick up things fast. Why not this?" Dammit, I'm good at just about everything– with the exception of sex, obviously.

"Slide back onto my thighs, and then fist my cock at the base." Grant's voice is steady, and his reassuring eyes never leave mine.

I do as he says. Sitting on his thighs, I look at Grant like he's a complicated binary code I can't quite figure out. I take a deep breath, and then grab his dick with my hand. My eyes pop wide in wonder as my fingers circle his flesh. I thought he'd feel different, rough and hard. But he's silky smooth and twitches in my hand. With every jerking movement, moisture flows over my skin.

"Is it normal for guys to be so–" Stroking his full length in explanation, Grant grunts and hitches his hips off the mattress. "Wet?" I splay my saturated fingertips, creating a webbing of sticky stuff.

"No," he rasps, body quivering. "Whittenhowers drip like leaky faucets, and are hardly ever soft. What's a blessing during sex is a curse the rest of the time, because we're horny bastards who always have wet spots on our tented pants."

"Oooh." Intrigued, I play around with his dick, trying to see how much precum I can get to flow. "Mmm…" I purr, stroking and caressing his dick, tugging at his foreskin. A giggle slips past my lips at Grant's reaction to me swiping at his hole.

"Regina?" Stomach muscles bunching, Grant looks on the edge of insanity. "Deflowering, remember? Grab my cock at the base." In a low, pleading tone, he begs, "Please."

I search his eyes to see if I did what he wanted correctly. His eyelids are lowered, casting half-moons shadows upon his cheeks. Ever so slowly, his eyes open, leveling a crystalline blue gaze on my hand. His lips part and he draws in a shaky breath.

"Now kneel with a knee on each side of my hips. Put your hand on mine for balance, and then lower yourself down onto me," he rasps roughly. "Go slow."

I lean forward and grip the headboard right over Grant's hand. Shifting on the mattress, I straddle him, then use my hand to guide his cock to my entrance. I gulp and dig my fingernails into Grant's hand as I impale myself down onto him.

Tremoring, Grant releases a primal grunt when he breaches my flesh.

Turning more animal than woman, a sound flows from my throat at the sensation. I tilt my head back at how incredible he feels, so hot and velvety. Grant's barely inside of me, and I want him all.

Stabilizing myself, I grip both of his hands on the headboard, and dig my fingernails into his skin. He shudders again, the wave rolling along his body, moving his cock inside of me slightly. With a deep breath, I abruptly drop onto him until our bodies meet. My flesh swallows his fully, quivering as it tries to adjust to the invasion.

I don't move— not even taking a breath as I reel from the impact of what I just did.

"I'm not a virgin anymore." I huff a laugh of pure shock and wonder. "Eighteen years was a long wait— goodbye to the last of my jaded innocence."

As my amusement fades, I notice Grant is quivering uncontrollably beneath me, making small, helpless noises in the back of his throat. Worried I've hurt him somehow, I can feel him beating inside of me, growing impossibly large.

Getting a clue, I grow suspicious when I feel scorching hot moisture trickling out inside of me. "You're not coming already, are you?" My voice is laced heavily with disappointment.

When I first came to terms with the fact that I'd have to have sex with Grant until I was knocked up, I wanted to do it as fast as possible. Now that I know it feels incredible in more ways than one, I don't want it to end.

I love how powerful sex makes me feel. How it pushes the grief and fear away. How every synapse in my brain is firing pleasure instead of pain. Sex allows me to forget.

"Coming? Not quite." Grant's skin blazes red. He turns his face and rests his cheek on the pillow. I tighten my grip on his hands until he'll explain. "It was an accident– I was too turned on after waiting so long. I didn't orgasm. I'm still ready whenever you are." Rambling and blushing, Grant's embarrassed.

"But… the stickiness? So that's not–"

"It's exactly *that*. Regina, please," Grant begs. The tone in his voice and the expression on his face has me moving against him.

"You feel so good, so why is this so bad?" spills unbidden from my lips as I ride him. "People make such a huge deal over having sex. We're told as kids to avoid sex– good girls wait, bad girls don't. All it takes is a second of having someone inside of you and you're no longer the same person you were an instant before. I don't get it."

"That's fear talking– bad versus good girl. But sex is a big deal, Regina. Don't trivialize it. It's about connecting." He flexes his hands underneath mine, and I dig my fingernails into his skin to stop him. He moans from the punishing contact.

"I like that." Grant groans deeply, speaking of my nails. "We connect, Regina. If you were with someone else, it wouldn't feel like this. It would still be pleasurable, but nowhere near the same."

"I don't want to think or talk about other people while we're doing this, Grant," I gasp out in annoyance. I try to push Grant's precious Gwen from my mind.

"Exactly." He grins up at me as if I just admitted something. "Either let go of my hands, or put a few pillows under my back."

"Are you telling me what to do?" In demand, I stop rolling my hips and glower down at him.

"I wouldn't dream of it." Grant's lips twitch. "I'm merely offering a suggestion. Just put the pillows under me and you'll see, Mistress."

I flinch from the verbal smack, head jerking to the side as if I was struck. As soon as the word registers, I move my hands off his and prepare to dismount.

How dare Grant call me Mistress?

Shame weaves through me, cancelling out the power I felt moments ago. I don't want to be reminded of what Grant changed me into while I'm doing it.

Grant laughs at me, large guffaws of amusement, but not like he's making fun of me. Growing bigger inside me, twitching, his face flushes, and I have a sneaking suspicion he's ready to erupt again.

"It's not meant in that context." Resting on the pillows, Grant shakes his head left and right while his laughter turns silent. "I'm talking about how a virgin who was thrust into my life against her will is riding me. Controlling me, making demands about not touching her and using imaginary restraints, all the while punishing me with her fingernails. I fucking love how your instincts complement my own."

"Your cock is leaking again," I bring to Grant's attention, not that he doesn't realize. He's swallowing back his groans and clenching his muscles to stop them from moving. "How many false alarms do you have in that billion dollar sack of yours?"

"Ha-ha," Grant mock laughs, but the heat smoldering in his eyes takes my breath away. "I called you Mistress, not because you're my lover, but because you're dominating me."

"You mean like a dominatrix?" I mutter in shock, mind conjuring up one of the working girls who has a ton of clients because she was a tough bitch.

"Precisely, Mistress Regina. You're off the charts dominant."

"I take it that's a good thing, judging by the fact that you're wiggling around beneath me right now," I mutter wryly, suddenly feeling more powerful than I ever have.

"Jesus Christ, Regina. I can't wait to see how you are when you're my age. You're superb now– just imagine with some more life experience under your belt. I hope I get to see it."

Grant flashes me a slightly evil grin, and I find myself grabbing two pillows and putting them behind his back. He charmed me into doing his bidding, and that's utterly terrifying.

"Just a suggestion for your pleasure, lean forward until our foreheads touch," he instructs.

Grant has earned my trust every step of this fucked up ride, so I instinctively know he's telling the truth. I slide forward, resting my forehead against his, pressing our chests together. A shudder weaves up my spine at how warm and comforting it is to have my breasts pressed against his chest– safe yet sexual.

Shifting underneath me until he's nearly sitting up, Grant thrusts upward sharply. Piercing me, I gasp at the foreign sensation. It's deeper and more intense. I hold still under Grant's rapid onslaught, not caring that I'm not in control.

Neediness sparks out of nowhere, causing me to want Grant to hold me, to grip my hips, to yank me off his lap and flip me around until I'm on my knees, and then pound into me from behind– hard.

Terror and confusion war at the mental image rolling on repeat in my mind. Grant's not capable of doing that, and I don't want that from him. Ever. He could physically move me, but he doesn't have the nature to conquer me. Knowing this, I don't tell Grant to let go of the headboard because he needs to earn it. I *need* him to earn it.

I'm so fucked in the head. When and how did this happen to me?

We both pant, our breath mingling, neither of us moving that last inch to merge our lips in a kiss. Instinct driving me, I begin to move with Grant in a primal dance, meeting him thrust for thrust. The clap of our bodies impacting echoes around my bedroom.

I didn't allow Grant to touch me first, nor will I let him kiss me first. I strike fast, merging our lips, and he cries out beneath me.

Mouths feasting, the cock inside of me goes wild. "Don't you dare come before I do, Grant," I warn with a bite of my teeth to his full bottom lip. He grunts, but doesn't release.

Riding Grant while he thrusts upward, our lips locked with dueling tongues, "Let me touch you," he pleads directly into my mouth.

"The more you beg, the longer you'll have to wait." I purr against Grant's luscious mouth, corners of my lips tilting into a taunting smile as I ride the wave of addictive power flowing through me. "I may have been handed to you, but you will earn every touch." I lean back, trailing my fingertips down his chest to his groin. "Every kiss." I recapture his lips. "Every fuck." I roll my hips to the point I lose my train of thought. "I'm not something you acquired, nor am I for your instant gratification, Mr. Whittenhower."

With a twist of my hips, my clit rubs over Grant's pelvis. The climax is instantaneous. No slow buildup– I erupt. Every muscle in my body clenches tautly, and then releases. A sharp, mournful cry flows from my throat as Grant fights my hold on his hands against the headboard, trying to steal a touch.

Heat flashes throughout my body as I fight Grant for the upper-hand. He grunts loudly and swells. A second later, he cries out and pours liquid fire inside of me, proving earlier was only a threat to what was to come. I press his hands with all my strength as I experience the strongest and longest lasting orgasm of my life.

Riding the wave of power and pleasure, I don't relinquish my position or release Grant's hands. I slowly roll my hips against his as I regain my breath. Intense heat spreads through me at the sensation of Grant's heart beating a rapid tattoo in his chest, fluttering against mine.

I smile against Grant's cheek, and he snickers at the euphoria infusing my system. Heady. I understand Kristal's comment about how sex can become addictive. When I started this dance with Grant and his family, I had no control. While I was avoiding them, it was an illusion of control.

I was meant to be here.

I think I just found the one thing that Grant wants more than his father's acknowledgement– ME. I will use me against Grant. I will make him love me. I will make him feel special. I will make him see that he is worthy. I will give him everything his father takes away from his soul– real pride. Then I will take Grant and my children away when I leave.

The Whittenhower brothers tried to dictate my life. As consequence, I will take from them what they hold dearest. They can keep their money. What good is it without family? I will do anything to survive.

The Whittenhower legacy belongs to me now.

"You have thirty seconds to get hard again, and I'll reward you by releasing your hands," I command huskily. I can't believe the words flowing from my mouth in a seductive voice that doesn't sound like mine.

I wonder what I'd look like in a mirror right now. A flush ignites along my skin, burning more than skin deep. My eyes must be sparkling bright. I've never been high, but I doubt it's better than the euphoric feeling roaring through my veins.

I rock on Grant's lap and he moans, growing inside me. On-demand, he proves my suspicions correct. Grant loves me controlling him just as his patriarchs control every facet of his life. But I can offer more than they can. One day, I'll have millions to my name that I will earn with my brains, but I can trump the Whittenhowers with children and dominating sex.

The Whittenhower's thought they were controlling me, yet now I control their heir.

Grant is mine.

Grant's children are mine.

The Whittenhower legacy is mine.

Mine.

Gasping against my lips, as hard as granite, Grant pistons into me. As reward, I abruptly release his hands. Without hesitation, he grips my hips and flips me over until I'm beneath him. With rough, forceful thrusts, he pile-drives into me, and I scream but it isn't from pain.

I fight Grant for control, and he smacks my hands away. Fingertips twisting, I yank his hair, and he whimpers but doesn't stop. I yank harder, startling him, and then slide out from beneath him. Arms and legs everywhere, I hop on Grant's back. Leaning forward, I bite his shoulder, leaving teeth impressions that will last for days, if not a week. I smile in satisfaction as his fingers flex on the sheets, body bucking.

Grant loves it rough– thrives on being conquered.

We play a very adult game with the enthusiasm of children. I giggle while clinging to Grant's back. He laughs wholeheartedly, and it softens me even more toward him.

Facial expression changing from elation to awe, "Mistress," Grant whispers reverently, lips fluttering against the shell of my ear. Suddenly serious, he cups my cheek with a warm palm, then leans in to place a chaste yet affectionate kiss to my parted lips.

Mood shifting from playful to powerful, I slide off Grant, and then try to pull him onto his back so I can mount him again. My fingers tighten on his wrists, denting his skin. Sound harsh, he cries out and flips around, pinning me with his melancholy stare.

A husky laugh rolls along my throat to purr out parted lips, thinking I finally won.

Patient and pliant, Grant lies still on the bed. As a reward, I crawl over him, dragging my skin against his, nipples etching a path of pleasure. We both shudder from the intense sensation. With slow movements, I straddle Grant's hips, no fears or worry that I'll be awkward this time around since I've had practice now.

With the rock of my hips, my pussy rolls down the length of Grant's cock, completely engulfing it. Eyelids fluttering shut, I relish the pleasure from the sensation of rolling my hips against Grant's. Palms resting on his chest, lost in the motion, I don't realize until it's too late…

With a squeak of surprise, I find myself smashed face-first into the mattress, with Grant gliding between my closed thighs. A guttural moan echoes around the room, one that spilled from my lips. Full, stretched to the limits, I nearly climax as Grant presses the length of his body on top of mine.

"You have to earn it, Mistress," Grant warns, panting roughly. "I won't relent so easily." We're both breathing in large gasps, more so from being turned on than from exertion. "If you can get out from underneath me and back on top, I'll be in your service for life." Grant whispers into my ear, nipping the shell with his teeth.

The feel of Grant's warm weight at my back is comforting yet terrifying. The hard length taking instead of allowing me to give has panic rippling through my body. Panic I find exhilarating.

I'm alive.

More than two years of my life have been committed to death.

Tonight I truly live.

In theory, I understand why Grant likes to be conquered. It's nothing I'm accustomed to and this will be one of the last times I experience it. This *will* be the last time Grant ever dominates me.

I lie motionless, imprinting the sound of Grant's breathing, the scent of his skin, and the rhythm of his body against mine into memory. Firsts. Grant Whittenhower was my first everything, except the kiss I so freely gave to Roman Alexander.

I vow never to forget– ever.

Whimpers are forced from my throat with every potent thrust. My fingers clutch at the sheets, twisting into the fabric. Restless, I release the sheet, only to grip Grant instead. Nails biting in, drawing blood, I brand Grant so he'll never forget this moment. Ever.

So close to orgasm, but for some reason it won't release, and I don't know why. Building. Building. Building as our bodies dance together. Incredible yet maddeningly frustrating, the pressure mounts with painful intensity.

Grant's movements falter, cock pulsing deep inside me. His breath heats the back of my neck as he harshly breathes in puffs of air.

I wait.

Lost to me, no longer playing a game, I'm not Mistress– "Regina," Grant moans, tone full of every imaginable emotion while on the edge of orgasm.

Making my move, I reach around to grip the back of Grant's neck, then flip us both over. I quickly scurry until I'm facing him again. Mounting him after my earlier practice, I take Grant back into my body before his need to release vanishes. I grind my pussy on him. Cock swelling, pulsing, he cries out my name as he spills inside of me.

I twine my fingers with Grant's, pulling our hands above our heads. I lean down and suck his kiss. "I own you, Grant," I proclaim, and then my orgasm hits with the force of a tsunami.

Releasing a primal scream, I realize I couldn't climax earlier because I wasn't in control.

Who the fuck am I?

What have I become?

Chapter Twenty-One

Eating breakfast as a family is a bizarre experience with questioning eyes lighting on me from all directions, especially from Grant's livid wife.

Did Grant and Regina consummate their relationship?
Is there an heir germinating in Regina's womb?

Sharing a newspaper while chatting with one another, the brothers have compromised on seating since the last time I was in this gargantuan dining room. Jackson is in the seat Daniel had occupied, with Daniel sitting where Priscilla had previously sat. Side-by-side, they lord over the table. Priscilla was bumped over a seat to sit next to Cora. I'm bookended by Grant and Whitt.

It's uncomfortable sitting in a massive room with seven people sitting at the end of the largest table I've ever seen. The Whittenhowers baffle the fuck out of me.

I'm just thankful breakfast is not *exotic*. I don't think I could have suffered through it along with the odd emotional climate in the room. Priscilla and Cora are eating fruit and cottage cheese, neither speaking to the other– you can feel animosity seeping from Cora's pores. Jackson is grumpily suffering through his bowl of oatmeal, while Daniel has dry toast and scrambled eggs. Whitt is humming and swinging his feet as he happily tucks in Cap'n Crunch– glad to see the child is truly a kid.

Grant and I are eating like we haven't eaten in a decade. Full breakfasts: meat, carbs, eggs, and fruit with coffee, juice, and milk. I was thrilled to discover Grant is an eater like me. Last night we raided the kitchen after round three, then again after round five. That man's dick never flags.

Every time I shovel in another forkful, Priscilla, Jackson, and Daniel share private smiles. At Hillbrook, I would have been ridiculed for being a fat ass. But at Misery Castle, it means a night well spent propagating the Whittenhower lineage.

"Where's Adelaide?" I ask the entire table. "I find it bizarre that my best friend hasn't even greeted me since I set foot into her house." I look around, noticing everyone is being tight-lipped. "I already called Fate, and Ade has no other friends."

Grant bumps my shoulder with his while darting his eyes in Daniel's direction.

Cold blue eyes latch onto mine. Mouth opening, Daniel bites his toast in reply.

Yeah, the bastard has his youngest daughter stashed away for some reason.

"Daniel, really?" Grant questions him. Instead of receiving the threatening toast routine, he gets an eyebrow raise.

Right now, Grant and Daniel look so much alike, it's no wonder no one has ever questioned paternity. I doubt anyone would believe otherwise without a DNA test, same with Daniel Whittenhower II being Daniel I's child. It's like seeing the same man during three stages of his life– unnerving.

"Haven't seen the waif in a few days– probably ran off to Shadow Haven to terrorize that Hunter boy again," Jackson mutters, eyes flashing a glare at the sticky mass in his bowl. "Martha, ya old cunt. Gimme something else."

Old? Not a day over forty, and showing the resemblance to her daughter, Kristal, Martha pops into the dining room from the wall panel. "No," she says firmly, grabbing for the bowl of oatmeal as punishment. "Oatmeal or nothing."

"Damn you, woman!" Jackson bellows, trying to fetch his bowl back but Martha's quicker. "I'm starving."

Daniel and Priscilla share a look, and you can almost hear their silent communication written in the air. What's left of the cottage cheese and fruit is pushed in front of Jackson, and a slice of dry toast is plopped on top.

Grabbing a fork, managing to smile in victory while pouting, Jackson tucks in. "Thanks, but I wanted some bacon." Wild hair sticking up in every direction, the maniac eyes my plate with intent.

From my periphery, a small hand sneaks a piece of bacon off my plate. We all wait for Whitt to toss Jackson a piece, but we hear the crunching before we register the kid popped it into his own mouth.

"You little shit," Jackson mutters with affection, then loud guffaws of amusement echo around the dining room. "I'll be in the study, working and starving my old ticker." Rising from his seat, he squeezes the back of Daniel's neck with affection, their equivalent of a hug. Then he kisses Priscilla square on the lips, and no one questions it.

Sure, it didn't look romantic, but still. Then again, I watched Jackson kiss Grant on the lips the day I met them both. I have the feeling Jackson lives to push boundaries and gets off on shock-value.

"I'll join you," Daniel murmurs, linen napkin landing on his plate. Once he's to his feet, Daniel's lips meet Priscilla's. It's not out of shock-value, territorialism, or jealousy. For one second in time, Daniel turns into a human being.

"What are your plans this morning?" Daniel breathes softly as he pulls away, thinking we can't hear.

Holding her husband's gaze, "Martha and I are going to Transcend to work on the accounts."

Jackson stops mid-step, then flips around to face us. "Alone?"

"No," Priscilla answers, rising to her feet. "Kristal is coming with us."

"Very well, then." Satisfied, Jackson waits for Daniel to walk with him. "The rest of you don't leave the estate today– Albert is too busy to babysit. Cora, you can do whatever you want, I guess."

"How gracious of you, Jackson," Cora slurs, eyes narrowed into lasers. "I'll be at my father's, just as I am every day, not that you care."

"You're right– I don't," Jackson says in parting, and Daniel doesn't even acknowledge the rest of us.

Priscilla rests a hand on Cora's shoulder. "You're welcome to join us today– your brother will be coming in this afternoon to help with the accounts. How such a young boy can be a wizard with numbers…"

In the face of someone so gracious, Cora thaws. It's odd to see a mother-in-law and daughter-in-law interact when they are so close in age– maybe ten to fifteen years separating them. Why in the world would they join a thirty-some-year-old Cora with their twenty-three-year-old son?

"I'll visit with Daddy this morning, then I'll ride into the city with Boyd this afternoon," Cora offers as a compromise. Yet another instance of someone showing a rare burst of humanity.

"I'll see you then." Priscilla squeezes Cora's shoulder one more time while her gaze lands on my bookends and me. "Any plans for the day?"

"Horrible day– Father and Uncle are teaching me finance this morning, but maybe Boyd should take my place," Whitt says way too sarcastically for a youngster, evidently not liking Boyd. His little cupid bow of a mouth twists into a scowl, dimples all but disappearing. "Then Grant said I'm having a visitor."

"Visitor?" Priscilla's blonde eyebrows raise so high it's almost comical.

"No worries, Mother. Young Daniel needs to play with kids close to his own age." Grant turns to me, and smiles brightly. "I thought we could walk around the grounds since it's such a gorgeous day today, and your Whitt's visitors are here to see you too. I want you to feel at home here, so I brought in people who will be a comfort to you."

"Who?" I gasp, shocked, heart beating out of control. "Fate's in West Virginia visiting her grandmother and aunt."

Smile satisfied, Grant murmurs, "It's a surprise."

"I know who, but I won't ruin Grant's surprise." Whitt's stormy scowl gets even gloomier, looking more and more like Grant by the second. "I'm sure you'll like her, but I hate her," he snarls, wiggling out of his chair. "Hate. Her."

"Oh!" Priscilla and Cora say in unison, releasing uncomfortable laughs. Hand covering her mouth, Priscilla speaks, "Are you sure this is a good idea after the last time?"

"They have to get along eventually, right?" Grant sounds hopeless.

"Maybe wait until they're adults?" Cora suggests. "It didn't go so well the first time Whitt met my brother, and he's a teenager."

I lean down to whisper in Whitt's ear. "Are they speaking in code?"

"Yeah," he mumbles back, a pout thick in his voice. "I don't play well with certain people, but Grant forces them on me anyway."

"One more try." Grant rises to his feet, and then gazes down at his son. "One more try, Daniel. But if you purposefully bait her, I'll make you have a weekly playdate for life."

"You can't do that!" Whitt shouts, no longer looking like the loveable child I know. "You're not my father. Daniel said it was a waste of time networking with a toddler!"

"Networking with a toddler?" Eyes bright, Grant snorts, choking on a laugh in the face of his only child shouting '*you're not my father*'. "That's a new one. Behave, and no more visits. Fight with her, and playdates for life," he warns, and even I can hear he means it.

"You can't socialize me like I'm a dog." Whitt stomps out of the dining room, turning into a nightmare. I smile, happy he's finally behaving like a child, even if the words out of his mouth are straight from his namesake.

"You should catch their playdate on camera." Cora and Grant share a conspiratorial look, one excluding Priscilla and me, and it makes my heart sink. "We could pass it around Maître–" Cora verbally stumbles. "–The founders meeting."

Married less than a year, even if they never shared a bed, they're still legally husband and wife. They will always know things about each other that I'll never learn. They've been in the same social circles since birth, and I cannot compete with that.

Priscilla flashes me a sympathetic look of understanding, and I realize for the first time that I'll never be her daughter-in-law. My children will be Whittenhowers, but I'll never be, even by marriage. I'll only be tolerated as a means to an end. Cora was welcomed with open arms. She was the one chosen to carry their lineage, and a disease ended that dream. Cora's loss, wasn't my gain. It became my curse, no matter how confusingly pleasurable it may be.

"Dear," Priscilla murmurs, purposefully ignoring Grant and Cora's banter about a subject going over both of our heads. "Would you like me to accompany you to sign up for classes next week? I'm alumni, and I can make sure you get into the classes you truly need, and advise you on the best professors."

"Thank you," I whisper, eyes stinging. Priscilla Whittenhower is truly a remarkable woman, seeing my pain and doing her best to erase it. "I'm looking forward to putting all of my energy into studying. I think I'd go insane if I didn't have a job."

"We all need a purpose in life." Grant alerts us that his conversation with Cora is over by butting into ours. Mouth twisting wryly, "You know, Mom, I'm also alumni."

"Thank you, Priscilla," I snub Grant, rejecting him. "I'd love your help. I'd be lost without it."

I receive a patented shoulder squeeze from the woman while she eyes Grant. I don't dare look at him, but I can feel his confusion wafting on the air, no doubt wondering what he's done wrong.

It's not about what Grant's done right or wrong. It's that this entire situation is batshit crazy, and I have to protect myself from charming yet terminally sad pretty boys who make my heart race, my lady parts weep, and my thighs clench.

Escaping, I mutter, "Cora," as I stride by her to flee the dining room. Her frail body turns frigid with my intentional use of her first name, because she expressly told me to call her Mrs. Whittenhower.

Never happening. I'll call my future daughter-in-law Mrs. Whittenhower first.

"*Reg-ee-na*," Cora draws my name out, emphasizing every syllable to be a cunt. Gone is the human being with a personality, and in her place is a bitchy heiress.

"You sound like a foreigner trying to learn English," I toss over my shoulder, refusing to catch Grant's eye. But I do enjoy Priscilla biting her lip against a laugh.

Cora strides by me, stilettos clacking loudly on the marble flooring. I watch as she stalks down the corridor, all the way to the front door. Attention split, I catch the tail end of what Priscilla whispers to Grant.

"Cats fight, and neither of yours are declawed," the mother warns the son. "I suggest you keep them separated like you do with Daniel and his siblings."

"I believe in socialization, Mother." I can hear the gigantic smile in Grant's voice– smug bastard.

"Your funeral– don't say I didn't warn you," Priscilla says in parting, striding toward the study where the Whittenhower brothers are holed up. Huge castle of a house, and they all gravitate to one another.

"You!" Grant shouts at me just as my legs move to make a run for it. "Don't even think about it." Catching up to me while my mind spins in indecision, he pins me to the wall, body boxing me in. "I thought you said you don't play games?"

To be a bitch, I meow directly into Grant's face, but his reaction is the opposite of what I expected. He kisses me. Hard.

Panting, fingers curled into claws against the back of Grant's shirt, I rasp, "What was that for?"

"Because you're capable of being a jealous woman after all," he mutters wryly, then pulls me into the powder room, where we work up an appetite for a mid-morning snack.

Chapter Twenty-Two

When Grant said we'd walk the grounds, he meant *walk* the grounds. I envisioned a couple strolling the back gardens in a book adaptation. How did I forget the boy was fit after exploring every inch of his body? Repeatedly.

Closing in on July, Misery Castle's grounds are luscious and gorgeous. Flower garden after flower garden is being tended by an army of groundskeepers. Fountains with stone benches. A flat area perfect for a picnic.

A motherfucking hedge MAZE straight out of The Secret Garden.

Grant pointed out the tennis courts and the pool, but didn't elaborate why, so I assume they're on his list of Misery Castle haunts.

Comforting yet creepy, Grant is like walking with a ghost– his shadow a half-step behind as we walk the perimeter of the woods surrounding Misery Castle, with our destination a pond in the foreground.

Reflective, half of his mind is on things I probably won't understand, while still managing to focus on me. Ever patient, Grant keeps reaching out to grab my hand, yet letting it fall to his side.

"Do you ever feel alone in a crowd?" Grant speaks for the first time in over an hour. Palm slipping inside mine, I realize it took him all this time to gather up the courage to do so. Heart clenching, I ache for him.

"Yes," I mutter emphatically. "All the time. I feel more alone when I'm with others than I do when I'm totally alone."

"Exactly." Grant squeezes my hand, smile thick in his voice. "People drain me– I'm an introvert," he whispers like it's a secret. "Daniel and my son are quiet by nature, but sometimes Jackson frays my nerves. I like to hide out in my tower and write when no one is making demands of me."

"With anyone else, it would be a metaphorical tower. But since you live in a goddamn castle, I have the feeling you're being literal." I mutter wryly, envisioning Grant locked in a tower like a damsel in distress awaiting his white knight. "The only problem with being alone– or not, as the case may be –is that you can hear your mind in the quiet. Sometimes I don't want to hear what it speaks."

"Very eloquent, Regina," Grant praises me like he finds me a crass, low-rent girl, and I pleasantly surprised him. "Stop– don't look at me like that. I meant you vocalize your feelings well, while I've always struggled to be heard."

"Oh," I mutter lamely, feeling like an ass. I squeeze Grant's hand in apology. Finally reaching the pond, I'm immediately drawn to the water. Smiling back at Grant, I drag him to a tiny dock. Falling to my backside, I tug off my sneakers, then dip my feet into the cool water. "Beautiful," I purr, blissed out.

Even though I interrupted the conversation that took him an hour to begin, Grant smiles brightly because this is the first time I've relaxed at Whittenhower Estates, outside of using sex to forget.

"This was Rebekah Zeitler's favorite place on the grounds– she said it reminded her of the lake at Serenity."

"Amazing…" I glance over the water rippling with the light breeze, not seeing the cloud shadow us overhead– the misery emanating from Grant. "What's wrong?"

"This pond was the last sight Rebekah ever saw," he offers as explanation. "I didn't get to truly express how sad I was to hear of your mother's passing. I know I saw you several times after the fact, but you wouldn't speak with me. I'll cherish the few hours I spent with Ella for the rest of my life."

Eyes stinging, if Grant's candor couldn't make me cry, nothing will. "You're a very soft-hearted person, aren't you?" Flinching next to me, I realized I've taken a misstep, similar to the ones Grant makes with me all the time. "I meant that as a compliment. Thank you," I whisper to the wind. "Thank you for caring, for wanting to get to know my mother, and for keeping her memory alive."

Turning away from me, gazing out into the distance at something that maybe once was or never will be, Grant struggles to have a voice again. So I offer him patience by being quiet and strength by reclaiming his hand.

"I overheard my parents– the three of them," Grant elaborates. Still staring at nothing, he mutters in a dead voice, "Jackson could go at any time. There is nothing that can be done. Rich or not, he's not on the organ transplant list after two rejected hearts. Daniel suggested murdering someone, can you believe that?"

I know I'm supposed to gasp, to act surprised, but all I can do is shrug because I'm not surprised.

Chuckling lightly, the sound sardonic, Grant continues. "Yeah, you're probably not surprised that Daniel would suggest it, but I'm surprised Jackson said no."

"What?" I do gasp, thinking he was joking all along.

"Daniel wasn't serious, but the Jackson I've known my whole life wouldn't have batted an eyelash at murder in order to survive. That crazy act isn't entirely an act. Living on borrowed time is hard on the family, but I can't imagine what it does to the person who is dying."

"Jesus Christ," is my only contribution.

"I idolized Jackson way before I learned he was my father. Larger than life, if it could be done, he did it. What's a death wish attitude to someone who is already dying? Jackson pulled a shit-ton of crazy shit and yanked me along for the ride. Seeing that I didn't find enjoyment in destroying other people, or driving like a lunatic in the fog at three a.m., he decided I wasn't the right heir for the job."

"Daniel would have probably been the right man for the job," I mutter, wishing I didn't believe it.

"Wilhelm Whittenhower believed the same, which is why my mother was married to Daniel instead of Jackson. My grandfather was murdered before he could change anything in his will, thinking he'd outlive his dying son."

"Oh..." It's my turn to look away, unsure if Grant was admitting to patricide in the family, or it was just a coincidence.

"It's a good thing my fathers love each other," Grant mutters absentmindedly.

Mind reeling, I'm taken aback. "Explain." Eyes narrowed, my voice is thick with suspicion and curiosity. "How the hell are you Jackson's kid, and what the fuck is up with your parents? The brothers aren't like... you know?"

Head hitching back, Grant's laughter echoes around the surrounding hills. Wiping at his eyes with the back of his hand, I said something he found infinitely hilarious. "Would you like to hear an epic love story between two brothers?"

Eyes bulging out of my head, "I've got the time," I manage to sound calm.

"Regina," Grant teases me. "Head in the gutter– I don't mean *sexual* love between the brothers. The founding families strive to keep their wealth and power in the families. As you've figured out, we either allow some fresh blood into the gene pool, or go slumming."

"Slumming?" I grumble, definitely considered that category by Daniel and Jackson.

"You're fresh blood," Grant informs me, because my face is twisted up into a grimace. "Yeah, slumming. The founding families weren't the only ones settled here when Dominion was erected. They had servants and laborers– a handful of lineages remained to work in our houses. But a few families managed to rise in class over the years, with the Simpson family claiming a founders spot. Not many girls in our social circle were born in Jackson and Daniel's generation. Being Whittenhowers, we got first pick on the draft, so to speak. Mother was raised in this house, with my grandparents living here until a car accident took their life a few years ago." Voice cracking, Grant gets choked up, but he continues on anyway. "It was better than handpicking from the staff to ensure loyalty, like some of the families had to do."

Thoroughly disgusted, I want to puke. "Why? Did they really betroth your parents when they were that young?"

"Yeah, they did. But if Jackson is fucking nuts, then Wilhelm was the goddamn devil," voice seething, dripping with vitriol. "He hoped to tear his sons apart. They were loyal to one another instead of to him– tight." Grant crosses his fingers in example. "Which is why as a partnership, they run this family like a well-oiled machine. The thing was, instead of tearing them apart, my mother's presence drew them closer together because they had a common goal– protecting their queen."

Baffled, I just stare at Grant's profile. "Seriously?" I roll my eyes. "No one is that fucking selfless. You saw me and Cora at each other's throats over you, and that was the polite version."

"You never met Wilhelm," Grant mutters ominously. "Devil," he whispers, voice haunted. Unfreezing, turning animated, he looks at me. "Besides, Daniel's asexual while Jackson runs off pure testosterone. No need to fight."

"Bullshit," I blurt, mind refusing to work that dynamic out.

"It's true. We fucked like fifteen times in the past eighteen hours, Regina. Jackson was no different. He likes to tease that he sucked up all the sex drive in their generation, leaving Daniel with none. Jackson's proud that I'm a horny devil, doesn't give two shits that his grandson might be gay, and says our branch of the line will continue to suck Daniel's branch dry, calling his nieces frigid bitches."

"Daniel has two daughters," I remind Grant. "*Not* frigid daughters."

"Daniel won't speak of his asexuality because he's a very private person, but Jackson explained it to me in-depth. Daniel sees his penis as any other body part, and sexual congress no different than eating, sleeping, or taking a shit. He gets erections because it's the body's natural response, and he drains his sack once a day like you'd take a piss or shit. It's impossible for him to look at someone and *want* them."

"But… but he still has sex with your mother?"

"Jackson said Daniel would forget to do it if he didn't remind him. They decided on specific days of the month- numerical so it falls on different days of the week, so my mother doesn't catch on and continues to believe Daniel is being spontaneous."

"What I don't get is why Jackson would want your mom to get it on with Daniel in the first place. He seems like the type to be selfish, and there is no way he left Priscilla alone all these years."

"Jackson has guaranteed faithfulness– he can't get it up, no matter how horny he may be. Heart medication does that, ya know? It takes blood to stiffen a cock. My fathers are a pair, aren't they? One would kill to have sex with my mother but can't, and the other doesn't care either way but does so his brother can live vicariously by watching their partner's pleasure."

"Jesus Christ, you literally meant an epic love story, as in a tragedy, didn't you?"

"Yes." Grant looks away, voice a quiet whisper. "And one is dying– hence the days of the month reminder so his lover would still feel wanted and loved forever, even when he's gone."

My eyes snap shut on the sight of tears streaming down Grant's cheeks. "Daniel loves my mother– purely and romantically. He enjoys the affection and connection, and doesn't mind the release. But since he's missing the essential spark that can't be ignored– the one that stiffens your cock or makes you wet, where you either fuck the person or go nuts –he's missing out on lust, on the excitement– the drive to mate. There are things about Daniel and Jackson I despise, but I respect and love them, no matter what, because I can't imagine walking through life or dying while wearing their shoes."

"But…" I stammer, face twisting up with indecision, eyebrows knitting. "But–"

Even with tears drying on his cheeks, the corners of Grant's lips curve up into a mischievous smirk. When he turns to me, he's wearing the most devastating smile I've ever seen, leaving me speechless.

"Ask, Regina," he orders in a taunting voice. "I can see the wheels spinning in your head. Rapid-fire those questions, and I'll answer them to the best of my ability."

"Really?" I squeak, unsure if I want to voice them.

"Mmm-hmm," Grant murmurs.

"How were you created if Jackson couldn't fuck?"

"Ah– excellent question. Before anyone knew Jackson had a heart condition, he was chasing my mother all over Misery Castle and its grounds. Sometimes he dragged Daniel along, trying to get a motor running that refused to be revved. Asexuality was a mystery to Jackson, and sexuality was just as baffling to Daniel. My mother had the pleasure of being their outlet."

"So Jackson was completing the task and Daniel wasn't?"

"Daniel wasn't even starting the task," Grant mutters wryly. "Imagine if your brother, best mate– partner –wouldn't chat about sex with you. We're guys; it's all we think about. Like I said, I don't know what Marcus likes, but he tries to figure it out by talking to Dexter and me. Anyway, Jackson tried to tease Daniel with my mother. When that didn't work, he tried other means."

"Like what?" I lean forward, intrigued.

"Guys," Grant says with a shrug. "Jackson said he was so horny in his youth, his favorite pastime was getting sucked off by guys because they had stronger mouths and didn't act like it insulted their delicate sensibilities." Shuddering, Grant seems confused by that. "Jackson identifies as bisexual– what a pair they make."

"Plus, guys can't steal and use your billion dollar sperm," I tease, earning me a chuckle for the effort. Clearly the joke has run its course.

"Anyway, Jackson would bring a guy around, checking to see if Daniel would get hard– obviously he didn't."

"And if he didn't get aroused by your perfect mother, then obviously he was broken," I mutter wryly.

"Undoubtedly," Grant mimics my tone. "Then one day, Jackson discovered that Daniel wanks in the morning to clean out the sack– Daniel's aspiration was to become a doctor, so he felt the pressure should be released, no matter what Catholicism teaches us about the sin of seeding the earth."

Palms covering my face, I fucking lose it. Laughing so hard I get a stitch in my side, I realize Grant is an impressive human being, and I truly enjoy spending time with him.

"Don't laugh, Regina," Grant teases me, eyes glinting deviously in the sunlight. "Believe it or not, this is the truth as Jackson tells it, and what I've seen with my own two eyes."

"I get the gist, that your mom was pregnant with you when she married Daniel, right?"

"Right," Grant affirms, including a head nod for added effect. "Wilhelm hated Jackson with a passion. Jackson was too wild and uncontrollable, while Daniel was cold, precise, and efficient. Jackson chased tail constantly, fucking the staff– boy and girl. Daniel's head was always in the game, either on business or reading his medical journals. Jackson was the heir, and my mother was betrothed to him. Then the heart condition was diagnosed after Jackson's first collapse. While he was in the hospital for a several month stay, Wilhelm forced Daniel and my mother to marry, not believing Jackson would outlive him."

"Oh, my God. Jackson probably wanted to kill him," I mutter in horror.

Freezing, Grant looks like a deer caught in the headlights. "Kill who? My grandfather?"

Eyebrows knitted together by Grant's reaction, I mutter, "No, Daniel."

"Oh… Jackson could never harm Daniel– ever. My grandfather didn't realize my mother was already pregnant with me, ensuring the line would pass down from Jackson to me instead of Daniel, even if he wished it so. Not realizing my mother was with child, Wilhelm enforced the bedding ceremony, where they have to witness the consummation."

"Oh, shit!" I yelp, envisioning it.

"Daniel's a trooper." Grant chuckles, taking on a sinister edge. "He'd spent a great deal of time cuddling with my mother, and found he enjoyed the kissing sessions Jackson forced him to perform. So, he drained his sack… into my mother."

"And decided he didn't mind it?" I pitch in, voice hopeful. "No, wait. Daniel's a miserable bastard, so I'm assuming he didn't like it."

"Jackson said Daniel enjoys sex. Some asexuals don't, though. But the act is pleasurable by design, and Daniel is all about anatomy and its uses. He has a penchant for genetics, and sex for reproduction falls into that category. No lust is felt, so no precursor to sex to clue him in that it's time to engage."

"That's so… sad."

"I imagine Daniel's mind is quite clear of clutter." Grant is quiet for a moment– reflecting. "When I call Wilhelm the devil, I mean it, Regina. His friends are still alive, and they are monsters too. Jackson, even with his heart condition, was strong, forceful. Daniel was eleven months younger, but there was always something vulnerable about him, Jackson said. This is an assumption on Jackson's part, but he fears that one of my grandfather's friends got to Daniel when they were visiting, probably when he was very young, and it flipped a switch to where body parts and their actions are clinical."

I would have to be dead not to cry at that. A sob is torn from my throat, remembering during breakfast where I saw Daniel, Grant, and Whitt as three stages of the same man. Only now, I see some pervert touching my Whitt. Crying, but no tears fall, I grip Grant's hand tightly.

"We don't know for sure, but it makes perfect sense. If you haven't noticed, Daniel touches no one but my mother, because that is socially acceptable. Like his mind doesn't know right from wrong, so he doesn't touch anyone."

"Good touch versus bad touch is taught in public school, but not in Hillbrook," I mutter, getting a clue about Ade's coldness. Fate and I will hold hands and hug, kiss cheeks, but a simple touch from Ade is monumental.

"Daniel doesn't hug the girls, and he's utterly terrified of touching my son with any affection. The only time Daniel has touched his namesake was in a moment of lost control, where he backhanded Whitt over his sexuality. He never touched me until I became an adult– he'll squeeze my neck or shoulder, but that's it. I was a sensitive kid, Regina. I craved love and affection, and my father wouldn't give it to me, so I thought something was wrong with me, when it was something wrong with him."

"Christ, Grant." Reaching over, I tug him into my arms, holding his shaking body tightly.

Whispering against my throat, "Jackson kisses us on the lips to hammer it into Daniel's head that it's the intent that makes it wrong. But Daniel is incapable of spotting the difference between sexual intent and affection, seeing everything clinically."

Grant's crying again, tears trailing down my neck to seep into the collar of my blouse. I pull a Jackson. Shock-value. "Are they a threesome?"

"Ménage á trois?" Grant asks in a perfect French accent, the bastard. I push him off me for being pretentious. "In the partnership sense, yes." He scrubs at his eyes with the backs of his hands, clearing away his sadness. "The three of them run our family, with Jackson making sure Daniel and Mother are equipped once he's gone. My son and I suffer with getting trained in all areas for the eventuality of taking over."

"Grant," I drawl, knowing he's purposefully being daft.

Yanking me into his arms, evil laughter flows into my ears. "Are you asking if the brothers are screwing, Regina? You and I are not the formal sort– just go for it."

"Fine," I bite out. "Are the brothers fucking? I feel like a goddamn pervert for asking."

"I hope not," Grant answers without hesitation. "And you're not a pervert, because that was the second question I ever asked Jackson. The first was how they managed to hide their relationship. I didn't find out until I was twelve when Jackson spilled the beans, and the girls to this day don't know. Pretty sure my son suspects since his day job is hiding behind the draperies. Anyway, their rooms are connected, with my mother's in the middle."

"About that second question you asked," I remind him, wanting the juicy shit.

"Jackson says no. He's only been able to have sex a handful of times to completion since my birth, and the doctors warn against getting his heartrate up by excitement. Sex starts in the mind, which arouses the body. Even if his body won't respond, his mind still needs sex. He did admit to entering the marital bed and pleasuring my mother–"

"With Daniel?" blurts out because I can't help myself.

"Mmm… hmm…" Grant hums, completely shameless. "Jackson prides himself on being a sexual deviant. Deviancy is in the mind, not the body. In this, I do think like my birth father, so I don't believe him. I won't lie, it terrifies me to think Jackson would take advantage of Daniel, because I see Daniel as a man who wouldn't be able to consent to Jackson because he'd never say no."

"You shitting me? C'mon! Daniel not saying no?"

"Sexually speaking, Daniel has been Jackson's puppet my entire life by living vicariously. It's not above the realm of possibilities, ya know? He's a dying man with nothing to lose, with the two people who love him more than life itself. The only consolation I have is the fact that Jackson can't get it up… I mean, yeah. I don't even want to contemplate the damage he'd inflict if his cock worked."

"Did you puke when Jackson told you all of this?" I get to the heart of the matter. All parents are asexual in the minds of their children. "Did you?"

"Yes…" Grant seems relieved to admit it. "Hearing about Jackson watching and instructing is one thing, being terrified he joins in has a young boy worshipping the porcelain god."

"You know I'm never going to be able to look them in the eye ever again, don't you?" I pull my feet from the pond, then sit cross-legged, not giving a shit that my shorts are getting damp.

"You? Regina Regal, not able to look someone in the eye with judgment?" Grant teases me shamelessly. "I still can't look Daniel in the eye, which makes him think me all the more worthless. Meanwhile, I'm envisioning him touching or being touched by someone he shouldn't. Every time he calls me an idiot, I want to blurt out that at least I know right from wrong when it comes to sex."

"Oh, that would be cruel," I purr, hating how I now have ammunition, should I choose to use it. For a moment, I feel like a horrible person for wanting to exploit their situation, but look how I got here in the first place.

Bastards.

"No more talking," Grant announces, lying back on the dock with his crossed arms cushioning the back of his head. Face turned skyward, he absorbs the sun with a smile of pure pleasure curving his lips. "Talking is exhausting. Let's just enjoy the beautiful day."

I follow suit, lying next to Grant. "I don't want to think." I ignore the pout in my voice– I don't pout. "Quiet means thinking."

Confusion heavily lacing his voice, Grant sounds disappointed. "I thought you said you understood, that you liked to be alone?"

"Oh, I do– but I have to keep busy. I like to work alone because it keeps my head quiet. When I'm with others, my mind spins out of control."

"Thinking is my favorite activity," Grant murmurs softly. "Other people talking interrupts my ruminations and it frustrates me. I don't even like to be touched when I'm thinking because I find it jarring." Face turning, blue eyes pin me in place. "I need to absorb some sun and let my mind wander so I can handle my son's playdate with his baby sister. You can play in the pond. I don't mind."

"Oh, thank fuck!" After a quick kiss to Grant's lips, I hop up from lying on the dock. "I can't be idle, drives me fucking nuts." I skip down the dock, spotting a decorative crate. Cracking the lid open, I find some goodies. "OH! Jackpot! Fishing pole."

Grant's soft laughter fades on the wind, warming me. Ghostly quiet, he keeps me company while I cast. With my hands busy and my mind concentrating on fishing, I only allow my mind to wander to my dad because he's the one who taught me how to fish. But a small part of me is curious as to what Grant thinks about.

I toss a look over my shoulder. Switch set to off, breathtakingly beautiful, sun casting light across his cheeks and creating shadows beneath his eyes, Grant looks too surreal for this life, and that thought terrifies me.

Another premonition hits me out of nowhere, and this time I listen to it. This amazing moment is fleeting– real yet not. This is yet another snapshot in my life that I'll never recapture, so I better enjoy it while it lasts.

Enjoy Grant, because he won't last.

Chapter Twenty-Three

Walking back to the house is ten times faster with Grant's brisk stride. He's sun-kissed and vibrating with anxiety. Slipping my hand into his sweaty palm, I don't bother asking what his malfunction is. My mind spins the possibilities. Brooding Grant surrounds himself with family, inside his estate where no one can enter without his approval.

Grant's anxiety ramps up mine. It didn't fall on deaf ears when he said Whitt was having a playdate with a baby sister. Since I know for a fact Grant hasn't popped out another kid, or else I wouldn't be here in this moment, I'm suddenly terrified I'm going to be face-to-face with Mistress #1.

Gwen.

"Yes!" I shriek, hopping up and down the moment our visitors come into view. "Oh, my God!" I flash Grant an enthusiastic smile, relieved I'm not meeting the one that got away. Then I'm pulling free from his hand to jog the last few hundred feet to jump into one of our visitor's waiting arms.

"Reggie," rumbles a deep laugh from Julio's broad chest. "I've missed you too… since yesterday," he mutters sarcastically as he settles me back on my feet.

"So good to see a friendly face." I grin up at Stanton Green's enforcer, eye catching sight of the presence leaning against a stone wall at his back. "Oh, hi," I turn bashful, finally getting a clue.

"Stanton. Julian." Grant nods to each of them. "My father will release the kid once Bianca gets settled."

Too young and too devastating, Stanton smiles at me like he's amused I'm intimidated by him. He steps to the side, but the toddler clinging at the back of his thigh won't let go. After removing tiny fingers that have turned to claws, he extracts his daughter.

Crouching, I try to coax the angel to me. "Binks, c'mere." Back in our neighborhood, the girl would have flown into my arms, chatting about this and that. But the oppressive air of Misery Castle is affecting the girl.

"Daddy?" Huge pools of blue flick from her father, to Julio, to Grant, and then to me, and I finally see the resemblance. The chestnut hair and slightly tan skin were obviously Stanton's genetic contributions. Those eyes…

"I brought my ballerina," Binks mutters shyly, presenting me with her dollbaby. "Want to play with me, Reggie?"

I glance back at Grant, finding him spreading out a blanket on the lawn. "Yeah, c'mon, baby." Settling onto the blanket, I create a space between my crossed legs for the four-year-old to sit. "Tell me all about your ballerina."

Leaning against my chest, Binks is comfortable to chat about this morning's dance lessons. Her voice is melodious, and a chill flows in my veins.

Gwen. If I ever meet her, I'll probably want to kill her on sight.

Jealousy crashes over me, nearly taking me down.

Released from the back doors leading to the study, a tiny man strides across the lawn toward us. He's wearing a three piece suit, with his blond hair parted on the side in a miniature version of his namesake. As if summoning all the misery in the castle to create a storm cloud over his head, Whitt is more powerful and destructive than Daniel, yet more morose than Grant could ever be.

One day, Daniel Whittenhower II will be the king of this castle, his grandfather, uncle, and father be damned. Of all the premonitions I've had, I'm most certain of this one.

"Shit," I hiss, not caring that Binks heard me cuss, because she is a mafia princess in training and Stanton doesn't filter anything from her. "What happened to *my* Whitt? Does he know?"

"No," Grant and Stanton mutter in unison. "The oldest kids know. The rest we try to socialize for the future when they find out."

"Why not just tell them?" Julio finds my question hilarious for some reason, and earns a chastising look from his boss.

"They'll find out when it's time," Grant murmurs quietly while Stanton talks over him. "Bianca knows," he says with a shrug. "And she knows to keep her mouth shut, don't you?"

"Yes, Daddy." She chirps from my lap. "Mommy told me."

"Has Whitt met his mother?" flows from my mouth without thought.

Grant's, "No."

Stanton's, "Fuck no."

Julio's evil laughter mingles with Bianca's trailing giggle.

Step after step, crystalline blue eyes turn stormy, latching onto me like I'm betraying his trust.

"My son is legally Daniel and Priscilla's son," Grant reminds me. "He's having a playdate with this little lady."

"Deep down, all of 'em recognize each other on sight." Julio's voice is sarcastic as all get out. "Never seen kids hate each other instantly. The oldest are buds because they share both parents, and their little sister doesn't know but hates them both. Bianca is laidback... but Daniel." Julio cackles. He actually cackles just as Whitt gets within hearing distance.

"Should we sit, or wait to see if your son is going to try to murder my daughter like last time?" Stanton says jokingly, voice teasing, but there is a note of truth underneath.

Grant doesn't breathe as his son comes to a stop before me.

With the tips of his leather shoes kissing the edge of the blanket, "Regina," sounds like the word *traitor* from the six-year-old's taut lips. "You," is pointed at the little girl in my lap, and I can hear how he's restraining himself from harming her.

"Hi," Binks replies shyly in her melodious voice, and that only seems to infuriate Whitt more.

"You kids should be kids." I pick Bianca up, and then set her on her bum on the blanket. After crawling to my feet, I lean down to whisper in Whitt's ear. "Behave, little man. I've known Binks since she was born, babysitting her from time to time. No matter what, you'll always be my favorite person in the whole wide world."

Whitt visibly relaxes, and I learn so much from his reaction. Poor fella thinks he has to beg, borrow, and steal love and affection, not realizing he deserves it simply because he exists. Palm curling over the top of his head, I mess up his too perfect hair because it was freaking my ass out. Tugging, I tilt his head back, and then plop a smooch to his forehead.

"Kids are kids," I remind the adults, but receive an array of disagreeing looks. "Back off and let them be." Walking away, I call over my shoulder, "Yo, Julio, let's chat. Grant's too quiet and I need to release some words."

Settling on the top of the low stone wall surrounding the picnic area, Stanton's deep chuckle is infectious. "Reggie's got you pegged, Grant." After a second, Grant reanimates himself to join Stanton on the wall, leaving the kids to work out their differences.

"So, dish," I order Julio as we pace the grounds around the picnic area. I'm going to need to soak my feet after all the walking I've done today. "What exactly happened last time?"

Whiskey-colored eyes flick down to gaze at me, while a smirk curls at Julio's large lips. "I thought the first question you'd ask would be about Roman, and the second about your possessions," he mutters knowingly, guessing I was waiting to shove those questions in so it wasn't so obvious.

My eyes flick away guiltily to concentrate on the beautiful landscape. "It's surreal, being here, when my usual view was of your building and the dealers and whores hanging on the streets."

"Whole 'nother world, isn't it?" Julio mock-punches my shoulder. "Okay. First of all, you're walking funny, so I guess Grant was the lucky bastard to pop your cherry."

"Ugh," I grunt, annoyed more at Julio ignoring my questions than at the teasing. I pull another Jackson. "Fifteen times. We've been fucking like rabbits. I'm probably pregnant already."

"Dayum…" Julio drawls, thinking I'm exaggerating. "As you no doubt figured out, Stanton and I knew what was up but had to keep out of it. Sorry about that."

"If you're so sorry, you'd answer the important questions." Pouting, when I don't pout, I plop down on a stone bench overlooking the rose garden, finding it the perfect view of the picnic area. Grant and Stanton are chatting, eyes never leaving the two silent kids having a staring contest on the blanket.

What an odd dynamic Stanton and Grant make.

I don't share.

"I can hear you thinking, and no, you don't want to meet Gwen." With a sigh, the large man sits next to me. "Roman is good, going about business as usual. I'll let him know you asked about him. We all pitched in and boxed your stuff up nice and safe, and Stanton took possession of it. We delivered it to Albert when we arrived."

"Oh," I clutch my heart at the thoughtfulness. "Thank you."

"Okay, now that I answered that, how about you tell me how you are?" Julio wraps an arm around my shoulders, easily comforting me since he's a huge guy. "How are you handling the culture shock, Reg?"

"Priscilla is taking me to sign up for classes." Excitement and anticipation stir in my belly. "I think when I have a goal to meet, with work to be done, I'll feel better. I spend most of my time trying not to think about my situation. My parents keep popping into my head, and that's worse. So, no, I wasn't joking about the constant sex. Grant's insatiable, and I like not thinking."

"School will definitely do you good," Julio agrees. "Grant's a weird one, but he'd never hurt you or anyone else."

"Himself, maybe?" I guess.

"Yeah..." Julio pauses, balancing what he should and shouldn't say. "I know you and everyone sees me like an underling, but in a way I'm Stan's partner in life. I was born to be his companion. All the founding families have someone like me. Albert, Martha, and Kris are the Whittenhower's... yeah, don't have a word for it. Anyway, I've known Grant since I was born because I go everywhere Stan goes."

"You were born with a purpose, just as my child will be." I rest my palm on my belly, cupping an invisible or imaginary baby. "None of you are free, are you?"

"Freedom is overrated if you're not a goal-oriented person, Regina. Freedom leads to a lot of lost souls who buy my drugs." Julio's voice may be sad, but it's not tainted with shame. "I like my life because Stan and I are equals– we listen to each other. There is no corruptible force like in other families. Albert gives it right to Jackson and Grant. Martha doesn't take anyone's shit, and we expect Kris to behave the same when she grows up. As Stanton's most trusted adviser, I save him from himself, because if Stan fucks up, my life goes down in flames too."

"No retiring for you?" I remember my first drive through the gates with Albert, and the guard joked with him.

"Sure there is," Julio purrs, a smile thick in his voice. "Either when Stan kicks it or retires. My old man was Caleb Sr.'s enforcer. Right now, Papá's living the high life, fixing cars and cooking Mamá tasty meals. I'm gay and have no plans for kids, so I see Bianca like a daughter, and I've enjoyed helping raise her. I *am* Stanton's family, and he's mine. I don't want to retire if that means he's gone, but I'll happily retire when he does, but only if Bianca has someone to watch over her."

"Albert can't retire, can he? Because once Jackson's gone, Grant doesn't have anyone glued to his side."

"That bastard is a control freak– Albert. The only way he'll retire is in a body bag. He calls himself the keeper of the Whittenhower legacy. He shadows Jackson and that little boy over there–" Julio points at Whitt. "As I said, Grant has his own death wish, refusing to have anyone look after him. While Daniel and Priscilla share Martha. Kris is supposed to be watching after any children you have, by the way."

"Jesus," I gasp, shocked. "So cloak and dagger. I don't get it."

"As I said, The Green family is *my* family. Albert and Martha had a fling and made Kris, in case you're curious. They were born here, have lived here– the Whittenhowers have been *their* family for generations. You didn't leave your mother's bedside, and none of us are going to leave our families."

"Watching over them for what? What evil force are you protecting them from?"

"From themselves," Julio answers without hesitation. "Aside from the families involved with organized crime, the rest are sheltered idiots who know nothing of the world at large. They get bored and do destructive things that would implode our world. Everyone on this planet was born with a purpose, and I believe I'm to protect what the original founders built, even if it means protecting it from their descendants."

"Fate and Faith, who's protecting them, then?" I raise an eyebrow in challenge, never seeing anyone glued to them like Julio is to Stanton.

"Faith? Amelia Simpson, the aunt she lives with in West Virginia. The Simpsons were underlings like my family, but Tom's a financial genius, so they gave him a house in the Gates. Fate? Were you blind and deaf at Hillbrook? Every student has a purpose. The dang place is crawling with legacies and their companions. That psychotic Ezra kid? He's got three of the fuckers shoved up his ass. One of 'em, Cort, he doesn't even realize he was born with a purpose. Ezra's so unstable, we have someone watching out for Cort, fearful if something happens to him, Ezra will go off the rails and burn Dominion to the ground."

"I just don't understand," I mutter. "I lived in the hood and protected myself. Why aren't they self-reliant?"

"Ha!" Julio's head jerks backward as laughter spills forth. "You lost everything to your name, but were going to Hillbrook. No one stepped in to offer support as a test to see what you'd do to survive. It wasn't a coincidence you found an apartment across from Stanton. Jackson didn't want to upset Priscilla if anything happened to Rebekah's precious scholarship student she was sculpting for the future. I didn't stand on the sidewalk day in and day out. I popped out there on command when you were supposed to come home, making sure you were safe, okay, and on time. If you were seconds late, I would have had one of my dealers search for you. Stan owns the buildings that house Digital Nation and Beans 'n Bags. I mean, c'mon. Who else would have named a coffee shop that? Stan's got a wicked sense of humor. Your wages weren't actually garnished–phony paystubs."

Eyes held wide with fright, my world tilts on its axis for the billionth time recently. Fingers curling into claws against my thighs, I shrug my shoulder to flop Julio's arm off me. "Nothing is real. Nothing."

"Sorry, chick. But that's the truest thing you've ever said. Everyone is playing god with someone, and someday you might get to be the overlord who actually has a heart to go with that huge motherfucking brain in your head. Most of 'em are ignorant to what's going on around them, thinking it's reality. As I said, we underlings have a conscience, a heart, and a brain. While those we protect from themselves, the ones who are trying to destroy everything, all they have is too much time on their hands, with a brain capable of creating havoc, and the money to be evil."

"This isn't the life I'm going to lead, nor will my children." I stand up, having to do... something. "No!"

"Stan says the same thing. He took an entire floor in The Green Building, hired a bunch of tutors and dance instructors, just so Bianca wouldn't ever set foot into Hillbrook and be corrupted. She won't be a part of this life until she's ready. She'll get to be a kid and to explore her passions. She won't be murdered slowly like Grant has been. At least young Daniel is strong enough to fight for what he wants."

"I-I-I–" stammering, I'm rendered speechless.

"50/50 on whether or not your children live like this, but they won't be a doormat like their dad because of you, so there is that," Julio tries to comfort me, but all it does is sicken me further.

"I want to run away from here, and take Grant and Whitt with me. Grant always looks on the verge of slitting his wrists, and Daniel is not the little boy I thought he was."

Julio grabs my wrist, wrapping his large fingers around tightly but with caution. "Ah, when Bianca and Daniel first met..." a sadistic snicker flees his lips. "We left them alone to play, and within minutes we heard growling and snarling. They were rolling around on the ground, yanking each other's hair out over a toy neither wanted to share. Daniel was calling Bianca Toddler, and she was calling him a prick."

"I just… I just don't see Whitt behaving like that," I murmur, examining every interaction between me and the little boy.

"That's what's so bizarre." Julio tugs me to his side, wrapping his arm around my shoulder, steering us back to the tableau. "The kid is reserved like Daniel, quiet and brooding like Grant, and once and a while he's bright and cheery like–"

"Gwen," rolls off my tongue, thick with bitter jealousy.

Brown eyes scrunched together, "Fuck no," Julio is taken aback. "Gwen is a damsel in distress, slit your wrists, psycho cunt. Anyway, sometimes the tiny Daniel is like how Grant used to be–"

"Sunshine," I cut him off again.

"Yes." I relax because I didn't piss Julio off for interrupting him. "Exactly. To the point those who know the truth about Grant's paternity thought maybe a DNA test was in order. But the second young Daniel saw Bianca, he turned into Jackson. Lethal. Brutal. Without mercy. He was going to off his competition to not only the Whittenhower throne, but the Meyers, purely on instinct. We didn't stop it because we were baffled. Then the kid just stopped trying to choke his baby sister, made sure she was okay, and then just stared at her with disgust."

Eyeing the siblings on the blanket as we approach, I mutter underneath my breath, "And this means what, exactly?"

"Daniel has self-restraint and emotional control, and Stanton believes he'll make one helluva elder someday. Oh, and that the kids should never be left alone, especially when they're adults. Sometimes you just hate someone and it's soul deep."

Eyes still glued to their children, Grant and Stanton are holding a conversation about how to improve Transcend. Looking exhausted, I can tell Grant's social battery is drained and blinking red.

Bianca and Whitt aren't saying anything. Each are holding a toy, and both are staring at what the other has in their possession.

"Daniel, share," Grant orders firmly, sounding exactly like a father should.

"NO!" Whitt shouts, sounding like a spoiled, rotten brat of a child, just like he should.

In response, Bianca curls her arms around her dollbaby, trapping the ballerina to her chest. Stanton doesn't chastise his daughter for not sharing.

"Daniel," Grant's voice lashes out. "Share."

"NO!" Tiny fingers curl possessively around a red Matchbox car. "I got this for my last birthday."

"Jesus Christ, Daniel." I can tell Grant is at the end of his rope. "You didn't get the Matchbox; you got the real thing. The Roadster is sitting in the garage."

"Who the fuck gets their kid a car for their sixth birthday?" I whisper out the side of my mouth to Julio, and he releases a silent laugh in reply.

"But only Jackson will let me drive it," Whitt whines, giving me heart palpitations. "So Daniel bought me this, and you know he doesn't buy gifts."

Hand clasped to my chest, I hurt for the little boy. Grant moves to take the toy away, and I find myself intercepting. "Let Whitt keep the car."

"Regina?" Grant gasps, shocked at what he's hearing.

"Just hear me out, okay?" I kneel on the blanket near both kids.

"But Daniel has to learn to share," Grant stops me.

"Why?" Stan and Julio say in unison, but Stanton continues on. "Ballerina is Bianca's favorite toy because Caleb bought it for her before he left for the country. Daniel is emotionally attached to the car, so why share?"

"Because the children should be taught not to be sociopaths like their grandparents," Grant reminds Stanton cryptically.

"Making sacrifices is an important lesson to learn," Grant tries again, but even I think that cost is too high for children so young.

"I'm not sharing. Not this–" Whitt curls his fingers tightly around the car. "Not with her. Daniel says everything is a negotiation, but you have to have something to negotiate with. What if I give her the car but she doesn't give me the doll? Then I'm left with nothing and she has all the power. Don't try to tell me we'll trade at the same time– that never works. Last time, Toddler ended up with both toys and wouldn't give me mine back."

"Liar," Binks mumbles dejectedly.

"Bianca," Stanton cautions. "Apologize to Daniel. We all know he's not lying. I found his flipbook in your toy box last month."

"Sorries." Binks sniffles alligator tears. "It had pretty pictures, and when I flipped the pages the picture moved."

Head perking up, my sunshine breaks through the clouds. "Thanks– I drew them."

"Really?" Bianca looks to her father to see if Whitt is lying or not.

"Yeah, I'll make you one with ballerinas if you promise never to touch my car."

"Deal." Binks flashes the sweetest smile.

"Or anything else important to me. I don't share. Ever." Commanding yet snotty, Whitt turns into a combination of both Daniel and Jackson. "Especially with you."

Grant glares at me, silently screaming *Don't parent my son!*

I wasn't parenting Whitt. I was being real with him. Adults don't share, but they sure as fuck demand. I'm not about to teach Whitt to be a doormat, never saying no, having everything he values ripped from him by those who only asked for it as a test to see how weak he truly is.

You don't share because it's asked of you. You give because it wasn't.

No doubt the instant Whitt hits his bedroom, he'll be making his adversary the best dang ballerina flipbook he possibly can, all because he wants to share a gift that wasn't demanded or expected.

The car is precious to Whitt because he never expected Daniel to give it to him. Why should he share simply because it was asked of him, especially when Bianca didn't need it and never planned on sharing her doll with him?

Grant is miserable right now, yet everyone else is happy. Even the kids are letting each other look at their favorite toy, but not touch or take. With patient eyes, I show Grant I don't care if he's pissed at me, and I can tell that confuses the hell out of him.

"Grant's gonna crash," I mouth to Julio, who nods his head in agreement, then does this creepy silent conversation with Stanton.

"Well, as much fun as this visit has been." Stanton slides down the wall to land on his feet. "I've got to get back to work, and it looks like Grant needs to be put down for a nap before his temper gets the better of him," he razzes a frazzled Grant. "Maybe have a potty and a snack afterward."

"A story and a cuddle, I suspect," Julio joins in. "Tucked in nice and tight. Nighty night."

At Grant's glare, Stanton adds, "We'll go so Rapunzel can hide in her tower."

"Regina," Grant says my name sharply. "This is what happens when children don't share. They end up being assholes."

Laughing heartily, Stanton reaches down to pluck his daughter off the ground. Hands cupping beneath her armpits, Bianca finds herself hoisted to her father's hip. "And look what happens to those who share too much," he mutters in Grant's direction, no doubt over the fact that Bianca calls him Daddy yet Grant's son calls Daniel Father.

Wandering away, Julio calls over his shoulder. "We shared Reggie with you, you ungrateful assmunch. She's one of ours. Say thank you, then go take a nap."

As soon as our guests are out of earshot, Grant goes off at the mouth. "Don't ever question me in front of... people like that." Glaring at me while pointing at Whitt, "Either of you. After Jackson passes, I have to be Stanton's equal, not your bitch."

"Wow," I mutter quickly, harshly, as Grant strides across the lawn toward the house. "Just wow." Simmering anger boils over in my belly and flows out my mouth. "Unless it's in my bedroom or the powder room, right? There you want to be my bitch!"

Grant's strides falter but he doesn't stop.

Giggling like he gets the joke, and it's possible he does, Whitt slides his tiny hand into mine– the Matchbox car pressed between our palms.

"Don't ever share what you value most," I warn Whitt, eyes still staring at Grant's retreating back.

"Because it's stupid?" He replies as we begin walking toward the house.

"Yeah, it is. But because to share what you value most is to lessen its worth. Cherish this car, take care of it, and only share it with those who understand its worth."

Whitt's hand flexes in mine, and I know he understands an undeniable truth that Grant has never learned.

Chapter Twenty-Four

As we approach the doors leading to the study, raised voices reach my ears, one of them Ade's. "Why don't you go make Bianca a ballerina flipbook?" I coax Whitt, not wanting him to hear something he shouldn't. "Use the front door."

Not amused, blue eyes roll up to mine. "If you turn the knob to the left, it makes no noise as it opens. The draperies are closed, so no one will notice you enter the study. If you lean to the right, you'll be able to see through the crack between the fabric panels."

After schooling me in the finer points of stalking like a sociopath, Whitt strides away to do as I asked. I bite my lip against a bitter laugh. Father and son, they walk identically, their backs taut with fury because of me.

"Are you ready to apologize to Cortez Hunter, Adelaide?" Daniel's voice is calm yet authoritative. I slip into the study, using the curtains as camouflage. "Or do you want to be locked back in the punishment room?"

Taking a chance, I tilt to the right, sending a little prayer up above that Whitt wasn't so angry with me he'd lie to get me caught. Daniel comes into sharp focus, sitting behind his massive desk with Jackson lounging next to him with booted-feet sprawled on top of the desk. Daniel is stiff with anger, but Jackson clearly doesn't give a shit and is bored.

"Your daughter's tantrum reminded me of me," Jackson muses, eyes burning a hole into the side of his brother's face. "Anything I should know?"

Daniel narrows his eyes but otherwise doesn't comment. "Adelaide, you are a young woman." I follow the direction he's facing to find Ade sitting in a chair, looking ten pounds thinner and worse for wear. "Young women don't get involved in altercations with young gentleman."

"Gentleman? Pfft! Cort is trash." Ade's haughtiness is at an all-time high. "He's no better than the staff."

"Be that as it may–"

"Listen here, you little bitch!" Jackson cuts Daniel off, boots landing on the floor with a *BOOM!* "If I ever hear you speaking of anyone, especially the staff like that again, your father's swats will be nothing in comparison to the solid thrashing I'll administer. Do you understand me, Adelaide Theodora Atwater Whittenhower?"

"Yes, Uncle Jackson." Ade gulps, never having sounded so submissive.

"What is this about?" Daniel demands, one eye trained on his daughter with the other on his brother. "Explain."

Eyes gone wild with fury, Jackson could burn you with just a look, but Daniel is immune. "The Hunters have been on this soil as long as we have. They are a founding family, even if they are only here to serve. Cortez Hunter is not trash, and I won't allow my niece to draw unnecessary attention to us. Did you somehow forget Ray?"

"Raymond's gone." Daniel's voice breaks, and I never thought I'd hear that. "Diane hasn't seen him since…" he trails off, sounding haunted.

"Gone. Pfft!" Jackson mimics Ade. "I know shit you'd never in your worst nightmares wish to learn– a universe of evil I've kept away from you. So I expect your daughter not to bring it to our front door by antagonizing Cortez Hunter."

"I'm trying for an amicable resolution, Jackson," Daniel mutters dryly. "Calm yourself– think of your heart."

"Shut up!" Jackson palms Daniel's entire face and shoves like a bully. "Even if Raymond stays out of it, Adelaide needs to stop enraging Ezra."

"Enraging Ezra?" Ade blurts out, clearly taken aback. "Ez has never raised his voice to me."

"Because the kid's a psycho. The quieter he talks, the more you should run. If he doesn't speak, you best piss your goddamn pants, girly."

"Don't talk about my future husband like that!"

Jackson rolls his eyes. "Future husband? Not if you don't stop antagonizing his partner. Ezra and Cortez are a package deal. If you want to make us proud, drop to your knees and get to sucking like an heiress should."

"Daddy!" Ade shouts at Daniel, who looks dazed and confused.

"I really don't know what to say to you right now, Jackson." Steepling his fingertips on the desktop, Daniel is at a loss for words.

"Most men operate with their dicks. I get that Ezra is a fag, but Cort might like pussy too. Ya never know. But either way, all men love a warm mouth wrapped around their cocks, no matter what's between the mouth's legs."

"This cannot be appropriate," Daniel mutters, eyes darting around like he's looking for Priscilla. "Don't–" he points at Ade to stop her from speaking. "The boys are children, so no dropping to your knees. The only reason you should open your mouth is to apologize to Cortez, and then say no more since only vitriol spills forth in that boy's direction."

The door to the study opens, and in walks an ethereal being. Tall and willowy, with both hair and skin a pale white. The angel walking on Earth must never go in direct sunlight. Gunmetal eyes fall first on Daniel, pass over Jackson in a snub, and then land on Adelaide.

"Has Adelaide broken yet?" Voice light and tinkling, her vindictive words belie her innocent appearance. "The more you push Cortez, the worse my son behaves. I will not suffer his lunacy."

"Apologize to Diane, Adelaide," Daniel orders sternly.

"I-I-I– I'm sorry, Ms. Holden," Adelaide stammers, voice pain-filled like she's staring into the sun and it's frying her brain. "But I can't help myself."

Kneeling next to Ade's chair, with her delicate hand resting on the armrest, the woman I assume is Ezra's mother gets into my best friend's personal space. "Trust me when I say this. Cortez is the easier to handle of the pair. He's very sweet– malleable. I realize you and Ezra have the same nature, but it's baffling how you behave toward Cortez."

"He instigates it," Ade grumbles like a child, relaxing the longer Diane Holden gives her undivided attention. "He gets jealous and acts like an asshole, baiting me until I snap."

"Why do you allow it?" Jackson barks. "You're a Whittenhower. We don't allow others to influence our emotions. The more Cortez Hunter baits you, the more you should verbally put him into his place. Men have fragile egos, but strong bodies. Slaps from bony hands don't hurt us, but make us feel small…"

"Jackson?" Diane levels a glare in his direction. "Did you suddenly forget you're speaking of my ward?" Attention returning to Adelaide, "Ignore Cortez and treat Ezra with respect, that's all I ask. But if you don't, our future is going to be misery."

"I'll try my best," Ade promises. "It will be easier when I get to California. I'll call Ezra when Cortez is busy."

An unladylike snort fills the air. "Cortez is always shoved up Ezra's ass–"

"Quite literally," Jackson interrupts.

With the patience of a saint, Diane ignores the insinuation. "Besides," she purrs seductively, a talon curling beneath Ade's chin, "Cortez has no reason to be jealous. One single utterance from you would stop all of this unnecessary angst."

"I can't. I-I-I'm not ready," Ade stammers, looking terrified.

"Understandable, darling." Rising to her full height, Diane places a kiss to Ade's forehead. Voice changing from lulling to punishing, "Don't fuck up our happy future," she warns, eyes lasering onto something I can't see. "Who did this?"

"Not it!" Jackson shouts like a child as Diane moves the collar of Ade's blouse to the side. I can't see what they see, so I lean forward.

"I did nothing that wasn't done to me when I misbehaved. The punishment fit the crime. Adelaide struck Cortez, and then tried to choke him."

"He *did* choke me!" Ade shouts, flinging Diane's hand away, causing her blouse to fall open. "I was defending myself."

"Bloodthirsty, I think Daniel has some explaining to do," Jackson purrs.

"Adelaide *is* my daughter," Daniel snarls. "Everyone calm down. Adelaide will behave around Cortez and Ezra from now on, and our alliance is strong."

"As my father, you should kick his goddamned ass for hitting me first!" Ade lunges to her feet. "But then again, look what you did to me, Daddy!" She tears her blouse off, turning to face away from me.

I'm charging out of the draperies in an instant. "What the fuck did you ruthless assfucks do?" I grab Ade's bony arm, flipping her around to get a good look at her. Raised welts crisscross her back from where she was lashed in punishment. "You make me sick," I snarl at Daniel.

"Who the fuck is this?" Diane points at me, angelic face twisted up comically. "Jesus, she popped out of the draperies."

"Grant's mistress," Daniel murmurs drolly, while Jackson whispers, "Our salvation."

"Damn!" Diane nods her head a few dozen times, looking perturbed. "I always took Grant for the type. Hmm… little young for a budding mistress, but she's got moxie."

This beautiful woman doesn't mean mistress in the traditional sense, like I truly am. Diane means the powerful woman who erupts when in the throes of passion. Flabbergasted at their behavior, I tug Adelaide toward the door.

"Hey, girl!" Diane calls after us. "You look like you could survive my son."

We flee Jackson's words. "No scabbing the baby-maker, Diane. Regina probably already has a Whittenhower in her incubator. I'm sure we can find you a fresh-blood breeder somewhere who thinks they can fix crazy."

"Congratulations!" follows us up the staircase.

"You need to get the fuck out of here." Hands on her upper arms, blouse left behind in the study, I pull Ade toward my bedroom. "Stay in California and never come back. Maybe move to Europe after you graduate. That's where the art's at. You're brilliant enough to be a curator at a major museum."

Leaning heavily into me, "What about you?" Ade's words are listless.

"Don't worry about me– I could survive a nuclear holocaust. The founding families? Pfft!"

Using the last of her energy to laugh, "Liar," then she collapses.

Drawing Ade to the floor, I slip my hands behind her shoulders and knees and lift her into my arms. Long strides cutting down the corridor, I kick open my bedroom door, and then bolt the deadbolt behind us.

Chapter Twenty-Five

"Are you sure you're okay?" I ask Ade for the third time. After the awful scene in the study, I dragged Ade back to my bedroom. I needed to know how badly she was hurt, so I ran her a warm bath while she took off her clothing. I never want to see anything like this again– on anyone.

Adelaide is covered in thin lines, punishing lash marks. At least a hundred bruises, welts, and red marks. I asked her what type of object caused it. Embarrassed, she wouldn't tell me.

Terrified of exacerbating her bruises, I wouldn't let Ade turn on the jets in the bathtub, even though she said she wanted to use them to soften her achy muscles.

"I'm fine." Voice drowsy from exhaustion, injury, and the warm water, her head lulls from side to side.

Gathering up her blonde hair, I run a brush through the strands in a soothing motion to calm her. "How many times has Daniel done this to you?"

Ade rolls her eyes up to me and smiles sweetly– her real smile, not the haughty one she uses at Hillbrook. "Twice. It's not that bad. Honestly." Her blue eyes are clear, and I see no deceit, but I can't fathom how the beating wasn't bad.

"I don't like it, but it's tolerable. Daddy doesn't enjoy it, and he talks to me more than ever while he does it– I feel connected to him, and that takes the sting out of the punishment. My grandfather used to do the same to him and Uncle Jackson, and they told me the lessons they learned from it."

I don't know how Wilhelm Whittenhower died, but I'm starting to get a clearer picture.

"So the second time was because you attacked that baby-faced charmer?" Voice incredulous, I run the brush through Ade's hair a few more times. "Cortez seems like a good kid, like he'd try really hard to please you. Except for you, because... ya know– you're trying to steal his guy."

"Cort's territorial." Eyes slipping shut, a faint smile tugs at her lips. "He brings the worst out of me, but I bring the worst out of him."

"Well, you have two options, because if Daniel lashes you ever again, I'll kill him," I mutter in a cold voice, causing Ade to freeze because she knows I mean it. "You can go about your life. Go to California, get an education, and then find a life of your own after you graduate. Travel to Europe and meet people who make you feel good."

"Mmm…" Ade sighs, snuggling down deeper into the warm water. "That sounds nice, but it's just a dream. Reality is, a girl in my position has to think of family first. I have to marry Ezra."

"Okay, I get that– I do." I pause, brush gripped in my hand but stilled against Ade's hair. "I've learned a lot in the past forty-eight hours," I admit. "So I do understand your need to make Daniel proud. So I suggest you get along with Cortez for Ezra's sake. There will be no ditching the boy. Cortez is going wherever Ezra goes, even if it's to Hell."

"I don't believe that," Ade murmurs, completely in denial.

Julio's words filter into my mind. Cort doesn't realize he was born with a purpose because Ezra wanted him as a partner– lover – unlike the connection Julio has to Stanton. No one is cutting the connection between any of them, especially Ade.

I lean forward, using my hand to smooth her hair rather than the brush. I tread softly, "What did Diane want you to admit?"

Eyelids popping open, revealing startled blue eyes, Adelaide looks terrified. "I like girls," is blurted out rapidly, almost violently. She challenges me to react with negativity or disgust, but all the tumblers in my mind align, making perfect sense.

"Ah…" is my brilliant response, confusing us both. Ade's tiny, blonde eyebrows knit together, but her eyes never leave mine. "It will make your life easier. Now I understand why the match took place. It's the perfect arrangement, if only you'd get along with Cortez."

Eyes falling shut, cutting off our staring contest, "I know," Ade murmurs. "But I can't help how I feel when I look at Cortez. I want to tear his throat out, and he wants to do worse to me."

"I guess you'll have to learn." I sit back on my heels. "Jackson was right, ya know? You're allowing Cortez to bait you. You should be in control of your emotions at all times. You can loathe the boy, but never show it. You can murder him a billion times over inside your mind, but it better not show on your face."

"Easier said than done— you don't understand." Voice lost, Adelaide doesn't realize she's putting me down.

"I don't understand?" I mutter incredulously. "*Me?* For four years I had to hear about the interloper scholarship girl, and I managed to look my bullies in the eye. I'm living in your house, after being coerced and blackmailed during and after my mother's death. I'm able to sit at that gigantic table and not wedge a butter knife into your father's carotid artery, like the street trash that I am. If anyone understands, it's me."

"I'm sorry." Voice warbling, lips quivering, Adelaide releases the tears. Pessimistic of me to think, I don't know if they're real or not.

Niggling suspicion blooms into outright disgust. "You said twice," I remind Adelaide, and she freezes. "Daniel lashed you twice. What was the first time for?" Voice level, it's not really a question. We both know it was because of me.

"Not because of you— for you." When nervous or upset, Ade babbles, which means the flow of tears are real. "There is a distinction. You're my best friend. My sister. Just as I know you'd protect me, I'd protect you. Uncle Jackson and Daddy wanted to know everything there was to know about you to prepare the attack and for your resulting arrival. I wouldn't tell them, so they had to break me like my grandfather would break them."

"Ade!" I cry out, reaching for her because she looks ready to break for real.

"Don't you get it?" she shouts, flailing about in the bathwater. "You're here, in this house, in my brother's bed. I *did* break! I let you down. I couldn't protect you from my own father. Blame me!"

Curling around the bathtub, I try to hold a sobbing Adelaide, not caring that I'm getting sopping wet. But she truly is Daniel's daughter, and affection confuses her, especially when she's naked in a bathtub. Pulling away, guilt and shame are etched across her features.

"I'm sorry." She touches her fingertips to the back of my hand. "So fucking sorry. I'll hate myself for the rest of my life because I broke."

I say the only thing I can say. "I forgive you." Because even though I don't blame her, Adelaide blames herself, and arguing that fact isn't going to change it.

Drawing on my experience with Grant, I let Ade rest for a few minutes. Quietly crying, I know she's beyond upset, so I drag my nails through her hair, scratching her scalp. I always loved the sensation when my mom would do this to me, and I hope it brings Ade comfort. I don't know if she likes it, but she doesn't protest.

"I've never been touched like this before," she says shyly. "I-I-I... liking girls, I don't know how to handle it. I know I'll be expected to do what you're doing with Grant because Ezra's family will need an heir. I don't think I'm as brave as you are. Marrying is one thing. Letting Ez touch me is another."

A sixteen-year-old girl shouldn't be worrying about marrying a fourteen-year-old billionaire. She shouldn't be a high school graduate ready to depart to California with thrash marks covering her body. She should be at the mall, lounging around her pool, or gossiping with her girlfriends, and she should do that for a least a few more years.

Two years younger than me, I want more for Adelaide than I have.

"Ezra still has years and years of Hillbrook left, then he has college. Just because you're betrothed doesn't mean you have to get married right away. Live your life to the fullest, knowing in the future you'll be the mother of his children. That could be fifteen or twenty years from now, Ade. You shouldn't hold back, because the little prick sure as shit isn't. Do you think he thinks twice about banging Cort? Sorry to disappoint, but you're nowhere in Ezra's head in the moment. So don't stop yourself from finding a girlfriend and living your life."

"It's not fair, though." Ade sits up in the bathtub, and I divert my eyes from looking at the water spilling over her breasts. I swallow down the bile threatening to erupt from between my lips. Ade's breasts are tiny buds, proving we shouldn't be discussing marriage and babies. I'm a grown woman, but Ade is most definitely still a baby in body and age, but not of the mind.

Those little bratty boys should be keeping their dicks in their pants, even if they're only doing each other. What the hell is wrong with these people? Why is Diane allowing it?

"What's not fair?" I busy myself by getting a towel.

"You didn't get to do that, Regina. So why should I? My family forced–" Ade gulps. "You were forced into Grant's bed, and I don't know how to handle that. He's a good brother– someone had to kiss our boo-boos. So I just can't fathom you and him... *doing it*, or him making you do it." Her eyes track across my face, looking for a difference between last night's innocent Regina and today's jaded version. "Did my brother hurt you?"

"I'm tender, but not because Grant hurt me." I chuckle at how I manhandled Grant in the powder room, but there is no explaining that to Adelaide. Not yet anyway. Maybe when she's older and has some experience. "It was mutual."

"You just told me to wait with Ezra until I'm ready. You didn't. I mean, I know you couldn't wait, but why was it good since you didn't?" Ade's confused and genuinely curious.

"I was ready, Ade. Your brother woke something up inside of me that had lain dormant. I've only ever seen two guys and wanted them. The rest of the time, I just felt sexually numb, I guess."

"I've never felt numb, so I don't understand." Ade steps out of the bathtub, so I hold the towel out to her. "I've liked girls, and obviously I couldn't say anything about it, but I still felt *something*."

I try to explain while Ade dries off. "Maybe it was because I was so focused on studying or taking care of Mom. Or maybe it was because I'd seen so much destruction caused by sex for the girls in my neighborhood. My building was teeming with screaming, shitting, starving babies. Girls I grew up with are on their second or third child already. They kept thinking the next man would keep them, and that disgusted me. The guy would fuck and flee, leaving a kid behind. I lost more friends than I can count from telling them they were the problem, not the deadbeat daddy. If you pick a dude who has a string of children, expect to be the next he leaves behind. I kept telling them not to have a kid so the man would take care of them both– they needed to take care of their goddamn selves."

I rise to my feet, getting heated, still reeling over all the girls repeating this cycle over and over again, expecting to have a man take care of them, but they're left taking care of not only themselves but a couple of kids they can't afford. Then I get even angrier at myself because I could be pregnant already. The chemistry between Grant and me is explosive, and I can only guess how that translates into reproduction.

"I think seeing all that numbed me. There were no relationships to be seen. Whores trolling the streets waiting for married men to pull up to the curb. The jackass guys who were fucking my friends– all of them. One dipshit knocked up six girls at one time, then he disappeared, leaving the friends and sisters to hate on each other, when their kids are siblings."

"Your world is–"

I cut Ade off. "Well, yours is no better, girlfriend." I toss her my robe. "Nothing I do in life will ever erase the fact that I'm your brother's mistress. So, now I'm able to see both sides with fresh eyes, and I want to go hide out in the middle with the normal folk."

Belting the fabric around her miniscule waist, Ade captures me with her gaze. "You said two guys," she challenges. But she breaks our stare by grabbing the hairbrush and looking into the mirror.

"That boy who dropped me off at school– the one you asked me about. Roman. I kissed him goodbye– really kissed him. My first kiss, actually. I think I needed something just for me, instinctively knowing what would happen when I arrived here. But I'm not going to lie; what I did with Grant last night felt incredible. I was in charge the entire time, with everything my decision. But, mostly, what I did with Grant felt right."

Hairbrush clattering to the tile with a loud clack, Adelaide starts to sob hysterically. I'm at her side in a second, reaching for her. "What's wrong now?" I demand. "What did I say wrong?" Pulling Ade into my bedroom, I settle her on the foot of my bed.

"You're not just saying that to make me feel better, are you? I can see it in your face, but I'm not sure." She hiccups the words. "I'm so relieved."

Flustered, I say something I shouldn't. "I don't know how to say this anymore plainly. I fucked the hell out of Grant– dominated him. I'm sure I drained his balls dry." I sound annoyed, frustrated that I have to explain this at all. Ade is my best friend, but Grant is her brother. This is a conversation I can only have with Fate. "What's the matter?" I'm angry because I can't help her if she doesn't tell me what's wrong. I want to fix it.

"As I laid in bed last night, I spent the whole time imagining Grant forcing you. I mean, vividly imagining him raping you in great detail. It was bad enough I was locked in a guest room as punishment."

"Ade?" With a palm, I brush away the damp hair sticking to her forehead, then wipe her tears on the towel.

"Let me finish, okay? I'm selfish enough to admit that I'm happy you're here with me, no matter the circumstance. I'm glad the two people I love most in this world have a connection, so I don't feel as guilty." Tears drying on her cheeks, blue eyes glinting with pleasure, she begins to ramble again. "You guys are perfect for each other– you'll make each other happy."

"Whoa… slow your ass down, girlfriend. That's crazy talk. Grant and I aren't together." I protest, trying to remind myself. "I barely know him, and he's still married. He'll remain married. As gross as it sounds, I know I'm his mistress."

"Regina, if you could see your own face as you talk about my brother… and that's after twenty-four hours. Imagine after five years? I mean it. I want you both to finally be happy."

"Happy is me not being coerced into producing Whittenhower heirs. Happy is finding a boyfriend who doesn't want anything from me. Happiness is not using sex to forget my troubles, especially when it's with a married man always on the brink of offing himself. The only thing that will make Grant happy is being left alone."

"See? You do know my brother." Delicate face turning serene, a dreamy expression etches across Adelaide's features. "You'll be my sister for real. I know you can't be married, but eventually you'll be married in your heart."

Sighing at the foolish notions of a sixteen-year-old girl, I lay on my back next to Ade. Staring at the ceiling in stunned silence, I contemplate all she said.

I don't want to fall in love with Grant– I can't risk it.

A quiet knock snaps me out of my reverie. Lunging to my feet, I flick the deadbolt. "It's open," I call as I step backward, gazing at Ade over my shoulder to see her tightening the robe.

Chapter Twenty-Six

The door opens, and Whitt's baby-blue eyes are at doorknob level, peering at us from the crack with his tiny fingers clutching the knob. I smile at his cuteness and he takes it as an invitation to enter.

I sigh when I see what's attached to Whitt's hand– Grant. Seeing them hand-in-hand is shocking, even knowing they are father and son. Whitt is a cloned version of a miniature Grant. Everything about them is identical, even their mannerisms.

"Hi," Grant mutters warily as he helps Whitt onto the bed. "I thought I better check on you both after Kristal found me." He looks at the child and doesn't say any more.

The look on Whitt's face screams Grant doesn't have to censor himself. Pouty mouth drawn into a taut line, dimples gone, Whitt's wearing a very adult expression of fury and outrage over Ade's punishment.

"Will you stay in my room tonight and let me read you a story?" Whitt asks Ade in his small, sweet voice, but beneath that is a little man wanting to protect and comfort Ade.

My heart fractures, creating a space to allow others in. When it mends back together, my world tilts on its axis.

I was wrong and I will admit it. Priscilla Whittenhower is soft and loving and she instilled that into her children. The fact that the bond survives their abusive, controlling patriarchs says just how strong the bond truly is.

Grant hands Ade a hardcover copy of *The Secret Garden* and winks. He keeps looking me over, making sure I'm not mad at him for his moodiness earlier.

"Okay, little man, let's see what troubles Mary and Colin will get into next." Ade stands, picks Whitt up, and settles him on her hip. "You two have a good night," Ade says, casting her eyes to the floor and blushing vibrantly at how that sounded.

"Don't let the bed bugs bite," Whitt sings as the door shuts tight, closing Grant and me in together.

"I'm sorry. By the time Kristal found me you were leading Adelaide up the south staircase. I knew you ladies had each other so I went back to my fathers." Grant's tone is numb and lifeless.

"Daniel lashed Ade over that Cortez kid." My ass meets the edge of the mattress, exhaustion beating down from all sides. "That can't happen again, Grant."

Grant surprises me. He walks to the adjoining door and bolts it. He repeats the same with the main door. Then he sits a respectable distance from me on the bed. I can tell he wants to touch me, but refrains. He knows that after last night, he has to be invited, especially with how he treated me after Stanton and Julio left.

"I can't imagine what you're thinking right now, Regina." Leaning forward, Grant rests his head in his hands. "Buyer's remorse, I'm sure. You've seen us at our worst, and now I'm terrified you'll leave."

"Grant, about earlier–"

"I have to apologize," Grant speaks over me, as if he has to get the words out quickly before he loses his nerve. "There's an odd dynamic between Stanton and me, you see. The founders meet every week and discuss Dominion and its residents. Only the heads of the family and their heirs, with their enforcers standing by. Stan's my age, yet he's the head of his family, respected and revered as an equal, even by those who are ninety years old. So their teasing bothered me, because I'm Jackson's underling, and I fear they'll still see me that way after he passes and I take over."

"Won't Daniel take over since he's Whitt's guardian? I thought you said you couldn't handle the Whittenhower fortune, so it will go to Whitt or our child."

"This is separate, Regina– I was born in it, and I'll die in it. It has nothing to do with business holdings and everything to do with the legacy. Daniel doesn't know about the meetings, and he never will. There are stiff penalties for what little I've told you, but I needed to explain why I acted like a jackass earlier. I don't want you to be mad at me, and I don't want you to think I don't respect your point of view." Grant looks up, crystalline eyes watery. "Because I do, Regina. I respect the hell out of you."

"I get it." I take a deep breath. "Men have egos, and they engage in pissing contests. But, Grant, Stanton and Julio *know* you. Mouthing off to me isn't going to change how they view you. Making sound decisions for your family will gain their respect quicker than you barking at me and discounting my opinions."

"You're right." Hanging his head, Grant looks devastated. "You're right."

"I'm sorry, too," I blurt out. "I had no right to speak to Whitt as I did. He's your son, and I shouldn't be parenting him. Next time, I'll do so in private, in a way that gets my point across, and he can take the advice or leave it. But just so you know, I can't bite my tongue when it comes to *my* children."

"I'm having a difficult time, Regina." Grant scoots closer, but he still doesn't touch me. "I've known Cora my entire life. She was a teenager when I was a little guy. I don't see her as anything but a sister. I need you to know this. So it's going to break something in me to have her be the legal guardian of *your* children. It's going to break me watching *you*."

"I don't see how your mother can abide by this." Seething with a broken heart, the reality of my situation finally sinks in. "Priscilla seems like a very ethical, compassionate person."

"She is! My mother honestly thought you were my lover after seeing how we both behaved when we met. She thought you and I had been seeing each other since then. Mother didn't agree when Daniel and Jackson forced Cora and me to marry. Jackson had told Mother that I had been courting you for the past month, and she wanted me to have a family and be happy. She thought you and I would raise our family while continuing to allow the public to believe Cora was my wife."

"Jesus," I hiss in pain. "What about Ade, though? How did Jackson and Daniel make lashing her daughter seem logical?"

"Kristal and Martha overheard what happened in the study– every wall has ears in this house. There are secret passageways connecting everything because Staff should not be seen or heard. Don't fear, Mother never agreed with the way Daniel and Jackson punish us, but she tolerated it because it was a consequence for our bad behavior– one we knew would happen when we acted the way we did. As I left the study, my mother was headed in."

Hand moving quickly, Grant wraps his fingers around mine, clenching tightly. Turning to the side, the bleak expression on his face spears me through the heart.

"I want to start school immediately." For the first time, I turn desperate, asking for help to survive a situation I didn't want to be in in the first place. "I can't wait until the fall. Sitting here jumping at shadows will make me insane. Can you make that happen? If I've got to be the mother of your children and your mistress, while Cora gets the respect by being your wife, you owe me my education so I can have a good future. Because, Grant, if anything happens to you, my children are coming with me." I'm surprised by the conviction in my voice.

Grant surprises me by seeming to find strength in my words. "Yes, after we're done talking I'll contact the Dean. To prepare for every eventuality, I'll place most of my earnings into your bank account. Daniel and Jackson have no access to it, nor can they bully their way into getting it. If something were to happen to me, you'll need the cushion to start a new life."

"Our children?" I remind Grant, noticing he was only speaking of me.

"If we have a son, Daniel won't let him go, no matter what you do," Grant warns, causing fear to rush through my veins. "You have no recourse, Regina. With your intelligence, I know you already realize this. I'm not saying you won't be his mother, but you won't be able to take him with you. Any other children, you could probably wrench away."

"I just–"

"You saw how my son asked Ade to spend the night with him, how he was going to read to her. Don't think for a minute that he wouldn't protect his own heir. If something happens to me, our son– yours and mine – becomes the head of this family, and will be protected as such."

"But what about Whitt?" Confusion warps my voice. "Shouldn't he be the head of the family?"

"In actuality, yes. Legally, I'm the first born son of Daniel I and Priscilla, and Daniel II is the last born child. Therefore, my first legal son will be the rightful heir. If it were to get out that Whitt is my son, all hell would break loose, and Daniel would lose all that he's tried to build to a child who potentially loathes him."

"Would Daniel harm Whitt?" My fingers tighten in Grant's at the thought of anyone hurting that precious boy.

"No, once Daniel gets an heir he can shape in his image, he'll leave Whitt alone. I know you think I'm obsessed with money, and that's why I won't leave. It's not that. I *can't* leave. My biological father is dying, and I fear for my parents when that happens. Daniel holds my son hostage. The founding fathers have me for life. They aren't above criminal acts to keep me in line. You've already experienced some of the milder tricks. Once the line is satisfied, you can go live your life in peace and I can finally be free."

Voice wavering, my fingers shaking, "When you say free, I suddenly become terrified for your longevity."

Stare filled with longing and desperation, Grant looks directly into my eyes for a few moments.

I want to hold Grant, to make him feel better, and to reassure him. I need to take that slit-your-wrists look from his eyes. But at the same time, I need him to hold me, and that terrifies me more.

"I need to take a shower? Will you be here when I get done?" I want to kiss Grant before I go into the bathroom, but I don't.

"Regina, if you need space, just ask for it," Grant calls me on my shit, but he doesn't seem upset about. I'd forgotten how he will just shut down like his power was switched to off. "I'll make a few phone calls while you shower. Marcus is hiding your bank account from Daniel and Jackson. I'll need him to reroute my pay each week. Then I'll call the Dean and set up a time for you to meet tomorrow. Is this alright?"

I want to tell Grant he doesn't need my input or permission because he's a grown man, but I can tell that he really does need someone to tell him he did a good job. His confidence is zero, even though he's highly capable of running his own life.

"It's a plan, a very good plan, Grant. Daniel's wrong about you, ya know? I believe in you." I flash him a smile, then go into the bathroom.

Chapter Twenty-Seven

It's only early evening, so after my shower I gaze wistfully at the many nightgowns hanging in my closet. I long to crawl into bed and never come back out again. Reality is kicking my ass, but I can't afford to fade from it. I pull on a pair of ridiculously expensive jeans and a blouse. I feel sick to my stomach wearing clothing that costs more than the monthly expenses of the people I just left behind. I silently vow to help them all I can when I have the ability.

As I pass by, I try not to view my reflection in the mirror. My curvy body is accentuated by the fit of clothing that was specifically bought for me, instead of worn secondhand finds. My hair is smoother than ever from the concoction Ade bought for me.

As my green eyes regard me through the mirror, they're haunted and it makes me look as if I belong at Whittenhower Estates. All residents of Misery Castle wear that particular expression.

"Thank you," Grant says reverently. "You know how I get worried."

I fold myself in the center of the bed, tucking my knees beneath my chin while wrapping my arms around my legs for comfort, as I listen to Grant talk on the phone. I assume he's speaking with the Dean, and I'm not sure why the Dean would know how Grant gets worried.

"Transfer my royalties account to Regina's, and any future deposits as well. I would like a quarter of my earnings transferred weekly. Daniel shouldn't suspect that amount. He already believes me wasteful." His melodic voice holds a hint of thinly veiled anger.

Grant looks lost until he hears the reply. His face clears, seeming reassured. I have no clue who he's talking to. It makes me realize I know nothing of Grant outside of this fucked up house.

"Daniel caned my sister because of what happened at your house a few nights ago. Your wife was here, negotiating with my sister to behave."

Grant turns his back to me as far as the phone cord will allow, as if that means I can't hear him. Head bowed, his shoulders slope in shame. The buzz of rapidly fired words flows from the other end of the line. I have no idea what words are said, or who is speaking them.

Studying him, I watch as Grant listens to the person on the other end. Slowly, his shoulders broaden and his back straightens. His head raises and he turns back to me. I can almost see the confidence flowing through the phone line and infusing into Grant's will. It changes him into a stronger, more capable person.

"I need to see you, Marc." Grant isn't above begging. "Please, I need to talk to you in person, not over the phone." His begging gets more persistent, and it confuses the hell out of me. "I understand– I miss you, though. What about Dexter?"

The buzzing reply has Grant's eyes cutting toward me. He nods his head yes as the voice on the other end of the phone flows. I can hear the tone, but not the words. It's so soothing, I nearly sigh.

"Always." Pause. "Me too, Marc." Pause. "I'll wait for Dexter. Okay." Pause. "Thank you, Marc," he says reverently.

Grant hangs the phone up, trying and failing to hide his expression of embarrassment. Sun-kissed skin blazing red, he looks like I just witnessed him in an intimate moment.

Maybe I did– my tuition bitch is Grant's jerking partner in crime.

Sensing the direction of my thoughts, Grant smiles shyly at me and folds his hands in his lap. "That was my friend. I-I… um, I need to see Marc, but he said no."

Pouty, annoyed, and embarrassed, Grant's just asking for a thorough teasing. He reminds me of a petulant child, and I nearly laugh. I can see Whitt making that same expression. My lips twitch as I try to keep from smiling.

"Marc says I should come to you instead." Grant ducks his head bashfully, eyelashes shuttering his gaze.

If I wasn't a highly perceptive person, I'd think Grant was talking of sex or something equally salacious, but I do know Grant on this. He's talking of reassurance, a shoulder to cry on. Marc must be Grant's lifeline by keeping Jackson and Daniel's tight-fisted control at bay.

Leaning to the side on my elbow, I get into Grant's space. I gaze up at him with the most serious face I can muster. "Your cuddle and tug buddy said no to a fresh wank session?" I tease the ever-loving piss out of Grant. "What? Marc refuses to pay my tuition unless I take care of *business* for him?"

The crimson stain of mortification warps into the pale of horror across Grant's face. After a heartbeat, he realizes I'm teasing him. Head jerking backward, Grant releases the most intoxicating sound on the planet. All I can do is smile at the delight Grant displays, while ignoring the wrenching of my heart.

Crystalline eyes glittering with mirth, Grant shows his playful side. "That's exactly what we were talking about. I was trying to encourage Marc into a threesome with this hot bitch I know. She's a bit young for the both of us, but I told him she got off on the kinky shit. She'd totally cream for us if we allowed her to direct a mutual masturbation session."

Jesus Christ!

Blinking repeatedly, I manage to sound calm. "In your dreams." But my body is on fire, mind playing that scene in great detail. It takes a lot of effort to clear my throat. "That doesn't even remotely sound interesting. Boring, really."

"Mmm… hmm," Grant murmurs, shifting on the mattress to take some of the pressure off the tent in his pants. "Wanna know a secret?"

Flopping to my back, the bed bounces. "Yeah, I would. You and I could just fuck incessantly for the next five years, in between you'll disappear to your tower while I go to school, or we could actually get to know one another."

"As appealing as that sounds…" Grant lies next to me, folding his arms behind his head, one leg trailing to the floor. "I'm my fathers' paper-pusher. I get paid a ridiculous amount, but Daniel watches every penny while Jackson encourages me to be reckless. I majored in business, but it's not my passion."

Face glazed with lust, but not the sexual kind, Grant watches me for a moment, wondering if I care for him to continue. Shifting, he draws his arm down and begins plucking at a loose string on the hem of his pant leg.

Grant's nervous, more so than ever.

Taking the lead, I wrap my hand around Grant's nervous fingers. Shuddering, I close my eyes at the pleasant sensation zinging through my body at our connection. It scares the shit out of me, actually.

"I have a secret that only two other people know, neither are Whittenhowers. Do you want to be the third?" Grant's eyes are blazing with happiness and an underlying glint of deviousness. "I write when no one's watching," he whispers his secret. "I've published two books under a secret pseudonym."

Head jerking to the side, I stare at Grant in a mixture of shock and awe. He's the sensitive sort, perfect for the reclusive writer, but I didn't think he had it in him to cover up something that important.

I don't doubt Grant's ability to write a compelling story after growing up in this hell-borne family.

"What's your pseudonym?" Rolling on my side to face him, I fire questions out before he can answer the previous one asked. "What's the genre? Do you have a huge following? When do you find the time to write? How can you keep something so amazing private? You should feel proud of yourself."

Grant looks about ready to burst with happiness. "Nope, not gonna tell you my pseudonym– that's my secret. Only one person knows, and that's only because he's my in-between."

"Marcus," I cut Grant off before he can continue on. "It's fine. I'm not jealous. I understand how you and the cousins are tight. Just because we're sharing our bodies, and getting to know one another, doesn't mean either of us has the right to everything. I'm not just saying that, Grant." I utter my next words with conviction. "I mean it."

"It's scary, but I believe you." Grant whispers, words fluttering against my cheek. He sounds as awed as I feel about his writing career.

"My dad taught me that a woman shouldn't play games, and shouldn't expect one hundred percent, because every human deserves to save a bit of themselves for themselves. If my private thoughts belong to me, then yours must belong to you too. No double-standard. So I'm not jealous– I just like teasing you."

"Except around Cora," Grant reminds me.

Rolling my eyes, I briefly debate how to explain *that*. "Not Cora the person– what she represents. I'm jealous that she's something to you I'll never be, and I don't even want to be your wife. But I resent her more for having a legal right to my children. That's not jealousy."

"I'm sorry." Grant apologizes for the billionth time, words bleeding remorse.

Practical, I don't believe in beating a dead horse and expecting a different result. Move on and deal. "Enough of that." I scoot closer, enjoying the warmth Grant puts off. "Tell me more about your writing– what you're willing to share, that is."

Blushing, I can tell he never talks about himself. "Well, I don't make a lot of money at it. I know people think that if you write a book, you're rich. Writing is creation. It's just another art form. They don't call us starving artists for nothing. But I'd rather starve than do anything else," he says with pride.

My heart swells as I see the pride glow from Grant's face. This is who he's meant to be. If it weren't for his fathers, he would be immensely happy being a starving artist.

"You look pretty healthy to me," I tease, poking Grant in the belly. "But then again, your sister starves herself and she can afford to eat."

Grant growls, eyes narrowing. "I don't get that practice– at all. It's not sexy to grind against a skeleton, or comforting to hug a walking corpse." He rolls over on his side until we're face-to-face. "I'd give it all away in a heartbeat, ya know? The money. The legacy. The Whittenhower name. I'd hole up in a tiny place and absorb myself in my work. Life is too complicated, stressful, and it frightens me. I'd rather live inside my mind where I can control every minute detail."

The yearning in Grant's voice steals my breath away. I grab harder onto his hand, wanting nothing more than to sit in his lap and forget the world around us, even if it's only for a few minutes.

"I told you how you didn't know me, Regina. Not the real me. Everyone sees me as an extension of my fathers, but that's not me. It's why they're both so disappointed in me, terrified Whitt will turn out like me. Being sensitive and compassionate is worse than being gay in their eyes, and they fear I've infected my son. It's why they picked you, hoping your strength and pragmatism would overpower my weakness. Daniel wanted nothing more than a child created in his image, and he's never going to get that."

"Oh, I have a feeling Daniel and Adelaide are two sides of the same coin, and both of them wish she had been born with a dick. Not because Ade needs one sexually, but because a vagina is also considered a weakness in the eyes of your people."

"Too true." Grant's lips curl into a devious smirk. He watches me as if I'm now his world, and I can't hold his eyes because the depth of their gaze terrifies me.

I'm so screwed, both in a good *and* bad way.

"I want you to have a life outside of these walls, Regina. When Fate returns from West Virginia, she'll be moving here for a time to keep you company. Balance friendship with your education." Grant yanks my hand, causing my eyes to snap back up to his. "I'm keeping an eye on Roman Alexander for you. Even though it would pain me if you wanted to meet with him, I understand if you want to know if he's happy and healthy."

"Why?" Voice weak and thready, I can hear the tears in my voice, but none manifest.

"Welcome to the life of the rich and powerful, where you have to watch your back from birth. I know you had to be vigilant about your safety as you grew up, but imagine waiting for your nearest and dearest to stab you in the back to steal the power. I mean that in both the literal and figurative sense of the word. An ally is the most important thing in the world."

"Ally," I murmur, remembering the dozen times Grant called me his in the past few weeks. Lightning strikes, and I finally understand the odd relationship Stanton and Julio have. Julio said Grant had a death wish for not having an enforcer to watch his back and advise him. Grant wants that from Marcus, but something is holding him back.

Grant's next words prove my theory correct. "As much as I love and respect Marcus and Dexter, I can't count on them because I can't share things without major consequences. There's facets of my life that don't belong to me. After Jackson's death, when I take over, I'll be walking this life with adversaries who call me friend and family and not a single ally by my side."

"Grant." I try and fail to tug him into my arms.

"After some thinking." Grant clears his throat. "I can't allow you to become my ally, Regina. Because the calling of mother is more important– my children will need you."

"I don't understand," I mutter, confused.

"I know," Grant breathes across my face. "And it's best you don't. I love my siblings and mother with all my heart, but they're corruptible because they can be coerced or used against me. Roman. Even though I know you can trust your friend, and I believe I can trust him, I can't trust *you* around him. Roman's too big of a temptation for you."

"Grant, I'm not going to screw Roman and mess up your bloodline. It'd be a bit obvious if the kid popped out Native American when its parents both have recessive traits." It takes a few heartbeats before I understand what Grant's trying to say. "I'm sorry– I get it. If your wife entered your bedroom tonight, you'd wake up neutered with your billion dollar balls served to you for breakfast. No Roman. I got it."

Crinkles form at the corners of his eyes as Grant grins at me. "Allow me to ease your mind where Roman is concerned. Stanton is going to give me updates on him for me to pass on to you. Today's update was that Roman was in the usual place at the usual time, found reading a paperback and playing with his perfect hair," Grant mutters wryly. "Julian and Roman packed your belongings, and Stanton delivered them this afternoon. Albert put them in the garage, should you wish to catalog anything for later."

Curling into the fetal position, I hide my face. My chest aches, my skin hurts, my eyes sting, but the sob that spills from my chest is empty of tears.

"I miss them so much," I weep, body wracked with sobs. Grant sucks in a sharp breath at the pain in my voice. "I miss my parents. I miss Dad the most. Before he left us, Dad was my rock. When he died, I became my mother's rock and had no one else left to hold me. I like the feeling I get from being strong enough to shoulder the pain, but sometimes I need someone to hold me up. I'd forgotten what it felt like, but then Roman offered me what I was missing."

Voice restrained to hide his true emotions, "That's understandable, Regina. Everyone needs someone from time to time."

"I don't want to hurt your feelings, Grant, but I miss Roman, too." I look up at Grant with watery eyes that refuse to unleash tears. I expect to see anger, but his face is filled with understanding and compassion.

"Roman is loyal, correct?" I nod my head emphatically. "You trust him with your life?"

"Of course," I utter without question.

"I understand exactly what you're saying, Regina, and you're not insulting me or hurting my feelings. No one knows my true nature more than I do. But if a man is strong enough to hold up the strongest person I know, then he's a man of worth." Grant closes his eyes, muscles relaxing. With a relieved breath, his eyelids snap back open, pinning me. "Thank you."

"For what?"

Grant simply says, "Just thank you." After a heartbeat, he continues. "Thank you for being my echo and hearing me. I know you, Regina. I know your pain because I feel it too. Every waking moment of every day, but especially in the quiet of night." Voice thick with tears, his smile is filled with agony and loneliness.

Grant's body is taut with tension, and I know he wants to hold me but is waiting for permission. I finally give in to my body's need that is screaming by crawling on top of him, into his lap, and then wrapping my arms and legs around him. He buries his face into my hair and inhales loudly– sigh warm, ruffling the fine wisps of hair at my nape.

We don't speak.

Grant cries silently for the both of us, because I'm incapable. His tears slide down my neck in a cooling line to my breasts. His compassion and pain humble me.

I want to take the torment from his mind, to make him feel safe and wanted. I want to give Grant all the things I need, because no one will give them to me, feeding off of his security and comfort.

My fingers knot into the back of Grant's hair, and I pull until he looks at me– his blue eyes glow with trust, and it's my undoing. With a rush of air past my lips, I lunge upward, fusing our mouths together. I force all my pain, my frustration, my fear into our kiss. Fingers knotting tighter and tighter into Grant's wispy hair, the kiss takes on a violent edge, and I terrify myself with the intensity I'm giving off.

Breathless, "You may touch me," I flutter across his kiss-swollen lips.

Grant's eyes widen in surprise and delight. Tentative, he reaches out slowly, as if terrified I'll take permission back and yell at him for touching me. The anticipation kills me. Panting, I expected Grant to unleash all of his pent-up frustration and attack me as I had him. But his fingertips hover over my skin, barely a whisper of sensation. I close my eyes and sink into the oblivion known as Grant.

Rolling on top of me, I whimper when my tender mound comes into direct contact with the hardness between Grant's thighs. Forever the apologizer– "Sorry," he murmurs and moves away from me slightly.

Nibbling at my neck with blunt teeth, his fingers quickly unbutton my blouse. He accidentally bites me hard when he finds the lace and silk contraption that barely covers my breasts. I flush pink in embarrassment.

A noise that doesn't sound like me, escapes my throat when the warmth of Grant's mouth finds my nipple through the fabric of my bra. His teeth capture the enlarging bud and pull. Spiking pain and pleasure, his mouth is pulling and pulling and pulling, leaving me a writhing mass of pleasure. A loud groan is torn from my throat as the ache between my thighs turns into a raging fire of need.

My jeans disappear because I can't stand the restrictive feeling any longer. I throw them and hear the thump as they land, already forgotten.

"I can make you feel better. May I soothe you?" His voice is innocent, adding to the effect is his big round eyes and solemn expression.

I smirk at Grant because he's turned back into his devious, charming self.

I throw caution to the wind. Jaded Regina lies on her back on the bed in only her bra and an unbuttoned blouse. Oh, that's right...

I'm Jaded Regina.

A seductive, anticipatory chuckle flees my mouth, and I don't recognize the sound as mine.

"Is this what you want?" I tease Grant by drawing up my knees, then opening and closing them, playing peek-a-boo with my tender cunny. A throaty laugh spills from my lips— Grant looks gobsmacked.

Feeling no shame, my feet slide down the coverlet, and then I open my legs wide for him. I want his greedy mouth on me.

"You'll allow me to return the favor, right?" Voice cracking, I'm scared he'll tell me no. "I really want to." Ever since Roman tricked me, it's pretty much all I've thought about. I want to know what it's like to have a man at my total mercy.

"Regina, I may be a giver, but I'm still a man." Grant purrs wickedly while settling onto his stomach. His warm breath heats, then cools my flesh in a line along my inner thigh.

Groaning, my skin puckers, beading with goosebumps. Watching my every reaction, he softly blows on my tender skin, and every muscle in my body tightens as every nerve sparks to life.

"Obviously it's been awhile since I've done this, but I'm pretty sure it's like riding a bike." Peering up at me from between my legs, Grant flashes me a self-deprecating smile.

"Grant?" purrs from my lips. "If you tease me any longer, I'm going to explode before your mouth ever touches me."

Before I'm done speaking, Grant's resting his hot, moist tongue on my sore nub. Hips jerking forward from the sensation, I look down as he rolls his eyes up. Huge blue eyes stare at me through the thick fringe of blond lashes.

"Please," rolls off my tongue. I can feel his smile curve on my flesh rather than see it. All but what's happening in this bed flees my mind– I let go of the grief and fear. I'm lost in the waves of pleasure Grant's tongue, lips, and teeth elicit. It soothes the pain away and brings on a more demanding ache– one that will not take no for an answer. His fingers massage me from the inside while his lips gently suck on my greedy nub. But it's not enough.

"Grant, please," I plead in a throaty, needy drawl. "I need you inside me."

Blue eyes peek up at me in question. I'm too sore to ride him, but last night we found out I couldn't come unless I was in control. Grant waits patiently. However, I will never be patient. Reaching down, my fingers curl into his hair. Yanking hard, he groans in ecstasy.

Grant moves slowly– a puppet whose strings I pull. I watch in fascination as he undresses. My eyes feast on muscle-corded skin. A dusting of pale hair leads to his ruddy erection. The sight has need roaring through my system. He's pressed tight to his stomach, a line of moisture trailing down his length. I lick my lips in anticipation, my eyes stalking him as he crawls toward me on the bed.

I've changed my mind. I want him inside me, but somewhere else entirely.

I pounce, and he isn't prepared for my six-foot-tall body tackling him. He lays stunned on the mattress, wide-eyed and wildly panting.

For the second time in my life, a throaty laugh emerges from between my lips. The involuntary, husky sound stuns me for a moment. I couldn't make it if I tried, because it comes from somewhere deep inside of me when I'm at my most primal.

Straddling Grant's thighs, I hold him down with my palms on his abdomen. I flex my fingers, digging my nails into his sensitive skin, and I'm rewarded with a deep moan and a fresh drop of moisture on his belly.

My eyes roll until they connect with his. I need to know what Grant tastes like– that billion dollar fluid that has spilled from my body for hours and nourishes my womb. Leaning down, I lick his length and smile as it flexes to greet my eager tongue. Hands cupping my skull, his fingernails bite into my scalp, and I learn why he likes the nails so much– it awakens the skin to life.

I maintain our eye-contact as I sip at the pool that has collected in his navel. His nectar imprints itself on my cells– I'm instantly addicted. I will forever chase this taste.

Grant.

His back arches off the bed as the bulbous head parts my fervent lips. The heady sense of power I hold over this man inebriates me. Purely instinct, I attack Grant with my mouth, having no idea what I'm doing. I allow his moans and pleas to pull me into the direction to best pleasure him. I suck the tender, loose bits and he keens. I gently tug with my teeth, pulling them from his body. His shrill scream sparks guilt in my veins. Leaning away, his flesh falls from my mouth. I had hurt him, so I lave the precious bits in apology.

Grant's crazed eyes flash up to mine. Oh, he liked it. Blushing, innocent Regina tries to erupt, and he laughs at my reaction.

"Mistress, do it again. Harder this time. Please," voice pleading. The glint in his eye and the tone in his voice send a shot of need to my core. I clench my muscles and it strengthens.

My body moves on its own accord. I don't think. In the blink of an eye, I find myself straddling Grant's face with his cock shoved down my throat. A primal scream of ecstasy garbles around the flesh lodged in my mouth, trying to escape my lips.

Grant's cock lengthens and hardens further as he nips my bud with his teeth. The brutality of it almost brings my climax.

Yeah, this is my newest *forget the world* activity.

I fall into the rhythm of pleasure as I glide along his length. I'm invaded by two fingers– one in a place that has never been penetrated– and I bite him in shock. I worry I may have hurt him, but Grant shouldn't do that without asking.

Sucking my clit, thrusting his fingers in and out of both my pussy and ass, Grant pushes his cock farther down my throat. Groaning together, I learn something about Grant this instant– he craves painful touches mixed with the pleasure, while I must feel in control. What a pair we make.

My eyes roll back in my head, panting heavily, and I forget what I'm doing. Grant rests throbbing in my mouth, not complaining that I don't move. I'm lost to his touch– he sucks greedily at my nub, and I suffer the onslaught of his fingers. He caresses me, plays me to climax.

I never would have imagined that being filled at the same time in those two places could feel so good. With no build up, my orgasm hits me when Grant strums along the wall separating his fingers. I scream his name and buck against his face, tremors waving through my body, causing me to whimper with each one.

I fall to my back on the mattress and stare unseeing at the ceiling. *Holy Fuck!* I writhe every few seconds as aftershocks roll through me. "Grant." My voice is raw from screaming and from where he was pushed down my throat. I wet my lips and try again. "Make love to me– I need to see if I can get off while doing it. I don't want to be this freak all the time."

Grant doesn't speak, choosing to settle on top of me as his way of communicating. He glides his hands along the backs of my thighs, encouraging me to wrap my legs around his hips. He embraces me and takes a sip at my lips. The muscles in his back and ass flex underneath my heels as he arches to slide into me.

A low moan erupts from my chest as Grant slowly glides inside me. My flesh absorbs every sensation, every slide of skin-on-skin, and I tremble in pleasure.

His thrusts are deep and long. I melt into him, becoming one with him, and it utterly terrifies me. This can't last– it won't last– and if I fall into Grant, I don't know if I can survive the fallout of losing him.

Just as I was last night, I'm stuck at the precipice of release. It's painful– the fullness that refuses to spill. The pressure mounts and mounts but doesn't crest. I whimper, and he soothes my agony with a gentle kiss.

Grant chants my name with every roll of his hips. He strengthens inside me, and I know he's ready but won't let go until I do. I growl in frustration. "I can feel you're ready, Regina. Just let go. I'll be here for you," he promises.

"I can't!" I cry out. "I already did. It's your turn. Come for me, Grant," I hurriedly order.

"No," he disobeys. "Mistress, I'm here for your pleasure. Don't de-man me, Regina." Voice holding no frustration but a shit-ton of taunting, "It's not good for the ego."

"I'll stroke your ego another way," I tease back.

"Regina, if you need someone to fulfill your needs–" Stilling, his playfulness evaporates. "I'm okay with that." I don't like the sound in his voice, or the fear in his eyes. Just how Daniel and Jackson make him feel, Grant believes he isn't enough for me.

"Oh, Grant." I sigh, knowing I have to tread lightly. "No."

"I'm serious." He brushes the hair off my forehead so he can gaze down into my eyes. "If you need someone more like Roman, or Roman, I'll get them for you." Face twisted in a tortured expression, Grant's not fucking around. He means it, even if it would kill a part of him. "I just want you to be content and satisfied–happy."

"If I can't climax because I'm not in control, I highly doubt I'll be able to for someone who's controlling me." I try to laugh it off, but it comes out stilted and terrified.

"It's because I'm not strong enough to earn it, Mistress, not because you won't like it," he murmurs forlornly, that slit-your-wrists shadow rising from the depths of his gaze.

I close my eyes to the sight, and I wish I could remove the tone his voice held as he spoke those words. They keep replaying in my mind on repeat, and I want to kill everyone who shaped Grant into this insecure creature.

No matter how tightly I clench my eyelids or wish it away, it doesn't stop the scene from playing out in my mind's eye. A man larger than me, stronger than me, taller and more powerful, with bronze skin and eyes and closely cropped hair– he dominates me from above. Lost, apathy emanates from my soul– the emptiness. Sex becomes a conduit for pain, rather than pleasure. Unknowing to me, Grant, but not *my* Grant, stands out of sight as he watches the man take me raw. The look of pride in Grant's eyes takes my breath away yet simultaneously terrifies me.

I try to blink the vision away, but it's imprinted on my memory.

It's yet another premonition, not a fantasy, and I refuse to allow it to come to fruition. I will not spiral down the rabbit hole *that* far. Ever.

Unable to ignore the vision, my nails bite brutally into Grant's buttocks, no doubt drawing blood. With near violence, my pussy contracts around Grant's length. Sickened with myself, I nearly climax from the force of the vision.

Grant can't hold out as I relentlessly grip him from the inside. He cries my name and spills fiery liquid into my waiting, aching womb.

I learn one more lesson tonight– I don't need to be in control in order to climax. Grant's climax works just as well.

I keen deeply from that primal spot hidden inside me. Eyes popping open in a mix of ecstasy and panic, I stare up at Grant. His face transforms before my eyes– the pride, the satisfaction. The same expression he wore in my vision as another man fucked me into submission.

I ignore the premonition, and concentrate on Grant. This is the type of ego-stroking Grant needs. My release was found because of his, not because I was being a demanding kinky bitch– or so I tell myself. From now on, if it makes Grant happy, then it'll make me happy.

Chapter Twenty-Eight

After seven weeks of living at the sinister Misery Castle, I've yet to enter every room, which is pure insanity. However, I do have the lay of the land, for self-preservation's sake. Jackson and Daniel work just as much as I plan to, and we've reached a mutual level of begrudging respect over that fact. Time has gone by in a blur, albeit a pleasant blur. I've found out that money can indeed buy anything.

Even though the summer semester had already started, the Whittenhower name got me into the classes I wanted to take. With something productive to do, I'm unable to dwell on why I'm actually here, and I'm able to release the grief over my mother's death.

I'm moving on, but not forgetting a second of anything.

Albert drove me to school for the first few weeks, and I hated how dependent that made me feel. In the evenings, Grant taught me to drive the tiny sedan he bought me. On the weekends, Whitt volunteered his car as an excuse to ride in it. I hadn't expected the sense of freedom driving a ridiculously fast car could bring, especially with Grant and Whitt laughing in delight.

Whitt shouted, *"Faster! Faster!"* the entire time. He's going to be a maniac like his grandfather. All of us having busy lives, we cherish these unscripted, playful moments.

True to Grant's word, no one stopped me from driving myself to school, or anywhere else for that matter. But I'm not allowed to take Whitt anywhere without Grant, unless Albert is chauffeuring. The gate to Misery Castle opens and closes automatically, and the guards at the main gate to Crestview wave me in and out without question.

I'm not a bird trapped in an inescapable cage– Grant and Whitt are.

The summer session ended a few days ago, and the fall session begins in less than a week. After spending all of my free time with my best friend, I'm going to miss the hell out of Ade, because she's leaving me for California in the pursuit of knowledge– lucky bitch.

With Ade's help, I commissioned an empty room in the castle as my office. Being Grant's mistress has sickening benefits. I thought for sure someone would bitch that I just set up shop and made the space mine. But Priscilla asked Martha and Kristal to get me anything I wished. I didn't go overboard because it's gross, how if I snap my fingers, I get what I want.

Instead of letting it go to my head, I had Martha get me two more desks. I received a lot of odd looks when I used my newfound power to force Kristal to study with me, with the third desk belonging to Fate when she comes home.

With Ade leaving, my *maid* and my other bestie will be at my mercy. They'll learn pretty quickly that their definition of studying is not the same as mine. Fate is better than being an entitled heiress, and Kristal is so much more than the hired help. Both vivacious ladies are going to have a bright future free of their societal chains, even if it's over my dead body. Ade's going after her happily ever after in the big, bad world, and the girls and I are going to grab for ours too.

After being with Grant for so long, I've adopted his practices. No longer is it scary to be alone inside my head. I find the memories of my parents bittersweet instead of agonizing. So as we walk the winding corridors, it's not uncommon for us to do so in total silence. Most people would view our behavior as Grant and me not enjoying each other's company, but it couldn't be farther from the truth. We're *that* comfortable.

"I thought we'd have some fun tonight." Grant's excited voice startles me out of my head– it's not often that I actually hear him speak. He's returned to writing me notes now that we've bypassed the '*getting to know each other*' stage in our odd relationship.

"I've never been down this hallway." I comment, giddiness mixing with trepidation in my belly. You never know whether a dragon or dungeon will lay ahead. If it wasn't for leaving the castle to go to school, I'd fall into a time warp.

"I should have shown you sooner." Grant's eyebrows knit together, looking guilty. "I'm just not big on shows and movies. I'd rather spend my time with a good book."

"No joke," I tease him. If Grant's not working, he's either thinking, reading, or writing. I've yet to find the *tower* he hides in, and I doubt many know of its location. Sometimes I think the tower isn't even at Misery Castle. Grant will disappear into thin air, and reappear as quickly and silently as he left hours earlier.

"Welcome to the Whittenhower Theater." Grant gestures wide with his arm as he swings one of the double doors open.

"Of course it has a name," I mutter wryly as I enter a theater I didn't even know existed. It doesn't come as a surprise, seeing as I stumbled into a goddamn ballroom last week. A Ballroom.

A Ballroom.

Whittenhower Theater is an accurate title. It's not a TV room like in most houses, or even a movie theater like at the mall. It's a two-story, sloping, oblong room with a curtained stage at the bottom and red velvet seats arranged in rows lit by floor lights. Speaker boxes hang from black, soundproof walls, silently waiting to spill their secrets. No doubt converted for modern times, there is a screen at the back of the stage and a popcorn machine and snack bar near the door.

"Every room I enter impresses me more and more," I breathe in awe, eyes flicking over my shoulder to find Grant.

"And not in a good way," he adds, flashing me an ashamed smile. "The castle was the only source of entertainment while Dominion was being built. It may have been owned by the Whittenhowers, but it was built and used by all the founding families. Blame the ancestors for their ostentatious needs and wants."

"No shit," I mutter, shocked.

Sitting in the last row near the entrance, Priscilla is rocking a giggling Whitt in her lap. In the large space between the rear wall and the seats, Ade sits cross-legged on the floor while assembling a board game. Ahead, on the huge projection screen, a classic film plays on mute.

"Wanna play a game, Scholarship Girl?" Ade asks in a taunting tone, smirking up at me.

Voice light and playful, I tease her back. "And just what do the elite play for fun? It can't be Monopoly, since you play that every damn day. Not Chess, either– we are all but pawns to the kings and queens ruling our world."

"Global domination." Ade flips the Risk box up so I can see it.

"But of course." I grin. "Why play to own properties when you can roll the dice, engage in bloody battles, and take over country after country until you rule the world. Good choice, girlfriend."

With a wink, "Watch out, Whitt and Grant are creepy good."

I sit opposite Ade, and help divvy up the infantry, cavalry, and artillery pieces. "Who wants what color?" I chirp, stealing the gray for myself.

"I want blue," Grant murmurs against the shell of my ear, and I stifle a shudder. A kiss flutters against the nape of my neck, and I have to stifle the sigh that tries to slip past my lips, but this time I fail at stopping the shudder rolling along my spine.

Grant is *very* affectionate. Since we see each other less than I expected, moments hardly pass where we aren't connected in some way, even if it's only our gaze. He's in need of constant reassurance, but I find it a comfort.

At first, satisfying Grant's needs with his family and wife watching was bizarre and awkward, but they treat me with respect– they treat me as Grant's wife in private, but Cora gets treated with the respect and courtesy in public.

Cora and I are equally fucked. I become physically sick when Grant attends public functions with Cora, and no doubt she could spit nails on a daily basis as all the Whittenhowers and the staff treat me as Grant's wife within the castle walls.

Being the last Regal standing, with all of my family in the ground, it's the strangest feeling– the warmth that glows in my chest when we're all huddled up and behaving as a family. There are times even Daniel warms to me. Jackson is like trying to harness a tornado, and we're all at the mercy of his moods– he's a sloppy kisser/Daniel goader. After not seeing her for a few years, Katie and her husband, Kent, have been visiting more and more, spending all their time here when they aren't actively campaigning. I worried Katie would see me as an interloper, as less now than she used to view me, because I'm her brother's mistress. But she treated me as if no time had passed since her tenure at Hillbrook. Katie is the perfect politician's wife, only she's for real– firm yet compassionate.

"Well, aren't you handsome?" A soft voice flows from the doorway. "I haven't seen you since you were five. You're a young man now. How long have I been gone? Years? Did you miss me?"

Whitt's a charming flirt, just like his father, most likely just like his mother, but most certainly just like his big sister. The six-year-old scrambles off Priscilla's lap to greet our guest. Cupid cheeks blooming pink, "Miss Simpson, it's always a pleasure," he murmurs formally, extending his hand.

At least Whitt didn't try to choke this one.

I laugh to myself for many reasons, and those in the know join in with me. Hopping to my feet, "Fate!" I squeal, nearly tackling my teacup-sized best friend.

I haven't seen Fate since my mother's funeral. Faith got into a huge fight with their mother, Lara, and went back to West Virginia, so Fate followed for the summer. Supposedly she was to drag Faith back home to go to Hillbrook in the fall.

Fate's blue eyes sparkle and her skin is flushed with good health. She looks stronger, not as sickly thin. Her aunt must have been stuffing her with good vittles. "C'mon, let me hear the accent. You always pester Faith about it, and it's only fair that you picked it up this summer."

"I've missed you terribly, Regina," she sings without a drop of a West Virginia inflection– 100% snooty heiress. "Rusty Knob, West Virginia is a backward, little town, and I'm so happy to be back in civilization."

Fate's eyes are older, less innocent, and I wonder what I look like to her. What does she see when she looks into my eyes? Horror? Contentment? Contempt? Love?

"Thanks for coming, Fate," Ade calls from the floor, but makes no move to rise. "Regina really missed you, never shutting her trap about what you must be doing."

"It's a good thing you're not the jealous sort." Fate sticks her tongue out, being a brat.

I expect Ade to go ballistic, but she just rolls her eyes at me as she rises to her feet. Shocked, all I can do is stare as Ade lightly kisses Fate's cheek. My two best friends, who couldn't be in the same classroom at the same time, actually smile at one another. What is the world coming to?

"We've bonded over a common interest, it seems." Ade settles next to the game board again.

"You two have been speaking?" I ask Fate in surprise.

"Maybe," she gives as a noncommittal answer. The glint in her eye says they have, and often. "We aren't best friends or anything, but when one of us is somewhere else, the other steps in her place. Ade leaves for California tonight, and I step in– as I should. A lady needs her sisters by her side."

Turning away, I hide my eyes. I know they are red and glisten with tears- tears that refuse to fall.

"You're going to need us, Regina. Someday, we'll need you, too. So get used to having people watch your back." Ade leaves me in stunned silence. "You're not alone, and you never were. We've stopped waiting for you to ask for help. Now we're going to give it whether you want it or not."

Choking on emotion, I could just hug Fate for purposefully changing the subject. "OH! I want green!"

"Red!" Whitt calls, grabbing the clear, plastic bin before anyone else can snatch it. He tucks his prize to his chest and flashes a dimpled grin.

"Who ends up with piss-yellow?" Fate chuckles deviously.

"I guess I do, dammit!" Kristal exclaims as she walks into the room.

"Language." Martha pushes a rolling cart into the theater loaded with food, snacks, and drinks.

"Sorry, Ma. I guess you ignore the way Regina and Ade talk," she retorts with sarcasm.

"You're not them, Chica," Martha reprimands her daughter. "And we have a child in the room."

"Don't stop on my account. I can swear in five languages," Whitt announces, never looking up from where he's organizing his red pieces on the carpet. "Except French– I hate French."

I laugh into the back of my hand. That little shit.

"I think it's time for the moms to retire." Priscilla smiles at us and winks. "Have fun, and don't influence young Daniel too much." She knows damn well no one can influence the kid– he's already set in his ways.

"Martha, what do you say we watch a movie and eat a few slices of your famous sinful seven layer cake? I need to drown my sorrows with decadence while Daniel's locked in the study and Jackson is off being a reckless fool."

Priscilla tips Ade's face back and plants a kiss to her mouth. "Be safe, my baby girl. I love you."

"I will, Mommy. I love you, too." Ade replies in a small voice, quivering with emotion. "I'll miss you."

"And we will miss you very, *very* much." Priscilla says wistfully, "Go forth and prosper, but come home to us soon."

"Chocolate it is, Prissy." Martha takes Priscilla's elbow when she notices how distraught the mother is over her youngest daughter flying from the nest.

Martha reaches down and caresses Ade's cheek. "Give 'em hell, Miss Whittenhower."

"Mamá," Kristal whines.

"I didn't say I couldn't swear." Martha snickers mischievously. "The kid can swear in five languages. It ain't hurting his ears none. I just don't want you cussing, Chica."

Grant releases a string of words I've never heard before, and Whitt giggles hysterically. The boy offers his own in return, and Grant cuffs him upside the head.

"I don't even want to know how you know that phrase." Eyes held wide, Grant is awed. "I'll have to try that soon." He leers at me, and it makes Whitt giggle even more.

"Do I even want to know?" I ask, half afraid and half excited.

Grant replies smoothly with a phrase in Latin, causing me to blush so hard my earlobes feel like they've caught fire. I gaze at Whitt in shock, and he giggles again. When that kid is grown, whoever he hooks up with is going to be in for a huge surprise.

Whitt's a little pervert.

"Naughty fucking brats," Martha mutters under her breath as she escorts Priscilla from the theater.

"Remind me to invest in some liquid soap. Daniel's dirty mouth is in need of a thorough cleaning," Priscilla threatens, voice flowing in from the hallway.

"Food." Grant groans as if starve-gutted, and then attacks the cart. He lives off food, sex, and silence.

We all look to the clock ticking above the door. It's counting down the time until Ade flees Misery Castle. I hope she never returns. But selfishly, I don't want her to go.

Hours later, we lounge on the floor, with the game long forgotten. Grant keeps peppering me with butterfly kisses as a hint that he's ready for bed. Fate watches us with an amused expression as Kris fills her nails in with a black Sharpie.

Whitt's plastered to Adelaide, because he fears that if he lets her go, she'll float into the ether. Head resting in her lap, Ade's fingers feather Whitt's baby-fine hair.

Her face is scrunched with contemplation. "It's weird. I'm only sixteen, yet I'm entering the adult world," she muses.

"The kids in Rusty Knob are born working. Oh, the perils of being born into money." Fate makes light of Ade's statement, but underneath, it's laced with truth. It's not the same issues the urban children I grew up with are facing, or even the rural kids, but the water's just as murky with fiercer sharks.

Our heads turn as one when Albert comes to a standstill in the doorway. We take a collective breath. All of us will miss Adelaide, but we all hold different fears for her future.

"Nobody get emotional on me," Ade threatens, tears already glinting in her eyes. "I'll be back at winter break, and I bet I'll have a wicked tan." She crawls to her feet like this is no big deal.

"Wear sunscreen. Don't wanna see that pasty skin of yours filled with freckles or skin cancer," Fate cautions lightheartedly. "No worries, I'll take care of our girl." Darting forward, she makes a choking sound, then swiftly leaves the theater.

"One down." Ade jokes, smiling through the tears. "I really know how to clear a room, don't I? Kris." She pulls the spunky maid to her and squeezes so hard Kristal taps out.

I've spent endless hours with Kristal. She's the keeper of most of Misery Castle's secrets. I've watched her kickbox in the gym, dance while vacuuming, and not bat an eyelash when Jackson has a tantrum. Tough as she may be, Ade and Kristal have grown up together, and tears are streaming in a torrent down her cheeks, to the point she can't even respond to Ade.

"Stay outta trouble, Chica." Ade challenges, "If you can." Ade plants a smacker to the smaller girl's forehead, and then pushes her away. "Off ya go. No goodbyes." Kristal disappears the same way Fate went.

"Brother." Ade's voice cracks, fading, and then the floodgates really open.

Grant picks Ade up off her feet until they're eye-level. They watch each other, eyes darting minutely back and forth, communicating silently in a way I'll never understand or be able to achieve. I'm speared with a bolt of jealousy, not from their strong connection, but my lack of connection to anyone. I have no siblings– no family. I will never experience the connection they have.

Grant releases Ade without a word, then strides from the room. I can sense he didn't go far, waiting for his son.

"The world's *best* Daniel Whittenhower." Ade smirks through the wash of tears, kneeling down to Whitt's height.

"This is so you don't forget us." Whitt hands her a sealed manila envelope. "Don't open it until you get to your dorm room."

"Of course," she replies with the same amount of seriousness, tucking the envelope under her arm. "I love you, Daniel. Don't ever forget that, no matter what happens. *I love you.*"

Whitt runs past Albert and out the door. I watch as Grant chases after him, scoops him up, and jogs down the hallway in one fell swoop.

"Albert, can you give us a minute alone, please." Ade tries for polite, but it's costing her.

We wait while Albert closes the door, giving Ade and me privacy. I thought she was crying before– I was wrong. Sobs wrack her body, tears spilling so fast they drench her blouse.

"Sorry," Ade mutters, plucking a linen napkin from the cart. After she wipes her face dry, she continues. "A lot can happen in five months, and there are no guarantees I'll be back for winter break. I've thought of doing as you are– year-round schooling and a double course load. I might as well get it over with as fast as possible, ya know? We both need to be ready before the five-years are up. What we have to do is life-changing."

Adelaide drops to her knees before me, and I wince when I hear the clack of her bones hitting the hardness of the floor. She lifts my t-shirt, and stares in wonder at my growing belly. I haven't told anyone but Ade. Grant just knew since I missed my monthly, but we're not sharing the news until my second trimester. We must have hit the ball out of the park in the first week, because my doctor said I'm six weeks along.

"Hey, niece or nephew," Ade murmurs against my belly. "Your mama and I are going to make sure we get to keep you with us always. I'll burn this fucking earth to its core to keep you safe." She rolls her eyes up to meet mine– the intensity they hold would make enemies flee screaming in terror.

"Spend all of your energy growing our baby." Ade abruptly stands. "Keep my brother happy and you will be, too."

"I'll try." As lame as it sounds, it's all I can do.

"My present is waiting out there." Ade tips her head over her shoulder. "I guess I better go educate myself, because we've got a world to change in the future."

I've held myself in check until this moment. Through Fate and Kris crying, and even when Whitt's tiny sobs met my ears when his father picked him up to briskly whisk him away. Now, alone with Ade... a bereaved noise releases from my chest. I'm fucking scared shitless to go through this without Ade by my side.

I'm terrified.

"No goodbyes." Ade breathes, "I love you, Regina."

Ade silences any reply I would offer by kissing me on the mouth. Not a shock-value Jackson kiss, or a sisterly kiss. A passionate kiss Grant would give me. Eyes held wide with shock, I stare at her the entire time she sucks my kiss.

Ade flashes me a cocky smile as she pulls away.

Click… Click… Click… Tumblers click into place inside of my mind.

"Yeah, love's a cruel bitch– who would've imagined you'd be the girl I fell in love with," are Ade's parting words.

I stare at the open doorway for minutes, knowing our world has already changed. I don't remember walking from the theater to my bedroom, for which I'm thankful.

Once in bed, I huddle up between two halves of the same whole, giving and accepting comfort in equal measure. A tiny hand spans my lower stomach, with a larger replica overlapping it. Grant snores softly against the back of my neck, and Whitt's tear-crusted cheek rests against my breast.

If all goes correctly as planned, which is doubtful, this will be my future family.

I close my eyes with a smile. Adelaide is safe away from Misery Castle– free to pursue her dreams. Right this minute, she's flying over the vast span of our great nation to another coast and a new life.

Fate and Kristal are in Fate's new bedroom, bonding over girl talk. Martha is comforting Priscilla. Cora spends most of her time down in the Gates at her father's mansion. Jackson and Daniel are off playing Monopoly, Chess, and Risk with real currency, human beings, and countries.

It's telling of our values by where we end our nights.

Chapter Twenty-Nine

Today marks six months since I entered Misery Castle, and I don't recognize myself. I've experienced countless shifts in my reality, until Regina Regal of seven months ago would loathe the Regina Regal of today.

I'm in my second semester at school, and about to begin my third trimester in my pregnancy. School is going well, even though I've been threatened by Daniel that I won't be allowed to attend once I start showing. The jokes on him– I've been showing for months. What you learn on the streets stays with you forever. In Junior High, girls managed to go full-term before anyone noticed. I've become the master at camouflaging my baby bump.

Tonight though… tonight is pure torture. I've pasted a smile on my face and managed to not have my voice break when I speak. I know deep down that if I protest, or get upset, or get all girly and hormonal and beg and plead and ask Grant why he doesn't love or respect me, he'll break.

I deserve a goddamn Academy Award.

"I hate these parties," Grant complains as he adjusts his bowtie for the tenth time.

Devastatingly handsome in his tux, looking at Grant should be illegal. It would be a pleasure to say he's all mine, but tonight proves that isn't the case.

Refusing to upset him, I play along like nothing's out of the ordinary. "You're actually fucking your tie up more, not fixing it."

I bite my lip as I adjust Grant's tie back to where it was before he messed with it. It feels weird helping him get ready for a party I'm not invited to attend.

I can pretend on a daily basis. It gets easier and easier to forget reality while we lie in bed together cuddling while chatting about our future son. We tease how we'll name him something ridiculous like Zolt, when we know his name will be Daniel. Two generations of Daniels, with Grant being left out of the mix, when by rights, it should be three generations of Jacksons and my son given his own name. But that is nothing I can change. We've progressed to nicknames, because Daniel, Daniel, and Daniel need to know who is talking to whom.

The Whittenhower heir growing in my belly, being nourished from my life force, created from both Grant's and my DNA, will be called Niel.

Niel.

Every night we go to sleep chatting about the antics Whitt and Niel will get into, and it becomes too easy to pretend. As we go about the doldrums of daily life, discussing the stressors of work and school, it becomes more and more like reality.

But it's the most devastating fantasy.

Reality is that Grant isn't mine, nor is the child I'm carrying in my belly. The child is mine by genetics only. Niel and I will be connected on a soul level, but the Whittenhowers could give a shit less about your soul.

"Why do you hate the parties so much?" One more adjustment of Grant's tie, and it's perfect. "You're so fucking handsome, it's terrifying."

In one of his moods, the compliment washes right over him. "Sometimes I just want to run away and never look back," he murmurs as he walks away from me to sit on the edge of the bed. Leaning forward, he hides his face in his hands.

This is why I kept my trap shut on *my* feelings. Grant is the most loving, playful, mischievous, and charming depressive person on the planet. Which is why everyone I come into direct contact with tells me, "*As long as you keep Grant happy, you'll be happy.*" Because when he's not, I'm on suicide watch.

I enjoy being the rock, but sometimes I need to be a boulder to hold Grant up. On those days, I cry in the shower because I don't have a mountain shouldering my burdens.

"I wasn't meant to be a Whittenhower– I'm my mother's son. I love Ade and Whitt, and I'd miss them, but I could leave and never come back. This stress is killing me."

"What's worrying you?" I sit next to Grant, but I don't offer any physical comfort. I can tell that if I were to touch him, he wouldn't explain what's rattling around inside his mind.

"What isn't?" Blue eyes cut in my direction, like I've lost my damn mind. "I have to go downstairs, where two hundred guests await, wanting to congratulate Cora and me for the child that's inside *your* belly. I have to lie as I'm interviewed by the press, and as I talk to friends I've known since birth. I'm not strong enough to lie and not have it affect me. But most of all, I know you're torn to bits and trying to hide it."

The lonely, somber tone in Grant's voice has my hand on his back in an instant. I rub small circles in comfort, trying to lend him the strength I have in abundance– the strength he needs to get through the night.

Grant and I, we're in this together. I'm upset, and he understands why. So I try to think what it would feel like if I had to go down there and leave him up here. What it would feel like to hide the man I love while I pretended to love another for appearances. How I'd feel if neither of my sons' true parentage was known.

I couldn't do it– I wouldn't.

Grant doesn't want to do it, either. But the difference between him and me is that I have the balls to tell them all to fuck off.

"You'll do just fine. You aren't built to lie, but I've never met someone as charming and engaging as you. Just be yourself, and remember that the child they're congratulating you on is *yours*, and always will be. No matter what happens with me, Niel will always be your son."

Niel will always be my son too, even if he doesn't know it. Just as Whitt doesn't know Grant is his father, Gwen is his mother, and all those wonderful human beings are his siblings, my son will believe he belongs to Grant and Cora Whittenhower.

But nothing will change the fact that I carry Niel. My blood will always flow in his veins. Someday, when we meet again, Niel will know who I am because we're connected at soul depth.

I tell myself this every moment of every day, because to do anything less would be an express pass to Wintercrest Asylum.

"I love you, Regina." Words reverent, Grant means them. He loves me, I know he does. But not enough to make essential sacrifices he's not willing to give, and I don't fault him because I understand him.

Grant and I spend most of our time in silence. The longer we know each other, the less that needs to be said. We just get each other, even if we don't agree with it. I pull Grant into my lap, wrapping my arms around him. He cries silently against my breast, the tears soaking into my shirt and cooling my flesh.

"Grant, tell me how you see your life," I coax him. "Let's fantasize for a moment. If you dwell on what you're about to do, you'll make it worse."

"I just want to be alone. I want to write and be inside my own head. What I want is selfish," he curses.

"No, it's not selfish. You're allowed to dream of what you want. Tell me more," I urge him on.

"I wouldn't be a father or a husband, because children and a wife run on their own time, not my limited time. I'd lock myself away and create. When I was ready to see people, I would. But they wouldn't be the people who wait for me downstairs. Never them," he snarls angrily.

I don't do the girly, hormonal, over-emotional, irrational thing where I doubt myself because the father of my child just admitted he didn't want to be around me or our child. Where I scream and shout, call him a rat-bastard, and throw shit at his head. '*Don't you love me?*' bullshit. '*If you loved me, I'd come first!*' when everyone looks out for #1 while spouting selfishness. It's human nature, and the quicker we all come to realize this, the more peaceful life will be.

Grant's vision of his own future has nothing to do with me and everything to do with his need for serenity.

Practical, I'm not built like most women. I understand Grant's needs and wants belong to him, and his private thoughts and emotions are his to own. All of that is involuntary, and he shouldn't be judged on it. To do otherwise means I'm a narcissist who thinks Grant's world should revolve around me.

But I do have self-respect, so if I didn't understand why Grant felt as he does, I'd leave him as soon as I had the ability. Grant owns how he feels, just as I have the right to not put up with it. It's not my place to change Grant. It's my place to either accept him or leave.

This isn't the life I saw for my future, and Grant knows it. The difference between him and I is that I will get the future I dreamed, because nothing will stop me– not even a Whittenhower.

"I will get you that future," I promise Grant, and mean every word of it. "I love you enough to know what you need and why you need it."

"I've never doubted you, Regina," he whispers reverently, fingertips clenching on my belly above Niel. "But now I have to go downstairs and live the life I wasn't meant to lead."

Grant stands up, then smooths his hands down the tuxedo jacket. He pulls the lapels until the jacket forms to his perfect shoulders. A sight to behold, six months in and my mouth still dries up when I gaze at him. The combination of his blue eyes, blond hair, and the self-deprecating smile that brings out his dimples, is devastating while in a custom-made tuxedo.

Grant looks like a younger, hotter James Bond.

My fingers clench his lapels, pulling him down to my mouth. Fervent, I kiss him with all the passion he ignites inside of me. His moan stokes the fire to smoldering temperatures. I pull away before I'm tempted to toss him to the bed and mount him.

Goddamn pregnancy hormones have me horny all the time– it's ridiculous.

"I wanted to show you what's waiting for you in our suite." I whisper against his lips, "Hurry back."

I walk Grant to the door, and he looks a little lost and unsure. It makes me want to take his hand and walk him down to the ballroom. He reminds me of a child on the first day of kindergarten– no, a puppy, and I need to hold his leash so he won't get lost.

"You'll be fine." I reassure him, trying hard to buy it myself.

"Regina, I hate reality." He looks about ready to put his arms out, palms on the jamb, worried I'll push him into the hallway. "I don't want to live it. It's too damn stressful for me. It makes me feel crazed," and he does sound a little crazed with his voice cracking and wavering with every other word he speaks.

"I made you a promise, and I always keep them. This will *not* be your future," I vow. I abruptly kiss Grant. With him distracted, I shove his ass out the door. I push it shut in his face and lock the deadbolt. I can't hold Grant's hand and walk him down there, but I can give him a dose of tough love.

It's a good five minutes before I hear Grant get the courage to move away from the door and go meet his fate.

As soon as I sense his presence is gone, I freak the fuck out. I don't know what to do with myself. That tiny voice in my subconscious is screeching. Its siren screams that if being locked inside of a suite while carrying a man's child, as he's downstairs with his wife, doesn't make me a whore, then it doesn't know what one is. I can't avoid my reality just as Grant can't ignore his.

I *am* a whore.

I *am* a mistress.

I loathe who I've become.

I'm not the type of person who stands idly by. If Grant belongs to anyone, it's to me. I can't allow him to go downstairs by himself when he's feeling lost. The depression and desolation was thick in his voice. It's my job to make sure he's happy, and he sure as hell wasn't.

I forget my baby bump camouflage in my haste as I sneak out of my bedroom, ghosting down the labyrinth. I don't worry about anyone spotting me. The upstairs hallways are so confusing that it's taken me six months to learn its bends and twists, and I'm still unsure half the time. It's doubtful any of the party guests would come up here anyway.

I glue myself to the wall while I peek over the edge of the south staircase's balcony. Dozens of men and women in black-tie finery chat in the vestibule down below. I hiss a curse, and quickly hurry across the balcony, heading toward the back staircase leading down to the kitchen.

Mistake.

Whittenhower Estates has a huge staff, all of them knowing exactly who I am. But I hadn't realized that for an affair of this size we'd have additional help tonight. "Shit!" Pair after pair of eyes latch onto the crazy, pregnant woman who just popped into the kitchen from parts unknown.

My savior comes in the form of a spitfire, tiny Latina. Gripping my elbow, "What are you doing, Regina." Kristal smirks at me knowingly.

"The baby was hungry." I lie and grab a pastry off a silver tray as the server passes by. I'm not hungry, but I don't like looking like a jealous idiot of a mistress.

"Follow me," Kris says with a wink.

Tugging me behind the wall, Kris leads me through a few narrow passageways. She explains on the way how the staff aren't to be seen or heard. None of this is new information since I've seen Martha pop out the walls, nearly making me piss my pants. But I never had the balls or time to investigate.

It's creepy, dark, and it's so narrow the wall brushes against my shoulders. I guess they didn't plan for gargantuan pregnant women when they made the secret passageways. I shiver from their ominous feel.

Kris cracks open a panel, and the sound of the party hits me full force. The clink of crystal and the murmur of voices are accompanied by melodious orchestra music.

My version of Pandora's Box, I press my eye to the crack and peer out. Swallowing down tears that won't fall, my heart drops to the floor.

Hundreds of men wearing black tuxedos impede my view. A kaleidoscope of color swirls around the dance floor from the ball gowns. Priceless gems and glittering diamonds catch the light from the chandeliers.

It's a whole 'nother world from anything I've ever experienced, and I never will. Grant may love me, but I truly am his mistress in every definition of the word. Just as there is kitchen staff, office staff, I'm bedroom staff. It's why I'm celebrating a party thrown in the honor of the baby boy I'm carrying by peeking out of a crack in the wall.

The mistress doesn't get taken on dates, or invited to soirées, benefit dinners, and charity functions. We're hidden behind castle walls, used when wanted and ignored when not, and shamed as we should be.

I catch sight of Daniel and Priscilla. They're beaming, accepting well wishes from all of their friends. Jackson's a head taller than most of the guests– hair not even combed. His eyes have a crazy glint, like he finds the entire affair ironic and he's getting off on the fact.

Cora is preening like a bird underneath everyone's praise. Usually pushed to the wayside, not able to conceive, this is Cora's day. It's her time to shine, even if it's not reality. Her fake belly is patted by each and every well-wisher– her belly that in all rights holds my son– her son.

I try not to hate Cora, using empathy and compassion over the fact that she can't have children. But since it's my son, I fail miserably. I don't give a shit about false accolades and parties.

Niel is *my* son!

Once spotted, Grant holds all of my attention. He's miserable– a second away from breaking his champagne flute and slicing his wrists. Grant is dramatic enough to do it– stand in an ever-growing pool of his own blood, shouting, *"I did this for you! Is it enough yet? Is it?"*

Doesn't anyone else see what I see? How can anyone shaking his hand, or kissing his cheek, not notice the expression of pure, unadulterated torture written across Grant's face?

The urge to run to Grant, to bundle him into my arms and hold him, is almost unbearable. I need to reassure him that the world is a perfectly fine place to live as long as you follow your own path.

Petrified, a sob builds in my chest.

Grant can't leave me– he can't.

And then Cora puts her hand on Grant's forearm, and my blood boils to the temperature of the surface of the Sun. I hiss and bare my teeth.

When Grant flings Cora's hand away, my pride in him overpowers the insane territorialism that came with the pregnancy hormones. Cora glares at Grant, and when she turns to face her adoring crowd, she's glowing beautifully from her pregnancy– fake bitch.

Grant starts to panic, and I'm a hairsbreadth from opening the panel and running to his rescue. Suddenly a back blocks my view of Grant, stopping me from making a horrible mistake. A tall man with broad shoulders and closely cropped hair leans down and whispers into Grant's ear. I have no way of knowing what he's saying, but Grant visibly relaxes.

Grant's eyes fall shut and his face goes lax when a long-fingered hand rests upon his shoulder. I don't know who the man is, but he heavily influences Grant. Welling up, my instincts supply the name.

Marcus Zeitler.

A noise frightens me. So caught up in the scene in the ballroom, I hadn't realized Kristal was no longer with me. Hurrying, I slide the panel shut, then try to remember my way to the kitchen through the mazework of tunnel-like passageways.

I must have turned left when I should've turned right, and I start to panic. Trying to think logically, I backtrack and find myself in a completely different location than from where I started. Misery Castle is ginormous, and I could stay in the passageways for life and no one would be the wiser. I just need to find one of the many exits.

Logical or not, sections of the passageway are so narrow Niel rubs against the walls, and the ceiling brushes my hair. After a few close calls where I nearly shriek and piss my pants, spider webs no longer terrify me, as for the spiders...

I wander for what feels like hours, but it's probably only minutes. My feet hurt from carrying Niel along on my journey. I don't want to admit defeat, but my last resort will be shouting and hoping someone will hear me above the din of the party. As thankful as I'd be if I met a member of our staff in one of these tunnels, I'd probably piss my pants for real, should it actually happen.

A moan startles me, and I fuse my back to the wall, for all the good that does with my huge stomach sticking out in front. Like a hedonistic game of Marco Polo, the next moan is louder, and I use it to pinpoint the direction I need to go in order to get out of these walls.

I sneak up, not wanting to disturb whoever is making the sounds of pleasure. I force myself not to hurry even though my bladder is protesting– maybe I'll end up pissing myself after all.

Fingertips smoothing over the wall, I try to locate the exit. As entertaining as the moans sound, trying to locate a way out while some assmunch is getting his rocks off, kind of makes me want to tear his dick off when I get out of here– gotta love pregnancy hormones.

I have the ability to feel every emotion possible in under thirty seconds. I'm positive pregnancy is a reasonable defense in a court case.

Biting my lip against a victory call, I crack the panel open and peer out to see where in the castle I'm located. The wallpaper is gold, not taupe, so I must be in the north side of the house.

My fingers clutch the panel when a guttural moan startles me. A young man has another one pressed against the wall, and they're kissing passionately. Grinding, fingers yanking hair, they're really into each other.

It takes me a moment to realize it's the boys I met half a year ago at Hillbrook. The white-haired boy is Ade's intended, Ezra Zeitler, and the choking charmer is none other than Cortez Hunter.

I take a deep breath and prepare to leave the dusty passageway. These idiot fifteen-year-olds aren't going to keep me from a toilet. A man with glowing bronze skin and dark hair comes into view, causing me to freeze.

"There's a time and a place for this, son, and this is neither," he scolds the boys in a deep voice. The timbre of the sound makes my eyes slip shut, hitting me like a narcotic to the heart.

Son?

Jesus Christ, does this guy get around, or what? He's everywhere. It's my tuition bitch/Grant's cuddle buddy and savior. Marcus Zeitler.

Ezra's pale skin blooms crimson, but he steals another tender kiss from his boyfriend anyway. Cortez has changed in the eight months or so since I've seen him last. He's filled out, lost the baby fat, and the cocky air about him is real instead of put on. He takes the kiss and never blushes.

Then Cortez looks to Marcus with an expression I have no name for– it's almost taunting.

I've yet to see Marc's face, only his broad shoulder and the curve of his jaw. When Cortez smirks at him, his shoulders tighten beneath his black jacket.

"Don't push me," Marcus growls, the sound reverberating down my spine.

"Cort, behave," Ezra chastises, and then pulls his boyfriend down the hallway.

Marcus abruptly turns around, so quickly I can't take in any of his features, and then presses his eye to the cracked panel, connecting with mine. A suffocated sound fills the air as my breath hitches in my throat.

Neither of us moves. Marc holds my gaze and my knees weaken. He doesn't look away for what feels like an eternity, and I've lost the ability to blink. It's almost as if Marcus is trying to silently communicate with me. I see nothing but that odd amber eye flecked with gold and bronze. It reminds me of a full-bodied whiskey– Marcus is meant to be savored.

I'm breathing so hard, I can't catch my breath. Even though Marcus doesn't speak, his labored breathing matches and then equalizes with mine, fluttering my hair and filling my nostrils with his intoxicating scent.

Intense takes on an entirely different connotation.

Marcus leaves as abruptly as he came.

I hurry to my room, and by the time I get out of the bathroom from doing my nightly rituals, Grant is back. He is a mess– a complete disaster. Sadness and depression roll off of him in waves, filling the air and making it hard to breathe.

I've never seen Grant so despondent. His usual carefree playfulness is erased after two hours of playing the Whittenhower game.

Introverted, Grant usually hides in his tower to recharge, but he's so distraught he made his way to me instead. Not wishing to put him through any more undue stress, I remain silent, asking nothing of him.

I hold Grant all night long as he cries and frets. I lend him my strength to go on. Living the life of a Whittenhower is slowly killing Grant's soul. He's not strong enough to deal with the pressure and stress, because he wasn't meant for this kind of life.

I don't find Grant weak because of it. He's just Grant, and all I can do is accept him for who he truly is.

Grant will never be my knight in shining armor. But it doesn't matter, because I don't need one. I am Queen, and I was born to take care of those who can't care for themselves.

Chapter Thirty

"Why are you so obsessed with this computer stuff?" Katie, now demanding to be called *Katherine*, asks out of true curiosity. Sometimes I have to do a double-take when looking at her, because she's just a slightly older, softer, and hugely pregnant version of Ade.

God, I miss Ade.

I look around the room with pride. My office expanded from three desks to include a computer workstation, a table used to dismantle electronics, and people who invite themselves into my space and refuse to leave. Every morning, I get here early to work alone, but the room never stays empty for long.

Now, both Kristal and Whitt are tutored in here while I work on my studies. Every day, like clockwork, Fate arrives and settles in for a long study session of her own. I'm not stupid– I know they're keeping a watchful eye on me for Ade and Grant.

Right now, Fate has Kristal buried in her economics textbook. The maid won't be one for long. Six months under Fate's tutelage has brought out Kristal's true talent– numbers.

"Conjugating verbs sucks!" Whitt bitches and complains for the millionth time about how much he hates French.

We've moved on to Japanese because Whitt's obsessed with *Manga*– drawing his own version of the comic. Now I have to listen to the choppy fluidity of Japanese. French is prettier to listen to… *Que será, será.*

"It's the future, Kate," I explain, refusing to call her Katherine, but I won't insult her with the juvenile Katie anymore. She's a Junior Senator's wife, for heaven's sake.

I type in a bit more of my coding, and pray that it works. I breathe a sigh of relief when the computer does as I command. *That's right, bitch! I'm your creator, you do as I bid.*

"Someday the internet will be in every household and business, and we'll be connected wirelessly. It will be the world's largest source of information known to man. If you need to know anything–

and I mean anything –you can have it at the tip of your fingers in half a second. Just imagine how incredible that will be."

"Yeah, right." Kate snorts, but the rest of my cohabitants know never to insult my baby.

"Exactly," I pretend she wasn't being sarcastic. "We're lucky because we live in a major city. Most places have limited access to the web, and those who do find it extremely difficult to log on and have no idea what to do once they do. Jesus, the possibilities are endless. Right now, it's just intellectuals hosting sites, a few online stores, and a shit-ton of freaks and weirdos posting bestiality because no one is policing the sites. Computers are made for more than solitaire and Excel. I know you haven't upgraded to the newest mobile phone yet. So imagine your car phone, or that bag-phone you carry around, fitting into your pocket with no interruptions. Imagine your mobile phone with web access, and the ability to take pictures and shoot video."

Almost feverish, my face warms as my mouth spews my passion. I know I've lost Kate when her eyes glaze over with confusion. I shrug and go back to commanding the computer to do as I bid. I'm hooked to the net and trying to communicate with my professor's computer without him knowing. If I succeed, Professor Tindall will have to take me into his program. Hacking is illegal and uncharted territory, but if I accomplish it– no harm, no foul.

Finding my enthusiasm contagious, Whitt feeds into my insanity. "Do you think we'll be able to read comics and books on the internet someday?"

"No doubt, Sunshine. If you beg nicely, I may create a program just for you." I wink at him when he sticks his tongue out at me. "Casse-couille," I tease.

"What does that mean?" Whitt tips his head to the side and flashes me confused eyes.

"If you'd ever do your French homework, you may just find out," I taunt him.

Our good humor deflates the instant the wicked bitch of the Gates glides into my office. I nearly growl. This is my domain– No *call me Mrs. Whittenhower* shall pass.

"What the fuck do you want now?" rolls off my tongue with no concern for the listening minors in the room. To say that Cora and I hate each other would be an understatement. We actually went an entire month without seeing or hearing each other– that was a good month.

The mousy looking lady with pit viper fangs whips out a seamstress tape, and I cringe into my seat.

No. Fucking. Way.

"Measure me instead. We're both in our last trimester." Kate uses the diplomatic skills she's learned as a budding politician's wife. She and I are both due around the same time. She has a tiny, future Whitney Preston growing in her tummy. We've bonded over our pregnancies, hoping Niel and Whitney will be the best of friends since they'll be growing up in Misery Castle together.

Whitt is not impressed with the idea of having a little girl running around. Visions of the Binks/Whitt standoff play out in my head.

"My child," Cora stresses *my,* and it takes everything in me to restrain myself from killing her– I could always use pregnancy hormones as a defense. "Is that size," she points at my ginormous bump. "I need to know how big *my* Daniel is."

Cora walks toward me, causing me to lunge from my chair. "Listen here, bitch. I'm six-foot-tall and pushing one-eighty. Your freakishly thin body and mine are not the same size, no matter how you measure us. Use your sister-in-law." Kate flinches when I call Cora her sister-in-law. I flash her a shit-eating grin.

Cora's nothing to me but a casse-couille– a pain in the ass.

Our animosity erupted when I had to endure being in my room during a party celebrating the upcoming birth of Daniel Whittenhower III. I keep replaying the sight of her hand on Grant's forearm, and I see her impending death loom in my mind– repeatedly.

Today's visit is to measure for the newest baby bump pad. Cora has to look pregnant for the baby shower in two weeks. With all the socialites feeling up her bump, she can't use the Velcro pad thingy you use at the maternity clothing stores– nope, Cora's getting a molded, synthetic skin baby bump.

This will be Cora's third, because as I grow, so does she.

I glare at Cora as I retake my seat. Good luck getting to my abdomen, bitch. I cross my arms over *my* Niel. *Mine*!

Cora walks toward me, and I prepare to use my letter opener as a shank.

"Cora!" Grant's voice barks from the hallway. It's usually smooth as glass, but today it's as cutting as a shard. "Kate, please take Cora into the powder room and have her measure you."

"Grant?" Cora protests enough for all of us. I try to be empathetic, I really do.

God, I fucking despise the baby-stealing cunt.

"I wouldn't push my luck, Cora. Hormones are a wicked mistress. Entering a room with two pregnant women is a bad idea, especially when they both can barely tolerate you. Did your greed suddenly eclipse your sense of self-preservation?"

Grant walks into the room, avoiding Cora by several feet. He's right; if she were to touch him, I'd break her fingers. The closer to Niel's birth, the more mother lion I turn.

Territorial doesn't even cover it.

I'm in the nesting stage, completely irrational, and acting like a savage lunatic.

"How about we both take a break from our work?" Grant pops an eyebrow and dents his dimples, trying to charm me.

I roll my eyes at his efforts, but I rise from my seat. "You're in for it now, naughty boy," I mutter underneath my breath.

"Mistress, please punish me for my indiscretions," he whispers salaciously, knowing this is the only way I can release my frustration and anger, since I can't *actually* murder Cora.

We've learned to be a team, supporting each other in the only ways we know how. Because I'm such a serious person, when I'm on edge, Grant's playfulness balances me out.

"Don't regret what you've asked for," I say out loud as I leave the room.

Grant follows me like a well-trained puppy with Fate and Kristal's giggles following us down the hallway.

"You're waving your ass at me, just begging for a spanking," Grant murmurs near my ear.

"It wouldn't be *you* giving the spanking," I tease back. "Don't tempt me."

"Would you really be willing to do that?" Grant looks so eager, I huff a laugh.

Who knew?

"Do you want a pink ass, Mr. Whittenhower?" I tap Grant's behind with my palm as we walk down the hallway toward our rooms. "I can accommodate you."

"Yes," he breathes low and slow. His eyes dilate to the size of dinner plates and his skin flushes crimson in anticipation.

"I bet you can't wait until Niel's born so we can play rough again."

Grant's eyes clear as he sobers. "I want to wait for as long as he needs. There's nothing in life I want more than for Niel to be healthy and happy."

With tender affection, Grant's palm rounds my belly, causing my eyes to slip shut for differing reasons. We're hanging on a precarious edge. We either fall to our deaths, or pull ourselves to safety. The constant stress is killing me, and I try to hide it, because Grant feeds off of my emotions.

Our lives may not be hanging by a thread, but our happiness is.

Chapter Thirty-One

"You're such a good boy." I coo down at my baby boy, and he stretches his mighty arms. "It's too bad we couldn't have named you Curtis– you look just like my daddy."

"Will Niel's hair always be that red?" Whitt stands before us as we sit in the rocking chair. "His eyes are green– will they turn blue?"

A smile curls my lips. "Sorry to disappoint, but Niel won't be your mini-me in the looks department. His hair will lighten up a bit, maybe blonder. But it'll always have a tint of red to it."

Whitt fingers a puff of shocking red hair. "Niel will get picked on at Hillbrook." Eyes scrunched with intense concentration, the little man stares down at his baby brother, even if he believes him to be his nephew. "I'll always protect him– from everything."

Heart clenching, I breathe, "You're sweet."

"Most of the legacies at Hillbrook are blond-haired and blue-eyed." Whitt stares me down, mouth drawn tight with worry. "Father was teaching me about genetics– Grant and Cora couldn't have made a baby with green eyes and red hair. They're recessive genes. It's why they choose who marries whom, to keep the bloodlines pure."

Leaning back, I rest Niel on my thighs, displaying him in all of his glory. "I'm sure everyone already knows, but they don't care." We both get momentarily sidetracked by Niel blowing spit bubbles like a champion. "Does it bother you that he has red hair? The first thing you said about Binks was how she had brown hair."

Eyes narrowed, Whitt wears a faraway expression. Sometimes I wonder if he isn't precognitive, like maybe there's a reason he loathes that sweet baby girl. Stanton hasn't brought Binks for a playdate since the last time, and it's doubtful it will happen again.

"I'm glad Niel has red hair and green eyes. I want the world to know he belongs to *us*."

Whitt's *us* confuses me, but I let it go. "Niel's going to be a big boy, I just know it. Momma's little bruiser."

I thought for sure I was passing a full grown man. I gave birth at Misery Castle to a nine pound Niel, who's already pushing ten pounds a week later. If he's not attached to my nipple, he's kicking his feet and punching the air. I see no Daniel or Grant in my son whatsoever. By default, Niel looks nothing like Whitt.

Who I do see reflected in my son is his grandfathers. Jackson is missing the refinement Daniel possesses, and that quality was passed down to Niel. Muscular, with unruly red hair and green eyes, Curtis Regal is gazing up at me from the face of my son.

Bittersweet, Niel causes too many memories to erupt, but I'm beginning to channel it into comfort instead of grief.

"Do you think Niel likes me?" Whitt uses Niel's chubby arm as a roadway for his Matchbox car, with the destination of my son's clenching and unclenching fist. "I mean, will he like me when he's bigger?"

"Most definitely," I say with certainty. "Niel reminds me of Grant. Happy and playful–"

"Until he's moody and gloomy," Whitt murmurs underneath his breath, hurt in his voice. "I want Niel to have my car."

Getting choked up, I have to look away from the earnestness in Whitt's gaze. Sometimes I think he knows exactly who Niel is to him, and it kills me to lie when it's not my place to admit the truth.

"You said to share it with someone who would understand its worth." Whitt pries Niel's fingers apart, pressing the car to his palm. Making a happy sound, Niel closes his hand tightly, then begins pumping his little fist in the air. "He likes it," Whitt mutters in delight. "Niel will love me."

Reaching forward, I cup the little boy's face. "Everyone loves you," I remind him. "I always will." Leaning back away, I still haven't come to terms with having deep conversations with a small child. Mom had mentioned how she and Dad were terrified of how accelerated I was as a child, and now I can sympathize. Instinctively, I know Niel is going to be a regular little boy. Smart, but still a kid through and through.

The car slips from Niel's grasp, and he gets frustrated and starts to cry. "I think you should be the keeper of this." I pluck it from my lap to hand it back to Whitt. "You carry it around and give it to Niel to play with when he needs it. Okay?"

Whitt pockets the toy in a heartbeat. "I promise to be Niel's keeper," he purposely twists my words.

"Are you Whitney's keeper, too?" Kate gave birth at the same time I did, only at the hospital. Mistresses aren't given the same care as entitled heiresses, even if I was birthing the future head of their fortune.

But that's not Kate's fault, now is it? On a daily basis, I try not to blame Grant.

"Whitney has a mom and dad," is Whitt's reply. "She doesn't need me yet."

"Niel has a mom and a dad," I remind Whitt. Fingers settling behind Niel's back, I draw him to my chest. With a coo, he settles his cheek against my breast.

"Niel has me," Whitt corrects me.

Confused and flustered, "I–" Albert appears in the doorway to the nursery.

"Miss Regal, please bring the boys to the study," he says formally, voice tight with restraint, and terror flashes through my veins. Recently, Albert has been more relaxed around me, spending his downtime in my office to be near Kris. Sometimes he even jokes around.

"What's going on?" I rise from the chair, grabbing a burping cloth to drape over my shoulder. Niel is famous for drooling on my boob while waiting for his next snack.

Face ghost white, Whitt breathes, "It's time," and then bolts from the room faster than my eyes can track.

Having no idea what's going on, I trust Whitt's instincts enough to run after him. Supporting my son's neck and head, my long legs quickly eat up the distance between the nursery and the study.

Zipping into the study with Albert and Whitt at my heels, I grab the doorjamb to stop myself when I realize what's happening. Palm covering my mouth, "Oh, God!"

"Do you want me to take your grandsons, or can Regina stay?" Albert directs at Daniel.

"Stay. Shut the door, and don't let anyone else in here," Daniel cautions, voice tight with grief. Kneeling on the floor in front of his desk, Daniel cradles Jackson's head in his lap. "My brother deserves dignity unto death."

Jackson's always been larger than life, so it's horrifying to see him prone on the floor with his skin ashen, but nothing could prepare me for the expression of terror etched across Daniel's face.

Voice thready, Jackson struggles to speak. "All my boys are with me." Vivid blue eyes surf from one person to the next. First Albert, then Whitt, Niel while looking through me as if I'm not even here, then settling on Grant. Utterly silent, face a mask, I hadn't even noticed Grant kneeling at Jackson's side.

Everything in me is throbbing to run to Grant's side, to support him, but my feet are frozen in place. This scene is all too familiar. It hasn't even been a year since my mom passed, and now I feel more connected to Grant than ever.

In this moment, I realize I've never truly grieved the passing of my mother. I've pushed it from my mind, concentrating on the here and now, because it was better than suffering when I needed to be Grant's strength. Now that he needs me, I don't think I'm strong enough to hold us both together.

My father died in his prime. My mother died in her prime. Jackson is forty-four years old, body strong, mind stronger, will the strongest, but his heart is broken. Without a heart, you can't survive. As much as I resent the man, I've come to respect him but love him even more.

Jackson was the very definition of Joie de vivre.

"What about Priscilla?" flows from my lips without thought.

"We said our goodbyes this morning, darling." Jackson tries to flash me a smug smile filled with innuendo, but he doesn't have the strength. "I didn't want her to see me at the end– just my boys."

"Alby?" Jackson holds out his hand, and Albert is immediately falling to his knees. Head bowed over Jackson's hand, Albert places a kiss on the knuckles. "Watch over this family, even after Grant has chosen a new enforcer."

"Yes, sir." Albert places one more kiss, and then rises to his feet. "As the heartbeat of the Whittenhower family, you will be sorely missed."

"C'mere, young Daniel." Jackson holds nothing but love in his eyes for his oldest grandson.

A tiny palm slips into mine, shivering so badly Whitt's vibrating my arm. Clasping, our hands wrap around each other's tightly.

Tighter still.

I couldn't move for Grant, but I do for Whitt. I slowly walk him toward Jackson. Then I kneel on the floor, coaxing Whitt to come closer.

"Make me a promise, son," Jackson struggles to speak, and in the face of that, who could deny him anything. Whitt says nothing, just nodding his head over and over again. "It's your duty to take care of Niel. Do you understand?"

"Yes," Whitt meeps, petrified of the dying man who has shown him nothing but affection.

"Don't be scared," Jackson murmurs in a soothing voice, sounding identical to Grant in this moment. "Gimme a kiss goodbye, and then get your ass outta here."

Releasing my hand, Whitt crawls up his grandfather's body. Visibly shuddering, he shows strength by not crying or running away. "Goodbye," he whispers, and then kisses his grandfather sweetly on the lips. "I love you."

"Think of me every time you drive the Roadster– it was mine." Jackson swallows audibly, tears swimming in his eyes. "Drive like a bat outta hell with the wind whipping your hair, and remember all the fun we had together."

"I promise." Whitt slides off his grandfather's chest to land on the floor.

"Never forget." Jackson struggles to sit up, but fails. Daniel immediately shifts beneath Jackson, supporting his weight. "Never forget– I set you free because I love you, not because I felt you weren't worthy." Using all of his strength, Jackson points at the door and bellows, "Go!"

Unable to watch, I tuck my face against the top of my son's head, burying the sob building. Just as he's leaving us, I finally understand Jackson. The youngest Daniels weren't given the short straw by not being named after Jackson. Jackson wanted them named after the person he loves most. It's the same reason he set Whitt free. I guarantee, all the things we love about Whitt are the very things Jackson loves in Daniel. Since he couldn't set Daniel free, he does Whitt.

Once the door clicks shut, I raise my face from the top of Niel's head. With surprise, I find Grant reigning in his emotions. I thought he'd be a motherfucking mess, wailing and begging God to spare Jackson. But, instead, Grant kneels, eyes flicking between Jackson and Daniel with concern. I want to be disappointed that he's not once looked in my direction, or at his own son, but I'm not a selfish asshole.

With Whitt gone, secrets are no longer secrets. "Dad?" Grant comes closer, delicate hand wrapping tightly around Jackson's thick, masculine fingers. He presses his father's hand to his heart, while his other supports the elbow. "I can do this," he sounds like he's pumping himself up. "I can."

"I know." Jackson's face shifts to the side, sliding along Daniel's thigh. Father and son stare at one another, having a silent conversation while voicing another. "You don't want to, but know you're more than capable."

"I can't be like you." Grant's voice warbling is the first break in his composure. "I can't fill your shoes."

"I don't expect you to." Jackson struggles again, and Daniel is immediately supporting his head. "I expect you to walk in your own. We have too many alphas, when we need some compassion. Balance. You can balance the corruption."

"Jack?" Daniel leans down, eyes flicking between Jackson and Grant. "What's going on?"

Jackson and Grant share a look, their eyes darting toward Albert. "I knew I was at the end, so I spent the past forty-eight hours writing down everything you'll ever need to know," Jackson whispers in Daniel's direction, and I can guarantee there's a lot of information not included– things trapped in Grant's mind.

"Kiss me goodbye," Jackson demands of Grant.

"I'm not going afterward," Grant challenges back. "So don't waste your strength." Leaning down, Grant cradles his father's head, not noticing how he's touching Daniel at the same time. A quick kiss is dropped, then Grant is whispering fiercely in Jackson's ear, quiet enough no one but Jackson will ever hear. This goes on for long minutes, then, after another kiss, Grant sits back on his heels.

"I'm scared, Danny," Jackson mutters like he's a small boy.

A breath hitching ricochets around the study– Daniel.

"You're the lucky one," Daniel mutters wryly, his tone of voice belying the tears streaming down his cheeks. "I can run the business side of things, but I don't have a clue how to handle my wife, children, and grandchildren. They hate me because I'm practical."

I wait for Grant to protest, but he doesn't.

"I'm scared, Danny," Jackson repeats, trying to tip his head backward so he can look at his brother. "I'm going to Hell."

"No," Daniel and Grant murmur softly in unison. "Did you go to confession this morning?"

"Yes, but–" Jackson struggles to look at Daniel, so Daniel takes pity on him by curving forward until they're in their own little world. "I don't want to be alone. I've done evil acts, and no amount of confession will ever absolve my sins."

"If that's the case, you'll never be alone. We've created the same sins, so where you go, I go." Stunning me, Daniel leans forward, pressing a kiss to his brother's mouth. It's not a goodbye, or romantic or sexual, or even platonic. It's Daniel, and he doesn't touch anyone.

Ever.

My eyes flick away, feeling like I'm witnessing something so intimate I'll never survive it. I find Grant's eyes boring into mine, challenging me to feel disgust. When I don't give him what he wants, he looks away from me in shame.

"Never be afraid," Daniel is murmuring to Jackson. "You're reckless, so no matter where you go, you'll be the life of the party. You'll reign in Heaven or Hell."

I try to block out Daniel and Jackson's goodbye. I focus on Grant, but he's blank, totally shut down yet acting as if he can't look me in the eye for some reason. I gaze at the red puffs of hair dotting the top of my sleeping son's head, and I wonder if he realizes something major is happening.

"Life will never be the same without you." Daniel chokes on his words, showing emotions I felt him incapable of expressing. Jackson's unable to continue their conversation, too weak, so Daniel talks to his brother until he meets his end. "Who's going to remind me to have fun, or to remember Priscilla's needs? I'll be lost without you."

I've never felt that way toward anyone. Not my parents. Not my friends. Not Grant. Not even my son. I know I can survive anyone's loss, just by putting one foot in front of the other. I may be dead on the inside, but my mind and body will still thrive. When Jackson dies, he'll take Daniel's humanity with him.

With Daniel wrapped around him, Jackson struggles to speak one last time. "You'll do what's necessary," is directed at Grant, who's still cradling his father's arm to his chest. "I want our future to be the last thing I see."

Sobbing, Daniel kisses Jackson one more time, then reaches for my son. With great reluctance, I release Niel as a premonition steals the breath from my lungs.

Niel was never mine. He never was and never will be. My sole purpose was to bear the child, instill in him everything I know, and then release him to the world. Niel doesn't belong to me or the Whittenhowers.

Niel is *the* Whittenhower.

In the ultimate sacrifice, I release my son. History is being made. With Grant's compassion and passion, combined with my brains, strength, and ethics, Niel is our future with the ability to change it for the positive.

Awake yet content, Niel rests on Jackson's chest, being the one to feel the final heartbeat.

Jackson was proof there is no such thing as good and bad men. Just men. Men who do good and bad deeds.

Chapter Thirty-Two

Looking at Grant, "Sir?" Albert rises to his feet, crosses the room, opens the door, and then slips out into the hallway. In less than a second, he's back again, carrying a black bundle. "Should we move the body now?"

The body.

Once the soul flees, they always say *the body.*

Shuddering in horror, I reach for my son just as Daniel breaks. My eyes sting with tears, my stomach twists in pain, my ears reverberate with the misery flowing from Daniel's throat over the loss of his only brother. Grief-stricken, primal, that song of agony will haunt my nightmares for years to come.

Handsome face twisted into a gruesome snarl, "No!" Daniel screams while leaning over the body, trying to protect Jackson but he's already gone. Fingernails turning to claws, he scratches at Albert's hands. "What are you doing? Where are you taking him? Don't!"

"Sir?" Albert addresses Grant and enflames Daniel further.

With Grant's nod, Daniel erupts. "Don't touch him! Don't. Stop looking at Grant. Why are you looking at Grant? You listen to me, damn you!"

"Master Daniel, we have to take the body," Albert is firm, trying his damnedest not to let his emotions override his duty.

Head jerking up, for the first time ever, Daniel looks exactly like Jackson. Crazed with desperation. "Can't I have a moment with my brother? Jackson is not *the body.*"

I do the worst possible thing imaginable– I snort. The sarcastic, rude sound echoes around the study. Hand covering my mouth, "Daniel, I'm so sorry," I profusely apologize. "It's just that I said the same thing when my father died, and thought it again when my mother died. I understand– I do." I turn to Grant, who doesn't resemble himself at all. "Why are you taking Jackson away? Shouldn't we wait for the coroner?"

Yet again, Grant's refusing to look at me, to look me in the eye. In profile, I see no emotion written across Grant's features. While clutching our son to my chest, I realize I don't know this person at all. For the past year, I've imagined Grant breaking down worse than Daniel, sobbing and shrieking, and blaming God. How I'd be there for him, supporting him through one of the most trying times in his life. Instead, he's cold, stoic.

Strong.

Moving to the side, Grant tugs Daniel in his arms, whispers something into his ear, and then kisses his forehead. Standing, he gazes down at Daniel curled protectively around Jackson.

"Father?" Wiping at his face, Daniel gazes up at Grant like he's never seen him before. No, more like he's seeing a ghost. "We have to take Jackson away, but only for an hour or so. The founders need to say their goodbyes. Then we'll transport him to the funeral home to prepare for the wake."

Reduced to sounding like a child, "I just need more time," Daniel begs, tears rushing down his cheeks. "Please, don't take him away from me."

"There will never be enough time." Grant's voice breaks, and that bit of emotion comforts me and gives Daniel his equilibrium back. "Here, then gone, and I can't wrap my mind around how fast it happens. In an instant." Grant gestures to Albert. "Never enough time."

Scooting on my behind, I lean against Daniel's desk with Niel sleeping soundly against my chest. I don't know what surprises me more: Daniel sliding to sit shoulder-to-shoulder with me, or Grant and Albert transferring Jackson into a body bag. Unable to watch, I nuzzle the top of my son's head, ignoring the fact that Albert and Grant carry Jackson away, and that Grant never once acknowledged my existence.

Sitting with Daniel is bizarre, because it's reminiscent of sitting with Grant. Silent. My mind spins out of control, concentrating on Grant instead of grieving... anything is easier than grieving. The Grant I once knew is gone, replaced by a stranger. I begin to wonder what Grant would have been like if he hadn't grown up with the constant shadow of Jackson's looming death stifling his emotional growth.

Our lives shift again.

The light in Misery Castle was snuffed out with Jackson's passing. All I can hope is that the next generation of Whittenhowers will breathe life into these haunted walls.

Niel fusses, demanding attention. Leaning back against the desk, I scoot my ass down, and then raise my thighs for a place to rest the baby. Shifting him around, I tuck his butt on my belly, with his back and head resting on my thighs, and his little feet kicking my belly and breasts. Wiggly, he begins flailing his arms about, little fists of fury pummeling my knees and the sides of my thighs.

With the only sound in the study belonging to Niel, Daniel and I watch the baby instead of speaking about Jackson, or even Grant's bizarre behavior. We both study the features of my baby boy. The puffs of wiry red hair belonging to my dad. The green eyes coming from me via my dad. The tiny chin reminds me of my mom. The way his eyebrows knit in concentration reminds me of Grant. But mostly–

"Niel looks exactly like Jackson," Daniel finally speaks, sounding gutted. Then he admits, "It hurts to look at my grandson."

"I understand," I murmur so quietly I doubt Niel even heard me. "When I look at my son, I see my dad. I miss him so much– every day. It's bittersweet, but also a gift. Niel's grandfathers live on inside him."

"They do?" Daniel's voice pitches high in an upward inflection, like he didn't realize until now. "They do," he mutters with conviction. "I've never lost anyone before. I never knew my mother. My father's death was a gain, never a loss. I didn't understand when Priscilla's parents passed. I felt... off." Elegant shoulders shrug, seeming at a loss for words.

"I've never grieved anyone, because everyone I've ever loved leaves me behind. So I bury it, charging forward, and then move on by working."

"Does it work?" Daniel raises his hand, attempting to touch Niel, but then he lowers it. "I expect not." He does the hand routine a few more times, and a light bulb burns brightly in my mind. "I feel like I'm suffocating– dying."

"Would you like to hold your grandson?" I turn to Daniel. He and I have had some major disagreements on how life should be lived, but he will be a major part of my son's life.

"I've never held a baby before." Daniel shifts, body preparing for something he's trying to deny, even with his voice sounding eager and hopeful. "I don't know how. I don't even know how to hug anyone. I worry it's–" he doesn't complete his thought.

"Hugs, kisses, rubbing someone's back, that's called affection, Daniel, and it's not a bad thing." Now it's my turn to feel uncomfortable. "It's not sexual."

"I don't know what is or isn't sexual, Regina. I know you know I'm asexual." Daniel looks away, as if ashamed. "After– I have no idea what's right or wrong. What if I hurt Niel? I'd never want to hurt him. With Jackson gone…"

"Truthfully, there's a murky gray area I can't explain. But as long as sex parts aren't involved, it's not sexual." Ripping the Band-Aid off, I settle my son on Daniel's chest. Stunned, his hands are held out in the air. "I think it would be worse for Niel if you didn't touch him, and that's coming straight from Grant."

"Oh," Daniel huffs, as if he just had an epiphany. "I-I-I… Wilhelm was as cuddly as a rattlesnake. With no mother–" Daniel tentatively pats Niel's back with three fingers.

"Your affection came from Jackson, right?" I lean forward, coaxing. "Now you give and get that from Priscilla. It's not wrong to want to hold your children and grandchildren."

"I touch Grant because he's an adult," Daniel blurts out. "Now that he can say no if I do something wrong. But he's always so angry with me, I don't dare. I mean, he has every right to hate me. But I know not touching him bothers him more than when I do."

"Just go for it, Daniel." I watch as he awkwardly pats my son's back, getting accustomed to touching a little person. "Just go for it."

"I'm going to miss Jackson." Daniel cups the back of Niel's skull, fingers rubbing at his scalp.

"Me too." Leaning backward against the front of the desk, I close my eyes, willing tears that never come. I need the release before it kills me. "Life won't be the same without him."

"No, it won't." Daniel hugs my son lightly, testing the waters. Niel actually coos, cuddling deeper against his grandfather's chest. "But maybe it will get better."

My mind lights on Grant, and I mutter, "Maybe," but I don't believe it.

Chapter Thirty-Three

A black shroud has fallen over the castle. Not able to face Priscilla just yet, the moment I heard her enter the house, I hightailed it out of the study. But mostly, I was freaked out by how similar Daniel and I are emotionally, and that was utterly terrifying.

My first thought was locating a distraught little boy– nothing else mattered. Whitt wasn't in his bedroom, or my bedroom. Giving up on my search, I was going to call the staff and see if any of them had seen him, but when I brought Niel back to his nursery, it was serendipity.

Leaning in the doorway, I find Whitt. He crawled into Niel's crib, and is clutching his Matchbox car like a lifeline. "I have something better," I murmur as I break away from the doorway.

Whitt opens his arms, eyes stained red from crying. "Jackson's gone," I breathe as I settle Niel into his big brother's awaiting arms. "He was very brave, and you should be proud of him."

Throat contracting, Whitt swallows but is unable to speak. Leaning over the railing, I brush hair off foreheads and administer healing kisses. "Keep my son safe for me while I take a shower, okay?"

"Always, Queen," Whitt vows as if I'm asking something else entirely.

As strong as I seem, I never expected it to be Jackson's death to break me. I may not cry tears for release, but I sob so hard while the shower beats down on my shoulders, I begin to vomit uncontrollably.

I don't grieve for me. I grieve for the life lost, but more so for how lost Daniel, Priscilla, and Grant will be without Jackson.

I throw up out of fear for Grant. Fear his melancholy personality will get the best of him. Fear I won't be strong enough to guide him through a process I've never begun, let alone completed.

With some of the pressure released, my head is clearer even if my heart is throbbing like a sore tooth. Moving on, doing something is the best way to forget. But there is something about Jackson that demands to be remembered. No matter how badly I may wish to find something to divert my emotions, I allow it to roll over me and take me down.

Instead of watching TV, or taking a walk, or reading a story, I carry the boys in from the crib and place them in my bed. I crawl in after them, cradling Niel to my chest, with Whitt curled facing me.

Instead of ignoring the pain, I open up the floodgates and let the grief pour in. I accept it. I force Whitt to tell me stories of Jackson's reckless ways– I force him to remember. I tell him to recapture the memories in his drawings. I watch the little boy with the grown man mind silently cry while he laughs about his grandfather's outlandish antics.

Not having many stories to tell about Jackson, I add my own. Voicing for the first time, I speak of my mom and dad, hoping our humble anecdotes will take root and grow in the boy, and by extension, my son will someday hear these same stories from either me or Whitt.

Two worlds colliding, creating two boys who will be well-rounded individuals instead of brainwashed by their power and affluence.

Whitt and I swap stories for hours and hours, until what seems harrowing now becomes bittersweet. We don't stop until exhaustion overpowers Whitt and I allow him to fall asleep.

Staring at the tops of the boys' heads, I can finally pinpoint the sensation that's been bearing down on me. After sharing silence with him for nearly a year, I recognize the signature of Grant's presence. Must be Whitt and I were so far gone, neither of us heard Grant ghost into the bedroom.

After months and months of dealing with Grant's mercurial moods, I know my only recourse is to wait him out. If I add any pressure whatsoever, he shuts down and freezes my ass out.

I try. I try really hard, but when more than an hour passes, and I can feel Grant physically staring at me, I break the silence. "How long have you been here?" Turning my head, I spot Grant leaning his back against the door to the hallway, with only his silhouette and the whites of his eyes visible.

"Thank you," is all he says, voice thick with emotion. I can tell he's been crying– *is* still crying. "I'll write down everything you and my son said, and someday I'll give it to you, maybe share it with Daniel and Mother."

Every muscle in my body locks up, suppressing the urge to fling myself from the bed into Grant's lap. For the first time in a long time, I need comfort. There is a drive compelling me to seek comfort instead of offer it, and that doesn't happen often for me. But I can't be a burden when it was Grant's father who died tonight.

What kind of woman demands sympathy and comfort when she should be giving it to the family of the one we lost?

"I wasn't avoiding you in the study, Regina. My inability to look at you had nothing to do with you," Grant confesses, the darkness making it feel even more intimate. "I feared that if I looked at you, I'd break."

"Why did you act ashamed?" is at the very tip of my tongue, but I don't release it.

"Since my birth, I've been preparing for this moment. Similar in the way you prepared with your mother. *What do I do now?* But more so. When you're a little kid, you don't even register the meaning of death. When Jackson's borrowed time was brought up, I didn't get it. Not really anyway."

"But now you do?" I bite my lip, wishing I hadn't spoken. To interrupt Grant after he's found the courage to speak, there's a high probability he'll stop talking altogether.

"I've known," he admits, and I thank the heavens I didn't fuck this up. This is important, not only for healing but because it's Grant's release. "When my grandparents died, I learned the reality of death. From that moment on, I stalked Jackson like the Grim Reaper, knowing I would have to walk in his footsteps sooner rather than later. That's why I couldn't look you in the eye. Tonight I became someone you'd never respect."

"That's not true," I issue as a denial. "There is nothing you could do to make me stop loving you. How I feel about you is the very definition of unconditional. I've never tried to change you, taking all my time to truly get to know you."

"I watched Jackson bludgeon his own father during Mass, Regina," Grant blurts out matter-of-factly. "And patricide is the lesser of all the evils I've witnessed. When Jackson surmised that Daniel had been molested, I didn't doubt it for a second because I've heard of other little boys and girls being violated. If I hadn't been Jackson's son, I would have been another one of them– Whitt," Grant's voice breaks.

"Shit," I hiss with feeling, curling protectively around both boys.

"I was the passenger for twenty-three years. Now I'm the driver, making decisions that involve the lesser of two evils. Neither choice is ever anything I'd condone, but I can't stop it. All I can do is be the voice of reason, to find sane allies and make my vote count. That is why I said tonight I became a man you will never respect, a man who doesn't deserve you."

"I'm no prize," I mutter underneath my breath.

"Yes, you truly are, Regina." The rustling of fabric hits my ears as Grant finds a more comfortable position. "I don't deserve you. I think that's why I'm so hung up on Gwen. You call yourself The Mistress, while the mother of my first born is called The Whore. She doesn't think she deserves anything but pain. Gwen's father forces her to share any man's bed he wishes, including his own. She's tried to kill herself countless times."

"Don't ever hook up with her," I warn, and it's not territorialism or jealousy. Grant's self-preservation. Two slit-your-wrists personalities should be nowhere near one another.

"Mitchell Meyers is not long for this earth, if I have anything to say about it now that I'm in charge of my own legacy."

"Grant," I gasp out, shocked at how serious he sounds while speaking of murder.

"I warned you– this is why it will be very difficult to look you in the eye. Know this, what I just said is nothing in comparison to some of the votes I must cast. Life or death. To break a family or elevate it. To force two people to marry and make children. After surviving this game as the passenger, most drivers become vicious, punishing the families who hurt them the worst. But I can't survive it."

Preparing to roll away from the boys and go to Grant, he stops me before I can even move. "No, Regina. You have to stay over there, or else I'll never get this out. I can't tell you much more– I've already said way too much. I'm just feeling vulnerable tonight. I was ordered by the entire council to avoid my friends and family, because they knew I'd spill like a leaky faucet."

Hating everyone who suggested such a thing, fury boils in my blood. "You need us more now than ever."

"I do." Grant rises, gathering the courage to come to my side. I wait while he undresses down to his boxers, and then slides into bed. I curl, inviting him to spoon me from behind. Wrapping his arms around me until he's able to hold Whitt with Niel sandwiched in between us, Grant is the one who offers up the support.

"It's like," Grant murmurs against my ear. "It's like, when Jackson died, he gave me what little strength he had left, so I could be strong enough to survive the coming weeks." Holding us tighter, and tighter still, "You can stop now, Regina."

"Stop what?" I mutter in confusion.

"Stop trying to be strong. I can feel you hurting– your grief is battering me from the outside in. Release it. Please."

I do.

For the next few weeks, Grant becomes the Whittenhowers' rock. More silent than ever, he allows us time to grieve, to heal, to have a voice, and to come to terms with our new way of life.

When Grant senses we're strong enough to hold him up, he finally breaks… and it's worse than I could have ever imagined.

Seventeen years prior to the present

Chapter Thirty-Four

"Mrs. Whittenhower, please take your son from the nanny."

I wince inwardly when the photographer calls me the nanny, but it's the *Mrs.* Whittenhower combined with *your son* in the same sentence that has me on the edge of committing multiple homicides.

The photographer from Dominion's Insider is here to take a family portrait of Mr. and Mrs. Whittenhower and the heir to the Whittenhower throne– *my* son.

I lean forward to place Niel into Cora's awaiting, outstretched arms. I try not to touch her during the pass-off, because the thought makes me physically ill. But not nearly as sick as when Niel is settled into her embrace. Vivid green eyes gaze back at me in silent betrayal.

"What are you doing, Momma? Who is this bony lady?"

I haven't cried since my mother's passing, except for a rare, raw moment in the shower after Jackson died, even with the horrific year since his death, but placing my son into Cora's arms nearly brings the moisture to my eyes. Telltale pressure building, it prickles and burns almost as painfully as the fissure in my heart.

Pure. Fucking. Torturous. Agony.

I've felt death and loss deeper than anyone. The loss of my parents was crippling. Watching Grant suffer, watching Daniel try to support Priscilla, all the while grieving myself... but there isn't a word for the emotion I feel as I hand Cora my child for the very first time. I watch her hold Niel to her chest, and pose for shot after shot for the photographer.

The saccharin expression etched across Cora's face, as her thin lips stretch into a facsimile of a real smile for the camera, makes me loathe her. I've never hated anyone before, not even Daniel for trapping me into this situation. Jackson and Daniel's ploys gave me Niel. How could I hate anyone for that?

But, Cora, I loathe the bitch.

She was nowhere to be found after Jackson's death, not inside the castle anyway. She spent six months or more at her father's mansion down in the Gates. In the five or six months since, she's only popped in for public obligations.

Niel will be a year old next month, and Cora hasn't so much as looked in his direction. Not once. This is the first time she's held Niel, yet she's posing for a newspaper spread, because she was nominated for Dominion's Mother of the Year Award.

Mother of the year? To a child she did not contribute DNA, nor carry for nine months, nor birth, nor breastfeed for a year. She didn't have to suffer as her vagina healed for six weeks, or manage to wake for feedings and changings while everyone in the house was grieving. She didn't have to deal with Mastitis, or raw nipples, or the embarrassment of leaky breasts dampening her blouse at the dining room table. She didn't have to deal with a sick baby who managed the feat of shitting until it flowed out the top of his diaper and up his back, or have him puke in her face.

Mother of the year? To a child she's never once held.

Niel is only a pawn to Cora.

My son is no one's pawn. Niel is Daniel Whittenhower III, and he is destined to be king of Misery Castle.

I don't need the Whittenhower money, because I'll make my own. It took less than two years, and I'm already a blink away from my bachelor's degree, with my master's to quickly follow on its heels. I don't need to use children as props to get false accolades, or flash some man's last name around to get noticed, because my work speaks for itself. I'm already earning money by coding for a major corporation, not only at the top of my class, but in the world, and I'm creating programs with my signature on them– revolutionary programs that belong solely to *me*.

Money? Power? Influence? Who cares?

What I want is Niel in my arms. I want the world to know that that precious boy was created by his father and me. While it may have been forced in the beginning, it was still filled with mutual affection and attraction.

Niel's content demeanor is proof of our bond.

Every sense in my body collaborates into one single notion. Sickness. Sickness of the heart, mind, spirit, and body. I run to the powder room, and then violently heave into the toilet as I did almost two years ago.

Coming full circle, back then, I threw up at the thought of whoring myself out, and then having to give my child away. Now I throw up for a similar reason– reality.

Watching Grant and Cora cuddle up on the sofa while holding my son, drove home the reason I'm here. It's easy to get lost in the daily doldrums of life. While I study and work, Whitt is tutored or does his homework in my office while Niel naps. We eat together as a family. We read Whitt and Niel stories every night as they drift off to sleep. We talk about our hopes and dreams of the future. Grant writes beside me as I string algorithms together into usable sequences. Then we lie together in bed each night, and repeat it in the morning.

But it's not reality, because at some point we have to take a step forward. I can't live like this forever, where I'm Grant's pseudo-wife at Misery Castle, where his friends see me as his mistress, but out in the world at large, I'm nothing.

Cora Spencer-Whittenhower is Grant's wife.

While I go to work and school, raise my son, and am a part of Grant's family, nothing between us takes place outside of Misery Castle. No dates. No visiting friends. I've yet to meet Marcus Zeitler and Dexter Hayes– the two men I owe the past six years of my education to, thanks to their grandmother, Rebekah. The cousins are Grant's best friends, and I've never spoken one word to them, let alone held a conversation.

My world is concentrated down to a pinpoint, and it can't last forever. No matter how much I love and respect Grant, my need for self-respect demands that this is not the life I will lead forever. When I entered Misery Castle, I made a promise to my parents that while this may be my present, it will never be my future.

But at what cost? The cost of Grant? It sickens me to think, but I'm willing to pay it. The cost of Niel? I don't even want to contemplate that thought.

Heaving, acid burns my throat on its way out, terrified that the photographed fake scene will become my future reality– a future without Niel in my arms. A future without Grant's soft, calming voice, and his playful presence. A future without Whitt's mischievous wit.

The stress is crippling. I've held it together the best I could. When the anxiety overcomes me, I hide from Grant– I withdraw because he feeds from my emotions. If I'm strong, he's strong. If I'm happy, he's happy. If I show how afraid I am, he will undoubtedly become petrified. He's already stressed, and I worry about how he will deal with what I'm feeling.

After allowing myself the luxury of breaking down, I pull myself back together the best I can, then I return to the parlor. I lean against the archway and watch as Cora poses in different spots in the room, using my son as a prop.

My only consolation hurts me– Grant looks physically ill, so at least we're in this disaster together. He keeps looking at me to make sure I'm alright. I give him an impassive expression because it's all I can muster.

Kent Preston is campaigning again, so Priscilla joined Kate on the campaign trail, leaving Whitney behind at Misery Castle with her nanny. I'm glad they're gone, and that Ade is still in California, and Fate is living back at home with her sister, Faith. None of them have the stomach to witness this charade unfold, and I'd rather not have my shame on display.

Daniel's been off since Jackson's passing. Just downright bizarre. Emulating Jackson, he's trying to be more affectionate and open, but it comes off as creepy. But the one personality trait that has bloomed from Jackson's ashes is sarcasm. Daniel was never capable before– too black and white clinical.

Today, Daniel watches his daughter-in-law flaunt herself while wearing an ironic smirk that was more befitting Jackson than his handsome, gentlemanly face.

The photographer tries to have Daniel pose with Grant, Cora, and Niel, but Daniel has other plans. He pushes Cora out of the picture, smiling proudly when Niel readily snuggles to his chest– out of everyone, my son has attached himself to the coldest of Whittenhowers, and it's melted the man's frozen heart. Daniel makes a big production about how the three generations of Whittenhowers should grace the cover of Dominion's Insider.

I don't doubt for a second that it won't happen.

A not-so tiny hand slips into my palm, fingertips squeezing. Whitt's grown so much lately, body trying its damnedest to catch up with his mind. I believe Whitt will be tall when he's full-grown. At almost eight, the top of his head is already brushing Grant's shoulder.

The photographer poses Cora, Grant, and Niel on the sofa again, and Whitt makes a choking sound in the back of his throat. At least he wasn't here earlier, now experiencing a repeat. Face cutting to the side, we share a smile– Whitt will forever bring me sunshine and joy.

"Mr. and Mrs. Whittenhower, could you kiss for the camera? I think it would be the best shot." The photographer's voice vibrates with excitement. "Cover-worthy!"

In an instant, I find myself fleeing the room without a thought. It's one thing to hold my child and pretend it's your own, but it's another thing entirely to touch Grant in my presence. There was no way I could stand idly by and watch as something as intimate as a kiss be captured on camera. Especially with my child held in their arms, as if Niel was created from their love.

It's a fabrication of a life that doesn't exist. Every person who reads the newspaper will read the lie, see the phony posed family, and believe it.

Is it really cheating if you kiss your wife? What more do you expect from a man who has a wife and a mistress? Doesn't a woman like me deserve to be cheated on? After all, not only did I make a child with another woman's husband, I stole the life she should lead.

Honestly, I have no idea what Grant is up to most days. When he's not working, he's off in his tower– the tower I can't locate. For all I know, he's got a string of women on retainer. He's amorous enough to be able to service them all. But wondering, knowing, and seeing are different beasts.

It's easiest to assume Grant's ruminating in silence, then writing whatever he plotted. But that is hard to believe since he doesn't make me a part of his life outside of Misery Castle. But at the same time, it wouldn't surprise me if he didn't actually have a life outside of these walls.

It's a struggle for Grant to look me in the eye.

Strong Regina somehow turned back into an idiot girl when I hadn't realized it. My mind spins scenario after scenario in great detail as I run up the south staircase with Whitt on my heels.

Mind lighting onto my companion, I know Whitt won't leave my side, so I go to his bedroom for privacy. When my emotions are so raw, being in the room I share with Grant would be a disaster.

"That's wrong!" Whitt storms in angrily, slamming the door behind himself. "Grant can't do that! How can he kiss Cora? Someone needs to stop them."

"I'm trying my best, Sunshine, but I can't work miracles," I mutter, flabbergasted, because what I really want to do is tear people limb from limb.

"Grant's weak." Whitt stalks around his bedroom, nearly shouting. "He should stand up and say you're his wife," the child practically growls. "Grant let Cora touch Niel. Niel!"

Whitt doesn't sound like a kid anymore. A man's voice and words flow from a child's mouth. After all this time, I'm still not used to it.

"Grant is Grant," I defend, hating how unbeknownst to Whitt, he's putting down his own father– which is actually the point the kid is making, isn't it? "Whitt, you must accept Grant for who he is, not who you want him to be."

"I want him to grow a pair." Whitt slumps to his mattress in defeat. "If you were mine, and thought me worthy enough to give me a child, I'd never let you go."

Sitting on the edge of the bed near his feet, the words flow without thought. "Sometimes the things you say terrify me."

"Why? It's the truth. Grant's being a pussy."

"A pussy?" I arch an eyebrow, realizing Whitt and I have an odd relationship that is borderline inappropriate. We treat each other as equals, because if I treated Whitt like a child, he'd be insulted. "Stop spending so much time with Kristal," I suggest to halt his vocabulary downward slope. "People are different. It doesn't make Grant less of a man, just not a dominant one. Especially when I'm dominant enough for the both of us."

Frustrated that I'm not automatically agreeing with him, Whitt turns from me. Facing the wall while standing in the corner, the muscles in his back are quivering. I lay a gentle hand on his shoulder, and he flinches.

I know Whitt's crying, and he thinks if he does, he's not a *real* man. Daniel is huge on telling Whitt, and even Niel, what it means to be a man. Since Daniel's fucked in the head, most of the time he's wrong. It would be funny or cute if it wasn't so irritating.

"It takes a lot of courage to cry. A woman doesn't cry because she's weak; she cries to relieve the pressure. You're frustrated at Grant, and you're feeling like I don't hear you, and that's why you're crying. I envy you– I wish I could join you."

Full of myself, I was so focused on what this photoshoot meant for me, that I hadn't realized what it meant for Whitt. Even though Whitt doesn't know Grant is his father, he still looks up to him as such.

It's the four of us against the world most days.

Grant was having a family portrait with Cora and Niel, and Whitt felt forgotten and betrayed. His anger is not completely on my behalf, but his own. If Grant could ignore the fact that I'm Niel's mother, and how he's supposedly in love with me, then in Whitt's eyes, he's easily forgotten too.

I pull Whitt away from the wall, and this time he allows it. I settle him on the bed beside me, then drag him into my lap. Ever since I had Niel, Whitt won't let me hold him anymore. Every time I try, he informs me a man should hold the woman. I usually let it go, because Whitt's trying to figure out his own identity. But tonight, I hold Whitt, and instead of being passive like a child would, he holds me back.

"I'll be Niel's father if Grant can't be." Whitt sniffles against my shirt.

"Grant's doing a good job, Whitt." I try to hide the smile that creeps into my voice.

"Queen, I promise you, Niel will always have a father," Whitt utters in that ominous voice of his. It always reminds me of when a premonition chills my skin. But with Whitt, it's like he can read our fates before they happen.

"Thank you," I whisper against the top of Whitt's head, and then I pray.

Chapter Thirty-Five

All is right with the world as long as Niel is resting in my arms and suckling at my breast. Rocking back and forth in the chair, I stare down at the huge, green eyes gazing up at me with utter love, devotion, and trust.

The world at large might be fooled, but my son knows I'm his mother. So why the hell should I give a shit?

After watching us for twenty minutes, Grant finally detaches himself from the doorway. He had to gather courage and organize his words. "I need to apologize, and I know you get so sick and tired of me saying it. But this can't go on forever, so there is that." Grant's voice is soft and quiet in the near dark room. "I could feel your pain, and it echoed mine. I can't apologize enough, Regina."

When I don't respond, Grant rushes to my side. "I didn't kiss Cora. I stood up and told the photographer the session was over." Lips twisting sardonically, "Daniel told me he was proud of me once we were out of earshot."

All forgiven, chuckling, I lift my face for a tender kiss. Our mouths linger for a long time, until I grunt from a hearty pull at my breast.

"Niel's going to be muscular when he's older by the way he eats. If the flow isn't strong enough, he bites me." I murmur in wonder of the tiny man nursing at my bosom. "I know you didn't want to do that today, Grant. It's just one more reason why I wish we were the drivers of our own life, and everyone would just man up and stop being so controlling."

"I had a talk with Cora afterward, telling her if she didn't stop this shit, I'm going to go straight to her father. She's taking advantage of a situation none of us want to be in. Cora didn't want to marry me. I didn't want to marry her. Our families aligned– that's it. But it's until death do us part, which we both resent. Making our lives a living nightmare may make death a real option."

Shuddering, I think of all the times Grant makes odd comments, where you'd assume they were said in jest. But this is the first time he's said something and I fear he's being serious.

"Hi," Whitt's voice drifts from the cracked door, pulling me from my disturbing thoughts. I wonder how much the tiny stalker overheard. "May I say goodnight?"

"Always," I say with a smile. "You wanna burp?"

Whitt nods his head eagerly, never passing up a chance to help out with Niel. I gently pry my ravenous monkey from my breast, then cover myself with my shirt.

Protesting the end of his snack, Niel grumbles and punches his fists in the air. But the second Whitt has a hold of him, he simmers down immediately. With pride, I watch as Whitt cradles Niel like an expert, gently patting his back to coax out a burp.

Too cute– "You'll make an excellent father someday."

"I like boys," Whitt pouts, already understanding far too much, thanks to Daniel's thirst for spreading around his anatomy knowledge. There's no need for Sexual Education when the old man of the house makes you study medical textbooks for shits and giggles.

I stand, then offer Whitt the rocking chair. "Ask Daniel to find you some info on insemination and surrogacy if you want a biological child, or research adoption laws."

"You mean I could actually be a dad?" Whitt's shock is remarkable. The whole point Niel was created was because Jackson and Daniel didn't want to force Whitt to become a father by mating with a woman.

Guess the freak out was unnecessary, wasn't it?

"I'll just raise, Niel," Whitt mutters possessively, holding his brother like we'd have to pry the baby from his arms. "Niel will be my son– he's already *my* heir."

"Hey!" Grant swats Whitt upside the head. "*Our* baby." He points between me and himself. This is a daily occurrence– pissing contest between father and son over Niel and me. "My son. My woman. You'll grow up soon enough. Don't push it."

Whitt ignores us, pulling out his Matchbox car for Niel to play with. My son is usually quiet and pensive, but that's until Whitt enters the room. It's like sun shines down, brightening his world, and Niel seems to have the same effect on Whitt.

The Daniels have been inseparable since Niel's birth. Whitt even tried to witness the birth– didn't happen.

"You don't look at Whitney like that, Whitt. I'm starting to notice your nepotism," I tease. He always stares at Niel with the most serious expression on his face, like he truly believes Niel is his.

"They had to go and steal my name. I have to share my first name with everyone, then they take my nickname… for a girl!" Whitt's growl is not scary at all. "Whitney's safe with her parents. She doesn't need my protection," he says ominously, and I shiver.

"I can take care of my son, Daniel." He doesn't say anything. He just looks up at me in skepticism.

"I can," I say firmly.

"I don't doubt you, Queen. I just don't underestimate Father's need to keep what is his." Hearing the mature statement out of the mouth of a child with a man's voice is spooky, and very accurate. I wonder what Whitt knows about Daniel that we don't.

"I'm a kid no one notices because I'm not the chosen one." All of his anger, frustration, and jealousy infuses his voice, but I'm thankful none of it is directed at my son. "I can be in the room and no one sees me. They just keep talking." Whitt and Grant share a look, both of them having that particular issue in the family.

Standing from the rocking chair, Whitt gently places Niel in the crib, then pats his tummy in soothing circles. My son's eyes flutter shut, and then he drifts off to sleep quickly, feeling content, loved, and safe.

"Plus, Whitney screams when I touch her." Whitt flashes me a mischievous smirk with dimples. "Niel loves me already. Who would you rather play with?"

Ah– the logic of children.

Whitt comes forward and waits patiently. Sometimes I make him wait longer than necessary, just to see if he'll give up and walk away. Nope, he hasn't yet. Whitt can be more stubborn than Jackson ever was.

Smiling sweetly, Whitt gazes up at me, knowing we're playing battle of the wills.

I always give in first.

I bend down and kiss his forehead goodnight, and he sighs in pleasure.

"One day I'm going to be tall enough to kiss you goodnight," Whitt warns in a flirty tone, channeling Grant.

"You little perv," I mutter aghast, seeking Grant, whose eyes are bulging from their sockets in shock. "Eww… I'm like your mother."

"Yeah, and I like boys," Whitt mutters matter-of-factly, insulted. "And you're not my mother, Queen." He shrugs, and then walks over to the blushing Grant, who never knows what to make of Whitt, either.

However, Grant does cuff the kid upside the head again. I've often wondered, underneath his silky hair, if Whitt has a misshapen head courtesy of his father swatting him when he's acting like an ass.

Grant doesn't make him wait. He bends at the waist and pecks Whitt's cheek.

"No matter how tall you get, you're never kissing me goodnight." Grant taunts, trying to remove the uncomfortable air that has descended in the room.

"Gross," Whitt spits out, and then disappears to his own bedroom.

Leaving the nursery to enter my bedroom, I snort at that ridiculous exchange. "Troublemaker. I have no idea what Whitt's going to do or say, and sometimes he terrifies me with his intensity. Sweet, and such a good kid, but creepily possessive." Groaning in pleasure, I sit down on the edge of my bed. "I'm exhausted."

"I think Whitt wants me to know that if I don't treat you right, there will always be someone who will." Grant yanks his tie loose, and then starts unbuttoning his dress shirt. "*Him.*"

Creeped out, I lean back on the bed and try to enjoy the show. No matter how many times I've seen this rerun, it never fails to entertain.

"Next time, make sure you button your blouse after feeding Niel," Grant warns me with no judgment in his voice. "You're either going to scare Whitt off, or make him change his mind on his orientation."

Laughing at the mortified look on my face, Grant snaps me with his shirt.

"Ugh– I was covered." I defend, offended. Looking down at my chest, my shirt may not be buttoned, but it's overlapped. "Nothing's showing," I grumble in confusion. "Why say that?" I flick my gaze to meet Grant's, only to find him wearing nothing but a naughty smirk.

Hunger fills Grant's expression as he stalks across my bedroom toward me. "For me, there's not nearly enough flesh showing– take your shirt off, Regina."

The animalistic gleam in Grant's eyes has me scrambling on the bed. Suddenly playful, he tackles me from behind, sneaky fingertips tickling me brutally in all the right spots.

Trying to tap out, my palm hits the mattress. "Stop! Stop... no... no more, please," I beg, cry, and giggle. I'm highly ticklish and hate it. I pound my hands on the mattress and kick my legs in the air.

Leaning down over me, Grant whispers into my ear. "God, I love you, Regina." There's more affection than laughter filling his voice.

Suddenly heavy-lidded, my eyes slip shut from the warmth his words elicit. He gently kisses my neck as he peels my blouse from my back, then he kisses the path of the shirt. Panting, "Grant," I fist the coverlet, twisting fingertips in the fabric, as my body awakens for him.

I roll onto my back so I can gaze up at Grant, and I find that I've never seen him look so starved. "Oh, shit!" I hiss as warm liquid trickles down my stomach. Our exertion caused my milk to flow. I struggle to sit up without getting it all over the blanket.

"Shh..." Grant's voice is silky smooth. He pushes me to the mattress, an eager light shining in his eyes. Crawling over me, a pink tongue lashes out, then licks my stomach in a long, wet line.

"Grant!" I shriek in protest, struggling to push him away.

"I'm sure Niel won't mind– he wants to share with Daddy." A long lick swipes up my stomach, followed by a deep moan. "Don't be stingy and wasteful. Relax."

"You've always wanted to do this, haven't you?" Breathy, amusement is thick in my voice. "You've got some weird kinks. It's no wonder your son is a perv, and we have a budding one sleeping in his crib."

"Anything born of Jackson was bound to be a deviant." Grant's eyes shine with tears and mirth, still mourning the loss but finding comfort and amusement in the memory. "You have no idea how gorgeous your tits are, do you?"

"Oh, I remember dodging boys when they grew from buds." I laugh, remembering Roman's jaw dropping when I went from a leggy tomboy to chesty bookworm. He followed me around like a tail for months.

"I'm willing to share." He gazes up at me with the eyes of a predator, and my breath seizes. "So my son better share with his daddy." His hot mouth captures a distended nipple, sucking in as much of my tit as humanly possible.

"Oh, God!" I shout, back arching in pleasure. The movement pushes more of my tit into Grant's mouth. Suckling greedily, he takes deep draws from my breast. Writhing around on the mattress, "Ugh! I'm going to come from this– it's so damn wrong."

"But it feels so damn right." Teasing, I can feel his smile curve against my breast, as his eyes peer up at me with mischievousness. "I know I could come from doing this, too. My dick's leaking more than this awesome tit."

Another harsh draw has me demanding, "Fuck me while you suck me!"

"Now who's kinky?" Shifting onto his knees, Grant chuckles throatily. "Our son never had a chance."

"Hurry! I need you inside of me. Now." I rip my pants away, not bothering with the zipper. Clawing at the fabric, Grant laughs at my impatience.

"Shit, I need a condom." He crawls to the nightstand. "I haven't bought any yet. Have you?"

"My nightstand," I utter with impatience. "Fuck it! Grant. Fuck me!" Blood buzzing with an influx of hormones and need, I feel crazed. "It's been months."

"You aren't on birth control yet, Reg." Leaning over me, trying to reach my nightstand, "As much as I love our monkey, I'm selfish enough to go a few years without another baby getting in the way of us."

I sober up enough to wait the thirty seconds for Grant to retrieve the condom, but not enough to allow him to put it on himself. Transcend has a program where you learn with a plastic banana cock. During summer vacations when I was growing up, I was the idiot who taught other girls and guys how to put a dang condom on– yet I'm the one who has never used one myself.

Impatient, I grab it from Grant's hand and tear the wrapper open with my teeth. "Don't ever do that– it's against the rules. But since I don't give two shits right now…" Gripping his dick in my grasp, my hand is saturated to the point his sticky stuff is on the outside of the condom.

"Sorries." Grant chuckles the entire time I roll it on. His giggles are mixed with moans as my hand skims his cock.

Grinning like a villain, I mutter without shame, "Don't forget the tits."

"You drive me fucking crazy, Reg." Grant pushes me to the bed, pink tongue peeking at me, mouth opening in anticipation of feeding–

*RIIIINNNNNGGGGGG... ... ... RIIIINNNNNGGGGGG... ...
...*

"Are you fucking kidding me?!?" I bitch in frustration as Grant actually lifts the receiver. "I swear to God, if this isn't life or death, I'll find you and make it life or death."

"You heard the lady," Grant laughs into the phone. In an instant, his amused expression turns solemn.

"Stanton? Shit." His mouth twists into a frown as he listens. "Be right there."

"Regina, get dressed, please." I mouth *what?* And Grant shakes his head no at me. I quickly wipe my chest, then grab for my clothes I flung all over the bedroom. He redresses one-handed while listening to Stanton speak. Then he just hangs up and offers no explanation.

"Come on, hurry," he mutters breathlessly, rushing from the room while still buttoning his shirt. I struggle to catch up as he jogs through the labyrinth of hallways. We emerge in the garage, and then slide into his Mercedes.

"What is going on, Grant?" My voice warbles with worry as he drives far above the legal speed limit. Dizzying, the twisted drive from the castle to the Gates is at breakneck speeds.

Punching a button on his cellphone, Grant barks, "Open the gate. I'm not stopping." Without waiting for a reply, he tosses the device on his dash. Taking the straight and narrow street through Crestview at ninety, he barely slows to exit the gate. "Call my mother– let her know to keep an eye on the boys."

"Shit!" I curse, as I dial Priscilla. "I'm a bad mother for not thinking of that."

"It's understandable, Regina." Speeding up, we're doing over a hundred miles per hour on the single road leading from Crestview to Dominion proper.

I quickly give a rundown to Priscilla, which isn't much, considering Grant isn't telling me anything.

"He's alive," Grant waits to say until after I'm off the phone with his mother. "There was a shooting tonight." Voice solemn and tight with emotion, "I'm sorry, but there are no guarantees."

"Who? Stanton?" As soon as the words are out, I realize how stupid that sounded because Stanton is the one who called in the first place. "Grant, answer me."

We ride in tense silence for a few minutes as he slows to highway speeds while driving through Dominion traffic– his

NASCAR driving skills would have made Jackson proud. Pulling into the hospital parking lot at breakneck speed, he slams the brakes. We both slide forward, and then back from the force.

With hurried movements, Grant unhooks his seatbelt, and then reaches over for mine. The look in his eye utterly terrifies me as he bundles up my hands in one of his.

"Fuck!" he curses, pounding his palm on the steering-wheel. "I'm sorry, Regina. So fucking sorry." Eyes glistening with tears, Grant yet again tilts my world on its axis. "It's Roman– it's Roman, and they don't think he'll make it."

Too stunned to think, let alone move, I sit in silence as Grant slides from the car. Opening my door, he pulls me from the seat, and then escorts me across the parking lot to the hospital entrance.

I ghost in a fog through the walk, the information desk, and the ride up the elevator. Reality seeps in as I enter Roman's room in Intensive Care.

"I can stay out here." Trusting and respecting me, Grant offers me privacy, but I need his support. I nod into the room, and he follows after me.

After Dad, then Mom, then Jackson, I don't know what to expect when I see Roman. I breathe a sigh of relief that he's breathing on his own. Even though he has oxygen wafting from the tubing at his nose, he isn't intubated.

That's a good sign, isn't it?

Grant rests a palm on the small of my back as I gaze down at my childhood friend. "The bullet nicked close to Roman's heart. A centimeter closer, and he would have died instantly. Roman's stable, but he lost a lot of blood, so it could change at any moment. The doctors told Stanton it was 50/50 odds."

Nodding my head yes, I don't need to ask why Roman was shot. It's a hazard of the job. Yet another person I loved who had the Grim Reaper at his back every second of the day. Even Grant's depression worries me.

Everyone I love dies, leaving me to fend for myself and walk this life alone.

Scared, heart beating erratically, I approach Roman slowly. A memory flashes through my mind of him leaning against the wall in the alley with a huge, sarcastic smile on his face– his skin vibrant with health.

A sob is torn from my throat, but there is no release because the tears don't accompany it. How many times do I need to go through this in my lifetime? How many? But this isn't about me, I remind myself.

Aside from being hospitalized, Roman looks different to me. I study his features, noting the changes. Obviously he's older by two years, looking more like a grown man than a teenager. He looks peaceful in his sleep, albeit deathly pale. I wait with baited breath for his lids to open and reveal the blazing blue-green of his eyes.

It doesn't happen.

Fingertips tentative, I move Roman's hair from his angular cheek, tucking it behind his ear just the way he wears it. The silky strands slide through my fingertips. Pulling away, I smile when the rasp of his stubble scrapes my knuckles.

"You finally grew some whiskers." My whispered words are filled with pride and fascination. "I didn't think you ever would." I close my eyes and pray– beg.

If there is anyone out there, please allow Roman to live.

I stare down at Roman's sleeping form for a very long time, imprinting every physical trait into my memory bank. I wish I could hear his voice again, to be able to feel the zing that flashes through my body at our touch.

Acting on instinct, I dig around in my purse until I find my checkbook. I hover over the rolling bedside table and scribble the contents of my bank account onto a check written in his name.

"Do it, Regina," Grant supports me. "It's the right thing to do. It's only money to us, and we can always make more. But you know for someone like Roman, it's the difference between a new life and a death sentence."

With Grant's approving encouragement, I scratch my signature on a check worth more than twenty thousand dollars– all money I'd earned writing code. I scrawl a note for Roman, praying he'll wake and read it, then I fold the check inside the paper.

I loosen Roman's grip, slide the paper into his palm, and then push his fingers to hold it in place. Allowing myself just a moment more to say goodbye, I bury my face into his neck and inhale his scent. Even near death, he still smells intoxicating– clean and fresh. I pull his scent into my lungs and promise myself never to forget.

"I would have fallen in love with you, Roman," I admit, voice cracking with emotion. "I think I was already a little bit in love with you when I left." I whisper, "Survive," directly into his ear. Then I kiss his dry lips, lingering to feel his breath flutter against my mouth.

I turn to Grant, finding him leaning against the doorframe. I expect a look of betrayal to mar his handsome face, because he undoubtedly heard every word I whispered, and he watched me kiss another man. But he looks at me with patient, understanding eyes and offers up his hand. Without hesitation, I knot my fingers with his, and I don't look back as we leave Roman behind.

It's up to fate now.

"If Roman survives and has the courage to change his life, your offering will make the difference." Grant tries to reassure me as we walk through the hospital to the parking lot.

Grant's support is a pleasant side-effect of our growth over the past two years. The longer we're together, the stronger we both are.

"I owed Roman for all the times he did right by me. He kept the boys away, he bought my mom's pills, and he was by my side as she drew her final breath." A mournful noise erupts from my chest, and Grant pulls me into his arms. "But it wouldn't have mattered what he did or didn't do for me, I would have given him the money anyway."

"You can't buy friendship like that, Regina." Grant squeezes me tightly, pressing my cheek to his neck. Sensitive, he's crying for the both of us. "I believe Roman is a very loyal person, which is one of the reasons why I had Stanton give me updates on him. All of it was for altruistic reasons– I was never jealous. Basically, I knew you would want to know if Roman was alright or not."

Shuddering, I press my face against Grant's neck, inhaling his scent to anchor me to the here and now. "Grant, promise me something." I pull away to connect our gaze, needing to make sure he can see that I'm serious. "I don't want to know if Roman lives or dies. It'll kill me if he doesn't make it… and with how raw I feel right now, if he does survive, I'll want to contact him again."

"Are you sure?" Grant leans back, trying to take me all in with a single look. "Wouldn't the wondering kill you?"

"Promise me," I repeat, but more firmly. "If Roman dies, take the money out of my bank account so I won't know either way. Donate it to Transcend and help another kid just like Roman… just like me."

"I promise," Grant vows, and I know he'll never break it.

"Thank you." I squeeze my eyes shut tightly and release a universal truth. "I'm a curse on all those I love. If I love them, they die. I'm a pestilence."

"Oh, Regina," Grant mutters forlornly, gutted by my words because he knows I love him most of all– he never doubts it.

"I mean it, Grant. Don't. Tell. Me." I twist my fingers in the front of his shirt and draw him to eye level. "You tell me, and all bets are off. Have I made myself clear?"

"I promise," Grant repeats, sealing the pact with a tear-laced kiss.

Escape from Misery Castle

Fifteen years prior to the present

.

Chapter Thirty-Six

After six days of this shit, I have officially gone insane. I want to scream *stop!* At the same time, I want to fix it, but I don't know how. It doesn't matter which room of the seventy-three rooms I enter, the chaotic energy has infused into the stone and mortar of the entire estate, and it follows me around like a storm cloud of anxiety.

Sitting in my office, I'm trying to create a website for a client. It's difficult to get anything done with a nine-year-old and the two three-year-olds playing *Candy Land* at my feet– there seems to be something about me that is a child magnet.

Kate is yet again pregnant, which seems to be contagious, and I'm stuck with Whitney while she's off doing whatever politician's wives do. Not that I don't find Whitney precious, because I do.

Make children, drop them with their aunt, and then disappear while incubating another child, I suspect is what politician's wives do. Wash. Rinse. Repeat. I'll have another child that isn't mine to raise in a few months. Grant and I live like any other married couple inside these walls, and there is something about me that must scream *Mommy!*

But it's the adult children of Misery Castle who are making me want to tear my hair out at the roots, and I feel for them… I do. I just wish they would go elsewhere. The distraction is Grant and Adelaide. I flee from them, and they seem to ricochet back to me like a boomerang.

Too apathetic for my comfort, Fate and Kristal are just as annoyed as I am. At least I understand, try to offer comfort, and generally feel horrible about what's going on. Emergency disaster aside– we need some breathing room. It's been one thing after the other lately, and panicking and fretting changes nothing. Fix the problem, and if you have to wait, then go do something productive in the interim.

Practicality.

After dealing with Jackson's passing, Fate's life bottomed out. She's officially a resident of Whittenhower Estates. I have no doubt that this event had something to do with pissed off founders removing an annoying member from their ranks.

Thomas Simpson was the master criminal of a Ponzi scheme, and was murdered while residing in federal prison awaiting trial. All of the Simpson assets have been seized. Fate's mother couldn't handle the stress, and hung herself from the balcony of their home. But it got worse, because the rope broke and Lara fell three stories to the pavement drive. The coroner couldn't identify the body without Fate's help.

After losing both of her parents, I thought for sure tenderhearted Fate would need my comfort. But just as Grant can't seem to look me in the eye, neither can my best friend anymore. Fate was upset, but not how I imagined she would be.

Meanwhile, we've had an exhaustive search for Fate's younger sister, Faith. At sixteen, she dropped out of Hillbrook and vanished without a trace… and that was well over a year ago. Whitt and I attended the girl's sweet sixteen party, and I haven't seen her since. I just hope the newest disappearances don't mirror Faith's.

A group picture of everyone who attended Faith's party was printed and passed out amongst us. For reasons Whitt won't understand until he's an adult, we hung it in his bedroom so he could look at his older siblings– the only picture he has with most of them all together.

With her freshly printed degree in business, Fate is avoided like the plague. I don't blame the citizens of Dominion for not hiring a financial advisor who happens to be the spawn of the biggest crook in the city's history. So we hired her instead.

We. *Empowerment*. Fate, Kristal, and me.

I'm forming an internet startup company with their help. Which leads me back to my current predicament. Creativity and work would flow better if we didn't have the Whittenhower siblings radiating terror into the mortar of this house. I swear I can feel an earthquake building from their energy.

We all watch them pace identical lines across the carpet. It's as fascinating as it is disturbing. Grant is beyond distressed since his best friend's adoptive son and ward have gone missing, along with another boy named Aaron.

After not sleeping for the past six days, Grant doesn't need to explain. I'm not stupid– I figured out the connection, just not the why. Ezra Zeitler was kidnapped, and two of his enforcers followed.

Vanishing into the night without a trace, Ezra Holden Zeitler was abducted from his bed. The search for the missing eighteen-year-old Hillbrook Preparatory student had stalled until new developments arose. Two nights ago, two more residents of Shadow Haven were taken from their beds. The minors' names have been withheld, however, their ages are fifteen and seventeen years of age. If you have any information regarding the disappearance of the three missing teens, please contact local law enforcement immediately.

I've read the article over and over again in shock, even while the reality of it was breathing down my neck.

It was only a few weeks ago that Adelaide and Ezra announced their courtship to the community. Now my best friend paces the room, wondering if she'll ever see her future husband again. But at the same time, I can't imagine anyone outsmarting the strong, intelligent, young man.

The first time I met Ezra was during his freshmen orientation. Then I saw him in the hallways of Misery Castle, and later at Faith's birthday party. I can see Ezra's face clearly, and it brings a wave of nausea. So much potential– so much loss.

I close my eyes and silently pray that Ezra and his friends are returned safely home to their families. None of us can survive after suffering so many losses.

Obviously one of the unnamed teens is Cortez Hunter. I remember his poor attempt to charm me at Faith's birthday party, and I hope he has the opportunity to grow into himself. I want to weep for those boys, not knowing whether they're alive or dead at this very moment. I hope they didn't have to watch the other suffer. I could tell years back that they had a strong affection for each other. I can't even fathom how I'd feel if someone made me watch as Grant was harmed.

Since I can't find the boys, fix it, or help out in some way, I want to avoid the situation at all costs. It makes me feel useless and weak. Powerless. I tried to comfort Adelaide, and she brushed me off so she could engage in her nervous fretting. I've tried to get Grant to talk it out, and I hit a brick wall.

Grant said, "I can't talk about it." So we didn't, and we still don't, but I'm the one who has to watch Grant suffer through the depressive effects of not talking about it.

Now I want to work to forget. But since they have invaded my office, I can't concentrate enough to work. I have a dozen problems scrolling through my mind on auto-pilot.

The biggest problem *I* face is the sinus infection I had two months ago. I wish I had the balls to tell Grant so he could shoulder some of my stress.

I want to kill the doctors, the pharmacist, and my own ignorance. I'm ashamed because I didn't know something so important. From only my mind, I can conjure a computer program that has the ability to change the lives of millions, but I didn't know that antibiotics and birth control don't mix.

I rub my swelling tummy and silently thank my six-week-old fetus for the nausea and wild hormones.

My last nerve is about to snap.

Unborn baby and I can't stand it one more second. Grating sounds pour into me from all around the room. Whitney squeals in a high-pitched voice over Whitt cheating, causing Niel to shriek in protest. Whitt counters it with a deep, "You're just a baby. Shut up!" Kristal's throaty voice, sounding smug and slutty as she tells Fate about her newest sexual conquest.

…And feet– four feet shuffle across the carpet, scuffing at the nap with annoying intensity.

"SHUT UP!" I bellow at the top of my lungs until they burn. Seven sets of stunned eyes look to me as I grip the edge of my desk. No one speaks, no one dares to breathe, as they stare at me and I stare back.

Rabid, I seethe for no good reason.

Mozart's Symphony No. 40 blares in its electronic glory from someone's cellphone. On a normal day, that sound is annoying at best. On a day like today, it is smash-worthy.

"Whose is that?" I hiss, eyes roving the room's inhabitants.

Without apology, completely ignoring my tantrum, Grant removes his cellphone from his pocket. Patient eyes meet my dagger-filled glare as I tower over my desk.

"Grant Whittenhower speaking," he answers smoothly. I grip the desk harder, digging my nails into the pulpous wood. Does he not see how badly I want to hurt something? Is he testing my patience?

"Oh, thank God." Grant collapses into the nearest chair and ends the call.

Grant doesn't explain. You can't just say something like *that* during a phone conversation, and then not share. You can't!

Now we're all looking at Grant, begging him to speak, and he closes his eyes like he's saying a silent prayer.

Mother fucker!

After too long, "They're safe," Grant whispers in obvious relief. "The boys were found outside of a campground in Pennsylvania, right on the New York State border." He closes his eyes and his head droops in exhaustion.

"Oh!" Ade shouts, making a mad dash for the exit. But Grant grabs her arm as she charges by, nearly taking it out of its socket.

"No, don't go over there yet," Grant warns. "They're physically healthy, but that is it. Ezra will call you when he's ready to talk." His fingers tighten on her arm, and she winces. His voice picks up a tone I've never heard before. Dominance. "I mean it, Ade. Don't interfere. You'll never make it past the front door."

Fleeing the room with tears streaming down her face, we can hear Adelaide's sobs all the way down the hallway.

Grant's eyes track his sister's movements until she's out of sight, and then seek me out. I flinch when I see what lurks beneath the surface.

Haunted, tortured– ruined.

"Oh, those poor boys." My throat contracts, and I manage to lift the wastebasket to my lap before I empty my stomach. After heaving a dozen times, I wipe my face with a few tissues, then swish my mouth out with bottled water.

"Whitt, watch Niel and Whitney." Grant demands as he pulls up from his seat, not trusting Fate and Kristal to take care of a house plant, let alone the Whittenhower heirs. "Come, Regina. You're obviously not feeling well, and I'm in need of a shower and a nap. Afterward, we need to talk."

I want to rebel and lash out over Grant's tone of voice and the way he's commanding me around, but it somehow douses the fire smoldering inside me. Defeated and exhausted, I stand, then follow Grant to our rooms.

Chapter Thirty-Seven

Grant allowed me to shower while he made some more phone calls and got some more answers. But truth be told, I think he wanted me out of the picture so he could speak freely. I know he's hiding something major from me, but I know better than to push.

When I got out, Grant even took his cellphone into the bathroom with him.

Curled up in a cowardly ball in the center of our bed, I pretend to be asleep. Grant has never used that tone with me before. Is he angry at me? I don't think I've done anything wrong lately.

Maybe Grant somehow knows about the little monkey growing inside my tummy and he's furious.

…Or maybe I'm being a paranoid, selfish idiot who is making everything about her. Maybe Grant is on the phone with Marcus, trying to console him over his son's ordeal. Maybe Grant's on the phone with Stanton, trying to figure out how to keep the founding families' children safe, including ours.

But it doesn't matter the reason, because I still feel rejected.

I close my eyes and try to even my breathing when Grant pads into the bedroom from the shower, bringing the scent of sandalwood and a steam cloud with him.

I'm not ready to talk.

The bed dips, and my labored breathing no doubt betrays me. Something soft taps on my nose. I still the twitch, and continue pretending. Another few taps, now at my eyelids, my cheek, and my lips. Grant's playing with me because he knows I'm awake.

I crack my lids, and burst out laughing. Grant taps the tip of my nose again, and chuckles at the gobsmacked look on my face.

Forever the naughty pervert, Grant hums a tune and wiggles his cock in my view, tapping me a few more times with the drooling head.

"Why, Mr. Whittenhower, what do we have here?" I lick down his length, getting a potent taste of his jizz, and my stomach revolts. I groan and collapse back onto the bed.

So much for playing– baby says no.

"I guess my tummy isn't up for that." I mutter sadly, understanding why Grant wants to connect with me physically to forget the ordeal, to celebrate being relieved, and to just connect with someone who loves and understands him.

I need it, too. Badly.

"Sit up with your back against the headboard, Ms. Regal." Supporting me with his hands, Grant helps me get into position.

"You're not telling me what to do, are you?" I arch an eyebrow, mocking him.

"Wouldn't dream of it, Mistress. I'm merely offering a suggestion." Grant repeats the phrase he said to me during our first time. I smile up at him, and he rewards me by denting his dimples into a devastating smile.

Massage oil magically appears in his hand, and he squirts it all over my chest. I meep when the cold, slippery fluid hits my skin. Both of us shutter our eyes in pleasure when his hands massage the oil into my quivering flesh.

"It's been weeks since we've touched like this. I could have napped, and then we could have gone back to work just like every other day. Life's too short for that. I wanted to touch you, connect with you. So I am. The world can wait for us for once."

I sigh my agreement as Grant massages the ache away from my tender breasts. They already feel heavy and full from the pregnancy. I'm sure Grant appreciates it since he's a titty-man.

I tilt my head back, close my eyes, and enjoy the pleasure Grant's giving me. He groans deeply from his chest, causing my eyes to snap back open. I stare down in amazement– I didn't know you could do that there.

"Ah! I surprised you," Grant murmurs in delight. We watch in fascination as he rolls his hips, causing his length to slide between my slippery breasts. Fingertips denting into tender flesh, he holds my tits firmly together while thrusting into the cavern he created.

With a sharp grunt, he admits, "I won't last long."

Throbbing persistently, I can tell Grant won't last much longer. I tilt my head back, studying his body as he moves in jerks and starts. Neck arched, mouth parted with his tongue peeking out, pupils blown and eyes glazed with need, he glides his ruddy length against my breasts and takes his pleasure without giving.

I feel so damn proud of Grant for finally giving himself over to his wants and needs without worrying what anyone else wants or thinks. Grant's a man– a gorgeous, virile man, whose body is taut with his coming release.

"Oh, Mrs. Whittenhower…" Grant groans, and a heartbeat later he's spilling his billion dollar seed on my chest and neck.

Words finally registering with my brain, I freeze in confusion and hurt, not able to enjoy the sight of him writhing in the throes of orgasm.

With a devious grin, Grant stares down at me, and I know he can read my hurt. "Marry me, Regina," he murmurs softly while stroking my cheek. "I would be proud to call you Mrs. Whittenhower. You've earned the name more so than I have. Please, do me the honor of becoming my wife."

After a long pause, where I don't answer, Grant's features wash over with fear, and his eyes dart around, trying to get an emotional read on me.

"You already have a Mrs. Whittenhower, Grant," I whisper, reminding him of the only problem we have in our relationship. If Cora was gone, we could go public as a family with our children. We could celebrate our love for real, instead of with the taint of me being his hidden mistress hovering over us.

"Cora won't be my wife for much longer, Regina." Grant's laugh is jovial and intoxicating. "I have a meeting arranged with Cora's father, and I have some ammunition should he deny me the divorce."

I feel wild, wide-eyed and flushed, but that niggling premonition sensation suffocates the high. "I don't know, Grant. I've got a bad feeling about this."

"Don't worry." Grant peers down at me with nothing but unconditional love in his eyes. "Say yes, Regina." He kisses my mouth so tenderly that I would weep if I could. Then he trails kisses down my neck and laps at my chest.

"You're a kinky fucker, Mr. Whittenhower." I tease Grant as he cleans his own jizz off my tits.

"It's a good thing I am, Mrs. Whittenhower." He keeps getting kicks out of calling me that, and I haven't even said yes to something that is only a possibility, not a reality. Grant's the dreamer while I'm the pragmatist. "You wouldn't love me any other way. You feed off my hedonism."

In a wet line, Grant trails his tongue down between my breasts, and then rims my belly button. "Say yes, Regina," he commands against my tummy.

"I'm pregnant," I whisper underneath my breath, terrified of his reaction. I know he hears me when I feel his lips curl into a smile.

"I know, and I love you." Grant whispers back, then lays tender kisses along my rounding belly. "I hope we have a girl this time, and we'll name her after your mother. Maybe someday we'll have another boy, and you and I can battle it out over Curtis and Jackson." Eyes dreamy, Grant wrecks my world and rebuilds it with what he says next. "Ella Whittenhower? That has a beautiful ring to it, doesn't it?"

"Yes," I moan as Grant's tongue delves between my aching folds. "Yes! Hell, yes!"

"Yes, lick my pussy, Mr. Whittenhower?" He laps at my slit, causing my back to jackknife off the mattress with a sharp cry. "Or yes, I'll be your Mrs. Whittenhower?"

Grant pops his eyebrow, making sure I'm watching him. With slow precision, he extends his tongue ever so slowly, then swirls it around my nub.

I combust.

"Yes! I would be proud to be your wife, Grant. All I've ever wanted was to be the Mrs. Whittenhower to your Mr. Whittenhower."

Grant's eyes glint with victory as he lowers his face to feast. At first I think he's being playful, teasing me as he usually does, by whispering, "Echo, Echo, Echo," against my spasming flesh. But then I feel the cold slide of metal over my left ring finger, and I know he's reminding me of what connects us in the first place, something directly from one of the first letters he'd ever written me.

I hear you, Regina, because you're my echo.

I fall asleep in Grant's arms, after all these years, finally realizing what he meant. All else is infatuation and lust, but to be understood, is to be unconditionally loved.

ॐ•ॐ

With a happy smile curling my lips, a nudge to my shoulder pulls me from sleep. The fingers are too bony to be Grant's elegant ones.

"Ade?" I mumble drowsily.

"You have to wake up and get dressed, Regina." Ade's voice is rough, and my body instantly goes on high alert. "You're needed in the study."

"What's wrong, Ade?" I reach over to turn the lamp on, and discover it's four in the morning.

What the hell?

Where's Grant?

Ade looks down at me with red-rimmed eyes, and I bolt upright from the bed and almost pitch forward and beam myself in the forehead on the footboard. Her hand clasps my upper arm, stabilizing me.

"You're pregnant," Ade states. Her eyes drink in my naked form, noticing the swollen belly and breasts. "And there's a ring on your finger."

"Grant just asked me to marry him, and I'm six weeks pregnant." I look around, trying to get my bearings. "Where's Grant?"

Adelaide turns her face from me, trying to hide her devastated expression, but I can see tears flowing down her cheeks to soak her light hair. Without looking at me, she pulls my robe from the chair and hands it to me. On autopilot, I belt it into place, never taking my eyes from her profile.

"What is going on, Adelaide?"

She slowly closes her eyes and whimpers in agony. "Come–" her voice cracks and she swallows hard. "Come with me." Her solid grip returns to my arm, pulling me from the bedroom. Then she drags me through the maze of hallways, down the south staircase to the foyer, down another hallway, and into the study.

"Please sit, Regina," she requests, and the lock clicking on the double doors has me flinching.

I don't sit.

I scan the study.

I haven't set foot into this room in three years, not since the day Jackson died. It was too difficult, seeing and hearing the memory as if it were happening in real time.

Daniel was the opposite– he never leaves the study, trying to be closer to Jackson, I assume.

"What's going on, Daniel?" He looks more like Jackson in this moment– wild and reckless.

Broken.

"Force Regina to sit, or she'll fall," Daniel says in concern– concern that utterly terrifies me.

"You know Regina won't, Daddy." Ade crumples into the closest chair she can find as I stand before Daniel's desk, waiting for answers.

"Where's Grant?" Ade's wail jolts me, but I can't wrench my eyes from Daniel.

Daniel is a man who is cold, practical, just like me. But he's also a man who doesn't show emotion, and has a difficulty showing affection to anyone besides his wife, Grant, and Niel.

The shiver starts in my toes and spears my heart– Daniel has tears glistening in his eyes.

"Where's Grant," I command, and Daniel winces.

"Cora was beside herself with grief when Grant asked for the divorce. She poisoned herself, then called Grant to say goodbye–"

I cut Daniel off before he can say another word. "Bullshit! Cora has known from day one this was a business merger type marriage, and nothing more." Taking a deep breath, I ask my next question since Daniel isn't going to answer the first. "Is Cora dead?"

"The last of the Spencer line was snuffed out tonight. Bereaved, when he found out about his daughter's suicide, Henry died on the spot."

"That's–" I try to wrap my mind around what Daniel is telling me, but I'm at a loss. "It's horrific, but Cora shouldn't have been so selfish. She shouldn't have killed herself– now Boyd's left all alone."

"Boyd was forced into marriage last year," Daniel reminds me. "Gretchen Wilson. They have a son– Torian. Now the Spencer legacy is being held by an imposter. Jackson is probably rolling around in his grave right now."

"Stop talking around it, Daniel! Cora's loss is disgusting, but that doesn't answer my question. Where is Grant?"

"He's gone," Daniel mutters matter-of-factly.

"Gone where? Grant asked me to marry him tonight. I highly doubt he went far." I hold up my hand to show Daniel the infinity band circling my left ring finger. "Where's Grant?"

"I'm sorry. As much as it pains me to say, you'll never be a Whittenhower, Ms. Regal." Daniel hides his face behind his upraised palms. "It's too late."

"What do you mean, it's too late?" My voice betrays my fear.

"Grant's gone." Daniel's voice breaks.

"What do you mean, Grant's gone?" Tears prickle my eyes and release for the first time in five years. "NO!" I fist my hands in my robe over my belly.

"Grant's dead. My son is dead." Daniel's hand covers his mouth, and then he screams long and low– mournful.

I don't want to believe it, because I still feel Grant with me. My heart doesn't ache as it does for my parents. Grant can't be dead, but the primal scream erupting from Daniel's throat confirms it. In this very room three years ago, Daniel didn't make this nightmarish sound for Jackson, not to this intensity.

"I don't believe you," I mutter in denial, voice shattering. "How?"

Calming himself, Daniel states the facts. "Poison– we think Cora poisoned a water bottle and he drank some." He looks like he doesn't want to believe it as much as I do, but he's too much of a realist to hope. "The effects were like acid on contact."

"I want to see him!" I demand, voice shrill on the edge of a scream. "I won't believe it until I see Grant."

Standing from his desk, Daniel leans forward and bellows directly into my face. "They won't even let me see him, and I'm his goddamn father!"

"I just– no." Head shaking rapidly back and forth, I realize Daniel is making the same gesture of denial. "I *will* see Grant– I have to see him to believe it. It doesn't feel real, and I need to say goodbye."

Through our mutual grief we still battle one another.

"You may see Cora if you don't believe me." Daniel's eyes close as he speaks. He knows that isn't good enough, and that it doesn't make any sense. "I know my son is gone, because Marcus came to me with Grant's blood all over him. Marc was covered head to toe, and he was nearly catatonic."

"If Marcus was catatonic, how did he tell you anything?" I challenge, hope sparking.

"The paramedic was a friend of Marc's named Levi, and he confirmed it. Grant died and was resuscitated in the ambulance, then died again but couldn't be brought back. My son fought hard to live. Marcus was beside himself with grief, but loyalty demanded that he make the announcement in person."

"How can you just trust his word?" Sucking in air at an exponential rate, I release it in a violent gust. "HOW?"

"Grant is dead, Regina." Daniel falls into his chair, devastated. "I'm so sorry– so very sorry."

Still refusing to believe it, "I *will* see him."

"No," Daniel murmurs softly. "I was told it wasn't wise because of the acid– Grant's gone. His suffering is over, and that's all that matters."

Without Grant, there is no fantasy– reality wins.

A blood-curdling scream erupts from my throat, and I fall to my knees, head bowed to the floor. Keening Grant's name until it echoes around the room, I wail until no sound leaves my throat. I cry all the tears that have refused to fall since my mother's death, and yet I feel numb inside and out.

I'm a pestilence to those I love– to those who love me.

Daniel tries to cover his ears to my onslaught while silently weeping. Adelaide's curled into a ball, rocking back-and-forth, chanting gibberish on the hardwood floor.

Eons later, we all sit in stunned silence in honor of the silent Whittenhower we just lost.

"This is your fault," Daniel hisses with venom lacing his voice, on the verge of snapping in his state of grief. "You knew coming in that Grant was married. Everything was going well. You and Grant were happy together. We were all getting along. Your son is not only thriving but happy and content. But you wanted marriage, and Grant knew it."

"What was so wrong with that?" I roughly rasp. "You married Priscilla, and you love her. Didn't you want the same for your son?"

"My only son would still be alive right now, Regina, if it wasn't for you." Panting, chest moving up and down rapidly, Daniel is about to break. "If Grant hadn't asked for a divorce, he'd still be alive." Voice raising in crescendo, "It's your fucking fault my son is DEAD!"

Rage fueling him, moving with lightning speed, Daniel picks up a *Steuben Glass* paperweight off his desk, and throws it like a softball at my head. Jerking to the side, he misses but hits my shoulder instead. Pain erupts and my flesh splits from the force.

I don't even react.

I allow the pain to roll over me, because nothing could possibly hurt more than the loss of Grant.

"I won't leave without my son." I utter hollowly. Channeling Grant, I'll live for my children, but the prospect of the blessed release of death sounds inviting. "You'll have to kill me first."

"Oh, I can fucking arrange that, Regina," Daniel seethes. "Don't tempt me, but it's unnecessary, nevertheless. You have no legal rights to Daniel Whittenhower III. His legal parents died tonight."

Palm raised out, I beg. "No, don't do this, Daniel." The loss of Grant is debilitating, but the loss of my son...

"Niel's mine now. You cost me my son, so your cost is yours." Mouth opening wide, Daniel screams so loud the foundation rocks. "GET THE HELL OUT OF MY FUCKING HOUSE!"

"NO," I protest. "No."

"Your cunt partners are being escorted off the premises as we speak. Fate is a leech on the teat of humanity, and I don't give two shits that Martha and Albert are Kristal's parents– you can take the trash with you."

"I'll go, but first let me say goodbye to my son– to Whitt."

"I don't negotiate with terrorists, Regina, and that's precisely what you are." With a deep breath, Daniel razes my world to the ground. "If you contact any minor Whittenhowers, I will have you thrown into jail. You will not say goodbye to my *sons*– either of them, in any capacity."

"Daniel, don't," I plead, tears streaming down my face.

Lost.

"GET THE FUCK OUT OF MY SIGHT!" Daniel picks up another figurine– his favorite. The eagle Grant bought him when he was a boy. Thoughtful yet premeditated, Daniel puts it down and selects another, then cocks his arm back.

Appearing out of nowhere like the angel of death, Ade steps in between us, because I would've just let Daniel stone me to death for my sins. Daniel arcs his hand at the last instant to avoid hitting his daughter in the head, and connects with a stained glass windowpane instead.

The shatter is deafening.

Ade crouches down and rapidly whispers into my ear while Daniel selects another Steuben Glass paperweight from the top of his desk. Examining it with his insanity. "Niel and Whitt have each other– they'll protect one another, and they'll have Kate's daughters as companions. Niel will be treated as a king."

"No, Ade," I whine, crying so hard I can barely speak. "Don't ask this of me– Grant wouldn't have ever wanted this."

"Regina," Ade issues sharply, sounding petrified for me. "Daddy will do no harm to Niel. He'll leave Whitt alone for Niel's sake." She rests her palm on my budding abdomen. "You have this one to worry about. All it will take is for one paperweight to hit its target, and the last living piece of my brother will die."

Queened

Mistress & Master of Restraint #6

The long-standing Mistress & Master of Restraint series is dark and mysterious, with a warped sense of morality. Erotic romance fans, would you prefer something just as twisted, but not as dark? Try the Blended Series, beginning with Good Girl. For a mix of both styles, try the Rusty Knob series.

To purchase any of Erica Chilson's titles, please visit her website (ericachilson.com) for details.

Acknowledgements

A lot of work goes into writing a novel, and it isn't just by the writer herself. **My parents:** for their unconditional support. **My readers**: thank you for reading my twisted words and spreading my books to the masses. For without you, no one would have ever heard of my stories. My readers are my lifeblood. A shout out to the members of the **M&M of Restraint Group on Facebook**: thanks for the endless entertainment and inspiration. Thank you to my street team: **Erica Chilson's Deviants!** You guys ROCK! **Wicked Reads**: (in all its incarnations) **Angela G.**, thank you for taking over and making Wicked Reads better than I could have done by myself. & thank you for helping promote my work and the work of other authors. Angela? Have I told you lately how much I appreciate you? A huge thank you to the **Wicked Writer's Betas** for keeping me grounded and encouraging me to keep trudging along when I get frustrated. Your thoughts and observations are invaluable. ((Hugs)) Beta readers: **Kris | Suz | Darcy | Sandy | Di | Angela | Diane | Jacki | Linsey | Alexis | Alicia | Billie Jo | Shelby | Tassie | April | Caroline | Judith | Jodi Lynn | Jodi | Lakecia** | Someday, I'd love to meet you all in real life– it would be the experience of a lifetime.

About the Author

Erica Chilson does not write in the 3rd person, wanting her readers to *be* her characters. Therefore, writing a bio about herself, is uncomfortable in the extreme.

Born, raised, and here to stay, the Wicked Writer is a stump-jumper, a ridge-runner. Hailing from North Central Pennsylvania, directly on the New York State border; she loves the changes in seasons, the humid air, all the mountainous forest, and the gloomy atmosphere.

Introverted, but not socially awkward, Erica prides herself on thinking first and filtering her speech. There are days she doesn't speak at all. If it wasn't for the fact that she lives with her parents, giving her a sense of reality, she would be a hermit, where the delivery man finds her months after expiration.

Reading was an escape, a way to leave a not-so pleasant reality behind. Reading lent Erica the courage she gathered from the characters between the pages to long for a different life. Writing was an instrument of change, evolving Erica into the woman she is today– a better, more mature, more at peace thinker.

Erica has a wicked mind, one she pours out into her creations. Her filter doesn't allow all of it to erupt, much to her relief. Sarcastic, with a very dark, perverse sense of humor, Erica puts a bit of herself into every character she writes.

I love hearing from readers. If you would like more information on release dates, works in progress, teaser chapters, and random bits of madness, please visit my Facebook Fan Page: https://www.facebook.com/thewickedwriter my website: ericachilson.com or please contact me via email: wickedwriter.ericachilson@gmail.com
DEVIANTS ONLY, if you'd like to join Erica Chilson's closed Facebook group, M&M of Restraint: https://www.facebook.com/groups/MistressandMaster/

www.ingramcontent.com/pod-product-compliance
Lightning Source LLC
Chambersburg PA
CBHW071229250626
47163CB00001B/105